I0612805

FATED TO THE SCARRED WOLF

The Hunted Omegas

Book 5

APRIL L. MOON

THIGPEN-
GANDY
PUBLISHING

Copyright © 2025 by April L. Moon

All rights reserved.

No part of this book may be reproduced in any form or by any electronic or mechanical means, including information storage and retrieval systems, without written permission from the author, except for the use of brief quotations in a book review.

The story, all names, characters, and incidents portrayed in this production are fictitious. No identification with actual persons (living or deceased), places, buildings, and products is intended or should be inferred.

For inquiries, contact April@aprillmoon.com.

Edited by Linda Ingmanson.

Cover by LLewellen Designs.

 Formatted with Vellum

What Came Before

The his is book five in an interconnected series. It is not a stand-alone, and while it does have an HEA for the main couple, it's highly recommended that you read the previous books before this book. If you choose to forge ahead, there will be spoilers, and you will be missing quite a bit of context. **Pretty please, start at book one!**

DESIGNATIONS in this world begin with alpha, as in most wolf packs. But they proceed all the way down the pecking order from alpha, beta, gamma, to the lowest of lows, the psi wolf.

Almost.

There is one designation more hated than all others: the omega. Deceptively last on the hierarchy, omegas were rare and blessed throughout history with extra gifts from the Moon Goddess herself. They lived and used those gifts for their packs quietly for many, many centuries. Until one omega went bad, causing war to break out, nearly wiping certain magical species off the map.

The rest of supernatural kind rose up together to overturn the wolves. The Interspecies Governing Council (IGC) was created, and the Omega Defense League (ODL) was formed to prevent another like Narcissa from rising ever again. From that day to the present, omegas have been hunted to extinction. Every brand-new wolf-shifter baby must be tested by the ODL, and any omega daughters are killed by their third day of life.

But now Brielle and her pack seem to have been specially touched by the Goddess, blessed with powers of fertility and healing that have potential to bring wolves back from the verge of extinction.

If they can survive.

FATED to the Wolf Billionaire

After surviving multiple vicious attacks and a vampire's bite, Reed and Fiona have celebrated their bonding under the moon. They are forging a new path ahead together despite the uncertain times the pack still faces and how little they know about Fiona's djinn powers. Brielle now holds the first piece of the omega stone needed to ground her powers, with four remaining to be found to make the stone whole and useful. Shay's fae powers have grown, and she's finding new and stronger ways to exercise them as time wears on. And Leigh is about halfway through her pregnancy, little Poppy still safe and sound, despite the troll attacks and long journeys. Their mates stand staunchly at their sides through it all.

Olivia is the odd one out, omega marked, but quietly alone. She was on the verge of asking Kane to pack her back off to Alaska—where she could safely hide away from the males who would want to breed her for her mark—when a racket at the gate calls them away. Her healer's powers are needed when the missing Lucien and Samuel from Pack Blackwater arrive gravely wounded, bloody and battered from a run-in with Petró Varga's vengeful pack. The men seem stable enough under Brielle and Olivia's care, but the first time Olivia brushes against Lucien's skin, his wolf comes to life—claiming her as his mate.

Present day...

Prologue

Lucien

One day prior to full moon

Dominik Varga was a man of unchecked rage. The thought was dulled by his fist slamming into my face for what had to have been the hundredth time. Petró Varga's shit stain of a cousin had yanked me from the street a few weeks ago and chained me up in his little hidey-hole to question me about Pack Blackwater's sins.

Hundredth? Maybe thousandth. Although, to give the man credit, he was creative. He didn't waste all his punches on my face. My entire body ached and throbbed, the aftereffects of his diligent attentions when I refused to give him anything useful. My face was the worst, though, second only to my bloodied hands and feet, which were missing many fingernails and toenails, and all those tiny bones you didn't think about until they didn't work anymore because they were broken.

My wolf did his best to heal me between rounds of abuse, but with no medical care and little to no food or water, my energy stores were sorely depleted. Wounds that should have taken minutes to heal were taking hours, days.

I would give my left kidney for a real bed, a plate of hot food, and a shower right now.

But as the fucker in front of me drew a wicked, curved knife from his bag of demented tricks, I knew that was a distant fantasy. He had me squirreled away in a dirt-walled pit, chained in the darkness.

I didn't know if I was under the Hungarian pack mansion or just in the woods somewhere, because I'd woken up chained underground to the concrete floor, and a metal hook overhead where he looped my handcuffs when he was ready for his next round of torture. No one but Dominik came here, which meant I had his undivided attention.

I'd tried to shift and escape the first night, but the bastard had used spelled silver cuffs, and any attempts to call my wolf resulted in blackout pain. I'd tried to grit my teeth and do it anyway after about a week when I realized the pack wasn't going to find me any time soon, but I'd woken up hours later with intense burns under the cuffs, still fully human.

As the endless days wore on, my chances for escape and revenge grew slimmer, and those revenge fantasies had started to fade along with my energy. Dominik's torture had become significantly more brutal the more time wore on, and I'd come to realize something.

Dominik Varga was going to kill me.

I was never escaping this pit. He knew it, I knew it, and yet still the motherfucker didn't have the decency to do it quickly. Somehow, that knowledge didn't stop me from running my mouth.

The more annoying I am, the quicker he's going to end it.

"Oh, good," I slurred around a fat lip and bruised jaw. "You realized you missed that spot. I wouldn't have wanted to be too pretty when your arm got tired for the night and you left me to rot. Petró would be disappointed if his favorite lapdog not only failed to get dirt on the new high alpha, but didn't even do the job right." I spat, the bloody gob landing somewhat adjacent to Dominik's booted foot.

Damn. I was losing my aim.

Petró didn't want to get his hands dirty during his campaign to be the new high alpha, so he let his cousin—the new third of the Hungarian pack, since Petró's father died—do the truly nasty stuff in privacy. But I still heard him barking at Dominik in angry Hungarian from somewhere up above. I knew he was the mastermind behind my torture, and in between Dominik's visits, I envisioned all the ways I'd like to take my anger out on Petró, Dominik... his entire pack of dogs that leapt to do his evil bidding.

Dominik responded in thickly accented English. "You're a masochistic bastard, and I respect that." His feral grin sent a chill down my spine. He was bloodthirsty; that was nothing new in the weeks I'd grown to know him intimately as my torturer. But something about him was slightly unhinged today, and that *was* new. Concerning, perhaps, if I still had the capacity for concern in the muddle of painful fog that always surrounded me now.

But all I had left was sarcasm.

"Are you really his cousin, though? There are some juicy rumors floating around that you're actually his bastard half brother."

Dominik scowled and ran a meaty hand over his buzzed head as he circled me where I hung limply from the chains shackling my wrists, his left hand twitching as if it couldn't wait to get around my throat and shut me up for good. A shark circling his next meal. My feet were also shackled, but they were window dressing. I no longer had the energy to kick or fight back. So there I hung, like sausage on a meat hook for my bloodthirsty butcher. He'd come well prepared for the job.

The table of torture implements was practically bursting with options, over against the wall. At this point, they were all caked in my dried blood, but that didn't make them any less effective.

Frankly, I preferred when he used the knives to the hammers. Hammers did a lot of damage quickly. The knives stayed surface level until he got bored and decided to cut deeper.

It wasn't the first time I'd suffered abuse, and if I lived through it, it probably wouldn't be the last. My father had beaten into both my mother and me the idea that we were nothing. I couldn't do anything about that back then either, but I never let the bastard touch my baby sister, Lilly.

Her sweet face swam before my eyes, seventeen and golden, eyes full of twinkling mischief. True pain lanced my chest, the old memories of her more damaging than anything Dominik could do to me.

"I do wonder, would you still be so cocky if you knew it was permanent?" His nearly black eyes lit with unholy excitement that didn't bode well for me.

And what the fuck did he mean, permanent? Unless he chopped off a limb, I'd heal. And if he *did* chop off a limb in this hole, I'd bleed out, and his fun would end. I refused to dignify the threat with a response.

He teasingly ran the wicked, rusty blade along the line of my jaw, nicking me a few times in his haste.

"Not the throat, not yet. You see, Petró and I agree that you've got information we could use to tear down that murderous prick, Kane. Like, which bitch is the omega, and how they're hiding her. That's information many would pay handsomely for. And while you've stayed strong so far, there is more to torture than just pain. Weak men break for pain. Strong men? Strong men have to be *mentally* broken. And I've been doing some digging into you and your past. It seems the ladies *love* you. Fucking two, three bitches a weekend after your council sessions ended, sometimes in the same night?"

He tutted, as if he were some paragon of morality, while he held a blade to my battered throat. The temptation to lean into the blade's razor-sharp edge was strong.

I'd had enough pain and suffering to fill a lifetime much longer than mine already. Something stopped me, though.

Maybe I was a masochist.

I leaned a hair closer as I spoke. "I must take after your uncle. Father, whatever. Word on the street is he fucked his own brother's mate, and that's how you came to be. How *does* it feel to be the bastard of the family? No wonder you're only Petró's third, even though you're blood."

The backhand came hard and swift, making my ears ring and my nose drip blood from the impact.

I just laughed, even though I was too exhausted to lift my head.

He was too easy. Psycho, but predictable. It didn't matter who a man was, you couldn't talk bad about his mother without pissing him off.

Dominik yanked me up by a fistful of my matted hair. "For that remark, I will enjoy this." His ugly mug blurred before my eyes, the leering face of my father looking down at me with disdain instead.

If I could have shaken myself to clear the image, I would have. Even Dominik's soulless eyes and filthy clothing were better than remembering my father.

He enjoys all this. Always has. The thought was fuzzy as my father/Dominik raised the knife to my face, and it wasn't until it hovered above my right eye that I realized it was now coated with something black and sticky.

The knife burned hotter than hellfire as it split my skin like a ripe peach, and a scream tore itself from my raw throat as it blazed a trail down my cheek.

Merciful blackness swallowed me, and the pain was no more.

"LUCE? YOU DOWN HERE?"

I was dreaming again. Though, the splitting pain in my face was still present, as well as a sickly feeling in my guts, like I'd eaten a bucket of live worms and they were trying to crawl out of me in protest. This was a sorry-ass dream.

"Lucien, holy Goddess help us. You look like shit on a stick, man. How long have you been down here?" The voice sounded familiar, but too distant for me to place. Oh well. Dreams were dreams.

I tried to blink, tried to move, but there was nothing left in the tank. Whatever had been on that knife Dominik had used on me had really done a number on my already weakened system. Attempts to rouse my wolf were fruitless, and the first true shot of fear flooded my system.

What had that fucker done to me?

"He's got you cuffed, but I think I can get them out of the ceiling and floor. The idiot used magic cuffs but regular chains, which is good for us. Hang tight, okay? This is probably going to hurt like a bitch."

I tried again, but still got no response from my wolf.

With herculean effort, I finally got my good eye open. A blurry man who smelled familiar stood before me, hands half shifted and fur running up his arms as he gripped the chains attached to my ankles and pulled, veins cording in his neck with the effort as he used his wolf's strength to separate the links halfway between my ankle and the heavy bolts anchoring them to the bare cement floor.

"Hell yes. Okay, three more, and we're out of here." The man grinned triumphantly up at me, and I finally placed him.

Samuel. Pack Blackwater. He was ruddy cheeked, and his thick thatch of brown hair canted down over one eyebrow.

Tepid relief tried to work its way in, but I was too beaten down to feel truly excited. We weren't out of this hellhole yet, and the chains were making a lot of noise as he snatched them apart.

But in another moment, both of my feet were free—cuffed, but no longer attached, at least—and that was more freedom than I'd had in weeks.

To my shame, tears prickled my eyes as my arm came down, the muscles burning and protesting as he lowered my shoulder to its normal position for the first time in more than a day and night.

Dominik hadn't bothered to release my arms since he hadn't fed me in days.

I swore under my breath, and Samuel grimaced. "I'm really sorry, Luce, but I've got to get you out of here quickly. It's just me and you, and if Dominik catches sight of us, he's going to send the whole pack after us. There's no signal in these woods to call for backup, but I didn't want to hike back and leave you down here any longer."

"So we can't get caught. Got it," I wheezed as much as spoke the words, probably from that broken rib Dominik gifted me with yesterday.

Although, I hadn't been wheezing before, so maybe he broke something new while I was still out? Didn't matter. Samuel found me. We had to get out. There was no time to think about anything else.

I might get my revenge after all. The thought was fleeting, pain clouding out any chance of more as I had to take my own weight.

He made pretty quick work of the last chain and, with a shudder, released the call on his wolf. The fur faded along his arms, and the sharp claws faded into blunt human fingertips.

"Can you walk?"

I was barely standing, but like fuck was I going to admit it. "I'm good. Let's go."

I only made it one step before my knees buckled, and I would have face-planted into the nearest wall if Samuel hadn't caught me up under the arms.

"Okay, tough guy. New rule: you be honest about your condition, so we don't make stupid mistakes."

I grunted with half acknowledgment, half pain as he looped my right arm over his shoulder to hold me up. Our ascent out of the weird dirt cave I'd been held prisoner in was slow, my body protesting every single step.

But I wasn't looking a gift escape in the mouth, so I bit my bottom lip until it bled, and knuckled under. Samuel took most of my weight, but even so, every step was excruciating. In my feet, yes, but by the time we made it to the surface, the pain in my face and abdomen was white-hot and throbbing. I didn't know what Dom did to me this time, but I must really have hit a nerve with the line about him being a bastard.

That, or he really had been possessed by the spirit of my depraved father there at the end.

I must have made a noise, because Samuel looked down at me and frowned.

"Shit. Why didn't you tell me you were bleeding?"

"Been bleeding for weeks. Not worth mentioning." The words came out too quiet, and my head felt light, like a balloon trying to float away. I was so out of it, I couldn't even appreciate the fresh air and sunshine, which I'd so badly missed over the last few weeks. If I passed out, he'd have to carry me, which would take twice as long and double our chances of getting caught.

Samuel hobbled us over to the nearest tree and sat me down where I could lean against the trunk, lifting my ragged, bloody shirt to get a better look at my abdomen. Sitting down *did* feel better, but we couldn't afford the break. He and I both knew it.

"Fuck me."

"What is it?" I asked, not bothering to lift my burning arms to check for myself.

There was a long pause, and I could see his decision to lie to me play across his features before he intentionally blanked his face. "It's nothing. You're just more busted up than I realized. We've got to get you to a medic."

Yeah, whatever was going on with my gut? It wasn't nothing. But if we didn't get out of here, it wouldn't matter because I'd be worm bait.

"Hoist me back up. I'll live." *And if I don't, I don't want to kick it here.*

To his credit, he didn't pussyfoot around and claim it was going to be roses. He pulled a crinkled water bottle out of his back pocket and shoved it into my hands, and as soon as I had taken a few blessedly cool swallows, he was back to business.

Samuel's mouth was set in a determined line as he pulled me to my feet and used the momentum to heft me all the way onto his shoulders into a fireman's carry.

He grunted as my full weight hit him, but a moment later, he pressed back up to standing, and then we were running.

Every step jolted and jarred things that really couldn't handle the impact, but I gritted my teeth and hung on the best I could while he dodged trees and periodically stopped to listen for pursuit. I considered it a win that I stayed conscious.

Eventually, we hit a small clearing, what looked like the very rough end of a remote logging track. A black Jeep sat facing the road, and I breathed a sigh of relief as we broke out of the trees.

Until Samuel went stiff and slid me off his shoulders. I swayed on my feet as he whispered, "Just get in the truck and lock the doors. Don't let them get their hands on you, and if you have to, leave me."

Yeah, right. Even behind the wheel, I wouldn't make it far before I passed out. The bottom of my shirt and the left leg of my pants were saturated in thick, sticky blood. Running through the woods had been faster, but it hadn't been easy on my battered body.

But Samuel didn't give me a chance to argue. One second, he was a man, the next, he was a wolf, bolting into the forest back in the direction we'd come.

Angry howls pierced the air, and I got moving. If we had to make a hasty getaway a second time, I'd like to be in the damn Jeep, where I could pass out in peace.

Progress was painstakingly slow, and twice I stumbled and fell to the ground, each time harder to get back to my feet than the last. But my eyes were locked on the passenger door, and somewhere inside, the burning will to live urged me forward. Okay, live *and* get revenge on the fuckers who did this to me.

When my fingertips finally met the blessedly cool door handle, I could have wept with relief. I fumbled a bit as I pulled open the door and hauled myself into the tan leather seats, which were about to be destroyed by my filth.

"Hopefully, he got the rental insurance," I muttered, pulling the door closed with a satisfying snap. I wanted to close my eyes and sleep for a hundred years, but I forced myself to look around, see if there was food or water to help my wolf heal some of these wounds.

Thankfully, I didn't have to go far. There was a still-cold bottle of water in the cup holder, and the center console was full of beef jerky and protein bars with writing on the wrappers I couldn't read.

Hot damn, I'd never been so happy to see a piece of meat as tough as shoe leather. I chugged half a bottle of water, not wanting to push it, and then chewed my way through three pieces of jerky before Samuel showed up.

He was bruised, bleeding, and naked, but he was still a damn sight better off than I was. He slid into the driver's seat and threw the Jeep into Drive without bothering to put on a seat belt.

I glanced up as he pulled away, catching sight of something in the rearview mirror. It was a shifter, no, two—one arguing, pointing our way. The other, holding him back.

I blacked out before we made it out of the forest.

ONE

Olivia
_____

L ate on the night of the full moon, Maiden's Enclave
    Mate. He'd called me his *mate*.

The word hung in the air, making my head spin and my pulse pound.

I stared down blankly at Lucien's grip on my wrist, shock filtering through me, slowly at first, and then all at once, making me shake with the intensity. My own wolf paced restlessly in my chest, the complete opposite of her usual easy quiescence—and yet, she wasn't *disagreeing* with Lucien's proclamation that we were his mate.

Before I could even begin to process, his eyes lost focus, falling closed as his grip on my wrist went slack, and Brielle swore, using words I didn't think the polite doctor even knew.

"He's fading. I'm not sure what's wrong!"

Her panicked words spurred me out of shock and into motion, the ludicrous idea that Lucien and I were mates instantly shelved to deal with the medical crisis in front of us.

Brielle used her newfound strength to tear off his bloodstained shirt, not bothering with the medical scissors that were tidily packed into one of the drawers around the room. The problem became immediately evident.

A huge, gory wound in his abdomen, puckered red with infection, and ominous black streaks leaching from the edges out across his chest.

My eyesight sharpened with my wolf's presence, the problem registering in my brain without any conscious effort from me. It was my turn to panic and blurt, "They dosed him with wolfsbane! If he loses his wolf, there's no way he'll be able to heal from this. We need the antidote."

Brielle and I both spun away from the table, dragging open drawers and cabinets, ignoring the medical supplies scattering like chaff. Wolfsbane poisoning was an emergency, even without the grievous injury. Wolfsbane destroyed the wolf if left too long untreated, and suddenly, Lucien's wolf making a last-ditch appearance to grab me made a lot more sense.

I nearly wept with relief when I pulled open the last cabinet on my side of the clinic, spotting the well-marked autoinjectors with the antidote.

"It's here, I've got it. Get his pants off so I can get to his thigh!" I shouted in my haste, spinning back toward Lucien's side with sweaty hands and a racing heart. I didn't know if it was too late to reverse the damage, but as I bit the cap and yanked it off with my teeth, I didn't waste a single second. Brielle and Kane worked together to lower his tattered pants, lifting the hem of his black boxer briefs to bare his thick, muscled thighs for the needle.

I didn't let myself consider the fact that if we *were* too late, I lost my mate. The needle sank painfully deep, but his leg didn't twitch or jump beyond the force of the impact when I slammed the injector against his flesh.

His *feverish* flesh.

Brielle already had her hands on either side of the wound,

eyes closed as she poured her omega powers into his still, life-less body.

When the injector was empty, I cast around aimlessly for the cap, tears blurring my vision. A tanned hand appeared in my line of sight. Kane, holding out the red cap wordlessly.

I took it and covered the needle, then on autopilot dropped the whole thing into the wall-mounted sharps bin. Hesitating there by the wall, I braced my hand on the doorjamb, giving myself a single moment to breathe, reset.

I couldn't heal anyone with tears in my eyes.

Frankly, I wasn't *that girl*. The one who got all choked up over patients. I cared about them, of course. I'd dedicated my life to healing; you'd be a pretty damn awful healer if you were completely detached. But I had a certain clinical wall that allowed me to function in high-stress situations. It didn't come down until I was alone, back in my empty apartment, the crisis passed. That was when I let myself cry, when there was no one around to see or judge me falling apart. Not now, in the thick of things. It was unprofessional and ineffective.

Granted, finding your mate and the fact that he had been tortured, wolfsbane poisoned, and might lose his wolf and die all hitting you in a minute flat was a lot more to process than normal medical stress. This was an emotional moment, not just a clinical one.

I gripped the doorframe hard enough that my fingertips hurt, willed the tears away, and then spun back toward our two patients.

Brielle was still hunched over Lucien, pouring everything she had into him to try to fight back the infection and the wolfsbane. Which meant there was nothing else I could do for him that she couldn't, not yet.

Cleaning, bandaging, poultices—those could all come after he stabilized. I turned toward Samuel, their other pack mate, and offered my best healer smile.

"Okay, then, let's get you fixed up. What hurts?"

He tore his gaze away from Lucien to look at me incredulously. "Shouldn't you be working on him? He's out, and I'm at least upright. Nobody dosed me with wolfsbane, so I'm pretty sure I'll heal up eventually."

Typical alpha male, didn't want to visit the healer, even if we could help his wolf along.

"I'm sure you will, but an exam will confirm that and tell me if I need to clean any wounds or if you need any herbal assistance. I see a few bloody spots on your shirt. Do you have wounds under there, or is that someone else's blood?"

He glanced down, shrugged. "It's mine."

"That's what I thought. Can you remove it, or do you need my help?" I arched one eyebrow, wondering how far he'd take the tough-alpha routine.

He snorted indignantly, but I had my answer as I watched him try not to wince as he pulled the shirt off, revealing a bloodied but heavily muscled torso.

My shoulders loosened a little as I examined the various gashes and punctures, some from claws, some from fangs. Regular shifter fighting injuries; no sign of wolfsbane, infection, or other taints. His breathing was clear and even, as were all his vitals.

"Okay, these look pretty straightforward, and as long as this doesn't hurt." I pressed over a suspicious-looking rib, and he hissed through his teeth. "Yep, broken rib. I don't *have* to bind it, but you'll need to stay in bed for at least forty-eight hours until your wolf can heal it."

"I need to report to the high alpha as soon as we're done here. A binding would be appreciated."

I nodded, not at all surprised he wanted to jump back on his feet. Most wolves did.

"That's fine, if that's what you'd prefer. I'll get these cleaned up first and then put the binding on, and you'll be okay to move around. But try not to overdo it, or you'll be coming back to see me."

He nodded his agreement, and I went to work.

Gathering wound-cleaning supplies was second nature. Wolves got into a *lot* of scrapes—literally and metaphorically —so eighty percent of my job was tending flesh wounds, so there were no complications while natural healing did its thing. After I'd gathered what I'd need, including the wrap for his busted rib, I allowed myself to spare a glance for Lucien.

My mate.

The thought shook me to my core as I took in his pallid features, the big, jagged scar forming over his eyebrow and down his cheek. It was angry, scabbed, and puckering in places, but not fresh.

As a wolf, that meant someone who'd know what causes scarring for shifters had done it intentionally. They wanted to bring him low, tear him down. That one would be as much a mental wound as a physical one.

Wolves fought, yes. But we didn't intentionally maim each other. It was another level of evil that would be a lot harder to heal from internally than externally.

If he survives to find out about it.

I forced myself to turn back to Samuel with a neutral stance, trying to keep my own thoughts and feelings tamped down, safely below the surface and off my face.

As I worked on cleaning the largest gash first, my mind wandered as my hands did the familiar task. Was I imagining the pull toward Lucien's bed, or was that the first sign of the mate bond?

Had I been pulled toward him back in the castle because of the mate bond, but my own shyness and his disinterest had kept us from discovering it?

We would probably never know.

I blinked, realizing the wounds and blood were all cleaned, and stepped back to drop the used supplies into the trash.

"Okay, lean forward for me as much as you can without tweaking your ribs, and I'll wrap them."

Samuel sat himself up straight without complaint, though I was sure that rib hurt. I bound his ribs, putting some extra gauze for padding over the one I suspected was broken. There wasn't much point x-raying a wolf unless his lungs had problems. Within two days, he'd be fully healed.

"You're all set. Also, as your healer, I'd like to suggest you report to the high alpha from the bed. He's four feet away. Let him come to you." I gave him a pointed look while being careful not to make direct eye contact because of my much lower rank. He had the good sense to look a little abashed at the scolding, so I decided to make it easier on him and called Kane over myself.

"Alpha? He's ready to make his report, but I'd like him to stay in bed for a few days. Do you mind just talking to him here?"

"Of course." Kane smiled at me, then walked over to Samuel's bedside.

They spoke in hushed tones, so I stepped away to give them privacy. There wasn't far to go without hitting Lucien's bed.

Part of me wanted to cling to his hand, while the other part knew that it would be crossing a professional line in a big way.

His wolf declaring me his mate wasn't the same as the man telling me he wanted to date or initiate physical contact beyond his basic care. I would keep it clinical until he woke up so we could talk; that seemed the safest and most ethical way to go about it.

When I stepped up to his bedside, though, the burn in my side from when he'd first grabbed my wrist flared again, and I rocked back on my heels. What the hell *was* that?

Brielle was still working on him, her eyes screwed shut, and

I could see a tiny bit of improvement on the black lines trailing out from his wound, proof that the antidote was starting to work. Making a split-second decision, I excused myself to the small, attached bathroom off the clinic.

It was barely more than a toilet, sink, shower, and a single bare bulb overhead for lighting. But there was a filmy old mirror over the sink, which was all I really needed.

Reaching down to the bottom of my shirt, I lifted it, looking at my hazy reflection to see if there was anything obviously wrong. I could be clumsy sometimes when I was in the zone, so maybe I'd just run into the side of the table without realizing it.

But I didn't see a scrape or a rash, nothing like a simple bruise from banging my hip against the metal treatment tables.

I saw my mate marks, covering the whole of my side in vibrant red lines. But while most mate marks I'd seen on pack runs were smooth, swirling graceful lines, these were not.

Big, bold, red splashes of color covered my right side, swirls and slashes disappearing up under the edge of my shirt, so I stripped it off to see the rest.

When I could finally see them all, they wound all the way up to cover the top of my shoulder too.

But somehow, looking at the vibrant red lines, I wasn't filled with joy. There was only one word I could use to describe them, the emotion welling up deep within not my own. It was his.

Rage.

TWO

Lucien

I came awake with a gasp, the pain searing my abdomen the first thing I noticed as I sucked in oxygen as if it was my last breath on earth, every muscle going tense as my fight-or-flight instinct roared to the surface. The second thing I noticed was the sweetest perfume I'd ever smelled, hanging in the air like a delicious, seductive cloud. It was fresh, citrusy orange with sugary peach, and something earthy. Cotton? Yes, that was it. Summertime and desire all rolled up in one sweet package.

Something niggled at me, something that felt important, but I couldn't place it. All I felt was pain, pain and cold hands plastered to my chest. And the damn magic cuffs that were still on my wrists.

As my awareness came back fully, I realized that those cold hands belonged to the omega healer, and her magic was cool, fighting against the burn filling me from the inside out.

We made it out. Relief had me sagging deeper into the bed, even as my body protested the tiny movements.

"Brielle?" My voice came out as a dry croak, but it got her attention. Her eyes flew open, and when she saw that I was indeed awake, her shoulders slumped with relief and fatigue.

"Thank the Goddess. You've been out for a while, and I was starting to worry..." She trailed off, seeming to think better of whatever she'd been about to say. "Let me go get Olivia. She just ran to the bathroom, and I'm sure you'll want her with you while you're recovering."

Her kind smile was confusing.

Olivia?

It took me a moment to remember the other healer, and I squinched up my forehead when I realized who she was talking about.

Why the fuck would I want her at my bedside?

Olivia was stunningly beautiful, sure. Most wolf females were gorgeous, so it made sense that she was no exception. The first time I'd seen her at the pack castle was imprinted in my brain like a photograph.

She'd been standing in one of the big, old windows, like some romance movie bullshit. But the way the light highlighted her cheekbones, the shine of her red hair... She was an angel, and I knew in that moment that she was too good for the likes of me. Too *pure*.

I'd decided then and there that I would never touch her. She reminded me of someone I'd loved, someone too innocent for a bastard like me.

Poison. You poison everything you touch.

I gritted my teeth as my father's words echoed in my brain, forcibly putting them aside, as always.

But the lovely, timid female couldn't do anything for me that Brielle couldn't, as far as I knew.

Whatever floats her boat, I thought idly, deciding not to question it. I was still fuzzy, my hazy memories of how we ended up here not sticking with me at the moment. It was torture, Samuel's appearance, a Jeep, and then nothing.

Weeks of torture would do that to a man.

The pain and the heat came back to the forefront, and for a

few moments, I just lay there, staring at the ceiling and wishing for some cold water as I dragged every breath through a sandpaper throat.

Cold packs. Popsicles. Jell-o. Hell, I'd lick an icicle at this point if that was all that was available.

I must have a fever.

Before I could ponder the implications of that, Brielle appeared back at my bedside, grinning as she pulled the other healer along with her.

"Here she is!" The announcement was unnecessary. A lot of my body was busted to shit right now, but my eyes worked just fine. She was every inch as breathtaking as the first time I'd caught sight of her. *And the scent was hers.* Fuck, why had I never noticed before how mouthwateringly amazing she smelled?

I kept the thought to myself, though, because it was unwise to piss off the people who handled your medical care. Best to stick with the basics. Even if the she-wolf in question had crystal-green eyes I wanted to get lost in. Her hair cascaded over her shoulder in soft red waves, hints of gold shining from them even without the sun to light her up. Little freckles dusted her cheeks and nose, and I was suddenly overcome with the urge to pull her down closer, so I could kiss each one.

What the fuck? I did not kiss noses and wax poetic about eye color. Delirium was a bitch.

"Could I have some water?" I snapped the question, unnecessarily harsh, but the healers didn't flinch.

"Of course! Olivia, you stay with him. I'll run and get some ice from the kitchen." Before either of us could protest, Brielle darted from the room with speed I'd never seen her use before. *Wolf* speed.

Part of me knew that was an interesting development, but I wasn't quite sure why in my haze. I was going to have questions when I felt better.

Damn, I hoped I felt better soon. Every part of me hurt like

26

I'd been run over by a train, tossed off a cliff, fallen down a waterfall, and hit every damn rock on the way down. I raised one arm, scratching at my eyebrow. It also burned, but in an itchy, distracting way.

"No, don't do that. You don't want to pick at a scab while it's healing." Olivia's soft voice sent a shiver through me, a tingle down my spine that was surprising given my wrecked physical state.

A scab? I wanted to scoff, but with my slow healing right now... I supposed it was possible I'd have marks. It wasn't going to stop me from scratching them.

She grabbed my hand, easily stopping my weak efforts to scratch, and it was like the whole room shifted around me.

I blinked once, slowly, trying to urge my sluggish brain to figure out what was going on.

Mate.

My wolf's voice startled me so badly, I actually jerked on the table, the motion bathing me in fresh agony. My wolf rarely spoke. Rarely enough that I could count on one hand the number of times in my long-ass life he'd done it, and never since Lilly.

He hadn't responded to me before when I'd tried, so there was no small measure of relief that he was back despite the pain jerking around had caused my fresh wounds.

But *mate*? What the fuck did he mean by that?

Maybe I was hallucinating. It made more sense than my wolf trying to tell me my mate was in this room. I was ninety-seven percent certain that my not finding her in hundreds of years meant I didn't have one, or maybe she'd already died before I got to meet her.

Life was a bitch like that sometimes. But I didn't *want* a mate when it boiled right down to it. That was just another person to lose.

"Shh, it's going to be okay. Try to hold still. You're really banged up, and moving is going to make everything hurt worse."

No shit.

I didn't lash out at her, though, sending angry thoughts to my wolf instead.

We don't have a mate. What's wrong with you?

I didn't expect an answer, not really. But his response would have knocked me on my ass if I weren't already lying down.

The red-haired female is our mate. She bears our marks.

Holy hell.

The red-haired female could only be—

"Olivia?"

"Yes? Do you want a pillow? Hang on." She set my hand carefully at my side, moving slowly so as not to jostle me, then jogged over to a cabinet, pulling a plain white pillow from inside.

I watched all of this in silent shock, barely remembering that I should lean forward a bit and help her tuck it behind me when she held it up for me with a soft smile curving her lips. I shifted a few times to get it settled, and the pillow actually was better than lying flat on my back on the barely padded exam table, but my brain was too scattered to focus on it.

There was no way. My wolf was desperate to latch on to a female because I was bad off or something. This sweet, young female couldn't be mine. She practically radiated innocent, never-been-kissed energy. I rode a motorcycle and fucked like a demon every chance I got. Not to mention, I was old enough to be her great-grandpa, times a few extra greats, and she was what, *maybe* twenty-five? Goddess's tits, if my wolf was right, something had gone cruelly wrong in the universe.

Brielle returned with the water, wordlessly proffering the cup and bendy straw. I took a few pulls, but my gaze was fixed on Olivia.

My mate.

The thought was strange even inside my head.

It just couldn't be true.

I spat out the straw, needing information more than hydration. "How old are you? Twenty-five? Thirty?"

She blinked at me as if I'd sprouted a third eye. "Twenty-four. Why?"

I closed my eyes and let my head fall back against the pillow with an ungraceful *thunk*.

This had to be a joke. A very sick joke. Twenty-four? She was barely out of her teens.

"My wolf is just confused, that's all."

"Your... wolf is confused. Okay. Well, confusion can be normal after the kind of beating you've taken. A concussion can make you forget a lot of things. What are you confused about? Maybe I can fill in some details."

Nothing but kindness, despite my off-the-wall reactions to her. Typical healer. What the fuck was I going to do with a *healer* as a mate? Was she going to be happy with my lifestyle? No, and there was no way in hell I could change enough to make her happy.

I chuckled, the sound too dark to be real humor. "I must have cracked my head pretty damn hard for him to be insisting that you're my mate. Right? You're practically an infant."

Judging by the crushed expression and slump of her shoulders, not to mention the way my wolf snarled his displeasure as soon as I saw her reaction, I'd put my foot in my mouth. I instantly hated myself for it.

But maybe it was for the best.

It was flippant and probably rude for me to say it like that, but that was who I was. Nearly four hundred years into my existence, I wasn't changing anytime soon. And maybe, just maybe, the part of me that was pissed off at the world right now wanted to lash out at someone.

Even if that someone was young and beautiful and innocent.

She didn't answer right away, her eyes fixated on her linked hands as if they held the secrets of life, and the whole room grew so still, you could have heard a flea jump.

"It is just a concussion, right? There's no way you and I could be a match. It's absurd." It was an asshole move, doubling down after I knew the first remark had hurt her, and I knew it before the words left my lips. But some sadistic part of me wanted to push her away, even as everything inside me screamed to hold her close, to cherish her.

I had to, though, to save her from me. Everyone who was good in my life died, and she wouldn't be an exception. She was too pure, too soft.

I was damaged, tainted. And nothing about my life was soft or good, ever.

She took a step away from the bed, then another, and, without a word, ran from the room. I watched her go, wanting to call after her as remorse twisted in my chest, but I didn't. All I'd said was the truth; my wolf was confused, and she was way too young for me. Too *sweet* for me. It was for the best that she left. It was in her best interest that she stayed the hell away from me so her wolf didn't get tangled up, like mine. There was no way she wore my marks.

A pretty, young thing like Olivia? She had a mate out there somewhere. A good, upstanding, respectable one. Fuck, maybe Samuel. He was the straitlaced type.

I pointedly ignored the jealous surge in my chest at the thought. My neck ached as I scanned the rest of the room, my gaze falling on Samuel sitting on the side of his own bed, Kane at his side. They both stared at me with horrified expressions.

Samuel—who I knew briefly from our time running from Petró's pack and a few brief meetings before they'd left Romania to establish Pack Blackwater in Alaska—was the first to speak up. "What the hell is wrong with you, man? She's a nice girl. You can't just go around saying shit like that. You're going to have to apologize when she comes back. *If* she comes back."

I snorted. "You haven't known me very long, but I never apologize for the truth. My wolf is just jacked up about the torture. It'll pass."

"I don't think it will," Brielle said, a grim tilt to her mouth from where she stood next to the cabinets full of medical supplies. "Your wolf grabbed her while you were unconscious and claimed her as his mate. She's got marks down her side that she didn't have this morning. I picked up on it through the omega seal while she was in the bathroom checking them out."

My palms were suddenly sweaty, and blood rushed through my ears in a rapid *whoosh whoosh whoosh*. The acrid scent of astringent was too loud in my nose, suffocating. Everything was too much, even the silence that followed the omega's words.

Olivia was my mate.

The red-haired beauty was my perfect kryptonite and also the only female my wolf would ever want for the rest of my life. But there was no way I would claim her.

I *couldn't* let my wolf claim her.

Just fucking perfect.

THREE

Olivia

I slammed my bedroom door behind me and wanted more than anything to sink down to the floor behind it. But I couldn't let myself do that now, could I? Because then I'd be exactly what he thought of me: an infant.

His thoughtless words had played on repeat since the second I heard them.

There's no way you and I could be a match. It's absurd.

No wonder he hadn't noticed me at the pack castle; he thought I was barely more than a toddler. Fury mixed with the humiliation pulsing through my veins.

It wasn't the first time I'd been written off; not even close. I dropped onto my bed instead of slipping to the floor, determined to prove him wrong in the tiniest of ways, even if he wasn't here to see it.

Yes, I was only twenty-four, but age was just a number for most of a wolf's lifetime. We physically matured as quickly as humans, which meant I was a full-grown adult, and he didn't look a day over thirty, no matter how old he *actually* was. Wolves got mated with large age gaps all the time, so it wasn't even unusual.

Which meant it wasn't that we would be physically incompatible. No, he must sense some greater defect, a personal flaw he didn't like that made him think I was too young for him.

Immature.

Screw that noise.

Restless, I jumped back off the bed and paced around the room. It wasn't until I spared a glance at the clock on the bedside table that I groaned.

It was after three in the morning.

I was exhausted, blood smeared, and royally over it all. And that was before you considered the fact that a nu like me mated to an alpha like him was always going to cause trouble, even when he didn't think she was an infant.

How old was his grumpy ass, anyway?

It was a question for tomorrow. *All of it can wait until tomorrow,* I decided with a bitter edge even in my thoughts.

I climbed into the shower and then into my latest borrowed bed. But despite the weariness seeping all the way to my bones, it wasn't really a surprise that sleep didn't come for a long, long time.

FOUR

Lucien

After a meal of hearty soup and some rustic bread, and two of the maiden priestesses *finally* removing the cursed silver cuffs from my wrists and ankles, I slept fitfully and woke with the first slanting rays of sun through the clinic's window. Surprisingly, I felt halfway decent, my wolf rapidly repairing damage now that I'd seen a healer, had another meal, and gotten some uninterrupted rest.

I sat up, feet dangling off the side of the bed and eyeing the distance to the tiny clinic bathroom, when Brielle backed into the room with a tray absolutely laden with hot, steaming plates.

"Oh! You're up already. You definitely shouldn't be getting out of bed by yourself yet." Her stern tone stayed my movements until she slid the tray onto the counter and turned to help me ease off the side of the bed.

Her grip on me as she guided me to the bathroom was unexpectedly strong, and she had no trouble holding me up when I leaned on her more heavily than I would have liked. Or admitted in alpha company.

"You seem to have powered up since the last time I saw

you." I wheezed a little as we made it to the door, leaning heavily against it as I waved her off.

"Just a bit. Do you need my help to, ah..." She gestured toward the toilet.

I scoffed. "The day I can't hold my own dick is the day you can put me down, Doc. I'll manage."

She rolled her eyes but turned her back, giving me privacy as I shuffled across the small space. Luckily, it wasn't all hubris this time.

I still hurt all over, but I was steady on my feet, if slower than a turtle and half as enthusiastic. When I finished and hobbled over to the sink to wash up, I froze midstep, and would have lost my balance if it weren't for the cold porcelain sink my hip crashed into.

All my attention was locked on the mirror. Horror, thick and sickly, consumed me as I gripped the side of the basin. My face wasn't *mine* anymore.

An ugly, knotted, red, scabby scar ran through my right eyebrow, narrowly missing my eye as it cut down my cheek, ending at the bottom of my jaw, slightly altering the shape of my mouth as it clipped the corner of my lips on the way down.

I flashed back to the sight of a rusty blade descending toward my face, oily black liquid dripping from it. The breath-stealing burn, and Dominik's wicked grin as he asked how I'd feel if it was permanent.

My breathing was rapid, too rapid, and my vision blurred as I held on to that sink as if it was the only thing tethering me to the earth.

He'd ruined my face. I was *hideous*.

If I hadn't deserved Olivia before, there was no way she'd want to be saddled with me now.

Dominik—and Petró, by extension—had taken away the one thing I had going in my favor. My looks. The outside matched the inside now.

My father would be so smug, if he were still around to see it.

You might look like an angel, but you ruin everything you touch. You're no angel. You're a devil in an angel's disguise.

The remembered jab was the final straw. A bellow of rage tore itself from my throat, leaving it raw, and had Brielle scurrying into the room, the sounds of more feet racing toward us in the hallway not far behind. I wanted to rip the sink out of the wall and smash it against the old, warped mirror. Smash *everything*. Make everything as broken as I was in the only way I knew how.

Maidens surrounded me and led me like a child back to the exam table, a flurry of conversation and worried glances surrounding me as hands pulled at me from every direction, but I ignored them all.

For the second time in my life, I'd lost everything. The first time, there was nothing I could do. I'd been helpless, a victim of circumstances outside my control.

This time? I was going to personally wipe the Hungarian pack off the face of the earth.

The motherfucker who did this to me was going to pay with his life, no matter the cost.

FIVE

Olivia

A knock on my door startled me awake, even though it felt like I'd slept for less than ten minutes.

I jolted upright in a panic, yanked from a dream in which my disappointed father was lecturing me in high school, only for his face to transform into Lucien's.

How old are you anyway?

"Olivia? All-hands-on-deck pack meeting. Five minutes, Bri's room. I brought you a coffee when you didn't show at breakfast."

"Thanks, Fi! Give me two to brush my teeth and throw on clothes."

She chuckled on the other side of the door, and I twisted the knob to wave her in as I sped past to clean myself up a little.

"Take your time. I think the males like it when we make them wait. Wolves love a good chase, after all."

I stalled midbrush, toothbrush foamy in my mouth as I considered her words. Was that true? I'd ask her later when we weren't running late to a pack meeting.

Despite taking an extra sixty seconds to drag a brush through my tangled hair so I looked halfway presentable, I was dressed and accepting the steaming cup of coffee from Fiona less than five minutes later.

She sighed, checking her phone for the time. "You're not very good at being late, are you?"

"Lateness wasn't a trait that was appreciated in my home pack."

"Yeah? You haven't told me much about your past. Ever since we met, it's been all about my weird magic. But I'd love to know more, if you're willing to share. All the intricacies of pack life are really fascinating, as someone coming in from the outside."

Her smile was genuine, an open, honest expression that told me she was sincerely interested. She wanted to be my friend, and somehow, that was a knife twist to the gut.

When had I ever had a true friend? My dad was the closest I'd ever had growing up, but now, everything was different.

I blew out a breath, sending the hurtful train of thought with it.

Digging up my painful past wouldn't help anything. But Fiona was still waiting for an answer, so I shot her a smile I didn't quite feel, buying myself a moment with a sip of the delicious coffee.

"There's not much to tell, really. I'm from Arizona, small pack. Things were quiet most of the time."

I ignored the stab of guilt I felt at her crestfallen expression and quickly changed the subject. "This pack, however, keeps us *all* busy. Any idea what the meeting is about?"

She snorted. "You're not wrong. I kind of wish Pack Blackwater was more like..." She gave me an expectant look, and I realized she was waiting for the name of my home pack.

"The Canyon pack." I was technically still a member of the Canyon pack, but, given my marked palm, well, I doubted I'd be visiting Arizona any time soon.

Not exactly like anyone is missing me.

"The Canyon pack. Excellent." She squeezed my hand, then pulled me through the open door to Brielle and Kane's room.

The rest of the pack had already gathered, and I watched an antsy Reed settle the second his gaze fell on Fiona, greeting her with open arms and a grin.

It was nothing more than a sweet moment between mates, and yet somehow, it made me feel lower than the dirt floor.

My mate was never going to look at me that way, like I hung the moon. Like he couldn't breathe when I wasn't with him.

But you know what? I had gotten along just fine this far without a mate, and that didn't have to change. He thought I was too young, then he could be single. I rolled my shoulders back, taking up a place near Fiona where I could lean against the wall.

"Thank you all for coming," Kane said with a smile. "We're only waiting on our last four, and then we'll get started."

Last four? I did another scan of the room, and all the usual Blackwater suspects were here, except—

"You waited for us? Well, you do know how to make a girl feel special, Alpha." Elodie sashayed into the room—without the cane she'd been using after her troll injury, I noticed—and blew kisses at Kane and Brielle.

Samuel walked behind her, enjoying the view of her swaying ass when he thought no one was looking, and Galyna walked behind him pushing a wheelchair. I averted my eyes, not wanting to see Lucien as he was wheeled into the room. Pale, but upright.

Clearly, sleep, an antidote for the wolfsbane poisoning, and Brielle's omega powers had done him a world of good.

The ragged scar over his eye, though, that hadn't improved at all. My chest went tight as I snuck a glance at him, quickly looking away before he could catch me.

He was pallid, still recovering from major injuries. But the fact that he was upright and alive? That meant we'd gotten him the wolfsbane antidote in time.

A part of me I didn't want to examine too closely—that primal beast inside who had claimed him as *hers*, dammit—was relieved. A wolf mate without their wolf... Well, they couldn't be a mate.

Granted, it had kept me awake last night that my own marks had appeared, but his torso remained completely bare. Or, at least it was while he was lying in the bed after his treatments.

What did *that* mean?

"So, most of you know already that we've got the first fragment of the omega stone, but we need four more to make it whole. King Cysernaphus ever so helpfully provided us a list of the species holding the other shards." Kane paused, wearing a wry expression.

"The centaurs make sense. They've long been leaders among the supernatural for their wisdom. Their headquarters are in Greece—on a little island off the coast where they can run without fear of their true forms being spotted—so someone will need to travel there, most likely. It's going to be delicate, extricating the piece without confirming Petró's condemning accusations to the council."

"Councilman Fortier isn't the leader of the centaurs. It can be done," Reed said. I couldn't help but notice the somber determination in the words and shudder.

"Let's hope you're right about that. The fae are also a sensible choice to hold an artifact of such power, but slightly less accessible. You can't buy a plane ticket to the fae realm. It's most likely being held by the queen herself, inside the Greater Fae Court."

Shay cleared her throat. "Dirge and I have discussed that at length, and we would like to volunteer to retrieve that piece. As you know, there is so much I don't know about my own past, and this seems like a good chance to learn a bit more about my heritage, while also securing the omega stone shard for our pack."

Kane and Brielle exchanged a loaded look, and Brielle spoke up. "We appreciate you both so much. Do you want another pair to come with you?"

Dirge shook his head, shoulders stiff with tension. "Priestess Lisanne said the fewer who enter the realm, the less likelihood there is of one of us getting stuck beyond the veil. It's best that it's only Shay and me."

"Then may the Goddess bless you on your journey." Brielle's bottom lip trembled as she hugged Shay, then Dirge in turn.

Sadness overwhelmed me as I watched them. Theirs was a friendship tested by fire, and it seemed the testing wasn't done yet. But to my surprise, Fiona wrapped an arm around my shoulders, pulling me close so she could whisper in my ear.

"They're going to be fine. Don't be sad."

I eyed my friend with curiosity. She was unassuming in so many ways, quietly brilliant, that it would be easy to underestimate her. But Fiona saw me when so many other people just glanced over me, like a ghost. It was uncanny at times the things she picked up on.

"So that's one piece off the list. Thank you both." Kane inclined his head formally to the pair of them and then continued, all business. "The last two pieces are a bit more... interesting. Goblins, while a very fecund species, aren't very powerful individually. Their strength lies in community, ingenuity, and purity of heart. But they are listed as protecting the fourth piece. Frankly, with how widespread they are, I'm not certain where that piece will be located."

"I've got some ideas. Councilman Lug was always friendly, and I'm certain he'd tell us the best place to start looking if we reached out discreetly." Lucien's voice was raspy and thin, but still sent a shudder of desire through me, as if he'd raked his fingers through my hair. When I realized I was bodily swaying toward the source, I snapped myself back against the wall, wincing slightly at the impact of my head against the stone.

A blush crept up my neck as he and Samuel both looked at me, clearly wondering why I'd just brained myself for no reason whatsoever. I kept my gaze glued to the floor and locked my muscles into place by sheer will, ignoring them both.

He didn't want a mate? He didn't have one. Easy-peasy.

Right?

Thankfully, the conversation moved on rapidly, and I didn't have time to wallow in my embarrassment.

"Excellent, Lucien. Perhaps after a few more days of convalescing, you could reach out to him? And whenever you're ready, I want a full report of your kidnapping. Why they took you, what they wanted, and then we can decide how we should strike back."

"Consider it done, High Alpha. As for the report, there's not much to tell. They wanted dirt on you, and to know who the omega is and how we were hiding her. It was Varga and his cousin." Lucien shrugged, as if the entire ordeal could be summed up in so few sentences.

"Thank you."

"Of course, Alpha." Lucien's response was gruff, as if he were unused to receiving praise.

There it was again, that traitorous desire to sway into him, into his voice. My wolf paced restlessly, not demanding escape, but *annoyed* that her mate was in the room and yet now wanted to recant his claiming of her.

Offended might have been a better word, and I latched on to that. I should be offended. He'd insulted me to my face and had rolled right in here without an apology or acknowledgment of what was going on between us. Somehow, being pissed at him made it easier to tamp down the inappropriate urges I was feeling toward a near stranger.

But was it reasonable to be pissed at a man who'd just been through as much as he had? For an alpha wolf to be in a wheel-chair, surrounded by *other* alphas... That would rankle any of them. Yet here he was, trying to keep his chin up and a brave face on.

He'd been through hell, and if I couldn't give him grace in this moment, the least I could give him was time. We hadn't even had a *real* conversation. Didn't we owe each other at least that much, a chance to get on the same page before lashing out at each other?

We absolutely did.

The realization settled both me and my wolf enough that I could focus on the planning going on around me.

"Phoenixes are nearly polar opposites of goblins. They've always been few in number, and at this moment, I don't know of any currently alive. We're going to have to reach out to other packs, and perhaps the other species we visit to see if any are willing to share the location of a living phoenix."

"So we're starting with the centaurs, then?" Leigh asked. You could tell from her posture she was anxious, the hand resting on her belly tense, even though she'd asked the question lightly.

Kane nodded. "That was my conclusion as well. The question remains, who is willing and able to go?"

Ah. That again. I looked sadly at Fiona. She'd been through so much since she joined our pack, but she was one of the few females who was actually able to go out safely with her mate.

Brielle couldn't leave the enclave, Shay was already going to get the fae piece, Leigh's pregnancy was now in the second half, and travel would get more and more difficult the further along she was, and I couldn't leave the pack without being attacked.

It was a shitty situation, there were no two ways about it.

No one seemed surprised when Reed cleared his throat. "Fiona and I are willing to go for the good of the pack. But based on our interactions with both King Cysernaphus and the vampires, we feel it's best if we have at least two additional pack mates to back us up."

"I wish it could be me," Brielle said, sadness seeming to clog her throat for a moment before she got it under control. "But we can definitely find someone to go with you. Perhaps—"

"I volunteer," Samuel offered, pushing off the wall he leaned against to stand up straight. "I'm already here, and I'm nearly healed from the run-in with the Hungarians. No sense sending me home just to bring another guy back."

Reed acknowledged him with a nod. I couldn't help it when my eyes slid off Samuel and down to my scowling mate in the wheelchair next to him. He was magnetic, drawing me in even when he wanted nothing to do with me.

"Are you all just going to pretend I'm not here? I can go. I'll be healed in another day or two, and I can be the fourth. There's no reason to send a pregnant female's mate on a dangerous mission when you've got two unattached men available right here."

I swallowed hard, forcing myself to look away. Damn him, and his *unattached* self. Apparently, I was the only one thinking I owed him a conversation before making any rash decisions.

There was a long, uncomfortable pause before Dirge cleared his throat. "You're not unattached anymore, Lucien. And while you've been away, we've uncovered some unfortunate consequences of the omega seal. Any unbonded female with the seal on her palm will be hunted by all unbonded males outside her alpha-omega pair's pack. So until you and Olivia bond, she's vulnerable and requires extra protection."

His words were like sandpaper over my skin, even though he said them with painstaking kindness. I'd never felt more like a burden than I did at that exact moment, as every eye in the room swiveled toward either me or Lucien, as if waiting for him to respond or for me to burst into flames from embarrassment.

The latter felt like a distinct possibility. I refused to cry about it, so bring on the flames.

After yet more silence, I finally stole a glance toward Lucien, his jaw tight, teeth ground together in apparent fury as a muscle ticked above his temple.

Just great. He wants even less to do with me now, the helpless infant he can't wait to be rid of.

"I'm sure we can work that out. You said extra protection. That doesn't have to be me, does it?"

Dirge's jaw actually dropped. Lucien's callous response carved away at my heart like a chain saw decimating a block of butter. "Well, no—she's safe with anyone under Kane's direct pack link, but surely—"

"It's settled, then. I can still go."

I could feel eyes burning into me, waiting for my response, but there was only one thought on my mind. One neon-glowing, obvious solution.

If I was such a problem, I'd just excuse myself from the whole mess. He didn't want me? Well, he wasn't the first. And I *certainly* wasn't going to sit around and be pathetic and needy where I wasn't wanted.

I lifted my chin, ignoring every person in the room except one.

"That's okay," I said, pleased to hear how steady I sounded despite the pain pulsing through my veins like a second heartbeat. "I'm actually going back to Alaska as soon as the jet's ready. I'll be safe with the pack there, right, Kane?"

SIX

Lucien

_____

Her response should have made me really fucking happy, or at the very least relieved to kick the whole *fated mate* can down the road. I pushed her away, after all.

The barb about me being unattached? Yeah, that was not at all smooth or subtle. I'd caught her flinch out of the corner of my eye, even though she tried to hide it.

So why did it feel like my wolf was about to tear himself out of my skin when she said she was leaving?

Not leaving just the room, where I could scent her sweet, floral perfume like it was my drug of choice. No, she wanted off the whole damn continent that I was on.

Could I blame her? No.

Did my wolf give a shit about why I needed to push her away?

Also no.

If my body hadn't been battered and broken so recently, I was pretty sure he'd have torn himself out of me and pounced on her, pinning her beneath us so she couldn't escape. But that was *insane*. I didn't even know her, and she was young enough to be my daughter. Many times over.

I had no right, even if my wolf was demanding that we had *every* right. "Ours" was pulsing behind my eyelids on loop, like a chant.

Ours ours ours ours ours.

"You would absolutely be safe with the rest of the pack back in Alaska. I just thought..." The high alpha hesitated, giving me a very pointed look, as if I was about to jump in and interrupt what he was about to say.

But was I? Was I going to stake some claim on her, pound my chest like a caveman?

My wolf wanted to, with every fiber of his being. Even after wolfsbane, he was practically ravenous to sink his teeth into her at every chance. But that wasn't normal. That was more proof I wasn't fit for a sweet woman like Olivia.

Not to mention, I was hideous now, and without my looks, I had literally nothing to offer a woman. The thought sent a fresh spear of anger through me, and I gritted my teeth, hating the way even the small motion pulled at the giant, still-tender scar on my face.

The darkness inside me right now was too toxic. I shouldn't stop her from running.

I cleared my throat, shook my head. "We should probably discuss those plans together." I cast a quick glance around the room and added, "Without an audience."

She nodded stiffly, and I knew she probably wanted to smack me for being an ass.

But it was for the best, damn it.

I didn't have any room for a mate in my heart, only revenge.

The group broke up quickly at that, and I ignored the stares I got from my pack mates as they left the room in a steady trickle.

I'd have to get used to the stares. There was no doubt I'd be stared at for the rest of my life, a monster fit to scare children in bedtime stories.

The outside matches the inside now.

The bitter thought was ringing inside my skull when Kane hesitated next to me, the last to exit the room.

He spoke in low, semithreatening tones meant only for me. "We're going to give you some space, but I don't need to remind you that she's a member of my pack, and I won't have you treating her or any female under my protection badly. You've been through a lot, and it's okay if you need some time and space to heal before you're ready to enter a relationship. But *do not* hurt this girl or be unnecessarily cruel just because you're angry. That's a direct order from your Alpha."

I had no doubt he could feel my turmoil through the pack bonds and knew the storm raging inside me. I gave him a tight nod of acknowledgment, not liking that he knew as much as he did. He squeezed my shoulder before walking out of the room and shutting the door quietly behind him.

There was a beat of utter silence, and then I cleared my throat, needing to break it.

"Are you going to stare at the floor the entire time? If you're not ready to talk..." Olivia hesitated, and I finally looked up from the carpet.

She was so beautiful, it was physically painful. The kind of beauty that radiated from the goodness inside her. I sucked in a breath through my teeth with a hiss, and she visibly recoiled.

The urge to comfort her, hold her, and apologize was nearly overwhelming. But I couldn't do that, or she'd get the wrong idea.

She looked so damn *wounded* by my mere presence, I needed to say something, and fast.

"Look, this is all new. And Kane's probably right, I need some time to adjust to everything." I waved with agitation at my hideous scar. "You and I are strangers. Mates? I—" The denial was there, right on my lips, but it just wouldn't fall, no matter how true it was. I snapped my jaws shut again, angry that I couldn't just man up and set her free.

"I know we're strangers, and I am very clear on the fact that you have zero interest in being mated to me. I'm not pushing myself on you at all. I'll leave, and make it easy."

She was doing a good impression of bravery, keeping a stiff upper lip, but her scent. That glorious summery perfume in the air around her soured, going from sweet, ripe peaches and oranges to bitter peel in a snap.

My wolf was not pleased that we were the cause of her distress.

Olivia gasped as my vision sharpened, and I knew he was shining through my eyes, demanding that his opinion on the matter be known.

I'm trying to do the right thing here! I practically snarled the angry thought at my wolf, but he refused to pull back, refused to let me speak if I was going to send our mate away.

Ours.

Stubborn ass.

I closed my eyes in frustration, not sure what the fuck to do if I literally couldn't speak to tell her what I needed to say.

When cool, delicate fingertips traced along the back of my hand, I froze, the touch unexpected and altogether too alluring.

A shudder racked me, and when I opened my eyes again, she was kneeling before my wheelchair, sympathy in her gorgeous green eyes, swimming with unshed tears.

"It's okay. You don't have to act like you want this. I get it. I'll be on the first plane, and maybe eventually—" The words cut off on a sob, and then she was gone, hand over her mouth to cover the sounds of her crying, as if she had anything to be ashamed of.

In that moment, I was lower than the dirt and the worms crawling through it.

"Olivia, wait!" I called after her, but by the time I wrenched the wheelchair around to follow her, Olivia was long gone, door hanging open behind her. The only thing she left behind was the ghostly touch of her fingertips, the phantom pleasure of the first touch we'd shared. That, and a blowtorch-level burn in my side along my ribs, which I suspected was my own mate marks trying to fill in despite my lingering injuries.

I had royally fucked it all up, and I didn't know how to fix it.

I didn't know if it was even possible to fix any of it.

But I knew with every fiber of my being that I wasn't done with her.

One touch wasn't nearly enough.

SEVEN

Olivia

T ears streamed down my face as I ran, not even caring
     where I ended up, so long as it was alone, far from the
pitying eyes of the pack.

I eventually ran out of steam at the very back of the
gardens, a quiet, seldom-tended corner by the looks of things.
There were chips in the stone wall, and overgrown bushes that
looked a little too wild to be domestic.

It was dark and gloomy where I settled beneath a giant tree,
but I didn't mind. I wanted to hide and lick my wounds in
private. So, I sat at the base of the tree, pulling my knees into
my chest so I could bury my face against them. How had everything gone so wrong, so quickly?

Wishing for a mate and being lonely sucked, yes. But it was
nothing compared to the rejection that lay over me like a
smothering blanket now.

He'd looked right into my eyes, and where there should
have been love, joy, and excitement, there was only regret and
rejection. And fury, I couldn't forget that.

I was hollow inside, that chain saw of his very effective on
my emotions, carving them right out alongside my heart. How

long I stayed under the tree, crying out what was left of my feelings, I had no idea. Dusk fell, and once or twice I heard someone calling my name, but I didn't answer.

When I left the garden, I had to face the truth. Do hard things. Like pack my stuff, tell my new friends goodbye, and fly to Alaska for wolves I'd never met before to babysit me.

Live among complete strangers, again. Be unwanted—an imposition—*again*.

If I had any emotional energy left, the thought would have pissed me off. I was a talented healer and herbalist; there were plenty of packs out there that would be thrilled to have me. Just not the one I left, and not Pack Blackwater with a one-of-a-kind omega healer.

I stared down at my stupid, glowing palm with unfettered disgust. If it weren't for that mark, I could go to any of those other packs, where I could be useful, wanted.

But no. Not an option if I didn't want to get brutally raped.

Slamming my palm on the ground, I resisted the urge to scream my frustrations at the sky. It wouldn't help, and the second I did, I would have company. I wasn't ready to talk to anyone, so I remained silent, fingers clawed into the dirt as I wasted the day away alone and drawing paltry comfort from the lush gardens around me.

But eventually, as the darkness began to thicken, the cold crept in with it. I considered shifting, because fur was a lot warmer than human skin. But also, all I'd done was delay the inevitable. If I wanted any chance of being on a plane tomorrow, I had to head back now and tell Kane my decision.

Or Brielle. Sure, maybe it was cowardly, but telling the high freaking alpha of the wolf world that you were so inferior your own fated mate didn't want you? It wasn't high on my bucket list. Negative five million on the list, actually, after unmedicated toenail plucking and licking a dumpster with a family of raccoons living in it.

Putting it off, though, wasn't mature. And no matter how much it sucked, the beauty of taking charge was that at least I could prove him a little bit wrong. I was a mature, capable woman who could handle her own business.

With that thought front and center, I shoved myself off the now-cold ground, brushing off my pants as I picked through the overgrowth back to the manicured garden path.

I didn't make it.

A single, sharp horn blast filled the air, and I froze. Was that an alarm? In all the weeks we'd been here, I hadn't heard it, even when Brielle's powers were chipping away at the wards. So, if they were sounding an alarm now, that had to mean... I didn't know. Did they think I was missing? Were we under attack?

Shit!

I raced toward the path, swearing under my breath as branches and thorns pulled at my hair and clothes, little rivulets of blood trailing down my face and arms by the time the paver stones came into view. Before I made it halfway out of the garden, a sword-wielding blonde maiden ran into my path. On second look, it was Dakota from the front gate.

"Fuck! There you are. Didn't you hear us shouting for you earlier?"

"I'm sorry, I—"

"Shut up. There's no time to talk now. We've got to get you out of here."

"What?"

"Just keep up!" she yelled over her shoulder, not bothering to sheathe her sword as she ran through the twisting paths at top speed. If anyone else was coming the other way, she could impale them, but that didn't seem to concern her.

My mind raced as fast as my feet, but she was scanning our surroundings as she ran, holding the big-ass butterfly sword all the maidens toted around like pets with a white-knuckled grip.

She didn't slow as we left the gardens, running toward the back gate, where Brielle's curse-removal spell had been done. But a minute later, I saw my pack mates crowded at the back gate, several of them shouting and gesturing angrily. Lucien was with them—looking too pale to be on his feet, but out of the wheelchair nonetheless.

What the hell is going on?

"We are *not* staying here like sitting ducks while Petró and his ODL sycophants pick us off. No. We have to leave," Gael shouted.

Oh, shit. Varga was here *with* the ODL? Terror zapped through me as if I'd been electrified. I was marked. While I wasn't omega, if they knew enough to search the enclave, they probably knew about the omega seal too.

Kane was stoically defiant, a wolfish glow to his eyes that was vaguely threatening his second-in-command. "The second we step foot outside the walls, they'll be able to sense Brielle."

"If they're here, they already know about Brielle, or at least know it's one of our females here under the maidens' protection. We're *all* in danger here," Gael said with a snarl.

Kane wasn't having it. "They suspect. They don't know anything."

Galyna inserted herself into the conversation with a bravery I admired. "I'm afraid my brother is right, High Alpha." Kane's head whipped toward her, upper lip lifting with a growl. She raised both hands in a peacekeeping gesture, but spoke quickly. "The barriers are only effective when the person you don't want sensing you is outside them. If they step foot through the front gate, they'll immediately sense her too. But the difference is, they'll know for a fact she's *inside the enclave*."

Oh, Goddess. This was really, really bad. "So what can we do? Is there anywhere else we can go that's safe?" I blurted the question, and Fiona looked over, relieved to see me. She offered me a hand, and I stepped to her side, opposite Reed.

It was a small comfort, but the touch grounded me in a way I desperately needed at the moment.

"You've got to get outside the walls before they get inside. We can stall them at the gates, and thanks to Fiona's vision, we've got a little bit of a lead on them, but not much."

Kane looked down at Brielle with sorrow etched into his features. "Or, we can make a stand. Right here."

She shook her head, glancing regretfully at all of us gathered around. "No way. We're not sacrificing our pack for our safety. This has to end, but not like this. We need to run. We've got a head start, and we're going to use it."

"If we start running, we're not going to be able to stop," Leigh said gravely. "Your powers are way stronger now, and they'll be able to detect you. And soon, Poppy too." Her voice broke on a sob, and Gael pulled her into his chest, closing his eyes as if her words were a dagger, twisting in his guts.

This was it. Our time was up. And if the pack fell, we *all* fell. Nowhere would be safe for me, with Brielle and Kane gone.

"Not Poppy" Fiona mumbled at my side. I glanced at her in confusion, but her eyes had turned amber, blue flaring out, tingeing the skin around them. "A rose in bloom, in the midst of a dry, cracked desert. She will live. She's... shielded, somehow." Fiona rocked back, sagging into Reed's strong arms as the vision left her, the blue fading away and her mismatched eyes returning to normal. I was close enough to tell her hands were shaking, and I scooped one of them up in my own, returning the comfort she'd just offered me.

"Thank you," Leigh said, tears streaming down her cheeks as she stared at Fiona as if she'd just thrown her a lifeline. "*Thank you.*"

Fiona nodded, hands shaking as she tucked a blonde lock behind one ear.

Samuel spoke up. "We don't have time for this. We've got to move, and move now."

Elodie nodded grimly, the usually jovial female's expression as grim as the rest. "There's a back road that we can take. It's rougher than the main driveway, but moving toward the ODL would be a mistake. If they think you're nearby, they'll have brought someone with omega-detection capabilities. Most likely a fae or warlock."

"I can't ask you to sacrifice yourselves for me," Brielle started, taking Galyna and Elodie by the hands. "You're family, but you're not pack. You should stay here with the maidens, where you're safe."

Galyna snatched her hand away, affronted by the suggestion, but Elodie was the one who answered. "Our swords and wolves are with you. Where you go, we go."

Brielle nodded, expression starting to crumble under the weight of it all. I don't know what came over me, but I stepped forward on autopilot, grabbing her hand. She gave me a watery smile as I squeezed it.

"It's going to work out," I whispered, believing it, even though all signs pointed to chaos and destruction.

"It's time to roll. The SUVs are here," Galyna announced, pointing toward a small back gate.

"Alpha! We need to split up. Shay and I need Lisanne to show us how to get to the fae gate," Dirge said, hesitating as the rest of us moved toward the rear gates.

Kane turned, clasping Dirge's hand, something unspoken passing between them as Brielle hugged Shay as if it would be the last time.

I climbed into the back of a black SUV, praying to the Goddess that it wasn't.

EIGHT

Lucien

One minute, I was lying in a shitty bed, eating my third giant steak of the afternoon and rehearsing what to say to my mate. The meat would help my wolf regenerate faster, but unfortunately, it wouldn't help me convince her that even though I was an asshole, I didn't want her to leave me for Alaska yet, even though I should send her away for her own safety. The next, an alarm was going off, and I was hobble-running toward the back gate.

As the conversation unfolded, horror filled me. Petró clearly found out I was gone from their torture chamber. But how the fuck did that translate into him being here? Did they track us without us knowing?

I glanced over at Samuel, and his expression told me he was wondering the same thing.

"Were we followed?" I asked in a whisper, and he shook his head.

"No fucking chance. I used every trick in the book to make sure that wasn't possible."

I nodded, falling silent as I considered the possibilities. Before I could suss out how the Hungarians had found us so quickly, though, we were running through the back gate, climbing into unmarked SUVs to make our escape.

It galled me to run, but this wasn't the time to make a stand. I was still weakened from the torture, and we had both a pregnant female and an omega female with us.

Not to mention my omega-sealed mate.

Olivia was magnetic, and I found myself climbing into the farthest-back seat to be next to her, ignoring her visible shock as I yanked the door shut behind me. Samuel and Elodie were in the seat ahead of us, while Reed drove, Fiona taking shotgun.

The rest of the pack was in the first SUV, leading the way down the craggy path off the mountain. I felt each bump through my sore, half-healed body, but it paled in comparison to the wave of mixed emotions coming off my mate on the bench seat next to me.

I turned to look at her, and she snapped her gaze away as if I'd burned her.

"I won't bite you." I murmured the words meant only for her, even though in a car full of wolves with exceptional hearing, they probably still heard. They seemed distracted in their own discussions, though, and I took the moment to just breathe her in.

She slowly turned to face me, arching one regal eyebrow before answering. "You've made that *abundantly* clear."

Fuck.

Sweet and innocent she may have been, but my mate had *fire* in her, and I'd be damned if I didn't like it.

Too much. My blood heated in my veins, and whether she knew it or not, she was basically waving a red cape in front of a bull. Or a juicy piece of meat in front of a starving wolf, because in that moment, my instincts to chase her down flared to life.

All my earlier protestations about how our wolves were confused meant nothing, not sitting this close to her heat and delicious scent, not when she was challenging me. There were no more righteous thoughts that she deserved better than a scarred, ugly fucker like me.

I slid closer on the bench seat, closing the gap between us as we continued the bumpy path down the mountain.

"We should talk."

"Now? You've got to be kidding." The exasperated look she sent me should have been a warning, but I didn't heed it.

I shrugged, ignoring the pull in my stomach wound as I did so. "We're not driving. What else are we going to do until we get to the airport?"

She pursed her lips like the sexiest librarian in the history of books, and I hated the fact that I could *feel* her not wanting to give me another chance. It was everywhere: her expression, her scent, the tense set of her shoulders. That only made me more determined. But I couldn't get the sounds of her muffled sobs as she'd run away from me out of my mind.

She might not want to talk to me, but I hadn't meant to hurt her. Not really. Everything was messed up since I got captured, since the torture. And she didn't deserve to deal with my shit.

"Hang on!" was all the warning we got from Reed as he hooked the SUV around a tight turn, sending us all sliding—I practically flew over the back seat, slamming into the car door with a grunt a split second before Olivia smashed into my other side.

My brain must have glitched as her curves pressed into my side, her hand flying out and landing on my chest as she tried to catch herself. That was the only logical reason for the fact that I let the next words fly out of my mouth.

"If you wanna climb in my lap, baby, all you've got to do is ask."

Olivia blinked up at me in surprise for a moment before shoving herself away in disgust. "Is this all just a sick joke to you?"

"No, of course not, I—" It was at that exact moment that I became acutely aware that we had a captive audience, both Samuel and Elodie, staring at me with angry looks on their faces. *They* hadn't forgotten to buckle up.

Olivia wasn't having my apology. She'd already scooted herself back to her seat, clicking her seat belt into place with cold finality as she sent me a scathing stare.

Yep, I had fucked it up again.

She wasn't some girl I was going to screw in a club bathroom and never think about again. She was my fated mate, and I didn't know how to handle a relationship that was serious.

Life-and-death, grow-old-and-gray-together, meet-the-family serious.

Not that I had any family left for her to meet, but I imagined she did somewhere, and I didn't need a crystal ball to know they wouldn't approve of me.

I ground my back teeth as I clicked my seat belt into place, giving her the space she so clearly wanted. As I stared out the window, I replayed the whole scene over in my head, kicking myself.

Why did I always default to asshole when I could have just helped her sit back up and kept my mouth shut? Samuel would never have pulled that shit.

Self-sabotage was the clear answer. I didn't deserve her, couldn't make her happy, and I knew that. So, I was going to keep shoving my foot in my mouth to prevent myself from ever having a real chance.

That was depressing as fuck.

But the more I thought about it, the more I saw a pattern. I didn't go for nice girls very often. One, because, believe it or not, I wasn't a monster who thrived on breaking hearts. It was just easier, cleaner when the woman knew up front I wasn't planning to stick around.

Two, because any time one got too close, I'd push her away

before anything serious could develop. If I ran my mouth, they'd eventually get sick of my shit and leave. Every time, over and over.

The sex kept the darkness at bay, and pushing them away kept me free, hovering about my issues closely enough to feel the threat of madness but not sink into the depths of my trauma.

But that wasn't going to work this time, not with a fated-mate bond dragging us together at every turn. We didn't have to fall into bed—or a relationship—but I could at least treat her with respect.

I owed Olivia an apology. As soon as we got a minute alone, I would give her one. Even if I had to corner her on the airplane to do it.

With that settled, my mind began to wander, the greenery passing by outside my window blurring with our speed.

When our tires finally hit pavement a while later, realization hit me.

"Hey, Samuel?"

"Yeah?"

"What's the likelihood they planted a tracker in those cuffs?"

He went still for a moment, then turned halfway in his seat so he could see me.

"Given that they showed up on our doorstep with reinforcements less than forty-eight hours after we got there? Pretty damn good."

"So, you don't think it's under my skin anywhere?"

"Brielle and I weren't looking for anything like that when we were treating you, so it's possible a tracker could have been overlooked. She was pretty exhausted just from helping fight the effects of the wolfsbane."

I was both surprised and pleased when Olivia spoke up, clearly wanting to help the pack, despite her well-deserved fury with me. But that raised a new concern. If there was potentially a tracker under my skin, wherever we went, they'd just follow.

"How can you check for that?" I asked her, willing her to see the apology in my eyes.

"Well, there are several ways. Scanners, physical exam—while they're small, some can be felt under the skin. With most of your..." She cleared her throat, shooting me an apologetic look before continuing. "With most of your scars healing cleanly, we should be able to feel the tracker under the skin."

After what I'd just said to her, she was *still* trying not to hurt my feelings by pointing out that the biggest, ugliest scar was never going to heal.

Damn, I was a fucking lowlife.

"When we get on the plane, we'll have them check you out. If there's still a tracker on you, we can destroy it in the air," Samuel offered.

On me was the nicer way of saying embedded under my skin, where they'd have to cut it out of me.

Joy.

"Don't worry, buddy, we won't let them track us to the centaurs."

I nodded tightly, keeping my eyes on the road as we raced toward the airport. Somehow, instead of smooth black pavement, all I saw was Dominik's laughing face as he loomed toward me, wielding a knife.

TIME MOVED STRANGELY when you were running for your lives. We were less than an hour out from the enclave when Galyna got a call from one of the maidens that Petró's people had arrived, and they were going to give them the runaround and keep them busy as long as possible.

After that, it was calm. Until we were about ten minutes

from the airport, and Reed startled me from my haunted staring at the road slipping by beneath us.

"Shit! We've got company. Somebody call Gael, in case he hasn't seen them."

Before we could dial, though, Reed's phone was ringing. Fiona picked it up and put it on speaker, so we could all hear.

"You've got somebody on your tail."

"Yeah, I noticed. They're not exactly being subtle. I changed lanes, and they practically fishtailed to stick to my bumper."

Gael growled, the sound low and menacing enough to raise my own wolf's hackles. "Do you feel comfortable trying to lose them, or are we going to deal with them at the airstrip?"

"I somehow don't think they've got any doubts about where we're heading. I'm more concerned about them ambushing us with more people at the airstrip."

Gael was silent for a beat, and then Kane's voice came over the phone. "I'll contact my security guy at the airport. Hang on."

The line went dead as he put us on hold, and tense silence permeated the vehicle as we waited, the single minute he was gone seeming to last ten.

"The airstrip is clear right now, but security will clear the private entry gate before we get there."

"Got it," Reed said, grimacing as the car behind us tried to zip past, get between us and the rest of the pack in the first SUV. They left the line open, but tense silence descended over both vehicles as we continued evasive maneuvers.

"These idiots are going to cause a crash," I muttered under my breath, to which Samuel nodded his agreement.

"I think at this point, it's highly likely your theory about a tracker is correct. We had a hell of a head start, but they're on our bumper. There are other airports in the area that would have been more obvious choices for us to leave the jet."

"Fuck me. Should we try to dig it out now, or...?"

"Absolutely not," Olivia snapped, surprising me yet again with her vehemence. "Digging something out of your body in the back of an erratically moving car is irresponsible. We could do more damage and set your recovery back significantly."

Her words were punctuated by the whole SUV shuddering and then jolting as Reed slammed the brakes and maneuvered around the sedan, the driver of which was doing their best to separate us from our pack.

"Point taken. But we're going to need it out as soon as the plane is airborne."

She nodded tightly, not pleased, but also with no trace of fear for what I could only assume would be a grisly task. "I will find it and get it out."

"Thank you." I held her gaze until she looked away, and I noticed her white-knuckled grip on the handle overhead. Taking a risk, I unbuckled my seat belt and slid into the empty middle seat, leaning in close so only she could hear me. "It's going to be fine. I won't let anything happen to you."

She froze like a fawn as my breath washed over her ear. When she turned to face me, it was slow, as if she was uncertain about what she was going to see when she looked back. The raw vulnerability in her eyes cracked something inside me, and all my protestations about how our wolves were just confused about being mates felt incredibly stupid. I could see the question. The *Can I trust you?* that she was too proud to voice.

Goddess help me, I wanted her to be able to trust me. I wanted to be that man for her.

Could I be?

It was a dangerous question.

Kane's voice over the phone speaker silenced my internal war for the time being. "Those are the gates! Every male, be ready to bail out. I want the females to stay in the vehicles until the area is cleared, and then it's straight to the jet. Our females are the targets and should all be presumed in danger. Is that clear?"

Echoed responses of "Yes, Alpha," filled both cars.

Fiona hung up the phone after that, pensively tucking it into her own pocket.

"When I slide out, I want you to get into the driver's seat. If things don't go our way—" Reed started, and Fiona shook her head, cutting him off.

"If you're about to ask me to leave you, you can knock that shit off."

He snorted, shooting her a smirk before refocusing on the quickly disappearing road between us and the gates to the airstrip.

"Yes, ma'am. But remember before you refuse me, it's not just you we're protecting."

Fiona nodded tightly, and I saw the moment her eyes landed on Olivia, and her stance softened. "I'll do whatever I have to."

"That's my Stormy Girl." Reed looked her way just long enough to run his fingertips over her cheekbone, and I felt dirty for intruding on the tender moment.

But it was over as quickly as it began, because the tall, razor-wire-topped gates were beginning to roll back, and we had an enemy hot on our heels.

NINE

Olivia

I knew what was coming, but when the moment came that all the men—and Elodie, who ignored the Alpha's order about females staying in the cars—bailed out of the SUV, I wasn't ready.

One moment, we were skidding through the gates at top speed; the next, they were all flying out, shifting in midair, and there was no one but me and Fiona left in our car, the doors slamming shut behind them.

Fiona quickly hit the lock button on the doors and slid into the driver's seat as Reed had told her to. "You should climb up here with me, just in case."

My hands shook as I climbed between the second-row seats in front of me to do as she asked. "In case of what?"

"In case I need to hold somebody's hand." The grin she sent me was lackluster, and I knew she was trying not to show her own panic for my sake. As condensation started to cling to the windows around us, it hit me that she was struggling to keep her djinn powers in check.

I took my place in the passenger seat and gripped her hand without another word. Within ninety seconds flat, battle had broken out all around us. The men had shifted, only the two warrior maidens swinging their butterfly swords in human form as they faced off against Omega Defense League enforcers. They looked like two vampires and two fae, with perhaps a different kind of shifter rounding out their group? I couldn't tell without catching its scent.

Goddess, help them.

The silent prayer felt wholly inadequate in the current situation, but it was all I could do without directly defying an order from the high alpha. When a Jeep pulled up and five more beefy fighters poured out—these in street clothes, not ODL uniforms—I gripped Fiona's fingers harder.

Fiona started murmuring, as if anything above a whisper would damn our men. "Ten to seven. Those aren't great odds, but they're strong fighters. I've seen it. Elodie took out three massive trolls by herself when we were in Neftheim. They've only got a couple of vampires, and I don't know what the rest are. I've only seen wolves, trolls, and vampires so far."

"Didn't Elodie also almost die because of that third troll?"

There was a beat of silence, and water dripped down the windows of the SUV as she struggled for control. "Yes. But she *didn't*, and that's what matters."

"I hope you're right. Those two are lesser fae, and they're pretty powerful." I caught sight of Lucien's wolf, engaging alongside Gael with one of the vampires. When he turned, I saw that his wolf had a fresh scar down over his right eye, and I knew it was him.

They were tag teaming the vampire, and when Gael leapt toward his chest, dodging a wicked-looking silver blade by less than an inch, Lucien sank his fangs into the back of the vampire's thigh, making him howl with rage and stab backward.

The blade never made it, because Gael used the distraction to leap for the vampire's throat, tearing it out in a spray of dark blood that made me wince as the vampire's head rolled free.

"Holy fuck, is that a *lion*?" Fiona shrieked and pointed to where, yes, the fifth ODL enforcer had shed his human skin in favor of tawny fur, golden mane, and huge canines of his own.

Kane was on him in seconds, Reed and who I presumed to be Samuel all attacking at once. The clash was bloody, fur and bits of gore flying everywhere.

"Cat shifters aren't big fans of wolves."

"No shit," she said with a gasp as the lion fell under their attack, eyes going glassy before his body shuddered, reverting to human form as he died.

All told, it was over quickly, but not without injuries to our pack mates.

The last two ODL enforcers fled once they realized they were going to die, one of them cradling a limp arm that gushed blood as he fell into the passenger seat of the black Jeep.

The gates had only just started to roll closed behind their retreating car when I leapt from the SUV, my healer's instincts taking over. Galyna was closest to me, so I stopped at her side first.

Perhaps I should have given them another second to register that the battle had ended before running to check their injuries, because before I could blink, I was frozen in place with a butterfly sword blade an eighth of an inch from my carotid artery.

"It's just me," I whispered. "I saw you take a hit from one of the fae."

She blew out a breath and dropped the blade from my neck. "Sorry. Never sneak up on a maiden."

"I won't make that mistake again. Where did it hit you?"

She grimaced. "It's fine. If you want to check me out, you can do it on the jet."

"But magical attacks—"

"Olivia!" The alpha bark had me wanting to cower with its force. I froze, instinct riveting me to the spot at having garnered an alpha's displeasure. "What the fuck are you doing? Get to the jet!" It was a direct order, but as recognition sank past my instinctual response, anger reared up in its place, and I spun toward Lucien, who was once again human, and stalking toward me with fire in his eyes.

He was also very, very naked. His muscles were bigger than I remembered as he closed the distance between us, bunching and releasing with every step. He was coated in a thin sheen of sweat and spattered with other shifters' blood. The scar on his face combined with his furious expression made me think of an avenging god from the old stories, swept down to earth in a cloud of power to exact wicked vengeance. He was all threat, all alpha.

I kept my eyes glued to his face, not wanting the first time I saw my mate that way to be him shouting at me and bloody.

"You have injuries. I'm a healer. This is what we do," I snapped, lifting my chin as he closed the distance between us, stopping mere inches from my chest and leaning down into my personal space.

"You do *not* ignore orders from the high alpha, and more importantly, you do not put your own life at risk!"

I opened my mouth to respond, but all the breath left me in a rush as he picked me up and slung me over his shoulder without even giving me a chance to answer. I was upside down, staring at his bare ass in shock before I even realized what was happening.

Shock and fury filled me as he jogged across the grass toward the airstrip, not waiting for me to argue as all the blood rushed to my head.

"Put me down!" I demanded when my tongue caught up to my indignation.

"I will not. I should paddle your ass for getting out of the car before it was clear!"

"You wouldn't dare." I surprised myself with the growl that followed the words, but my wolf did *not* like him trying to boss us around after he'd all but rejected our bond.

A fiery slap on my ass cheek shocked the hell out of me.

Oh, you are going to regret that, Lucien Vasilescu.

I kicked downward with my foot, as hard as I could with his arm banded over the backs of my thighs. I connected with something solid, and he grunted when my tennis shoe made impact, but he didn't slow down or retaliate with another spanking.

The grass beneath us turned to dark asphalt, and then he was jogging up the steps of the jet. To my surprise, though, he didn't drop me into the first seat. He charged down the aisle, still holding me captive, until we reached the back of the plane, where there was a small private bedroom.

Fear trilled in my veins, and I realized that I didn't really know this man from Adam. What was he about to do to me? I wasn't proud of the way the thought froze me, but he was a very dominant alpha, and I was nowhere near his strength, even recovering as he was. His injuries hadn't stopped him from fighting, that was for damn sure.

The door clicked shut behind us, and the world spun as he pulled me off his shoulder and set me on my feet.

"Don't you ever scare me like that again." His words were a harsh whisper, and then his hands were in my hair, dragging me forward as he pressed his lips to mine in a searing kiss. I was shocked into quiescence, my brain taking several seconds to realize that instead of fighting, we were kissing.

I knew the whole *time stood still* thing was a cliché, but damn if it didn't feel like we were frozen in time as the entire world tilted under my feet as I wrapped my arms around my very own vengeful god.

Shock quickly gave way to something instinctual as I was consumed by a rush of unfamiliar heat. Every part of me that was touching him was a live wire, heat pooling in my belly and lower. I tentatively rested my hands on his bare shoulders, and he groaned against my mouth before releasing my lips, pulling me into his chest in a bear hug.

"One minute, I was scanning for enemies; the next, I see you with a blade to your throat." He whispered the words into the top of my head, and I could feel the tension in his muscles under my fingertips. Taste the tang of fear in his scent.

He'd been afraid.

For me.

Suddenly, I wasn't angry at him for carting me off like a piece of luggage. Even if my butt still stung, and I was confident there was a handprint glowing on my skin. It burned like a claiming, not a reprimand.

"I wasn't trying to scare you or startle her. I was just trying to help." Tears I refused to let fall stung my eyes at the admission, and in hindsight, I could see that it was maybe stupid to jump out of the SUV and run toward the fray instead of the jet like we'd been told.

But damn it, I was a healer. It wasn't in me to sit by and let someone injured go untreated.

"I know. You're a little hellcat underneath all that innocence, aren't you?"

The way he purred the nickname had me melting, the heat that started with his kiss going from campfire to inferno in no time at all. I swayed toward him, bracing my palms on his bare chest. It was warm and solid and *safe* somehow under my fingertips. It was real. And I liked it.

It felt like the first moment of my entire life that was in full color, digital surround sound as I stared into his amber eyes, which burned with the same heat I felt inside.

He put his fingertips under my chin, guiding me up until I was staring into his eyes, seeing the devilish smirk he wore.

I was completely lost for words as I stared into his gorgeous amber depths, his gaze lulling me into complacency like a cobra in a basket. Until it finally registered in my brain that he was very, *very* nude and I was pressed up against a whole lot of bare skin and rippling muscle, not just his pecs.

A hard swallow was my only response, though he waited expectantly for me to answer.

Harsh pounding on the thin bedroom door saved me.

"Lucien! I'm coming in!" It was Kane, and he sounded pissed, with that alpha double timbre to his voice that meant trouble.

I leapt back like a teenager caught doing something naughty with her boyfriend, which wasn't terribly far from the truth. Except for the fact that I was a grown-ass woman and Lucien was my fated mate. You know, minor details.

Kane pushed through the door with the fury of an avenging angel. He looked rapidly between Lucien and me, as if gauging without words what was happening. When his stormy eyes finally landed on mine, I wished I could crawl under the bed and hide. It was like he could see straight through me.

"Are you okay?"

"Yes, I'm fine." It wasn't a lie. Physically, I was totally unharmed.

Emotionally? I was reeling from the sudden change in Lucien from indifference to over-the-top alpha protective. Possessive. *Passionate.*

I shuddered at the memory of our bodies pressed together, his lips hot and soft on mine, then blushed.

Kane shifted his gaze to Lucien, a dark scowl settling over his features. "Come with me. We need to have a chat about the appropriate ways to treat a female in our pack."

"Yes, Alpha." Lucien was the picture of compliance, but as

he trailed Kane out of the room, he cast me a heated look over his shoulder that told me he was remembering the exact same moment I was.

And he liked it as much as I did.

Holy shit.

I SAT on the edge of the bed, my legs suddenly shaky, when not even ninety seconds after the males left, the door to the tiny jet bedroom flew open a second time.

"Damn, girl. You've got that boy on lockdown. That was *impressive*." Leigh strode through with an unapologetic grin. "You're reminding me how much fun it is to piss Gael off. It's been a while, but let me tell you, the sex is never better than when I've been pushing his buttons." She fanned herself dramatically, and I blushed for the second time in as many minutes. Much more and I'd be a sentient beet.

"Leigh, don't be embarrassing. Nobody wants to hear that," Brielle huffed. "Especially not Gael's *sister,* who needs the healer."

"Fine, but I'm just saying…" She turned to me, waggling her eyebrows suggestively, thankfully in lieu of telling us any more about her sex life. She quickly found a spot to lean against the wall so Brielle—and Galyna, whose arm was slung over her shoulder—could shuffle past and into the small bedroom.

"Here, set her on the bed," I offered, jumping up and out of the way.

"Thanks," Galyna said with an uncomfortable wheeze as she exhaled. Her face was pale, her lips slightly blue.

I studied her with concern as she lay back on the duvet. "You don't look so good." Her entire demeanor was *significantly* worse than when we'd been standing outside. That was a rapid decline. Her usually hale complexion had vanished under the weight of the magical attack. Her dark hair was usually kept in a sharp, tidy braid, but now it was disheveled, as if she hadn't bothered exerting the energy to tuck the errant strands away where they belonged.

"Gee, thanks. You medical types always know how to make a girl feel all warm and fuzzy inside."

Brielle snorted. "Don't talk, you're wasting breath you don't have. Where did he hit you?"

When Galyna pointed to her upper left chest, I bit my bottom lip between my teeth. That was not a good place to take a magical hit, even for a wolf.

Fiona was half shifted and Elodie was as mussed as Galyna and twice as filthy—though otherwise healthy—when they walked in a second later and shut the door on the sound of males arguing in the main seating area of the jet. We all jolted on our feet as the plane began to roll forward, taxiing into position on the runway, no doubt.

"Oli, can you grab me whatever medical supplies are in that back cabinet to the left, there?"

I jumped into action, my worry of no use to anyone. "Of course." It was a pleasant surprise to find a fully stocked traditional first aid kit, but also a well-labeled herbalist kit, with all the most common herbs used to treat shifter injuries. There was also a bulky surgical kit, but I really hoped we didn't need that while we were in the air. Or at all, actually.

Though, I might need some of it to dig a tracker out of Lucien.

Shit.

I hurried over with the supplies, grimacing when I saw the blackened, burnt-looking flesh on Galyna's shoulder and chest now that she'd stripped out of her gore-spattered and slightly singed tunic.

"Is there any burn salve in here?" Brielle asked, hands

bracketing the area as she let her omega healing powers flood into the wounded warrior.

"No salve, no, but there are two herbs in the pack that I could make a quick balm with." Not that I knew what they were, but I rarely had to know an herb's name to be able to sense how it could help or harm. Thankfully, this time I didn't zone out, as that was embarrassing.

"That would be great, thank you." She never opened her eyes, too focused on her work, but she did smile.

I quickly mixed the herbs into a rough-and-ready balm with some almond oil. It had soothing properties for shifters, and whenever my hand hovered over the few oil bottles in the kit, my instincts told me that was the one. I only waited a moment after the blend was done for Brielle to open her eyes. As soon as she did, I proffered the container.

"If that's all you need for Galyna, I need to go see if I can find a tracker under any of Lucien's wounds. He thinks that might be how they found us so quickly."

Brielle nodded, expression grim as she took the balm. "If you need any help with extraction, let me know."

"Thanks."

I only hesitated for a moment before grabbing the surgical kit and the herbalist kit and heading for the front of the jet.

The men had quieted down, whatever Kane wanted to say to Lucien apparently over and done with while we worked on Galyna.

All eyes turned to me as I shut the bedroom door, and suddenly, I wished I'd sent Brielle out here. Her magic was a more obvious choice for the task at hand, plus she was a trained doctor. I hesitated, until Reed smiled and waved me forward. At least they'd all put on pants.

"Lucien and Samuel filled us in on their theory. Do you need a hand looking for the tracker?"

You could always count on Reed to smooth over an uncomfortable situation, and I was so relieved he was calm in that moment.

Not that I wasn't calm; I was a professional. But all the rapid changes in the past few days were taking an emotional toll at this point.

That, or was it just that I'd met my fated mate, and he was giving me whiplash between shoving me away, acting like a caveman, and then kissing me completely out of the blue?

And damn, that kiss. It was the best I'd ever had, my cheeks heating at just the memory. Not that it took much to make me blush as a redhead, but still.

Was that how it would be now? He was constantly looking at me like... like I was his prey? No, that wasn't it. He looked at me as if I were a delicious treat he wanted to wolf down in one bite.

I had to work twice as hard to keep my professional façade in place as I considered the best way to go about finding the tracker. Without a handheld scanner, I'd have to hope the tracking tech they used was large enough that I could feel it with my fingertips.

Everyone was still staring at me, and I realized they were all waiting for me to answer Reed while I'd been having a tiny conversation in my own head. *Awkward.*

"No, I don't think so. But I'll let you know if I find one and that changes."

"Sure thing." He smiled kindly, and I got my butt into gear, walking the length of the plane to where Lucien stood, arms crossed over his muscular chest, eyes burning into me with every step I took.

TEN

Lucien

O livia cleared her throat, staring at my bare chest and
carefully avoiding eye contact as I waited for her to tell
me what to do. That's when her scent hit me, the normally
sweet peaches and fresh cotton tinged sour with anxiety.

I was making her nervous, which was understandable,
given I'd just lost my shit and thrown her over my shoulder.

And spanked her.

Fuck.

Then kissed her.

Double fuck. I was not doing so well at keeping my distance,
but damn if seeing her with that blade against her throat hadn't
flipped a switch inside me. It was pure instinct.

"Can you four give us a few minutes?" I asked the
other men.

"Are you going to keep your head?" Kane's question was
sharp, scolding.

It rankled, but frankly? I couldn't blame him. He took his
protection over the pack females seriously, as he should. I was
all up in my head after the torture and the memories it had
dragged to the surface of my father.

Olivia and I... We were off to a rocky start. She'd been perfectly kind, and it was entirely my fault.

"I'm calm," I promised, though I couldn't completely hide my resentment of the question. I was older than Kane by more than three hundred and fifty years, and my wolf knew it. But dominance was a different beast, and there was no denying his overwhelming power.

Kane turned to Olivia, setting his hands on her shoulders and making eye contact. I could see her trembling under the weight of his gaze and instantly bristled. I had to resist the urge to insert myself between them so he couldn't make her shake like that. "If you have *any* trouble with him, we are within earshot at all times."

"Y-yes, Alpha."

Kane nodded, and the other four men walked to the back of the plane, where they could still see us, but we had a tiny bit more privacy. My wolf immediately calmed, preferring not to have other males around our unbonded mate.

Samuel was unbonded as well, and my wolf saw him as a threat, even if I knew logically he would never try to steal Olivia from me. Assuming I didn't literally run her off and cause her to reject our bond, at least.

My wolf snarled at the thought.

Olivia cleared her throat a second time, that nervous tinge to her scent making me question what the best next step was. She rolled back her shoulders as if gathering her courage, and I decided to wait her out, let her control the situation.

Another heartbeat, and her healer training seemed to take over, replacing the anxious she-wolf with a no-nonsense professional.

"Okay, there isn't a handheld scanner on the plane, so I'm going to have to examine you by hand, to see if we can feel any foreign objects under the skin." She gestured to the nearest seat. "You should probably sit."

I obeyed without ever breaking her gaze. I even resisted the urge to say something sarcastic or suggestive, which might make her uncomfortable. But I couldn't just let this go on between us. I'd been the one to push her away, and then I'd pulled her back in. It was all mixed signals.

"I'm sorry. I shouldn't have... I shouldn't have done a lot of things, but I definitely didn't deserve to kiss you after I acted like such an ass. And I'm sorry for speaking to you that way back in the SUV. I default to asshole, and that's not fair to you. Or your fault."

She blinked twice, slowly, as if she didn't quite know what to do with the unexpected words. When she spoke, the words were hesitant. "Thank you."

"It's the least you deserve. I'm just all messed up, after, well, you know what." I shook my head, not wanting to get into the gory details. She'd seen me when I first arrived at the enclave; she knew what had happened.

She nodded, kneeling down in front of my seat so we were at eye level. I couldn't read her expression, but she shocked the fuck out of me when she reached out, palm up in offering.

Hesitantly, I placed my hand in hers. She clasped my hand, the warmth and acceptance I felt at the simple touch astounding. Beyond anything I deserved, and it was humbling. Shame covered me from head to toe at how badly I'd treated this woman, when literally all she'd offered me was kindness and acceptance.

"Do you want to talk about it?"

My throat was too clogged with emotion to say a word, so I simply shook my head, hoping she could see what I couldn't say in that moment. My gratitude. My unworthiness. The desperate way I wished I could be good enough for her.

"Okay. I'm here if you change your mind. I'd better start your exam, though, because we don't want the Hungarians following us to Greece now, do we?"

"Fuck no."

She smiled at that, squeezing once before releasing my hand. But the memory of her touch, her unconditional acceptance, was never going to leave me. It was seared on my soul, a beautiful brand amid the mess of scars new and old that made up the rest of me.

Her touch was professional as she gently checked several of my wounds, and I managed not to wince through sheer force of will. When she paused at one on my shoulder, I looked up at her.

"I think this might be the one. The wound here was shallow and has already healed, but I believe there's something under the skin. I'm going to see if Brielle can confirm for me, because it's small, and I don't want to cut into you just to find out I'm wrong. I'll be right back."

A minute later, both healers stood in front of me, poking at the outer edge of my shoulder. Brielle briefly closed her eyes, then nodded. "Yep. Foreign object, about the right size. I can have that out in a few minutes. Do you want a local anesthetic for the pain?"

"No. Just get it out."

"Got it." Brielle was all business as she unrolled the mini surgical kit and swabbed my skin with disinfectant.

A quick glance up at Olivia, and I was acting rashly again. I held out my free hand, palm up, mirroring the gesture she'd given me a few moments before. She stared at it for only a second before stepping up and placing her hand in mine.

Unfamiliar warmth and longing filled me as I let myself get lost in her eyes, and I barely noticed when Brielle took the scalpel to my shoulder.

"Okay, you're good to go. I'm not even going to stitch it, because it's shallow and it's already starting to knit back up. I'll give this to Reed in case he wants to check anything on it before destroying it."

"Thank you," I murmured, clinging to the contact with my mate.

My mate.

It was such a surreal admission, even in the private shroud of my own thoughts. The rest of the pack was walking back up the aisle, and I heard Brielle whisper something as she handed the tracker off to Reed.

"Olivia, I—" Stabbing pain stole my breath, and I grabbed at my right eye and the scar over it as I hissed between my teeth.

"Lucien? What's wrong? Lucien!"

I couldn't answer, couldn't think, couldn't even stay upright as the pain paralyzed me, and the whole world tilted on its side as I slid toward the floor.

ELEVEN

Olivia

I tried to catch Lucien as he slumped over, getting a whole lot of bare skin and not a lot of leverage, and ended up on the floor myself, his head cushioned on my chest.

He clutched his face, his cries of pain having drawn nearly everyone—except Galyna, who was also in rough shape—to the front of the jet.

"What's happening?" I directed the question to Brielle, who'd knelt beside us and already had her hands on Lucien's shoulder, funneling her power into him.

"I'm not sure."

I didn't like the way her voice shook with uncertainty, not one bit. But before I could respond, fur sprouted along the backs of Lucien's arms, his fingertips turning claw tipped as they fell away from his scar. When my eyes met his, they glowed orange with his wolf, and long, sharp canines protruded from his mouth.

"Lucien?" His name was a terrified whisper on my lips, but he was mere inches from me, so he heard it.

His only response was a growl, harsh and threatening as he bared his teeth at Brielle.

Kane shoved between them in a flash, snatching the diminutive omega behind his much-larger bulk.

"Lucien! That's enough!" Kane's face contorted with fury as he lashed out with his suffocating dominance.

But Lucien didn't even flinch as his eyes began to flicker, the cool orange giving way to flecks of red.

"What's happening?" I didn't know who I was asking, only that I was afraid for Lucien.

I stared in horror at his eyes, possibilities running through my mind at a mile a minute. But the only time a wolf's eyes went red was when they were *feral*. There was nothing in this moment that should have caused that.

But a second later, when Lucien lunged away from me, it wasn't toward Kane. It was toward *Samuel*.

"Lucien, no!" I moved without thinking as Lucien leapt at the other male, throwing myself between them at the last second.

Everything happened at once. Lucien smashed into me, sandwiching me between their chests as he took a vicious swipe with his clawed fingers at Samuel's throat.

Samuel managed to dodge, but the strike caught me on the forehead.

For a split second, I felt no pain, only shock. When the agony broke through, it was terrible. I gasped and clutched my face, blood oozing between my fingers and dripping into my eyes as nausea roiled in my stomach.

Hands were on me before I could process whose they were or where they came from—big, masculine hands—and then I was snatched out of the way, the world spinning with the speed of it. Reed's face was in front of mine, concern etching his handsome features as he loomed over me.

"You're going to be okay. I'm going to carry you to the back so Brielle can come fix you up."

Thunder boomed ominously outside, and the plane shook under our feet.

"Shit," Reed swore under his breath. "Can you stay here for a second? Fiona is upset."

"What?" My brain was moving in short, staccato bursts, trying to catch up over the shock of my sudden injury. But he was already gone, grabbing Fiona around the waist and dragging her away from the two males, both half shifted as they tussled in the aisle of the jet.

"That motherfucker nearly took her head off! I'm gonna *kill him*." Fiona's voice dropped half an octave with the threat, her skin flashing blue faster than my blurred vision could follow.

"She doesn't want that! He's still her mate. And if you lose control, you're going to do more damage than he did. She won't survive a plane crash, Stormy, you know that!"

The growl that tore out of her throat was properly canine, and I had a moment of pride that my friend had so fully embraced pack life, which was quickly replaced by embarrassment as I violently puked into the nearest plush leather seat.

Brielle appeared at my side like an apparition, slapping her hand directly over my bleeding head wound as she murmured soothing things into my ear while I heaved up everything in my stomach.

The agony vanished almost instantly, but the nausea was a little harder to get rid of, with all the adrenaline coursing through me.

A fresh wave of alpha dominance nearly knocked me to my knees, but Brielle held me up, and then Fiona and Elodie were there, bracketing me.

The nausea finally left, winking out of existence as if through sheer force of Brielle's will.

"You're okay, you're going to be okay," Elodie murmured, rubbing my back and giving me a soft smile. "Nobody's going to let him touch you again."

"I don't think he meant to. His eyes—"

"There is *no* excuse for putting your hands on a woman. I don't fucking care what he's been through, he hurt you, he's dead to me." Fiona's voice was like ice, brittle and sharp as she cast a scathing look over her shoulder, where the men had formed an impenetrable wall between us and Lucien.

I couldn't see what was happening, and that was nearly as bad as getting cut. I knew they were all mad at him, but they hadn't seen his eyes. It was like something else had taken him over.

"I don't think he could help it. His eyes weren't right. And why would he attack Samuel like that? Samuel saved him from the Hungarians. He wasn't aiming for me. I don't believe he'd hurt me on purpose. *Please*," I begged, though I wasn't sure what I was even asking for. Fiona's amber-shifted eyes flickered, her usual mismatched blue returning for a second.

"Let the guys calm him down first, okay?" Elodie, ever the voice of reason, squeezed my arm supportively, and I wanted to weep.

Why was everything determined to go wrong between us? It was like unseen forces were yanking us apart, when mates were meant to be drawn together. And it made me furious, but in a way that made me want to curl up in a ball and sob for a week at the injustice of it all.

Reed was the first to turn toward us, his expression grim. "Are you okay?" he asked me.

Not even a little bit.

"I'm fine. I need to see Lucien."

He grimaced. "Are you sure that's a good idea?"

No.

"Yes." I lifted my chin, refusing to show how shaken I truly was. But I just *knew* at a soul-deep level that he didn't want to hurt me. Why he wanted to attack Samuel was a mystery, but he didn't want to hurt me, and that had to be enough for now.

"All right, hold on." He held up a hand and turned, talking quietly to the other men. It was a long, tense moment before he turned and reluctantly waved me forward.

I would be lying if I said my knees weren't jelly as I walked back up the plane aisle. But when I squeezed past Reed and Samuel, my heart broke, and I forgot all about my own fear. Because as soon as I caught sight of Lucien, flat on the floor, canines still protruding, partially shifted and stuck under the high alpha's dominance and Gael's knee... I had no doubt that he hadn't meant me harm.

I dropped to my knees at his side, resisting the urge to stroke back his hair as his eyes found mine, the only part of him he could move.

"What's happening? Are you hurt?"

He grunted, no words forming as frustration twisted his features.

I turned so I could see the high alpha, careful not to cause offense by making direct eye contact. "Are you keeping him from talking, or...?"

Kane shook his head. "No, just from moving, and only until he reverses his shift. We can't have him starting a brawl while we're in the air."

I nodded. He was right, even if I hated to see Lucien like this. His eyes still had those flecks of red, the feral tinge making me sad as well as confused.

"Can you guys give us a little space? I'm not saying let him up, just that I'd like to talk to him. See if I can help him calm down."

"Alpha, I don't know about that." Gael spoke up, rubbing his jaw anxiously. Then he looked at me guiltily. "Are you *sure*? I don't like leaving a female with a volatile male. Giving you space is what got you hurt the first go-around."

"I'm sure. He wasn't trying to hurt me, just Samuel for some reason."

"Clearly," Samuel muttered.

"Sorry, Samuel." I grimaced in his direction.

"*You* have nothing to apologize for. And for Goddess's sake, don't ever put yourself between two alpha males again." He eyed my still-bloody forehead with true regret.

"We'll give you space, but I will not let him up until he has control of his shift and you're clear. Even if he stays there the entire flight."

"I understand." Pain lanced me at the idea of him being kept prisoner the entire flight, after the captivity and torture he'd just endured. I had to help him.

The men moved back a little—not giving us as much space as before, even though Lucien was still pinned flat on his belly by Kane's dominance, despite Gael standing up and backing away. But when they stopped halfway down the aisle, forming a protective barrier between us and the rest of the pack females, I knew that was as good as we'd get.

Deciding to ignore them, I lay down on my side, getting face-to-face with Lucien, my back to the pack.

"Is it okay if I touch you?" I whispered the question, giving us as much privacy as possible.

There was no response, and then I realized he couldn't nod, and he wasn't talking. His eyes were fixated on my bloody forehead, and I just made a decision and went for it. I let my fingers stroke over his hair, which was usually styled back from his face, but was currently in disarray.

"I've heard that a mate's touch is calming, but as soon as you can talk, if you don't like it, I'll stop, okay?"

More silence, his eyes still fixated on my forehead where he'd cut me with his claws, so I continued to finger comb his hair, trying to think of what else to say. I wasn't the most talkative, even when I had someone else to hold a conversation with. But somehow, words poured from my lips in a soothing whisper without trouble. It was the regret in his eyes, the confusion. *It wasn't his fault.*

"I've never seen your hair without product in it before today. You're always so polished, I feel plain by comparison. But I like it this way too. It's free. And that's nice sometimes. It's really soft too, and nice to touch."

I kept rambling about nothing, keeping close watch on his features, in case he seemed to dislike anything I was doing, but the more I spoke, the less tense he seemed. His shoulders slowly relaxed, the fur and claws receding from his hands and arms.

The fangs disappeared next, and eventually, the last fleck of red vanished from his eyes.

"Hi, there," I said with a smile, once I could tell that *my* Lucien was back fully in control.

"Hi."

It was one hoarse word, but I felt it like a caress down my bare back.

"I'm so sorry. I will never forgive myself for hurting you."

"It's okay, I knew it wasn't me you were after." I forced a smile, though I could feel the tender moment between us slipping away already.

"There is *no* excuse. I—"

"Lucien." Kane appeared above us, hovering like a dark angel.

"High Alpha, I apologize."

"Good, and you will continue to apologize to the rest of the pack who you put in danger."

"Yes, Alpha." Lucien bared his neck, the small movement the first he'd made so far. And something about it shattered me just a little bit more inside.

My mate was broken, and from the shuttered look in his eyes, I knew he wasn't going to let me in to help put him back together.

TWELVE

Lucien

S hame over what I'd done was hot and thick in my throat as I watched Olivia back away, sadness marring her beautiful features. Kane finally allowed me back to my feet once she was behind Reed and Gael, clustered in among the women.

Protected from me.

The very first thing I did was turn to Samuel, who stood warily a few feet away and off to the side, where there were a few rows of expensive leather seats between us. "I apologize. I don't know what came over me. I— There's no excuse. But I truly don't know what happened."

"I think I do," Brielle said, tapping Gael's shoulder for him to let her through. She stepped up to Kane's side, giving me a sad look.

No, not sad. It was *pity*. And that burned hotter than the fucking sun.

"Based on what I felt, it seems the prolonged exposure to a lower dose of wolfsbane has damaged your connection to your wolf. It's not severed. If that were the case, you wouldn't have any access to your wolf or the ability to shift. But it was in your system long enough, it's had some negative impacts, causing you to lose control."

"Are you able to reverse it?" Kane asked.

She hesitated, twisting her lips with that pity again, and I knew. The words were merely bitter confirmation.

"No, I don't think I can. There's nothing physically left for me to heal. The connection with one's wolf is deeper, a bonding of two unique spirits. It's something that over time might correct itself."

Might.

She was trying to couch the blow in that patented way healers had, but I was no idiot. What she wasn't saying was that if it didn't, I would be a danger to my pack permanently.

Worse than that—my gaze swung to Olivia's coppery hair, the only part of her that was visible around the wall of alpha muscle between us—I would be a danger to my *mate*. I'd drawn her blood, could have permanently maimed her. She was painfully perfect, from her sweet citrusy scent down to the way she looked at me with those trusting doe eyes, as if I hadn't done a speck of wrong in my nearly four hundred years of life. And I couldn't bear to hurt her again, not even by accident.

"I understand. Thank you, Brielle."

She nodded, trying and failing to hide her emotions. Her still-water scent was bitter with the edge of sorrow.

But hers weren't the feelings I was most concerned about. Olivia had to be my top priority. I was a selfish prick, but even the little snatches of time with her had me getting attached.

If my wolf was a danger to her, I couldn't allow that. If there was even a chance of her getting hurt like... *No.* I viciously yanked my thoughts away from the painful past.

Letting myself go down that path was a dead-end road to sorrow, and I knew it.

I cleared my throat, lowered my voice for only my high

alpha's ears. "I'll keep my distance. I don't want to hurt anyone. Especially not her."

Kane nodded, and for the first time since I'd been hauled out of Dominik's torture pit, I saw sadness in his eyes.

But no amount of regret or pity in the world would rewind the clock. All it would do was form a chasm of pain, as the repeated impacts chipped away at the bedrock of who I'd been. It yawned before me, wider by the day. Uncrossable. Permanent. *Deadly*.

THIRTEEN

Olivia

The pack found a strange sort of unspoken equilibrium after that. The males formed up around Lucien, protecting him from himself as much as from us. The females gravitated back into the bedroom, giving us all as much space as possible. It wasn't lost on me that Samuel stayed as physically far away from me as possible on the same aircraft and wouldn't even face my direction, let alone make eye contact as we left the front of the jet.

It was a bit like being snubbed, even though instinctively I knew he was trying to prove himself nonthreatening to Lucien's damaged wolf.

The idea that another male could be a threat to a bond that Lucien so clearly wasn't sure he wanted... Well, it was ironic. It might even have been *hopeful* to that naïve part of me that wanted my mate's open-armed acceptance and devotion. The *wolf* knew he wanted me, even if the man didn't yet.

But the wolf was in danger, and I couldn't see that as a good thing. It made my own wolf restless in my chest, where she was usually quiet and meek. The whole thing was unsettling and had me on the back foot.

"Here." Elodie pressed a set of fresh clothes into my hand. "You've got a little—" She gestured to my neck and chest, and I absently lifted a hand to see what she was referring to. Sticky. I looked down, seeing the redness staining my fingers.

Blood.

"There's no shower on the jet, but there is a sink nearly big enough to bathe in. Once you get cleaned up, we should all get some sleep. There's no telling what kind of reception we'll get once we land in Greece, and we should be in fighting shape as much as possible."

"Smart," I whispered, forcing a smile I didn't feel. "At this rate I'm going to have to work off damage to this jet for Kane and Brielle." The joke wasn't really funny, but I didn't really feel like joking, so that tracked.

"Hey." She stopped me, hand on my shoulder, eyes serious. "It's okay to be fucked-up over this. You don't have to pretend with me. I can only imagine that finding a mate is tumultuous in the best of times, and these aren't that. This is... difficult. No one expects you to be okay. You're not a robot."

Tears rimmed my lower eyelids, threatening to fall in half a second flat. How did she see right through me like that? Was I so obvious, or—

She shook her head, not waiting for a response, just pulling me into her chest for a tight hug.

"You're going to get blood on your tunic," I protested, even as the contact settled me immediately. Exhaustion, heavy and thick, flooded my system now that I was safe and the crisis had passed.

Well, *imminent* crisis, anyway. No one had said how we were fending off the ODL now that we were outside the protection of the enclave. I tried really hard not to think that was because they didn't *know* how we were going to manage it. That thought was terrifying. If they found us and killed Brielle or, Goddess help us, Leigh and Poppy...

It didn't bear thinking about.

Elodie snorted, squeezing me tighter. "Oh, Oli. These uniforms are a dark color on purpose. The little bit of blood on you isn't going to hurt anything."

I melted into the comforting hug until she started to laugh. I pulled back, confused.

"This one time Lyna and I were sparring, and my bo staff slipped—"

"You bitch, it did *not* slip. That was entirely intentional!" Galyna groused from the bed, where she still lay looking pale and exhausted.

Elodie threw her head back and cackled like a cartoon villain, clearly not worried by her partner's ire.

Galyna's eyes narrowed, and I couldn't stop the giggle that bubbled up in my chest. They were ridiculous, the ensuing argument clearly friendly, even though the story unfolded that Galyna's broken nose had *not* been at the time. As tight as the two of them were now, I'd never have guessed their early partnership had been so contentious.

They were still playfully ribbing each other as I slipped into the bathroom, a tiny flicker of hope sparking in my stupid, betraying heart.

But I couldn't help but find reassurance in the fact that they'd had such a rocky beginning, like Lucien and me. Perhaps we could still find a little beauty in our own brokenness, eventually.

It was a single shred of hope, and I needed one of those with a desperation I didn't want to examine too closely.

TO MY SURPRISE, sleep took me easily that night, propped in a chair in the corner of the little bedroom with the hum of jet engines as a lullaby. My dreams were vivid nonsense, images of Lucien's feral-tainted eyes looming in dark forests, hunting me.

The one that finally woke me was of me surrendering to the beast. I woke with a gasp on my lips, frozen in half terror, half arousal as the fresh memory sent goose bumps flowing over my skin.

"Oli?" Fiona's soft voice snapped me out of the lingering dream, and I resisted the urge to shake myself to ditch the rest of it.

"Yeah?"

"You okay?"

I sighed. "Yes, I'm fine. Just a weird dream."

She laughed quietly, and when I finally sat up straight in the chair, I saw it was because Leigh and Brielle were both passed out on the bed, still snoring softly.

"What time is it?"

She blinked at me, then pulled her phone from the counter next to her. "Later than it feels. Leigh pulled down blocker shades on all the windows back here since it was so late by the time we were all ready to pass out."

That explained why it was still pitch black, but I felt like I'd slept for ten years.

"How long until we land in Greece, do you think?" I asked on a yawn.

"Less than half an hour, actually. If you want to get cleaned up now, we're going to have to wake them soon too."

She didn't have to tell me twice. One bathroom for four females meant you had to get in when you could. Especially when one of them was Leigh, who was a force of nature when pregnant.

By the time I'd cleaned up as well as I could and brushed my teeth with a spare toothbrush from the bathroom cabinet, everyone was awake and sipping coffees, and it was nearly time to land.

I paused before leaving the bedroom and going back out with the males. Galyna looked better this morning, sitting up on the edge of the bed, and the other women all seemed upbeat, but the question of the ODL still weighed on me.

"How are we going to stay under the radar if we're no longer protected at the enclave? Won't the ODL and the Hungarians be able to track us straight to the island?"

Brielle paused, midsip of her coffee. "We were worried about that, but Kane told me this morning that Nisí Mýthou has a special kind of ward on it to protect the centaurs. It's not that they won't be able to detect omega power through it—they will. But the centaurs' wards work by putting out *so many power signatures* that it scrambles and overloads any tracking equipment. And because there isn't a being alive who can sense an omega without the aid of a tracking tool or spell..." She shrugged. "My omega signature will get lost in the overload."

"And also"—Galyna interjected, wincing as she pulled her tunic over her head—"the trackers aren't so pinpoint specific that they'll know exactly where they lost us. They're general and only get more accurate if they're already close to you. So, they'll likely know we landed in Greece. But until they get to Greece, they won't be close enough to tell where we disappeared. Now, they might *suspect* the island, but there are enough other species with barriers nearby that they won't know for sure. Hopefully, that gives us time to get in, get the piece, and get back in the air before they can catch us."

I nodded, appreciating the explanation. It was *something*. But the worry was still there. "It's a pretty neat solution, instead of dampening the signals, to just amplify them all."

Brielle grinned, wrapping an arm around my shoulders in a half hug as we walked out of the bedroom. "Yes, it is. Ingenuity, huh?"

Lucien didn't say a word to me or make eye contact as we filed off the jet, and I tried not to take it personally. He had been through so much, and the stuff with his wolf last night was just one more blow to endure.

And pushing right now when we didn't have any privacy to work through things? Not the right time. Two large black SUVs waited for us on the tarmac, the drivers nodding to Reed, who presumably hired them. I hesitated until I saw which one Samuel was heading toward, and then climbed into the other.

If Lucien's wolf had been triggered by thinking Samuel was a threat, the least I could do was keep my distance until things worked themselves out.

I tried not to feel hurt a second time when Lucien sent a pointed look my way and then chose the lead SUV with Samuel.

But when Fiona slid into the seat next to me, muttering, "*Dick,*" under her breath, the tangle of emotions only choked me further. I hated that our mate bond seemed to be dividing the pack at a time when we could least afford to be divided.

However, I'd be lying if I said I didn't love her for being so firmly on my side. I'd never had that kind of ride-or-die friend-ship before meeting the women of Pack Blackwater, who'd so easily taken me in and folded me right into their pack with grace and acceptance.

To my surprise, our time in the cars was short, straight to a dock where a pair of speedboats waited. Although, Kane had told us the centaurs lived on an island. Somehow in the haze of the last few days, I'd lost that particular detail until faced with the little boats. Once again, Lucien chose the boat I wasn't in, and it stung.

The mist of the sea hitting my face was a small consolation, and I tried to let it all fall out of my mind. We were here on pack business, on the run, and my relationship or lack thereof wasn't the point of this. Our *survival* was.

The perspective helped, and by the time the little dot of

land in the distance grew to an island, I had found a measure of peace with my situation.

"Holy shit, that is—" Fiona gazed up at the sky above us, wonder in her eyes.

"What?" I asked, seeing nothing but a beautiful Mediterranean afternoon.

"That is quite a magical barrier." I squinted in the direction she was pointed, but saw nothing. But the second I stepped foot onto the soil, an uncomfortable ear-popping sensation hit me.

Barrier.

And then I saw them for the first time, and my jaw dropped.

Centaurs. Half man, half horse, galloping openly down the beach with polo mallets? Cheerful jeers were exchanged as they galloped and spun, swinging the mallets with sheer strength a human polo player couldn't hope to match. The ball they were chasing flew almost too fast for my eyes to track, and suddenly, I understood why theirs were painted neon orange, instead of the normal white ones I'd seen in polo matches on TV.

"That is so frickin' cool." Fiona squeezed my arm as she tracked the game with avid interest. "Have you ever seen a centaur before?"

"Uhm, technically yes? But he was wearing a suit in a council meeting, and I couldn't see his horse half because it was behind the table."

"Definitely not as cool as this."

"No, this is incredible." Two of the centaurs clashed into each other, fighting over the ball and bellowing angrily as one of them went down hard into the sand. Before I could get truly worried, though—horse limbs were fragile, and a break was disastrous—he had popped back up and was already chasing his opponent down the sandy beach with renewed fury.

"Welcome to Nisí Mýthou. Our leader is expecting you."

A female centaur had appeared so quietly—compared to

the raucous polo-playing males, at least—that I jumped when she spoke.

She wore a friendly smile on her tawny golden features, but it did nothing to diminish her imposing stature. I was smaller than most female wolves, primarily due to my naturally lower ranking, but even as tall as Leigh was as an alpha female, this centaur towered head and shoulders over her. Her clothing was fascinating as well. The males were all completely bare, sweat glistening on human chests, horse flanks heaving and dotted with patches of foam from their exertions.

But this regal female wore Grecian-inspired draped clothing, but modern. One shoulder was bare save leather cuffs at her biceps and a leather bracer on her forearm and wrist. A looped blue-green piece of fabric covered the other shoulder, stopping just under her breasts. Below that, she wore a leather weapons belt, studded with wicked-looking knives but with matching blue-green fabric carefully draped over her chestnut horse's chest. The leather quiver full of hand-fletched arrows over her shoulder completed the look.

Very stylish, while also obviously dangerous.

"I am Laurana, daughter of Herd Leader Asithius. I have been assigned to escort you to him." She gestured with one long, slim hand in the direction of a cluster of large, open buildings a short distance away.

"Thank you, Laurana," Brielle said with a warm smile.

"Of course, it is my duty." She ducked her head briefly in acknowledgment, but was that a flash of anger I saw?

It was hard to tell, she schooled her expression so quickly. But it made me uneasy, and I found myself drifting toward Lucien without realizing it.

His musky leather-and-almond scent was warm and soothing, and walking a pace or two behind him, I could easily catch it on the Mediterranean breeze. There was a bitter tinge to it that my wolf didn't like, but I put that down to him staying alert while surrounded by unknown supernaturals.

The buildings looked like they'd been pulled from the pages of a book on ancient Rome, only well maintained and clean. Giant columns supported arched stone roofs above, each one uniquely carved. I paused for a moment, staring at a particularly gorgeous carving of two centaurs at play, a smaller, young centaur trailing behind them with a ball.

The ground below us was grassy, even "indoors," presumably for the comfort of horse hooves. I was so caught up admiring the interesting architecture, I didn't feel the ground shaking under my feet until a weight like a freight train slammed into me, knocking me to the ground and my breath out of my lungs all at once as the herd of centaur males from the beach flew past so close by, my hair whipped in the wind they caused.

I stared in shock at Lucien above me, pressing me into the ground with an expression furious enough to melt paint. "You nearly got yourself trampled." He was furious, I could see it in his eyes. Felt it in the tension of his body caged over mine.

But my wolf? She practically purred under the attention, the close physical contact, all of it.

My breath hitched in my chest as I tried to form words, tried to tell him to get off me—the rowdy ball-chasing centaurs he'd protected me from had already galloped nearly out of sight, weaving through the columns and back out onto the beach. But damn it, he felt *incredible*.

The weight of him was warm, solid—making me want to rub up against him, not push him away.

I stared into his piercing amber eyes, unable to articulate exactly how I felt. His expression darkened, and he leaned in closer, erasing the distance between us in a way that was at once thrilling and terrifying. He buried his nose against my neck, just below my ear, and inhaled slowly, as if he never wanted to forget the scent.

"You keep looking at me like that, hellcat, and we're going to end up in bed together. And that's a *very* bad idea." He whispered the words against my throat, pressing a hot, firm kiss there before pushing himself up off the ground. I was frozen, the electricity in my veins after the erotic threat and the warm press of his lips... Goddess. I wanted to scissor my thighs together, chase the unfamiliar heat he'd stirred inside me again. If he could drive me crazy with just a kiss, what would it be like, falling into bed with a man as experienced as he was?

Would he mind that I was still a virgin? I bit my lip, the thought making me anxious. When was the right time to tell a man *that*? It just felt awkward no matter when it came up.

Lucien waited patiently, offering me a hand up from the ground, but I hesitated, staring at it like a snake about to strike.

We were dancing around the connection between us, and taking that hand... It felt like saying yes to something I didn't fully understand.

But I wanted to. *So badly*.

I placed my hand in his, the simple touch electric as he hauled me to my feet like I weighed nothing.

He didn't let me go right away, inspecting me with those unreadable eyes, that signature mysterious expression which was so uniquely *Lucien*.

"Come on, hellcat. Let's catch up to the group before we cause an interspecies incident." He tucked my hand around his biceps, keeping me close as we crossed the shady pavilion.

I knew it was for safety. He didn't want his mate to die stupidly under a thunder of hooves.

Reasonable. Kind. Understandable.

But my heart had taken the leap, and I was much more concerned about the thundering in my chest from such a small touch. Because my hand on his arm might have been innocent, but I wanted a hell of a lot more.

None of it innocent.

FOURTEEN

Lucien

The island of Nisí Mýthou was a beautiful contradiction: lush Mediterranean greenery sprouting from every nook and cranny, modern amenities designed for the centaurs' larger size and unique ambulatory needs, and all of it was crammed into classic Roman architecture.

But as Laurana droned on about what the various buildings were that we were passing, I didn't hear a word. Every inch of my being was fixated on the small, soft hand on my bare arm. Her touch was distracting in an unholy way.

I'd been with a lot of women in my lifetime. Hundreds, easily. When promiscuity was your coping mechanism, you stopped counting and started denying the facts.

So why did one little touch make me feel like I was a teenager all over again? It had to be the mating magic.

I wasn't one of those who believed the stories about your mate having the other half of your soul. It seemed illogical, if nothing else. Were we all supposed to believe we were wandering around half formed, until we found the elusive "one" right person? No.

Skeptic. That was me.

Except the pull toward Olivia—from her juicy, sugary scent to the way her touch calmed my wolf instantly—was anything but normal. And I couldn't deny that anymore.

Her allure was too much to resist, even though I knew there were about a thousand things wrong with us getting together.

The way she'd melted underneath me when I tackled her out of the way of the stampeding centaurs was going to live rent-free in my head for the rest of my life. Perfect submission and her devastating beauty were a deadly combination.

And I needed *more*. Now that I'd had her under me, knew what she felt like, how soft those curves were? Fuck, I wasn't going to stop until I got her under me again. With a hell of a lot less clothing next time.

But there was this innocence about her I couldn't shake. She was twenty-four, so I doubted she was a virgin, but I was no high school sweetheart boyfriend. I could seduce her. Convince her to follow me back to my room whenever the politics were done for the day.

The thought was incredibly appealing, on one hand. But on the other, she wasn't some quick lay I could forget about in the morning.

Not to mention, I'd already hurt her once by accident. The horror at seeing her blood on my hands was never going to leave me. To think I could now hurt her on purpose? No. Not going to happen.

She was mine, forever. And if I slept with her, the bond between us would only strengthen, and I ran a very real risk of my wolf refusing any other female company.

His furious growl in response to that thought confirmed that I was too late on that front—it was my hellcat or nobody.

I should've hated the restriction, but damn if I wasn't thrilled to have one more reason to pursue her. I shouldn't; I was damaged goods. But that hadn't stopped me so far, even if it should've.

But as riled up as my wolf was, I'd scare her off if I pushed things too fast. I'd have to take things slow, at her pace.

I could do that, right?

My wolf snarled again, but I actually found that one comforting. He wouldn't ever let me push her past what she was comfortable with. He was my guardrail, my safety net. There was a measure of peace in that.

"And here we are, at the leader's residence. My father has had light refreshments prepared for your party while you wait. Please help yourselves, and I will go ensure our guest lodgings are ready, should you need them." Laurana bowed, one horse leg bending, as she motioned with her arms, the move incredibly graceful before she trotted off.

We all exchanged glances, but after a shrug, Reed led the way inside.

This room was more closed off, well-placed floor-to-ceiling windows providing a stunning view of the Aegean sea, but keeping the private feel of the space. A long buffet was on one side, a beautiful array of food spread out on display. But honestly? I was enjoying watching Olivia's reactions more than the space itself. I'd seen plenty of beautiful places in my life, but never with her.

"Wow," she whispered, looking out the largest window with a view of the sea.

"Beautiful, isn't it?" I offered, leaning into the moment.

"Gorgeous. It's like glitter, all across the surface."

I wrapped an arm around her waist, pulling her closer and relishing her softness as she leaned into my side. "At the right time of day, it looks like diamonds. Did you live close to the ocean before moving to the Johnson City pack?"

"I— No." She tensed, giving me a forced smile that was about way more than the geographic location of her home pack.

Home is a sore subject, got it.

"Well then, island life will be a great experience for you while we're here." I decided not to push. We had enough trouble going on with pack politics without me adding to the strain.

"Yeah, this is amazing." She gestured to the luxurious surroundings, the plush couches—which were higher than any I'd seen before, with a built-in step probably meant to bring a guest's height up to that of a centaur's—and extravagant fixtures everywhere the eye could see.

"Are you hungry?" I searched her eyes a little too intently for such a simple question.

"I could eat." Those doe eyes pierced mine with an honesty, an innocence, that I couldn't wait to explore. I wanted to feed her. That was primal, for the wolf—protect, feed, care for your mate.

But I also wanted to know if her hunger matched mine. The hunger for *her*. To deepen the mate bond, explore all her secrets. Even if it wasn't smart.

Even if I was damaged goods.

I traced a fingertip along her cheekbone, and when she shuddered under my touch, I had my answer. "Wait right here. I'll make you a plate."

"O-okay."

I grinned at how obviously flustered she was by such simple contact. I wanted to push it further, maybe kiss her and see if she melted under my lips the same way she had under my body a few moments ago, but Fiona sidled up, squinting at me suspiciously.

"You okay over here?" The question might have been for Olivia, but her accusatory tone was all for me.

"I'm great. This place is so beautiful."

At that, Fiona's protectiveness softened just a little, even though I knew she'd still happily shiv me in the spleen after last night. "It really is. I've never seen anything quite like it."

"Yeah, I—"

I left them to their chat, crossing the luxurious space to the buffet, where I selected only the best-looking meats and cheeses. A little dark chocolate and fruit as well, because I thought she might like it. Some she-wolves had a sweet tooth, but I didn't know if Olivia did or not. I was looking forward to finding out. If I was throwing caution—common sense, perhaps—to the wind and pursuing her, I was going to treat her like a fucking queen.

My wolf preened inside as I presented her with the plate, and she smiled up at me as if I'd climbed Kilimanjaro to obtain the pork and personally handmade the prosciutto. "This is perfect, thank you."

"You're welcome."

While Olivia tasted some of the treats I'd brought her— straight for the fresh orange segments, I mentally noted for later—Fiona gave me the tiniest nod of approval.

"Pack Blackwater! To what do I owe this welcome surprise?" A booming voice interrupted our moment, and I turned on instinct, placing myself between the two women and the large male centaur who'd just stepped into the room.

"Herd Leader Asithius. Thank you for offering hospitality on such short notice." Reed greeted the leader smoothly, bowing at the waist with a practiced smile.

"Of course, the centaurs are always happy to host other species. We so rarely get to leave our paradise without complicated glamours to hide our true nature, we love when visitors wash up on our verdant shores. Makes things much easier. Though, from what I hear, you may be bringing a headache to my doorstep." Asithius arched an eyebrow and scanned our group, as if he could spot the troublemaker among us by looks alone.

When that scrutiny lingered on me, I had to admit he might be correct in his assessment.

Although, he could have been staring because I was ugly now. I could barely look at myself in the mirror when I took a piss; why should I expect a stranger not to stare?

Bitterness coated the back of my tongue, the desire for revenge against Dominik and Petró flaring back up to a visceral experience in my body, souring the previously pleasant exchange with my mate. I wanted to rip their throats out and drown them in their own blood. That wasn't the kind of fantasy a stable, loving mate to a sweet she-wolf like Olivia walked around with.

I might have been ashamed of myself had I not lived through every Goddess-damned moment of the torture. It still gave me nightmares, and that I *was* ashamed of. I didn't want to be a weak, broken thing. I wanted to put it all behind me and never give them another thought besides revenge. I'd pieced myself back together once before, when I thought it was impossible. But it had taken centuries to put the pain and loss behind me. Even now, they were as close as my shadow.

Whether I liked it or not, the Hungarians had broken something inside me, beyond the outward damage to my appearance.

It was part of the reason I didn't think I deserved her, my hellcat. She was so pure. *Perfect.* And some part of me knew that my hands on her would sully that beautiful perfection.

She deserved so fucking much more. So much *better* than I was. At least before, I had my demons, but I was handsome. Someone she could be proud to call her mate, have on her arm at pack gatherings.

But now?

Now she was Beauty, and I her hideous Beast.

Unworthy.

Unlovable.

"We don't intend to bring you any trouble, but trouble seems to be dogging our steps these days, nonetheless." Kane's solemn answer had me setting aside the self-loathing, at least for now, so I could do my job and help get this omega stone piece for the pack.

I cleared my throat, drawing their attention before speaking. "Herd Leader Asithius, if you speak with Councilman Fortier, I'm sure he would tell you that we've been working through legal channels, trying to forge a safer future for all wolfkind. Our visit today is in support of that, despite what our detractors may be saying."

Asithius nodded slowly, gesturing to the seating area for us all to sit on the elevated couches. Whether he was surprised by our forthrightness, I couldn't say.

Olivia looked at me expectantly as she sat next to Fiona, an empty fourth seat next to her. I hesitated, wanting nothing more than to claim my place beside her as a mate in full. But was that fair? We had so many issues, I wasn't sure my presence was a benefit to her.

I opted to take the seat next to Samuel, regret lancing through me as I saw the pain she tried to hide by quickly looking away from me.

Damn it.

"I appreciate that Pack Blackwater— or do you prefer Caelestis now, as you've taken on the mantle from your father?" Asithius asked.

Kane barely hesitated before answering. "I've taken both packs underwing. Either is fine."

Asithius ducked his chin in acknowledgment before continuing. "I appreciate that your pack has dealt honestly and aboveboard with the other species since you've come to power. That is frankly the *only* reason you were welcomed, after Cysernaphus called me and let me know the request you made of him."

Shit.

Of *course* the old bastard dwarven king had forewarned the other leaders we'd be coming. It was too much to expect that he'd only given us the list and let us make our own approach. One parting twist of the knife, just to be a dick.

"So, you're aware that we need the shard of the omega stone currently protected by the centaurs?" I asked, not daring to share that the reason we needed it was the fact that so many of our females had been Goddess touched. Despite the fact that Olivia and I were now mates, and she was marked, it didn't feel like my information to share.

If we never bonded and had a child, she could technically live safely inside the bounds of the current law. Brielle and Leigh, however... not so much.

"Yes, I'm aware that you *think* you need it. I'm not convinced of the wisdom of your plan. The world has been a much safer place since the stone was taken out of wolf custody and fragmented."

"With all due respect, Herd Leader, the stone is not rightfully yours. It was stolen hundreds of years ago, and Kane and I are the rightful holders of it in its entirety. The wisdom of wolves is the *only* wisdom that matters when it comes to the care and use of the omega stone." Brielle squared her shoulders and stared the centaur down as if he didn't outweigh her many times over, and she didn't give a fuck what he thought about it.

Asithius pursed his lips as if he'd just tasted something sour. "That may be so, but the omega stone was removed due to the destructive intent of wolves at the time. Whole magical species were nearly wiped off the planet, so I disagree that only your species should determine its care. Frankly, if the pixies knew I was meeting with you about this, they'd be pounding on my door before day's end. Returning it eventually *may* become necessary, but the wolf packs of today are no less fractious than those who lost the stone during the omega wars. Surely you understand why I would hesitate?"

I stifled a snarl at the blatant insult to not only my high alpha, but to all of us. "You malign our entire species under the guise of political expediency and call that a welcome? Tell me, Asithius, do you look down on all other species, or do you save your disdain solely for wolf shifters?"

Kane held up a hand, stopping my tirade in its tracks. But his expression told me he agreed with every word I'd spoken.

"My disdain, as you call it"—Asithius didn't bother to hold back his sneer as he addressed me—"is shared equally by any rabble-rousing species whose actions endanger my own kind. But no matter, because one centaur may not make such a momentous decision as this without the unanimous agreement of the governing herd."

"We would appreciate you taking this matter to them immediately. It's urgent, as we are unfairly hunted by our own kind. And I can assure you, Herd Leader, that you do not want Petró Varga to succeed in his quest to unseat me. He is the only rabble-rouser seeking control."

"Very well. I'll leave you with Laurana to be shown to our guest quarters. I will seek the governing herd's opinion, and we will notify you of our decision come morning."

"Thank you," Brielle said with a solemn nod. "I hope they will see that our only goal is to reunite the wolves and spare our species from further persecution. Because, Herd Leader, you were wrong about one more detail. The world hasn't been safer for *everyone* since the stone was taken. Our entire species has been in decline for centuries, and we're not the only ones. Make sure you tell your governing herd that."

Asithius was silent as he gestured us toward the door, a grim twist to his lips that didn't bode well for us getting this piece of the omega stone without a fight.

FIFTEEN

Olivia

Laurana was hovering just outside the door when I stepped through, seeming guilty as if she'd been eavesdropping.

"Sorry to startle you," I murmured as my other pack mates began to come through the door behind me.

"No, no apology necessary." Her smile was forced, and I wondered again how she felt about her place here.

"Your father told us you'd see us to the guest quarters. He's meeting with the governing herd, and we're supposed to hear back tomorrow."

"Of course. You may all follow me." She did the special bow again and then trotted off, leaving us to follow at a slightly too-fast walk.

"Something seem off about her to you?" Fiona asked quietly enough that only I could hear.

"Yes, but I can't put my finger on what."

She nodded, deep in thought as we traversed the island to the guest quarters. They were perched delightfully close to the beach, the building reminding me of a fancy resort. It was a long, low collection of rooms, each with a separate front door and back sliding doors that faced the gorgeous beach, the crash of aquamarine waves audible even from where we stood at the front of the building.

"There are enough rooms for each mated pair, and two spares for the maidens and your single wolf." Laurana nodded to Samuel, and my heart plummeted.

They expected me to room with Lucien? Lucien, who couldn't even sit on a couch next to me for a ten-minute conversation?

I anxiously bit my bottom lip between my teeth. Fiona wouldn't mind if I crashed with them or the maidens. Well, Elodie. Galyna barely spoke to me, but surely she wouldn't turn away a female in need?

Before I could ask, Laurana was gone, and my pack mates were beginning to wander off toward rooms.

Fiona, Goddess bless her, turned to me before leaving. "You want to room with us? Or Reed can ask Lucien to room with Samuel and give you your own space if you prefer."

"There's no need for that," Lucien said, his voice unexpectedly coming from just over my shoulder and making me jump. "There is a room for each mated pair."

Fiona's eyes flickered hazel as they narrowed at him. "That may be, but you two aren't bonded yet. If she doesn't want to stay with you, she's not going to stay with you."

Lucien raised both hands in an argument-diffusing gesture. "I'm not trying to start a war here. Just trying to treat Olivia as an equal, instead of putting her at the kiddie table like the rest of the pack does."

"You self-absorbed bastard," Fiona snarled, taking an angry step toward him. "You take that back."

"No. I stand by what I said. She's not a child. She can speak for herself about where she wants to sleep, and she doesn't need you, me, or *anyone* to take charge of her."

An oddly warm sensation filled my chest at his words. That

was a big leap from when he'd called me an infant at twenty-four to treating me as an equal. I liked it.

And I was also a *little bit* terrified, because I was a raging people pleaser, and it was not at all in my comfort zone to speak up and make my wishes known.

"Guys, please don't fight. I— It's not a big deal, really. I can stay with Lucien." I pasted on a smile, even though I absolutely hated the fighting.

"What's the problem?" Reed asked, stepping up to put an arm around Fiona's shoulders and squint accusingly at Lucien.

Why was everyone always so ready to accuse him of something? Okay, yes, he'd accidentally cut me yesterday, but that hadn't been intentional, and he'd apologized profusely. Plus, Brielle had fixed me right up.

But what was it about my mate—or me, I guess—that had everyone jumping down his throat?

"There is no *problem*." I tried again, stepping forward this time to get everyone's attention, even though I didn't really want it. "Fiona was just being kind and offering to let me stay with you two. But there's no need." I was proud of how firm I sounded, even though I was absolutely shitting myself about spending an entire night alone with Lucien. "If I change my mind, which room will you two be in?" I added, just in case.

Reed pointed to the room second to the end. "You two are right next to us."

"Perfect!" My cheer sounded fake to my own ears, but no way was I backing down and letting them fight again. "We're neighbors."

"If you need us, you come get us. Any time." Fiona stated again, her now fully shifted hazel eyes proof that she was still not happy about the whole situation.

I grabbed her hand, squeezing it to show her I was fine.

I *hoped* I was fine.

Reed led her away, and the warm bubble I'd been feeling

popped as nervousness consumed me. My belly was awash with uncertainty, and it felt as if I'd swallowed a handful of live spiders.

But, no. I'd just agreed to spend a night alone with my mate.

Whose marks were on my side.

Who was looking at me right now like he wanted to eat me, or perhaps like he regretted arguing for us rooming together? It was a toss-up.

It was all whiplash with this man. One minute, he was furious with me; the next, he was bringing me treats, and then turning right around and refusing to sit next to me.

Frankly, I was confused. And slightly hurt. Was I so undesirable as a partner? Why else would he be so hot and cold?

Well, he had just been through a major trauma, but wouldn't that make you want to lean *more* on a newly found mate bond? I could soothe his wolf in ways no one else could. But he had to give me a chance.

"Shall we?" he asked, offering me his arm again, as if he was all gentleman now.

Whiplash.

"Sure. I mean, yes." I hated myself for stammering as I looped my arm through his, the warm strength of him distracting.

The guest room was just as stunning on the inside as Herd Leader Asithius's quarters. It wasn't enormous, which meant from the front door, we could see straight back to the floor-to-ceiling glass wall at the back of the little apartment, framed by flowy white curtains for privacy. It was a stunning view, the muted sounds of the waves soothing.

It was all luxury, from the beautifully tiled floors to the gleaming fixtures with crisp white accents. The bed was enormous, set right next to the windows and piled high with white pillows and a fluffy duvet that looked like a cloud.

But when Lucien shut the front door behind us, the surroundings faded to leave only a single focus behind.

We were completely alone for the first time since we'd found out we were mates.

So little time had passed, and yet, it felt like so *much* had already transpired between us.

I leaned against the counter in the small kitchenette, resisting the urge to tap my fingernails on the stone countertops through sheer force of will.

Silence stretched for an interminable beat, and I held my breath as I waited for him to break the ice.

"So..." He drawled, the single, slow syllable making my stomach sizzle with heat like a pancake on a hot griddle, ready to be flipped.

"So?" I countered, staring at him intensely, as if his expression was going to give me any clue as to whether he was feeling anything close to as intense as I was.

"How do you want to do this? There's a bed, a chair, and the floor. I'll give you the bed, of course, but—"

"Wait, what?"

He paused, the confused expression he wore a little bit adorable. "What, what?"

I snorted, some of the nervous tension leaving me at the exchange. "We're just going straight to sleeping arrangements? Nothing else? You don't want to talk, try to get to know each other?" I sounded too hopeful, and I kicked myself for it.

"Oh. Right." He rested his hands on the countertop between us, and I avidly traced them, committing every tiny detail to memory, from the fine scars over his knuckles to the sheer breadth of them. They looked strong, masculine. So different from mine.

I could almost imagine what they'd feel like skimming over my body in that big old bed behind me. But not quite.

He ran a hand through his dirty-blond hair, and I noticed it had grown out a bit since I'd first seen him. It was no longer jaw length, but just past the sharp line of his jaw. It gave him a slightly more disheveled look, and I liked it.

But while I was admiring his hair, he spun away. "I get it. I'm ugly. But you don't have to stare, do you?" The words were harsh, as if he'd spat them from between clenched teeth.

"What are you talking about? I wasn't thinking you were ugly at all. I was noticing that your hair has grown out some since we first met. I... like it. It makes you look a little bit less perfect, in a good way."

His laugh was bitter. "Are you kidding me? *Less perfect* and you're happy about that?" He spun back toward me, rage simmering in the depths of his eyes, as if it was ready to burst out and burn the place down around our ears. "If you're looking for imperfect, well, darling, you've got the right mate." He defiantly turned his face so his scar was pointed right at me.

Ahh.

"Lucien, I'm not sure why you're so angry. I meant it. I wasn't staring at your scar. I don't care about that. I just see you."

"You don't care about my scar."

"Well, not in a bad way. I'm sorry that happened to you, because it was awful and painful. But, no, I don't care that you *have* a scar. Everyone has something. Some people's wounds are just under the surface."

He stalked around the island, and a spike of fear sent my heart speeding. Lucien boxed me in, his bulkier frame making me feel small as he leaned in close, that burning rage front and center in his gaze as those hands I'd just been admiring slapped onto the counter on either side of me.

His expression was dark, thunderclouds waiting to break. Or just to break *me*.

SIXTEEN

Lucien

_____

"Don't fucking lie to me, Olivia. Look at me. Just look at me!"

Later, I would be ashamed for alpha barking at my female. I knew it, but it didn't stop me from doing it.

"Can you honestly say you want to be mated to a monster who looks like this? I'm hideous. Lying isn't going to make it go away. If you can't handle it, you should run now, before it's too late and my wolf won't let you go."

Her fear was palpable, horror and terror in equal measure twisting her pretty little lips and turning her sweet, peachy scent sour. I hated myself for being an ass, even as I felt it was completely necessary. She needed to know who I was.

If she ran screaming now, my wolf would already be fucking miserable.

But if she kept dragging this out for months?

Fuck me.

No. I couldn't let that happen. If she was going to leave, she needed to just do it. It was a poor excuse for scaring my mate, but I ignored my wolf's howling and bared my teeth at her, letting the savagery that always boiled below the surface peek out for once.

But after a moment, something shifted in the air between us. The fear left her, even as I stayed frozen, snarling in her face like an uncouth beast. I was prepared for her to run, to slap me, call me a dick. I was prepared for a *lot* of things.

But not for her to reach up, capture my jaw between her hands, and press a kiss to my cheek.

No, not my cheek.

My scar.

The moment was strange on one level, but so achingly tender. It was as if she'd somehow seen through all my bluster, all the hot anger, and found the core of me underneath.

Fear. Pain. Ugliness. Revenge.

And just... accepted it.

I could feel myself flush, the bone-deep impact of such a simple touch rocking me to my soul.

"Olivia," I started, then immediately stopped. She hadn't let me go, hadn't done anything but rest her forehead against my temple, holding me. But at the same time, she'd given me everything. "I—"

Her fingertip rested on my lips, silencing me with no effort at all.

"I don't want your wolf to let me go. I don't think you're a monster or hideous. I'm incredibly sad that *you* feel that way, but trauma is a bitch."

The curse word sounded wrong somehow coming from the sweet little healer's lips. But she wasn't finished.

"We're fated. My wolf has claimed *yours* as much as your wolf has claimed mine. So if you want me to leave"—her voice shook, and I hated being the cause of it on a visceral level— "then I'm going to need you to come right out and tell me that. Not try to scare me off or be an asshole to drive me away. If you don't want to pursue our bond, *say so*. But if you tell me to leave, mean it. Because I'm not coming back. I deserve better than that."

Her hands trembled on my face, and I knew it cost her everything to pour it all out like that. To challenge an alpha male, and a pissed-off one at that.

In the end, the decision was achingly simple.

Did I want her, even if I was no longer a fit partner? Did I trust her to accept *all of me*, including my flaws?

Or did I send her away and end this forever?

There was only one answer.

I threaded my fingers into her red-gold locks, the soft silk of them decadent beneath my calloused hands, and brought my lips to hers in a claiming kiss. She tasted like honey and peaches, fruity and sweet and perfect, and I knew then that I'd only ever been kidding myself about letting her go.

Olivia was my little hellcat, and I was never going to be separated from her again.

She was stiff with surprise for only a second, and then she melted into me like the finest chocolate, dissolving on your tongue into pure bliss. Her hands wandered away from my jaw, looping around my neck as she leaned in, pressing our chests together as she took everything I offered and gave it back in equal measure.

I wasn't thinking as I led her away from the kitchen, guiding her toward the bed with our lips still fused together as if we never wanted to separate.

It wasn't until her thighs hit the mattress and she tensed under my hands that I realized I might have pushed things too far, too fast.

We broke the kiss, and I stroked her cheek with my thumb as I studied her expression. Soft, reddened lips, flushed cheeks, pupils blown wide. She was into it, but there was a little crease between her eyebrows that I knew meant she was thinking something that had her hesitating.

"What is it?" I murmured, pressing a kiss to that line between her eyebrows.

"I— I—" she faltered, chest and cheeks flushing brighter red. "I don't want to take things too fast. Physically." She blurted the last word as if it tasted bad.

"That's okay. We don't ever have to do anything you don't want. Just because we've both agreed we want to pursue the bond doesn't mean we have to jump into bed." I smiled, doing my best to keep things light and casual, even though my dick was pulsing to be set free just from that one taste of her. Her lips were addictive, and I knew that once I tasted the rest of her, I'd be hooked for life.

"No, I don't want you to take it the wrong way. I *want* to kiss you. It's just..." She bit her bottom lip roughly, and I could smell her sudden distress in her scent.

"Hey, now. Whatever it is, you can tell me. After the stunt I just pulled, and you forgave me, I won't judge. Ever. That's a promise."

It felt right too. Perhaps the very first thing I'd gotten right since finding out she wore my marks. Mate marks, which I desperately wanted to see now that we'd taken the plunge. But that was definitely a step too far if just kissing had made her nervous. I could wait. It would just make it all the sweeter when she was ready.

"I'm a virgin."

I blinked at her, the words sinking in slowly through my formerly ordered thoughts. "You're a virgin."

"Yes." She nodded, gnawing that lip as if I was about to freak out again. Which, to be fair, she had every right to be nervous about.

I needed to get my shit together so that my sweet little hellcat didn't have to look like she was tiptoeing through a minefield whenever she had to tell me something. That started now, no matter how fucking shocked I was at the news.

"Okay. Thank you for telling me."

"You're... Welcome?" I could hear the question in the words, and I cast around quickly for something else appropriate to say. But for all my usual political polish, I was completely unprepared for this bomb.

It was no wonder she radiated innocence at every turn. She *was* innocent. Part of me, the caveman part, was really fucking thrilled that nobody before me had ever touched her. The other part—perhaps the saner part—was appalled.

Not because there was anything wrong with being a virgin, but because it brought all those feelings of being too *dirty* for her back to the surface. I'd been with so many women, I literally couldn't count. And here she was, untouched at twenty-four.

It made me regret the faceless blur of women I'd previously slept with. Though surely she didn't expect me to be a monk at my age. But this wasn't about *me* right now. It was about Olivia. The thought grounded me, bringing me back to what she needed. My regrets could wait.

"So, we'll take things slow. At your pace." I cupped her cheek, noting that some of the tension left her at my words. Emboldened that I was on the right track, I continued. "Anything you want to try, anything you want to know, you can just ask."

She nodded, eyes wide at the possibilities. "But what if you don't enjoy it because I don't know what I'm doing?" Her expression seemed to crumple, tears building along her lower lids. My wolf did *not* fucking like it. "I've had boyfriends in the past, but nothing serious, and I don't... I know you've been with more experienced women. I don't want you to be disappointed that your mate is so—" She gestured down at herself, as if there was any damn thing wrong with her beautiful body, right as the tears began to fall.

"Whoa, now. Hold on." I hugged her tight, then sat on the

bed so I could hold her in my lap and stroke her back. "First of all, inexperience isn't a deficit. It's just a starting point. We can learn what you like together."

I paused until she nodded.

"Second of all, I could never be disappointed in you, hellcat. You're so much more than I deserve. You're fucking gorgeous and so kind. Even to me when I'm being an asshole and don't deserve a bombshell like you."

She chuckled, and the sound lit me up from the inside out as she finally got brave enough to meet my gaze again. "You're a really handsome asshole."

I snorted at her unexpected honesty. "Why, thank you. You're a perfect, kind, gorgeous woman who I can't wait to explore. From the tip of your head," I placed a kiss on her silky-soft hair, taking a deep drag of her alluring scent as I did so. "All the way to your toes." I kissed her forehead, then her nose, then her cheeks, before lifting her hand and kissing the back of her knuckles.

She caught her breath, staring at me as if I'd just rocked her world with the most innocent of touches.

"Does that sound good?"

"It sounds incredible. If you're sure you're not disappointed. That I'm not better. Older, more experienced?"

I shook my head, making eye contact so she'd hear me. "You can't be better than perfect. There's not a single thing I would change about you. If I could change anything, I would rewind the years I wasted without you, so I could have known you when I was younger."

She blushed, and I was starting to figure out that a beautiful bonus about my mate being a redhead would be reading every single emotion right on her skin. There was a deep flush working up her neck from the conversation, and I liked it a little too much. Reading her was becoming an obsession.

"Do you think we could just snuggle and talk for a while?"

"Absolutely. We've got all night."

SEVENTEEN

Olivia

Lucien leaned back against the headboard, taking me with him and settling me across his lap so I could see the waves. I felt so safe with him, so secure, in a way I hadn't felt since I was a very little girl. Which was absurd, given all that had happened since I'd met the wolves of Pack Blackwater. Absolutely absurd.

But here we were, warm and comfortable on a tiny Greek island, staring out at a beautiful sea in a gorgeous little guest room. *Safe*. Even if it was only temporary. And we'd taken a very big step today, acknowledging that we were going to work on our bond. On purpose.

Granted, he hadn't said the words, but the kiss had left no doubts in my mind. He wanted me as much as I wanted him, even though he'd been pushing me away. Even though he wasn't ready to *say* it. That was okay.

I leaned my head back against his shoulder, enjoying his slow strokes on my arm, and thought about what I wanted to know.

Everything, actually. But we had to start somewhere more accessible. Hmm. Nothing to do with his work that had led to the—still very emotionally painful—scar. So, something from before.

"Would you tell me about your family?"

The hand stroking my arm stopped. It restarted quickly, but it was too late, because I'd clocked the stutter. I looked up at Lucien, leaning back so I could see his face.

"Everything all right?" I asked, keeping my tone gentle, the same voice I used with little wolf pups with boo-boos who came into my clinic.

"Of course. Just thinking." He smiled, even as I could feel the tension in his muscles beneath me.

"Take your time. I'm in no rush. We've got all night. Besides, it's not as if I'm... How old are you, again?" I grinned as I echoed his words back at him, and caught the spark of a real smile in the line of his jaw, the twitch of his lips.

"A little smartass, are we?" He leaned forward and captured my lips with his, leaving me flushed and wanting more, even as he pulled back.

"No, of course not."

"A *sassy* smartass. I see how it's going to be. And I'm three hundred ninety-eight, if you want to be precise." He growled playfully, fingers skating over my ribs until they dug in with a tickle.

I gasped with laughter and tried fruitlessly to swat his hands away while processing. Holy shit. No wonder he thought I was too young at first. And while I knew he was deflecting, I was too busy trying not to pee from laughter to call him on it. My attempts to shake him off useless, I dove sideways, but he followed me, trapping me beneath him, a wide grin transforming his features as we were just silly together for the first time. It felt so good, so easy.

But when he settled over me, pressing me into the mattress, all traces of laughter fell away.

He was huge and warm and dominating, but somehow, I

felt just as safe under him as I had on his lap. My wolf was purring contentedly in my chest, approving of the close contact, the way one of his sweats-clad thighs pressed between mine, and that unfamiliar but welcome heat against my core.

I whimpered at the sudden burst of *need* that overtook me, the sound clawing itself from deep in my throat against my will.

"Easy, hellcat. Easy." He stroked the hair back from my face, the soft rumble in his chest soothing me on a primal level. But it didn't take away the hunger.

For more. For him. For *everything*.

Lucien leaned in, pressing his lips to mine with careful consideration, teasing lightly, taking little nips of my bottom lip before moving on to the corner of my mouth, my jawline, the sensitive spot below my ear.

All the while, need coiled tighter in my belly, like a spring ready to *pop* at the slightest push.

His hand was skimming over my waist, his fingertips just teasing the bare skin of my abdomen, when someone knocked at the door.

"Fuck," he whispered, dropping his head regretfully to my shoulder. He sucked in a deep breath, then leaned back, smiling at me. "Don't move a muscle," he ordered, dropping a sweet kiss on my forehead before going to check the door.

I rearranged myself just enough that I could see who it was. A towering male centaur, bare-chested but for a starched white apron, delivering a tray of food. I could smell the bitter promise of chocolate, and a tangy-sweet cheese, perhaps feta?

"Are you hungry?" Lucien asked when he turned with the tray, shutting the door behind him with his foot before carrying it across to the kitchen counter.

My stomach rumbled its approval of more food, even though my brain was still focused on the sexual tension climbing between us. He'd said we could take it slow, but nobody told my body or my wolf that.

Lucien chuckled. "I'm going to take that as a yes. It looks similar to what they had before. Would you like to come see, or can I bring you a plate?"

The question hung heavier than it seemed like it should. It was just dinner, so why did that look in his eyes send another shiver up my spine?

"I trust you," I said, feeling uncharacteristically bold.

His smile was worth it. Satisfied and hungry at once. He piled a plate high with meats and cheeses, then slipped a few more things I couldn't see onto the back of the plate before carrying it over to me.

"Thank you," I murmured, reaching for it. But he held it out of reach, shaking his head.

"How much do you trust me?"

"Umm..." That was a loaded question. *Complex.* But if I were honest, I trusted him more than I probably should. "Enough."

He grinned at my answer, and I held back a gasp at the fact that his canines were slightly elongated, proof that his wolf was pushing him, even though his eyes weren't glowing.

Interesting.

He sat the plate of goodies on the bedside table where it was within reach, but was careful to keep it turned so the thinly sliced cold cuts were pointed my way, still hiding whatever he'd put on the other side. Then he climbed onto the bed, settling between my thighs again. This time, he sat up, reached for a slice of ham, and held it to my lips.

Instinct took over, my wolf seeing the meat as a mate offering. I opened my mouth and ate it, bite by bite, until nothing was left but blunt, masculine fingertips. Before I could do something truly psychotic like lick those next, he reached for another piece, feeding me slowly until I was full and shook my head when he offered me more.

To a human, it might not have been erotic. But to a wolf? It was primal to feed your mate. *Survival.* Proof that he was a provider, which made her blissful on a whole new level. His eyes were glowing now, and based on the way my gaze skated over the sharp angles of his face, the way I could catch motes of dust floating lazily across the room, I suspected mine were too. Our wolves had joined the party.

Satisfied that I'd eaten my fill, he dropped to his forearms, lifting the hem of my shirt to expose a stretch of skin, which he traced with hot kisses that sent shock waves of need down, down, down to my core. It was distracting and wonderful, but something was still bothering me.

"You didn't eat," I said on a gasp as he traced his tongue lazily around my navel.

Lucien hummed, looking up at me from under his lashes, never breaking contact with my skin. "Not yet, no."

"Can I feed you?"

He groaned, as if the question physically hurt him. "Do you want to?"

"Of course. I— My wolf liked that. A lot." Why was I blushing? It was stupid, a sign of my lack of experience, but I couldn't stop it crawling up my neck at the admission.

"Whatever you want, hellcat."

I scooted up onto my elbows, choosing a slice of meat from the plate, and offering it to him. He growled, the rumble of it lighting me up deliciously where it buzzed against my sensitive inner thighs. Where I'd been carefully taking little bites, Lucien was all alpha.

He grabbed my wrist, pulling me forward where he wanted me. Two bites, and the roast beef was gone, but that didn't stop him. He sucked first my thumb into his mouth, swirling around it with his tongue as he held eye contact, then switched to my pointer finger. When he'd sucked me clean, he worked his way across my palm, nipping and sucking until he got to the inside of my wrist and froze, bowing his head as he huffed my scent from the pulse point there.

"Lucien? Are you okay?"

"I'm a little *too* good."

"What?"

He slowly raised his head, and I saw what he meant. His canines were fully descended, wicked sharp and gleaming with dangerous promise as they protruded over his bottom lip.

"My wolf liked you feeding me too. And if we don't stop, I'm going to devour every inch of this perfect body of yours before you're ready."

Another whimper escaped me at that delicious threat, and he closed his eyes, letting his head fall back as if he wanted to throw caution into the sea and pounce. Part of me wanted that too, but part of me knew he was right. I wasn't ready.

This was intense. Amazing in every way, but intense.

We still barely knew each other, though, and I wasn't the kind of girl who jumped straight into bed with someone. *Clearly.*

"Lie with me? And maybe show me what you were hiding behind the great wall of meat?" I suggested, gesturing for him to come lie next to me.

He climbed over me, stealing my thoughts with a mind-bending kiss, before doing exactly as I asked. He wrapped one arm around me, his impressive biceps a pretty comfy pillow as he reached over. When his other hand came into sight, a plump, juicy, chocolate-covered strawberry was pinched between his thumb and forefinger.

"How about dessert?"

EIGHTEEN

Lucien

After a long night of snuggling, I woke hard as stone the next morning, my cock notched against the sweet, tempting curve of Olivia's ass. Her hair was everywhere—spread across the pillow and tickling my nose as she slept, my forearm clutched like a teddy bear to her breasts.

It was sweet, sweet torture.

Everything about her was, really. And I was the lucky, undeserving bastard who got to enjoy these stolen moments with her.

I had to be careful after last night. I'd been so fucking close to the edge, I almost pushed her too far. Because when she asked me if she could feed me... Goddess's tits. I wanted to peel those pants off her and feast on her pussy until she screamed my name and painted me with her release.

Too much, too fast.

Thankfully, after I plied her with sugar, the exhaustion of the long day and night had caught up with her, and she'd drifted off to sleep quickly, her nose tucked against my neck where my scent was the strongest.

I'd lain awake staring at her long into the night, but eventually, the draw of a soft, warm mate had dragged me under into dreamless sleep, better than any I'd had since I'd been taken. Not waking up in a cold sweat with visions of my torturer looming over me was a vast improvement.

Olivia stirred in my arms, and I watched as her eyelids fluttered a second before she started to wiggle in my arms. When she froze a moment later, I realized why.

"Sorry. I'll move."

"No, it's okay, it's, umm..." A pretty blush lit up her freckled cheeks, and I couldn't hold back my grin.

"Does somebody like the feel of me pressed up against her in the morning?"

I pressed forward just a little, and I knew I was right that she liked it when she pushed back against my rock-hard cock with a tiny, perfect moan. But a second later, she sprang out of bed like a tennis ball off a backhand serve, and I found myself utterly alone in the still-warm sheets. Her scent was the only thing left behind.

That, and my raging erection.

She was as red as a stop sign, and the message in her body language was every bit as clear.

"Hey, it's okay. Your pace, remember? There's no pressure here."

She buried her face in her hands, shaking her head as she backed toward the bathroom. But it wasn't until she made a break for it, bolting into the other room and slamming the bathroom door with gusto, that I started to get worried.

"Olivia?" I climbed out of bed and knocked on the bathroom door, worry making me knock a little too loudly.

"Everything's fine, just go away."

Shit. Did I upset her? She seemed into it, but clearly I'd misread the situation. "Hellcat, if I hurt your feelings or upset you somehow, I need to know so I don't do it again. I'm sorry, I wasn't trying to take things too—"

She snatched the door open, hair pulled into a knot on top of her head, sleep shirt rucked up just under her breasts. Basically, she was the picture of sexy perfection for a lazy Sunday in bed. Until I got to her expression. Fury? Angst? It was unreadable, but it wasn't good, I knew that much.

"You didn't take things too fast, okay? I just got embarrassed, and now I'm embarrassed for being embarrassed, and also for *moaning* at you like that, I just..." She made a distressed sound and tried to slam the door again.

I slapped my palm against it to stop her before she could get it the last inch closed. "Okay, hold up. Rewind. Did you not enjoy yourself last night?"

"Yes, I did. Of course I did, it was incredible. But I—"

"No buts. You have absolutely fucking *nothing* to be embarrassed about. That moan? It was sexy as fuck. I want to make you do it again. And again. And again." I let my voice drop low as I said it, leaning into the little space she was peeping at me through. "I don't want you to do anything but what comes naturally to you. And if that's moaning when it feels good, well, hellcat, I want every single one of your moans. Just for me."

She blew out a slow breath, finally looking up and shyly meeting my gaze. "I'm sorry for running away."

"Don't apologize. You're perfect." There was something I needed to know, though I wasn't sure now was the ideal time to ask. I didn't want to keep scaring her off. "I know you're a virgin, but have you had *any* sexual experience with past boyfriends? Just so I know where we're at."

She bit her bottom lip and shook her head.

Ah. "Well, then, let me be the very first to tell you, it's hot as hell when you're into it. Even if it's something small. And I don't want you to hold back or feel embarrassed or in *any* way think you need to change what you're doing. Understood?"

Her small nod was all I needed to sweep in and kiss her again, tangling my fingers into the back of her shirt. This time, when a little moan escaped her, I growled my wholehearted approval.

AN HOUR LATER, we were dressed, had breakfast, and were waiting with the pack for Asithius in his lounge. This time, I'd learned my lesson and wasn't letting Olivia out of arm's reach. But when he walked in flanked by two even larger centaurs—one male, one female—we got even more than we bargained for.

"Welcome back! I hope you all rested well?"

Murmurs of agreement rose around the room, but everyone was too hyperfocused on the new additions to say much more.

"Excellent. You're going to need it. The governing herd has decided that if you wish to once again hold your omega stone, you'll need to earn it. Centaurs usually decide on requests from other species through challenges. I've brought with me our two current champions. If you agree to our terms, one of them will choose who they deem to be the worthiest opponent amongst your pack, and you'll face off one-to-one in a challenge. The winner keeps the omega stone. *Permanently*."

Shit. I'd known it wouldn't be easy, but I quickly sized up the two centaurs, and even the female centaur was heavily muscled enough to take down a large human male in an arm-wrestling contest. And depending on the challenge selected for you by the herd leaders, it would be nearly impossible to best either of them in feats of size or strength. I glanced down at their four horse legs and added speed to the mental list of complications. If that wasn't enough, they looked fucking *mean*. The male wore an expression that reminded me of a chained-up bulldog, hungry and looking to tear a bite of someone's ass.

That dangerous impression was fueled by the fact that they were both armed from head to hoof, leather weapons belts custom fitted to their torsos and horse chests, all in easy reach.

"Our females are not accepting a challenge. You can choose any male you want, but our women are off-limits." Gael was the one who snarled first, a protective arm around his pregnant mate.

"I agree." I stepped forward, putting myself between the three intimidatingly large centaurs and my small, gentle mate.

A moment later, we were all in a line, lips curled in a sneer.

"As I suspected. Flantia, your assistance won't be needed for this challenge." Asithius dismissed the female centaur with a bored wave.

Flantia smiled threateningly, bowing in the same fashion Laurana, had, but with twin daggers crossed over her chest. Formalities accomplished, she turned and galloped away, sending clods of grass flying into the room behind her.

"Flantian, her twin brother, would be more than happy to challenge a strong alpha wolf, wouldn't you?" Asithius clapped the male on the shoulder, and Flantian stared us all down, considering.

Other creatures might have thought us an easy win individually and made a flippant choice, but there was keen intelligence in his eyes. I knew instinctively that Flantian hadn't become the male champion through sheer might. No, I'd studied up on each of the species represented by the IGC when I'd taken the position, and centaurs prized ruthless cunning above all else. Their reputation was mostly put down to wisdom, but I disagreed. They were crafty.

He wouldn't choose the high alpha, because that would be an act of war. Gael's mate was visibly pregnant, so I doubted he'd choose him, despite his imposing stature. Centaurs valued family, and it would be seen as repugnant to potentially harm a male when his family needed him for protection. That left Reed, Samuel, and me on fairly equal footing.

When his eyes locked with mine, I knew before he even opened his mouth that he was going to choose me. And a moment later, he lifted a meaty hand and pointed directly at my chest, confirming it.

I tried my best to block out Olivia's horrified gasp behind me, the way her fingertips grasped the back of my loose shirt, as if she didn't want to let me go. I'd never faced a challenge with so much at stake; not just the stone, but a female of my own to fight for, to protect.

For our future daughter.

The weight settled over me like a mantle, visceral and almost suffocating with importance.

Failure was not an option.

"Excellent choice. Lucien, isn't it?" Asithius focused on me, gaze lingering once more on my scar in a way that made me grit my teeth.

"Yes, Herd Leader."

"Excellent!" Asithius rubbed his hands together, the picture of bloodthirsty excitement. "The challenge will begin one hour before sunset. You may wear comfortable pants, but no other clothing. You're allowed to bring no weapons beyond those you're born with. As you are a shifter, you may shift between forms at will. The challenge will be revealed when it's time to start, but you should know that it will be dangerous, even deadly. One winner will be determined by our governing herd, and you're allowed to choose your own representative to sit with them and cast a vote to ensure it's fair. Do you accept the terms of the challenge, knowing that the result is final?"

"I accept."

"We have an accord. Prepare yourself in whatever way you deem necessary, and be on the beach one hour before sunset with your representative."

"We'll be there," Kane said, the finality in his tone ringing through the room like a clarion call to war.

"LUCIEN! Lucien, please reconsider. You shouldn't accept this challenge." We were barely outside Asithius's door when Olivia grabbed my arm, dragging me to a stop, sheer panic written across her features.

"Hellcat, that's not an option. You heard Asithius. The champion chose me. I'm the one."

"You *can't*. It's too soon after your trauma—your wounds haven't fully healed yet."

"You don't think I'm capable?" The words were sharp, though I tried belatedly to soften them. It felt like she was questioning my abilities as a mate, not just in this challenge. If she thought I wasn't capable of protecting her, what were we doing here?

"No, that's not what I'm saying at all." She cast a glance at the pack who'd gathered around us in a ring, silently watching our fledgling relationship hit another massive iceberg. Her cheeks flushed, but she kept on doggedly. "You're extremely capable. But as a healer, I can't recommend it."

"I understand. But as an alpha of this pack, I can't reject the challenge." I took a step closer, gripping her elbows lightly, searching her face as I spoke again. "We need this piece. Not just we the pack, but *we* as a couple. That mark on your palm means that one day, our child will be an omega. Kane and Brielle need that stone to forge a future in which she's safe. In which *you're* safe. That's worth fighting for, and that's what will bring the rest of the packs to our side for the fight that's coming."

"I'm not going to let you kill yourself for some noble feelings over a child who doesn't *exist* yet!"

If she'd slapped me across the face, it would have been less shocking. Less painful.

"So you think I'll lose." I dropped her arms, taking a reflexive step back.

"I-I don't know. I think you shouldn't do this at all."

I shook my head sadly, knowing we were at cross-purposes.

"Then I guess I'll have to prove you wrong. I've committed now, and if I backed out for any reason, the piece would be forfeit."

"Please," she begged, taking a step toward me, which I dodged.

"No." I walked away, back toward our lodgings, where I could strategize with the males in peace before the challenge. Try to drown out the awful reality that my new mate might be into how I made her feel, but she still didn't see me as a capable mate and alpha to protect her or our future. But I didn't make it five steps before a searing pain in my face brought me to my knees.

A choked grunt left me as I held my scar, bending forward almost until my face was in the grass as I grappled with the agony that was wringing me inside out. It felt like being caught midshift, and it was excruciating.

"Lucien!" Olivia was at my side in an instant, Brielle on my other, cool omega magic flooding me as soon as Bri put her hand on the back of my neck.

But it did nothing to stop the onslaught.

Claws grew from my fingertips, hair sprouted along the backs of my arms as my wolf fought for control, fought for vengeance, even though there were no enemies here for him to attack. It was the broken bond, and nothing I could do would stop it.

I stayed frozen, unable to stop the change. All I could do was exert vicious control over my muscles, force myself to stillness so I couldn't harm anyone again.

Visions of Olivia's bloody face haunted me, and I refused to hurt her a second time. Kane knelt in front of me.

"Is the healing power working?" he asked.

I couldn't answer, but Brielle murmured something too softly for me to hear in response.

"Leave us. Elodie and Galyna, take the females back to our rooms and guard them. I don't think the centaurs are up to anything shady, but we're on neutral territory here, not friendly." Kane's order resonated with Alpha dominance.

"I don't want to leave him," Olivia argued anyway, closing her hand over mine where it was fisted in the grass. "I can help him."

There was a long pause, but Kane finally agreed. I heard the receding footsteps as the females left, and silence surrounded us once again.

Olivia and Kane stayed there with me on the ground, silent but supportive. Slowly, the pain began to recede, and I regained a measure of control.

As I came back to myself, I felt Kane's power through the pack bond, strong and steady, radiating into my chest like an anchor. A way to pull myself back to safe harbor.

When the last of the attack had left my system, I sat upright, every corner of my body protesting even the simple movement.

"Thank the Goddess," Olivia whispered, searching my eyes and apparently pleased with whatever she saw in them. She tried to throw her arms around me, but I stopped her, hands on her shoulders. "You should go. Let Gael take you to wait with the other women."

"But you need me. I can help. *This* is why you can't accept this challenge."

"That's what you don't understand, hellcat. I've already accepted this challenge. And that's why I need you to go." I stroked her cheek once with my thumb, then turned and gestured for Gael.

"Come on, Olivia. I know the others are worried. Leigh is frantic in our bond." Gael tapped his chest, no doubt where he felt his mate's emotions. When he gently took her by the hand, I couldn't meet her accusing gaze as he pulled her away.

If this was the last time I ever saw her, I didn't want to remember her looking at me like that.

NINETEEN

Olivia

I fumed in silence as Gael and I walked back to the guest residences. Every line of Lucien's body had been screaming that he knew it was dangerous, knew it was risky, but still, he was stubbornly determined to throw himself into certain danger.

And then, he'd sent me away, packed me off like so much luggage he didn't need. He may as well have shoved me in the attic and slammed the trapdoor shut.

The message was clear. *Buzz off*.

"They're all in our room, and they want to see you." Gael led me to a door farther down the row and opened it politely.

It was all polite avoidance with him, as if he were embarrassed for me. For *us*. We just kept screwing this relationship up any time we had a tiny bit of progress, and it was humiliating.

But as I walked into the room full of concerned women, all I could feel was fury. That and worry at his stubborn pride, his unwillingness to even *consider* a different path.

"Are you okay?" Fiona asked, wrapping me in a quick hug before pulling back to study me.

"Not even a little bit."

"Do you want to talk about it? Eat ice cream? Scream at the heavens?" she offered, and all I had was a pathetic shrug for a response.

"BD, Reedsy dear, I think you two might want to wait outside for this conversation. We need a testosterone-free zone for a little while." Leigh made shooing gestures at the men, who rolled their eyes but knew better than to argue with a pregnant she-wolf.

When the door clicked behind them, Galyna pressed a pint of ice cream and a spoon into my hand, not even bothering with a bowl. She had her own in hand, so clearly, this was a group sugar-up-and-vent session. I followed her to the area in front of the window, where the other women had all settled into a circle, some on the bed, some on the floor, Leigh in the chair.

I took a bite before saying anything else, letting the sweet, creamy bite melt and giving myself a moment to gather my thoughts.

"You asked me before what I want, Fiona, but what I want is for him to stop being stupid and realize that he shouldn't do this. But apparently that's not an option." I stabbed my ice cream with the spoon, definitely not imagining a giant, assholishly gleeful centaur's face as I did so.

"Oli, you know I love you, right? We all do. But I have to say something, and I don't think you're going to like it." Elodie looked nervous, and that made me nervous right along with her.

My throat tightened, and I was suddenly at a loss for words. I nodded stiffly for her to spit it out.

"I don't think you were right to ask him not to take the challenge. I don't blame you for being worried or upset, but if they'd challenged me, I wouldn't have backed down either. I'm a fighter. It's in my *blood*. My identity. And an alpha male? They're no different. It's in their nature to protect. Backing down from a challenge like that... I don't think any of those males would have been capable of it."

"So, I'm supposed to just watch him go off and do something reckless when he's still having attacks?"

"I'm not saying that. You can express your feelings, you can tell him you're scared or worried or don't want him to be hurt, but..."

"But what?"

"Do you want him to go into the challenge thinking you don't believe in him?"

The question burned like fire, because damn it, she was *right*. That was not what I'd meant at all, but I could still see the hurt way he looked at me, and then how he pushed me away from him as soon as the attack had passed.

I'd actually told him he couldn't do it. Regret climbed up my throat with wicked claws, making me feel instantly ill now that I was removed from the situation and looking at it with a clearer head. After everything he'd told me about how he felt like he wasn't good enough for me.

"Shit."

"Don't sweat it. We all make mistakes. You've just gotta own it and do your best to make it right." Leigh gave me a thumbs-up. "Also, it gets a lot easier when you can make it up to him with lingerie, just saying."

I imagined laying myself out on the bed in nothing but lingerie, and immediately, my cheeks heated. I wasn't ready for that yet.

"Lingerie isn't a Band-Aid. Ignore her," Brielle said, shooting a scolding look Leigh's way. "But I can see both sides of it. Your mate bond is so new, everything is heightened right now, and that includes your fears for him. Those won't go away, but they do get to be..." She waved her hands back and forth in the air, as if she couldn't think of the word. "Tolerable? I think the mental bond helps settle you a lot, because if you feel afraid for him, he gets that *emotion* through the bond, and it makes it a lot easier to know why you don't want him to do something. And also, that protective instinct kicks in when he feels your fear. Kane comes running like I'm a beacon when I feel afraid about something. It's really nice."

A pang of longing hit me with the force of a prize fighter. Everything she'd described about her mate bond sounded so comforting, and I wanted that more than anything.

If I pushed Lucien away by accident, I wasn't going to get there. But how could I make it right when he didn't want to see me?

"Should I go try to talk to him again?" I asked, trusting their greater relationship experience.

Leigh was the one to answer. "Before the challenge, yes, but right now, maybe not. Sometimes a cooldown for both of you is a good thing." She shrugged. "Gael and I fought like crazy people before we bonded, but we had shit to work through."

Brielle smiled at me encouragingly. "All of us have struggles to work through. Shay's not here, but I'm pretty sure she'd chime in right about now and mention that she had to deal with a feral mate at first. This isn't insurmountable."

"Thank you for that. I know it's fear... I just wish there was something I could do about the pain he keeps feeling from his scar. I'm terrified he's going to be in a dangerous situation tonight when one of those attacks hits, and he'll get hurt. Or killed." I buried my face in my hands, even the thought of Lucien dying in a few short hours enough to crush me.

That was the real problem. I was so fucking scared, I couldn't breathe, and instead of communicating that honestly, I lashed out, and he pushed me away.

I didn't realize it was possible for two people to be *so bad* at a relationship, but it felt like the two of us were setting some kind of record.

I did not want a gold medal for bad relationships. No way.

"Are you sure there *isn't* anything you can do?" Leigh asked, snapping me out of my pity party with her speculative look.

"What do you mean?"

"Well, Brielle's omega magic isn't working, but that pain is coming from *somewhere*. You've got your special herbalist talents. Maybe there's something herbal you could make to help numb the area, something to keep him from having an attack at least during the challenge. And you're his mate. Your touch helped him recover both times. If you make it, maybe you can imbue a little bit of that mate's protection into it, somehow?"

I had no idea if a plant like that existed, let alone if it was on this itty-bitty island. But if there was *any* chance I could help, make a difference in the outcome, I had to try. And hopefully, he would see the apology in it and know that I wanted to support him. Even though I didn't know how.

I was just so fucking scared to lose him.

"It can't hurt to try, right?"

"Hell yeah, there's my girl," Fiona said, squeezing my shoulders and almost making me drop the half-melted ice cream.

OKAY, so, the island wasn't as itty-bitty as it looked when we were pulling up in the boats. That was an illusion.

No, the island was *miles* of walking under the hot sun, looking for... I wasn't sure what. But I knew that when I got close enough, my weird plant thing would trigger, and I'd probably wake up with it clutched in my fist. Elodie was trailing me without complaint. She'd gotten the thumbs-up from Kane to go walking with me and seemed to be enjoying herself, while still giving me space to do my thing.

Galyna had stayed back with the other women, and I was glad. The walk was helping me think. But also, the other women hadn't *all* seen me do my weird zone-out thing, and I wanted to keep it that way. It was useful but embarrassing. No one knew why it happened or how it worked. My old pack had looked down on it as if there was something wrong with me.

Hell, maybe there was. I didn't know.

But right now, I needed it if I had any hope of helping Lucien stay safer during his challenge tonight. And I desperately wanted to give him something, something tangible, more than just an apology that was too little, too late.

Dealing with an alpha was different. I never expected to be mated to one, but that seemed to be the trajectory for all omega-marked females. Maybe it was part of what ensured I'd have an omega baby?

Food for thought.

I swiped a bead of sweat off my forehead before it could roll down into my eyes and sting, grateful as we stepped into a shady patch of low, shrubby trees with scattered greenery beneath them. They were in rough rows, as if they had been planted intentionally, but there didn't seem to be any close tending of the ground underneath. If I was going to find a useful plant, this was the most promising area I'd seen so far on the island.

Scanning the ground intently, I let myself get lost in the plants. Simple grasses were mixed in with various weeds; all useful in one way or another, though most people were happy to dismiss them. I was crouching down, inspecting a small flower more closely, when Elodie hissed.

"Someone's coming. I hear hoofbeats." She appeared at my side like a specter, hand on her sword hilt, though she hadn't unsheathed it yet.

"Hopefully, we're not trespassing. This grove was clearly created intentionally." I stood, swiping my dirty fingertips on my pants to clean them off a bit. Though as an herbalist, I didn't mind a little dirt under my fingernails, most people did.

"We have free rein of the island for the duration of our stay."

"That doesn't mean this isn't someone's backyard." I glanced around, spotting a small cottage on a nearby hill. As I watched, a female centaur galloped over the crest, coming right toward us.

"You may be right." Elodie dropped her hand from the sword, but her pose remained stiff, ready.

The centaur galloped to the edge of the grove, sliding to a stop with impressive agility. She was older than the other centaurs we'd seen so far, but still insanely fit. The graying hair pulled into a bun behind her head was the only sign I could see that she was older. Her abs were still a six-pack, and when she crossed her arms over her chest, her biceps were clearly defined, straining against the leather arm cuff she wore. "May I help you? I was aware we had visitors from the mainland, but I didn't realize any would wander this far from the island's center."

"Hi, umm, I hope we're not bothering you. We went on a walk, looking for some medicinal herbs. One of our..." I decided to be as honest as I could without potentially leaking that it was Lucien who had the issue. I wouldn't want to expose his weakness to his competitor. "One of our party has a wound that's giving him some pain, and I'm the pack herbalist."

She nodded, considering me, astute gaze landing quickly on my dirty fingernails. "I see. Well, you've stumbled upon the right place. The mastic tree sap is excellent for pain." She gestured to the grove, and I nodded. I'd sensed something from the trees, yes, but not quite what I was looking for.

"Sap collection takes time I'm afraid we won't have before we leave the island. Also, I wouldn't presume to tap your trees without permission."

"Good woman. But you're in luck. If you don't mind a bit

more hiking, I've got some left from last season's collection I'd be happy to part with."

"Oh! Thank you. We don't mind, right, Elodie?"

"Not at all. We appreciate you sharing with us."

"Well, then, come along." She turned and galloped off, not waiting for us to catch her.

We broke into a jog, trying not to be rude when she'd so kindly offered her help despite us wandering into her grove uninvited.

I was breathing hard by the time we crested the hill and got a closer look at the little cottage. It was tidy and cleanly kept, nestled into a small copse of scrubby trees. But most importantly—to me, at least—a vast, fenced garden surrounded it, having no trouble with the patchy shade cast by the trees. And my senses were pinging with the medicinal herbs tucked all around it.

The centaur waited at the gate, propping it open with her horse hip.

"Sorry for making you wait. I'm not quite as speedy as you are."

She snorted. "I'd wager you're not, in this form. Is it true that wolves lose their clothes if they shift?"

Elodie jumped in to answer her, holding the gate and waving me inside as she did so. "They don't disappear, but we do bust a lot of seams. What's your name, by the way?"

There was a pause.

"Flantiera. I hear you met my children today. The twins." Her back was turned when she answered, and I was thankful, because I blanched at the news that our good Samaritan was, in fact, the mother of the two champions.

One of whom was battling my mate this evening.

Shit.

"We did. That's pretty impressive that they're the two champions, both from the same family. You must be proud." Elodie kept the conversation going smoothly, giving me a much-needed moment to recover as we strolled down the garden path.

"Fighting is not the life I wanted for them. I named them after myself, but still they took after their father's interests. Warring and whoring were the only two things that got that man out of bed." She shook her head, whether from sadness or distaste, I couldn't tell.

Between one step and the next, I froze, turning toward the garden. It was like falling into a trance, though there was no hypnotist swaying a pocket watch in front of me. Nothing but a garden and a plant singing to me like sirens in the stories of old.

I veered off the path without thought, following the plant's song, willing to dash myself on the rocks of propriety if there was something in this garden that could help Lucien survive the night.

Thankfully, I didn't have to go far to see a little crooked weed, protruding from the cracks of a block garden border. Merry yellow blooms, conical in shape, with reddish-orange tips, shone up at me like little suns, drawing me in without hesitation. I knelt down, letting my fingertips linger over the blooms.

Spilanthes acmella, AKA the electric daisy.

I didn't know why, I didn't know how, but I knew what it was and that I needed it. It took me blinking several times to clear the haze from my vision and realize I was no longer alone.

"Interesting choice. Were you planning on telling me you were mágissa? That would have made things much simpler." Flantiera stood less than a foot away, her large hooves leaving indents in the soft mulch walkway I knelt on.

She could crush me with one of those hooves, and I didn't think it would be difficult. But instead, she observed, eyebrows arched and arms once again crossed.

"I have no idea what that means," I finally said.

"Your people don't know about mágisses? Interesting. Well, grab that up—with the roots—and follow me. I'll tell you while we work."

My shoulders slumped with relief as she turned and wandered toward the front door of the cottage, not offended that I'd been on the verge of helping myself to her plants.

Though, admittedly, the way this one was sprouting helter-skelter didn't appear to be intentional. Perhaps she considered it a weed. Elodie waited silently as I carefully dug out the whole plant, teasing as many roots as I could from between the block cracks.

When I straightened, carefully cradling the plant in my hands, she spoke. "So, care to tell me what just happened?"

There it was: the other shoe. How did I explain it without sounding crazy or pathetic? "I have... extra talents with plants."

"Clearly. What is that?" She pointed skeptically to the sunny little weed.

"*Spilanthes acmella*. It's been used for centuries for pain."

She snorted, giving me side-eye. "Yeah, that was a mouthful I'm not going to remember."

"Fair enough. It's also called the electric daisy or a toothache plant. It's not native to Greece, so I'm not really sure how it ended up here, growing through the cracks."

"The intrigue deepens. But I'm sure Flantiera knows. It's her garden, after all."

"True," I murmured, my mind already wandering from the conversation and on to how to prepare both mastic and electric daisy for pain in a way that was usable within a few hours.

Flantiera had left the front door open, waiting for us. After I stepped inside, it took a moment for my eyes to adjust to the dim interior, but as they did, lovely details began to fill in all around us. An enormous chair sat in a corner surrounded by bookshelves, and even from the door, I could see they were well loved and often used, a range of gardening manuals and herbalist tomes.

If I had any spare time, I'd love to spend it poking through those books. The overhead lighting was electric but simple, blending unobtrusively into the cottage's woodsy, earthy feel. We walked through a dining room with a table clearly meant for centaurs to stand around, decorated only with wreaths and horseshoe art. After that, we found the kitchen, where Flantiera waited, various herbalists' tools scattered over the clean countertop. Open shelves lined the wall above it, polished wood with neatly labeled glass jars full of various ingredients tidily arranged on top.

"Give that a gentle wash, and we'll get started."

It felt like being an apprentice again, but I didn't argue as I crossed to the sink and carefully rinsed the dirt from my prize.

Flantiera gestured to a cutting board and then began preparing the herb without waiting for my permission. Fair, given it was hers. I watched carefully as she first chopped it, then added only certain parts to a large stone mortar.

"Our island hasn't been blessed by a visit from a mágissa in a long time. But here you are, and with no idea what you are. I suppose it's not too surprising, as it's old Greek lore. But in English, it's like a witch or sorceress. But mágisses are always gifted with plants, as you are. They come in every species—including human, for the record. They have green witches with similar talents. But the centaurs haven't had one among us in decades, at least."

As I watched her expert preparation, dropping a crystal of mastic into the mortar as well as at least three other herbs from her jars, I wasn't sure about that statement.

"You seem more than talented enough for the title," I said, picking up several tricks just by watching her work.

She laughed, the sound a bit horsey on the back end, ironically. "I appreciate the compliment, but no. This is a normal skill honed over a long life full of menial labor. You have something innate, something I don't possess." She reached into an unlabeled jar and pulled out something dried. She made an impatient gesture for me to hold out my hand, then dropped the plant into my waiting palm. "What is that?"

"There's no label on the jar...?" I asked, feeling obtuse. Did she expect me to identify it purely by looking at the shriveled bit of green? Many plants appeared similar when dehydrated and chopped.

Her eye roll was that of a much younger centaur, and suddenly, she really reminded me of her daughter, Flantia. "You really don't know how any of it works, do you?"

"No. No one in my home pack knew where it came from or what it was. I was just weird."

Elodie made an annoyed-sounding grunt behind me, but I didn't turn around to confirm. It was all embarrassing, but Flantiera clearly wasn't letting it go.

"So many gifts held by such uneducated people." She sighed, shaking her head before closing my fingertips over the herb. "Close your eyes. Stop staring at it, and *feel* it. It'll come to you."

I did as she commanded, feeling properly chastised even though she'd given me no instructions the first time around. At first, I felt nothing. But within moments, tendrils of energy I could only describe as feeling *green* tingled against my palm, tickling like feathers. But in their wake, they left an unpleasant sting.

My eyes flew open. "*Urtica dioica.*"

Flantiera nodded, the faintest twist of a smile at the corner of her lips. "Very good."

"Care to share with the class what that is in English?" Elodie poked her head over my shoulder, looking down at the small green crumbles I still held. "Looks kind of like parsley to me."

"It's stinging nettle," I answered, carefully dropping the sample back onto her countertop, well away from the mortar where she was currently pulverizing the medicinal herbs for Lucien. Suddenly, I wanted to know every single thing the helpful centaur knew about me and my oddities.

"What else can I do?"

"Good question. There is some variation amongst mágisses, but there are also some common skills. They can identify any plant by touch and, in time, without touch. You know how to properly prepare any plant for use and what its uses are without prior experience. If plants grew on the moon, I imagine you'd know how to use those too."

I blinked, thinking back. It was true I could identify plants when I fell into my strange sleepwalks, but I'd never done it on purpose before today.

"That's pretty cool," Elodie interjected. "Anything else? Anything a *warrior* might find interesting?"

Flantiera nodded, considering the two of us. "You can identify poisons inside a patient or on a weapon without a sample of the plant that did the poisoning. You'll also be drawn to the correct antidotes."

"Well, shit, that's useful." Elodie grinned, squeezing my shoulder happily. "Just wait until we tell the others."

The thought of telling the others made my throat clog with unease.

I wanted to be useful, but what if Flantiera was wrong about me? What if I was defective? I'd never been able to do anything like what she was saying, but I'd also never tried.

"But the most important tool of a mágissa is their special ability. I can't say what yours is, but if you pursue the power, it will find you."

"Can you give us an example?" Elodie asked, all piqued curiosity with none of the anxiety that was currently trying to suffocate me.

Flantiera stared out the window into the garden, with her back to us, even though I knew she'd heard Elodie. She turned a potted plant on the windowsill just slightly before answering. "My mother's gift was the ability to grow anything, anywhere. With one touch, plants would bloom for her, unfurling from their seeds even in the most arid, rocky soils."

Somber understanding made me put a hand on her forearm. "I'm so sorry for your loss."

Flantiera's nod was full of graceful acceptance, but I could see the pain she was trying to hide in the taut lines of her neck, the white grip of her knuckles on the granite pestle. "She has been gone for many, many years. But the garden was hers. When I was a filly, I had hoped I might inherit her powers... but a mágissa's gifts are too fickle to be so simple. They appear when and where they please. Or so my mother told me."

"Thank you for sharing her memory with us."

She nodded once more before shoving the mortar my way and gesturing for me to look inside. It was a simple green paste, but I decided to follow my instincts and use touch as she'd directed me to with the nettle. I scooped some of it up on my fingertip, closed my fist around the goo, and waited.

A sense of deep soothing coated my palm, chasing away the sting I'd felt before. The names of each plant popped into my head in rapid succession, but I found myself easily able to remember each one and knowing the reasons she'd included them. It was... magical.

When I met her steady gaze, I knew mine was tearful. But I couldn't stop it. I was so damn grateful. "Thank you for teaching me. If we're here a few more days, I would love to come back and spend some more time with you. If that would be okay."

"Of course, child. But for now, you'd better go. Your man is going to need that before sunset, is he not?"

I snapped around to look out the open cottage door,

dismayed to see how low the sun was trailing in the sky. The time we'd spent here felt like a short flash, but apparently, it had been longer than I'd realized.

While I'd been letting my senses analyze the ingredients in the mixture, she'd packaged it into a small bottle, corked for travel.

Elodie was already halfway out the door, but I paused in the doorway, turning back to where Flantiera stood, solemnly wiping her counter clean. "Thank you for your generosity. I won't forget it or what you shared with me."

"You're welcome, child. Now run, or you'll be too late."

TWENTY

Lucien

"I think it needs to be Kane. I can negotiate and Gael can fight, but they're going to be with the centaurs' leaders. They'll respect his opinion far more than ours," Reed said from his position by the window.

We'd all gathered in Kane's room, since the women were just next door in Gael's. We could hear their occasional laughter through the wall, and it was soothing to all of us to know they were safe and happy. Though personally, I had a hollow well in my chest that simple laughter couldn't fill.

The only thing rattling around in there was the memory of Olivia begging me to back out. To humiliate not myself, but our pack, and leave this island empty-handed.

To leave our future daughter at risk.

She had so little faith in me. But could I blame her? What had I shown her so far to give her faith?

Not much.

I dragged a hand through my already tousled hair, then waved toward Reed. "I'm fine with that. If it's a power play they want, we can give them one."

He nodded, moving on to another minute detail of their

planning that I wasn't truly interested in. I had a fight to prepare for, both physically and mentally.

And I was *not* ready.

Not with her words haunting me like so many ghosts.

You shouldn't do this at all. I'm not going to let you kill yourself.

My wolf was restless, but I needed his strength for whatever came later. I had no doubt I would need to shift, and we would need his pent-up frustration to handle the challenge before us.

I'd feel marginally better if I at least knew what the challenge was. But the centaurs had stayed true to their word, telling me nothing yet. Damn centaur pride.

"So there's no documentation on centaur challenges in the past? Nothing we can go on?" I scanned the room, but each of the males shook his head. I was going in blind, and I hated that with every fiber of my being.

"I even asked Gracelyn to check the pack records," Reed said with an annoyed flick of his fingers. "There was one vague reference to a challenge between a centaur and a lynx shifter. All that was recorded was that the lynx failed and was killed for his trouble."

A lynx had a lot of disadvantages compared to a werewolf, depending on the challenge. Size and speed, for one. Jaw size. But not all challenges were about brute force, and the lynx's failing could actually have been a point against me. The challenge could have been *more* suited to a feline, not less.

It was impossible to say.

A knock on the door interrupted our conversation. Gael was closest, so he strode over to answer it. But within a second of it opening, the scent of fresh peaches and soft cotton rolled over me like a physical caress, and I knew it was Olivia. The second of bliss—knowing she'd come for *me*, which made my wolf arrogantly preen in my chest—was quickly replaced by tension. Was this a last-ditch plea to get me to call it off? Again?

I didn't know if I had the strength to push her away a

second time, but I couldn't focus on all the ways this night could go wrong if I wanted any chance of winning this piece for our pack.

"Luce," Gael called, gesturing to my diminutive mate. I could immediately tell she was anxious, from the way she stood as if she was ready to bolt, from the way her eyes darted around the room we were gathered in. But to me, she was still a vision.

I never got tired of taking her in, from her wild, flyaway hair to her dirt-smudged shoes. She was my little healer. Mine to protect, mine to love.

Mine to teach.

I shoved the inappropriate thoughts of all the things I wanted to teach her away as I crossed the floor. Pausing for a moment, I joined her outside and shut the door behind me, giving us the illusion of solitude. Elodie was guarding her, clearly, but she'd stopped fifteen paces away, giving us the appearance of privacy, at least.

"Is everything okay?" I asked, taking in her disheveled and grass-stained clothing. There was even a twig in her hair. Now that I was standing closer, I could see a faint smudge of dirt down the side of her face. What had she been up to? My gaze came to rest on the little glass jar clutched in her hands, and I cocked an eyebrow in question.

"No, it's not. I'm sorry, I've been going over what to say for the whole time we were walking, but nothing feels right. About what I said earlier..." Her cheeks were pale, and her sweet, fruity scent was tinged bitter with... regret?

I rocked back, physically shaken by the sudden change. What did she regret? What she'd said, or how I'd reacted?

Only one way to find out. But I couldn't bear it, her scent heavy and bitter like that, without doing something to ease her discomfort. I reached out slowly—giving her ample time to back up or push me away—before resting my hands on the outside of her elbows, stroking her soft skin with my thumbs in a soothing motion.

She shuddered under the simple touch, her scent changing as quickly as the breeze. Sweet and pungent, with the merest hint of spicy arousal.

Damn. She was so responsive, it pulled an echoing response from me.

"It's okay. Take your time." I finally spoke, trying to distract myself from that tantalizing thread of arousal I knew she also felt.

She nodded, lower lip wobbling before she bit it into stillness. I watched her as if she held the key to every puzzle in my life, while she gathered her composure. Shoulders rolled back, chin lifted. Finally, she released her lower lip when she was ready to keep talking. It was fascinating the way she went from shy, reserved she-wolf to bold, brassy healer, but I'd watched the transformation happen, piece by piece.

Her healer profession gave her mettle, a strength she didn't feel otherwise. Hence the jar.

Interesting. I stole every bit of knowledge I could get about her, and I filed that tidbit away for later like a petty thief hiding a particularly shiny bauble.

"I'm sorry for what I said earlier. After I left, I talked to the girls... They all agreed I was wrong to ask you not to take the challenge."

You could have knocked me down with a Goddess-damned feather. *She* was sorry? For telling me how she felt?

"You don't ever have to be sorry for telling me how you feel. Even if I don't like it. I wouldn't ask that of you."

She swallowed hard, eyes skating away from me as if she couldn't really hear what I was trying to tell her.

I gripped her chin with my thumb and forefinger, pulling her face toward me so that there was no way she could avoid looking me dead in the eyes when I spoke. "You don't *ever* have to hide from me. No matter what. You're mine, and I'm yours, and we are in this together. Besides, my little mate has claws, and that's exciting, not a defect." I released her chin, opting instead to trace my fingertips along her jaw, down to the column of her neck where I could pull her closer.

Her eyes turned molten with lust, a faint, silvery glow I hadn't seen before telling me her wolf liked what I was saying, what I was doing. My own vision sharpened as my wolf showed up to the party, meeting hers tit for tat.

But fuck if it didn't surprise me when she pressed up on her toes, melding her lips to mine like they were made for me. Every inch of her softness molded to my chest as I loosely wrapped my arms around her waist, letting her take the lead. There was no hesitation in this kiss, no holding back, and my entire body was a live wire, electrified at the taste of her, the feel of her perfection in my arms. Even her scent was strong, sweet and sad all at once.

When she pulled back, her lips were puffy, eyes wild with arousal and uncertainty. She wanted more, but she didn't know more of what.

After this challenge was over, I would show her.

Fuck, the challenge. I'd gotten so wrapped up in Olivia, I forgot about the very real clock ticking down to when I had to go face off against a giant fucking centaur. A quick glance over at the falling sun told me everything I needed to know.

We were out of time.

She traced my gaze and, realizing the same thing I had, took a half step out of my arms that tore part of my soul with her. But it was okay. She held it carefully, just as I was learning to hold hers.

"I know you don't have long. But I think I have something that will help you. I was just so scared earlier, and I let the fear win. But that's not who I am. This thing between us is so new, the idea of anything happening to you while you're having one of those attacks…" She shook her head, that bitter hint of regret edging back into her scent. She was all business now, though, not letting it stop her.

Olivia had fire in her green eyes when she spoke again. "I believe in you. I think you're going to win. But you can't help what's happened since you got your scar. *That* is what scared me. Leigh suggested maybe I could use my herbalism to help you until the connection with your wolf is fully healed. So, I spent the afternoon with Elodie wandering this island to see if there was anything I could use to help take the pain away, at least for a while."

She held the bottle aloft, thick green goo resting in the bottom of it that I could smell faintly even through the cork stopper.

It smelled like somebody had emptied out a weed whacker and the dismal results were in that bottle.

"I don't have to eat that, do I?"

She dropped her head back and laughed, the sound so light and free, it made me feel buoyant too. I wanted to make her laugh like that a thousand more times so I could soak up every single moment and hoard them like a dragon's treasure.

"No, you goose. I'm going to rub it over your scar. It's topical."

It was going to look kind of funny if I showed up with green goo smeared on my face, but who had room for pride where their mate was concerned?

I didn't, not anymore.

"All right. Do what you need to do, then," I murmured, gesturing toward my face.

She didn't hesitate, turning my face and tilting it down a bit so she could see the scar better. When she removed the cork from the bottle, I was hit by an overpowering wave of medicinal stench so strong, it made my eyes water and my wolf whine.

Her gentle touch as she began to smear it over the still-tender skin distracted me from the awful odor, my wolf practically humming with glee at her caring touch.

I watched her as she worked on me, the determined set of her jaw and the efficient way she moved just as fascinating as her passionate kiss from before, the way she sometimes went timid and hid from me. She was a complex woman, and it made her all the more alluring.

"Okay." She recorked the bottle, then tucked it into her pocket before absently wiping her fingertips on her thigh to clean them off. "That's all done. I feel like... I want to try something a little different, if you don't mind?"

"I trust you." It was the truth, even though I didn't realize it until I said the words. Of any person on this planet right now, I trusted her the most. The realization made my heart pound as if I were running, even though I was standing stock-still.

I hadn't trusted anyone that way since my baby sister, and she'd been dead a long, long time.

And all that time, I'd been *alone*, no matter how many people were around, no matter how many women I slept with to take the edge off the darkness.

This was different. *Olivia* was different.

But while I was having my foundation rocked, my pretty mate was unaware, resting her hands on either side of my wound, much as Brielle had done when she was going to use her omega powers on me.

She closed her eyes, going still as stone. I didn't feel any different at first. No cooling rush like when Brielle healed you. But after a few seconds, an itch like fire ants gnawed over my scar, over the entire area where she'd spread the goo. I squinched my eyes closed, trying to resist the urge to smack her hands away and scratch.

"Holy shit, that's cool!"

Startled by Elodie's voice suddenly close by, my eyes flew open again.

"What?" Olivia asked, blinking slowly as she lowered her hands from my skin.

"It just... soaked into his skin. It's gone, look!" She pointed at my face, and Olivia squinted up at the area. Within a second, her eyes grew wide with shock.

"Holy Goddess, it *worked!*"

"Care to fill me in on what just happened, hellcat?"

"I— Well, it's a long story, actually. I promise to tell you after the challenge, okay? Right now, the Alpha is waiting for you." She gestured behind me, where Kane stood staring out the window, trying not to look like an impatient bastard.

"Right." I pasted on a smile I didn't feel, the nervous energy of the challenge flooding back into me, bursting our happy little bubble into a million shards sharp enough to cut. "Are you coming? I'd understand if you don't want to."

Her expression tightened, and she stepped forward into my personal space one more time, hand coming to rest on my arm, fingertips resting lightly on my bare skin. "Try to stop me."

"I wouldn't dream of it."

TWENTY-ONE

Olivia

All our pack mates came to the challenge, and I'd never been more grateful to have a group of wolves at my back than I was while watching my mate strip off his shirt and walk out onto the sand with Kane at his side. I wanted to chase him, but instead, I grabbed Fiona's hand and held on tight as I watched him go, sending up prayers to the Goddess that my newfound mágissa talents could protect him from a scar attack for the duration of the challenge.

He was tall and proud, the strong lines of his muscular body oozing danger with every step toward the waiting crowd of centaurs. If I lived to be one thousand and one years old, I'd remember the outline of him, burned against the sunset. But more than that, it was the lingering tingle of his kiss on my lips that I held on to, the bold, vibrant taste of *him,* imparted with a kiss that left my hair wild and my heart pounding.

"Welcome, Pack Blackwater!" Herd Leader Asithius greeted us with a booming voice that carried over the sand, over the waves. He clapped once, then rubbed his hands together as he surveyed Lucien, shirtless and wearing only black athletic pants, as instructed. I clutched a spare pair in my hands for him to wear after, assuming he'd need to shift.

I hadn't let myself take the time to appreciate his chiseled physique before, when we were saying goodbye. But now there was nothing for me to do but watch and drink him in. His hair was disheveled, and his muscles corded in the waning sunlight. He was ruggedly beautiful, eyes burning with intensity that the distance between us couldn't dampen.

My wild wolf. My own wolf rumbled her appreciation in my chest.

"Centaur challenges have long been a tradition among our kind and are only rarely shared with outsiders. You might be tempted to look at our challengers"—he waved to Flantian, who stood tall and proud a few feet away, with a small throng of admirers who put up a cheer at his attention—"and think that brute strength would win it all for one side, but that's untrue. Centaurs are known worldwide for their wisdom. As such, our challenges are crafted to present an equitable contest of both wits and might for both centaurs *and* the rival species."

I held back a derisive snort. Wisdom might be what was written about in the *human* books about centaurs, but that certainly wasn't what the supernatural world knew them for. No, that was their cunning. They were a brilliant, ruthless species with the physical might to do as they pleased. Only their hard-to-disguise form and slow reproductive rate kept them from ruling the world.

"Wolves are apex predators, and so we've made today's challenge simple. A hunt. Bring us an infernabist for our celebratory feast tonight, and you win." Asithius spread his hands wide and smiled, as if we should all just believe this would be a walk in the park.

I watched Flantian from the corner of my eye as Asithius spoke, and even with only partial attention, it was impossible to miss the way his face paled.

Whatever an infernabist was, it wasn't good.

Fuck.

I didn't swear often, but this situation clearly warranted it. Wolves didn't hunt alone; we hunted in packs. And whatever this creature was, it was big enough to make a giant freaking centaur blanch. And Lucien would be facing it completely alone.

Alone and with nothing but herbs and my best guess at herbalist magic between him and another painful attack from his damaged connection with his wolf that could debilitate him at a dangerous time. I was numb with worry as I followed the stream of centaurs and my pack mates toward the finish line, where we would wait. Only the two champions and their representatives were left on the beach with Asithius for full instructions.

I cast one last look over my shoulder at Lucien before they were out of sight, his face grim as he listened and nodded along to whatever Asithius was now saying more quietly.

Shit, shit, shit, fuck.

TWENTY-TWO

Lucien

Asithius's words were a stream, and I was a rock, frozen in the flow, letting them wash over me, catching only snippets.

Extremely dangerous predator.

Four tusks, razor sharp.

Roam in packs, deep within the ghost forest.

Fast, vicious, with toxic saliva.

"Is everything clear?"

"Yes, Herd Leader. I will fight with honor for the herd." Flantian bowed deeply at my side, his fist over his heart and a grave expression knitting his brows together.

Asithius turned expectantly to me next. "Yes, Herd Leader. I will fight with everything I have for my pack."

"Excellent! In that case, the sun is just about in position. May the most cunning fighter win."

Between one heartbeat and the next, Flantian spun, flinging sand from beneath his hooves as he bolted away at a full, stretched gallop.

I turned and followed, not bothering to strip off the pants before shifting into lupine form. My wolf burst free with all the pent-up vigor of a young boy with his first slingshot. Taut, ready to snap, and with arrow-like precision.

Asithius had told us the ghost forest was on the far end of the island, so part of the challenge was just not letting Flantian run away with the whole thing, his longer legs and equine speed giving him a slight edge. I didn't fall into the trap of sprinting, though.

He might want to make a big show as we raced past his fans, but I couldn't give two shits about showmanship. This was pass/fail; we didn't get points for flair. Reserving enough energy for a fight was crucial, and I wasn't going to get sucked into the showboating.

Still, a thunderous roar rose from the crowd as we streaked past, and my wolf's sensitive ears ached at the uproar, flattening protectively against his head. But no matter how hard they screamed, how high they jumped—he was laser focused.

To my surprise, it was more than the standard lock-on to the hunt. It was a burning drive to *win*, to impress our mate with our prowess.

On that, my wolf and I were in perfect sync.

We chased the centaur down the length of the island, the terrain changing from sand to rock to sparse, sharp, crunchy grass under our paws as a dark forest loomed ahead. Flantian released a bellow—of rage or warning, it was hard to decipher in my wolf form—and slowed to a canter at the edge of the trees.

Probably wise for a beast as tall as he, for I could see low-hanging branches, thick with thorny, knotty dangers.

I arrowed past, leaving him in the dust before allowing myself to slow to a crawl, expanding my senses into the under-growth in search of the elusive infernabist. My wolf could hear and smell a festival of things unknown to humankind. Trace scents on the air, in the dirt below.

Deer scat.

A bird's nest, with the distinctive, earthy scent of fresh-hatched babies and their discarded shells. Interestingly out of season, but perhaps a by-product of the magic inherent in this island.

The soft snap of a hoof on a twig, some distance behind. *Flantian.*

That last one made my wolf preen, glad to be the superior predator for this environment.

But *I* knew that this might feel easy at a surface level— perhaps even that I had an inherent advantage—but there was no way that was true at the core of the test.

The centaurs *wanted* me to fail because they thought the world was safer while they held part of our stone. But it wasn't. Not for my mate, for our future daughter. And I couldn't afford to lose sight of that.

With that in mind, I forced my wolf to stop, drop to his belly, and *wait.*

We didn't know what an infernabist smelled like as it was something we'd never experienced before. But if it had tusks, like a wild hog, that was a clue. Something we could pick up on the breeze because we'd scented it before.

The wait was driving my wolf insane, as the centaur's sounds behind us became louder, distracting. I had a harder time than usual getting him to wait patiently. More effects of the damaged link between us? It seemed likely, but I was grateful my shift had still been seamless.

There was the distinctive rasp of wood over stone now, repetitive and uncomfortable to the ear, but right when I thought my wolf would howl his protest, we caught it.

Earthy, rank, with the shifting of the wind—*hog.* But different. Sulfur?

Go. Carefully.

The second I let him off the leash, my wolf arrowed toward the new, discomfiting scent. He dodged underbrush with the ease of a lifetime's practice, making good time through the deepening dark of the thick forest. The tree trunks in this area were gnarled, and I could see why they called it the ghost forest. It was exactly the kind of place children would be scared of in bedtime stories. From the knotted, ugly trees to the deep shadows cast by the thick canopy overhead, the terrible picture was complete with the dangerous beasts living under the boughs.

The thick scent of sulfur and musk grew to crowd out all others in my wolf's nose, and he slowed, dropping to a stalking crouch as we peered around the next bush.

To my disappointment, there was nothing but an empty cave, reeking with the ripe stench of many, many sulfur pigs.

A thought struck me. What if this *wasn't* the infernabist? I hadn't been shown a photo or provided a scent. Only told they lived in this forest and were highly dangerous. Although... the description was clear enough.

I would wait and see if any returned to the burrow. If whatever came didn't have tusks or didn't fit the description, I'd resume hunting.

Judging by the fresh scat in the small clearing ahead of the cave, they hadn't been away from the burrow for long.

My wolf lay down to wait, content with my reasoning this time, even as he kept his ears pricked and senses on high alert for movement around us. We were utterly alone, save for a single, surly crow that kept hopping around on the upper branches of the tree we lay next to, cawing periodically. His eyes held keen intelligence, and there was a whiff of magic about him. Not enough to be a shifter, just enough to be *other*.

For a long time, there no other sign of life. What remained of the sun's warmth leached away, leaving my wolf's belly cold against the damp earth and my patience growing thin. Even the rasping noises stopped, and I wasn't close enough to hear hoofbeats as Flantian continued his hunt.

Right when I was on the verge of losing my nerve and changing plans, a thunderous pounding shook the ground. *Hoofbeats.* Coming in fast, from my left. My wolf leapt to his feet, spinning toward the oncoming centaur.

But as I listened, I realized there were many more than just four feet.

Flantian had found the infernabists, and they were running straight toward me.

The rotten, sulfur smell was stronger in the wind, confirming I'd found the right species, at least. But when the herd of infernabists broke through the underbrush, I nearly lost my breath as disgust made my wolf shake.

The creatures were huge and hideous, indeed looking loosely like pigs—if they were pigs out of a nightmare. They were four times the size of a prize hog, their skin tomato red with scattered patches that looked charred, as if it had been burned by something terrible. They reeked strongly enough to make my eyes water, and their four tusks, razor sharp and as long as a woman's forearm, protruded over blackened snouts in a crisscross shape. They'd have no trouble gutting an unlucky wolf in battle. And that was before I noticed the *spikes* protruding down their forelegs.

No wonder their name meant *hellish beast*. They looked like they'd started running at the gates of hell and never stopped.

And they were heading straight toward my hiding spot.

I briefly considered trying to take one by surprise, but if I leapt out and grabbed one by the throat, I'd be stopping in front of a charging centaur, who had a crudely shaped, thick wooden spear hefted in his left hand. He was as likely to trample or spear me as I was to take down a beast that big on the first try.

No, I'd let them pass, then join the hunt. I could pick off a straggler, so long as it was large enough to feed the crowd.

Though the idea of *eating* one of these rotten-smelling

things was utterly abhorrent. The herd of roughly fifteen infernabists zipped past with bone-jarring impact, the ground shaking like an earthquake under their split hooves. As soon as Flantian's tail streamed past my nose, I leapt out of my spot, pounding after them.

I racked my brain for a way to bring down an animal that size, with that much inherent weaponry, without getting gored or gutted.

Flantian's superior height and rough weaponry were a *definite* advantage over my size and fangs. So I'd just have to get creative.

I didn't have to wait long for an opening. He threw the spear, the rough-cut tip glancing uselessly off one of the beast's shoulders. But the insulted infernabist squealed with outrage, the sound as ear-piercing as a harpy, and sent the herd scattering in every direction.

Flantian cut hard left, and I cut hard right, each of us singling out our own beast to hunt. I saw in his right hand a small carved spear, this one only about eighteen inches in length, the perfect size for close-up fighting.

I didn't envy him trying to face off against one of these sulfur pigs without the benefit of fangs. But I couldn't worry about him as my target zigzagged through the forest. I kept hot on its tail, hoping to wear it down a little with the run before I made my move. But as time dragged on, I realized it showed no signs of flagging, but *every* sign of making a run for its burrow. The underbrush was too tight in this part of the forest for me to have a clean shot to tussle with it, but I'd have seconds between it breaking into the clearing and disappearing into the cave.

That meant there was one shot, or I'd lose the beast and have to start from scratch.

It meant I would *lose* if I missed. That wasn't an option.

I dug deep for an extra burst of speed as I scented the now-familiar cave the infernabist herd called home. Three more strides, and the clearing came into sight. I bunched my muscles to leap, ready to land on the ugly beast's back and hopefully grab it around the neck and bring it down safely out of reach of its tusks and leg spines.

A masculine scream of pain rent the air as I leapt. My claws scrabbled for purchase as I landed on the beast's back, my jaws clamped around the back of the neck, the foul taste of its rotten-corpse-scented flesh even worse in my mouth than I'd imagined.

There was no fucking way these centaurs wanted to *eat* one of these disgusting creatures. But despite the fetid taste, I clamped down harder, relishing my successful attack as its pace faltered, and it sent us both careening to one side.

As it fell, I jumped free, not wanting to get pinned under its tremendous bulk. As I flew through the air, I spotted Flantian also in the clearing, battling with his own infernabist. Horror struck before my paws even kissed the earth.

Where I was triumphant, holding the upper hand, Flantian was down, a foreleg twisted in a clear break, a deep, gushing gore wound across his human abdomen. And the infernabist he'd been hunting was turning, ready to make another run at his hunter.

Fuck.

My pig was down, stunned from the sharp snap to the back of the neck—but that was *seconds*. It would recover and bolt into that cave, where I'd be on the back foot.

But could I really win and let my centaur challenger die?

This was no battle to the death. And the honorable thing to do was to save his arrogant ass. But what would Kane want?

I didn't have to waste time thinking. I knew exactly what the high alpha would want, cost be damned.

And so I leapt and hoped Olivia would forgive me for making the choice I had to make.

TWENTY-THREE

Olivia

The centaurs led all of us except Kane toward a viewing platform. I was confused at first—it was an open-air stone plaza, like the rest of their architecture in the city. But within moments of our arrival, screens began to descend from the roof overhead, each with a different camera angle. One-half of the platform was fixed on Flantian, the other, my mate.

Lucien's grave expression as Asithius's voice boomed over the crowd, detailing the horrible beast he was to fight, made my chest feel tight with anxiety. He stood tall and imposing, but something was off. Was he distracted? Did the paste I'd put on his scar burn?

I didn't know, and it was too late to ask. Too late to kiss him one more time. It felt like mere seconds—though it was probably longer—before the two charged past, cameras keeping pace as they raced toward the deep forest. I'd thought we might lose sight of them at the tree line, but the camera angle shifted, and suddenly, we were catching flashes of them between the trees.

Hidden cameras.

The whole forest must have been wired, because we never

lost sight of Lucien for more than a few seconds as he raced and wove through the underbrush.

Fiona clutched my hand tighter, leaning in to speak quietly close to my ear, so that only I could hear amid the rowdy crowd. "You should be proud. He's shown incredible bravery for our pack."

And it was true, he had. He'd proven himself once again to be a worthy male, a worthy *mate*. He was doing this for me, not just for the pack; there was no denying it.

I felt better since we'd talked outside his door, since I knew I'd sent him off in the best way I could. At least we hadn't left things broken between us to distract him. Because once he'd shifted into wolf form, all traces of distraction had fled.

He was a hunting machine. No, he was a *killing* machine. I shuddered, my nerves climbing as I watched him freeze on screen, the clarity so good and the screens so enormous, I could see the faint twitch of his nose as he scented something unknown in the air. And then, to my surprise, he dropped down and waited.

And waited.

And waited.

It was torture not knowing why he'd stopped. The cameras focused on him, not showing us his surroundings. But he looked calm enough.

I turned around, seeing that Flantian was working on a rough spear, not charging deeper into the woods unarmed, which was smart. He didn't have a wolf's fangs.

The initial energy of the crowd had waned a little, several groups of centaurs wandering off, as if the challenge had ended.

"What's going on?" I asked Reed, because he was standing closest in the crowd, beside Fiona.

"I'm not sure, but I overheard a few people say it was going to be a while. The infernabist might be nocturnal?"

Elodie spoke up. "I'll go mingle, ask around. Maybe we can get a little more intel on what to expect."

"Thank you." I gave her a grateful smile, even though it felt weak. Everyone else might be bored, but the other half of *me* was on that screen. And I wasn't going to take my eyes off him, not until he came back to me, healthy and safe.

I didn't care if he won, even though I knew I should. But who the hell cared what you *should* do when your mate's life was on the line?

This thing between us was so new, so fragile... the idea of it being severed so soon was soul crushing. So I watched him, and I willed every bit of my strength, my hope, my fledgling feelings toward him. Maybe the Goddess, the Universe, was listening.

Eventually, Flantian finished his pair of differently sized spears and trotted deeper into the forest. Lucien was still lying in wait when Elodie returned to our group over an hour later.

"So, apparently, they don't tell the challengers, but they watch the infernabists' migration patterns to know where they are and where to send the contestants. They intentionally put them in the forest at the opposite end of the ugly buggers, to give the contestants time to either prepare or grow complacent. It shouldn't be long before the herd starts to move, and we'll see more action."

I nodded as she spoke, thinking that all made sense and lined up with what we were seeing. It made me wonder where Lucien had decided to wait, but we wouldn't know that until he began to move again.

"Did anyone say what one of these looks like?"

Elodie grimaced. "No, they all grinned when I asked. Nobody would say anything other than 'You'll know when you see it.' I don't think that bodes well. Apparently, they only live on this island or in the nine hells. One of the centaurs tried to spin me a story that Hades sent them up from the underworld to punish a great hero of the past who'd pissed him off."

Dear Goddess, please let him return to me safely. The silent prayer was paltry, but with shaking hands and terror in my heart, there was nothing else I could do. The endless waiting was maddening, even though wolf-Lucien looked cool as could be on the screen.

Gael snorted. "The Greeks and their mythology, eh?"

"Yep," Elodie agreed, falling silent as she rejoined our watch party.

An announcement came over the speakers. "Greetings, watchers. The infernabist herd is on the move. Contact expected with a champion in ninety seconds. As a reminder, this is a sacrificial challenge," the voice said with a chipper lilt before abruptly cutting off.

"What the fuck is a sacrificial challenge? Aren't they just supposed to hunt a giant demon pig?" Leigh asked, glancing around with arched eyebrows at the gathered centaurs.

To my surprise, a barrel-chested male with slicked-back hair turned our way and answered her. "A sacrificial challenge is rare. It's only issued when the elders have something of grave importance on the line, worthy of sacrificing a challenger's life."

"Umm, what? They're going to kill one of them?" I hated the way my voice squeaked on the question, but the mental image I had wasn't good.

"No, but infernabist saliva is toxic. The challenge here isn't truly the hunt. Flantian's instructions were different from those they gave your pack mate. Flantian could never hope to bring down an infernabist with a weapon as paltry as a sharpened stick. Their cursed hides are nearly impenetrable. His task is to sacrifice himself to one of the beasts. If your pack mate knowingly abandons Flantian to pursue his own hunt, he has lost, even if he succeeds in the herculean task of felling one, which is unlikely."

Fresh horror swallowed me, creeping up from my toes and closing over my head.

They were willing to sacrifice one of their own in order to keep the stone from us? Did *Kane* know the rules? Had he agreed to test Lucien this way? Or had it been sprung on him after it was too late to stop too?

My grip on Fiona's fingers tightened, the simple touch the only thing keeping me upright as I swayed on my feet. A strong grip on my shoulder had me blinking upward to see it was Elodie who had bolstered me.

"He's going to be fine. He's a good male, underneath all his cheeky bravado. Remember that," she whispered, giving my shoulder a supportive squeeze but not letting go.

Within minutes, the sound of earsplitting squeals and racing hooves dragged our attention toward the other half of the plaza, where Flantian ran, dodging branches with acrobatic ease, spear in hand, a ferocious determination in the set of his jaws, the flat look in his eyes.

He was a man resigned to a gory, brutal death, and I didn't know how I'd ever missed it now that I knew. The cameras didn't show the infernabists yet, and my anxiety swelled yet again at the amount of noise they were making.

I turned away, unable to bear another second of staring at Flantian's doomed expression.

When I blinked back up at the screen, Lucien's wolf was on his feet, staring intently to where I was sure he could hear the oncoming herd. And a moment later, I almost lost my lunch at the sight that unfolded above me.

The most horrifying beings I'd ever seen scrambled into view, their stubby legs churning up the earth, their rotten, charred-looking flesh something out of a zombie film or a horror flick. But still, I couldn't look away as Lucien tensed, waited, poised to join the hunt. He let Flantian gallop past and then fell in, waiting for his chance.

He didn't have to wait long. Flantian threw his useless spear, startling the herd into splitting, and then the champions were separated again. I watched, barely breathing, as Lucien chased his foul prey through the deep shadows of the forest.

Wolf shifters—especially alphas, like Lucien—were no small creatures. But the pig beast towered over him, at least half as tall again and nearly twice as wide. His great bulk alone was a danger, let alone the wicked spines on his front legs or his evil curved and crossed tusks.

I didn't know how much time had passed as we watched, all clutching each other as if our pack mates were life rafts, the only thing to cling to in a sea of uncertainty. The wind picked up and began to gust, and when I spared a glance for Fiona, I saw her eyes had gone amber. The skin around them was dark blue as she fought for control of her djinn side.

"Easy, Stormy." Reed's murmur was the only sound on the viewing platform now, as we were held captive, victims to the hunt in our own way.

A pained scream tore itself from the crowd behind us, the sick crunch of bone telling me the sacrifice had begun. But I couldn't see Flantian anywhere on Lucien's screen. It was only the infernabist, and I watched, rapt, as Lucien's wolf leapt gracefully atop the giant creature's back, fangs sinking into its thick neck like a hot knife through butter.

And that was when I saw Flantian. The corner of the camera caught him in the clearing, losing against his own demon pig. Blood soaked into the ground, one of his beautiful chestnut legs bent at an awful angle.

I couldn't bear to look, but I also couldn't stand to look away. They were both in grave danger, and there wasn't a damn fucking thing I could do about it.

"Please, please, please," I whispered, on the verge of tears as I watched it unfold. Lucien took down his beast, executing a clean jump away before the beast could crush him with its excessive bulk as it fell.

I knew the moment Lucien spotted Flantian, wounded and under attack. He had no time and a terrible decision to make.

Lucien's head turned back toward his prey, and then, he was airborne.

Not toward his fallen beast, but toward Flantian's, which was charging in to take another chunk out of Flantian's flank, now that his abdomen was bleeding like his skin was a sieve.

Lucien's attack startled the beast, and it squealed, trying and succeeding to shake him off, since the angle wasn't as good as Lucien's first attack had been. Lucien flew sideways, crashing hard into the twisted trunk of a tree.

But rather than follow, the startled infernabist charged toward a cave across the clearing, its stunned counterpart doing the same a moment later, leaving the two challengers alone.

Lucien shook himself hard, staggering back to his feet as if winded, and limped over to Flantian's side. A moment later, his fur receded, and a very naked Lucien loomed over the downed centaur, dropping to his knees to apply pressure to his wound.

"Do you have a way to call for help?" he asked, and I nearly wept with relief.

He was alive, and he was passing the test. But on top of that, vibrant red marks curled over his side, disappearing around to the front of his chest. I knew without a doubt that they matched the lines on my own side. I let my eyes rove over his masculine beauty, enjoying every splash of color now painted over his chiseled physique. They made him look even more fierce, and as his eyes glowed soft orange with his wolf, he looked like a wild man from a fairy tale.

Lucien had gotten his mate marks.

TWENTY-FOUR

Lucien

I held my hands over Flantian's gaping stomach wound, distressed as his blood continued to ooze between my fingers. He groaned at the contact, taunting me even as he lay dying.

"You're an idiot. Isn't this important to your people? If your species is dying—" His words cut off on a vicious cough, blood gathering at the corners of his lips as his shoulders hunched with the force of it.

The blood between my fingers oozed faster, and I gritted my teeth as I pressed tighter, leaned in with my forearms to stanch more blood.

It felt hopeless, but fuck me if I was going to lie down and let him die.

He wheezed, laying his head back against his arm as if he were too exhausted to continue holding it up, but still, he taunted me. "—f your blessed Moon Goddess is depending on your sorry ass to save her daughters, shouldn't you... be... hunting?"

"Moon Goddess save me from assholes like you," I muttered under my breath. "I didn't know it was possible to be so sarcastic on one's dying breath, but if you'd shut up while I'm trying to save your sadistic hide, I'd appreciate it."

The bastard just laughed, sending a thin trickle of blood spilling down his chin as I scowled at him.

He was sickly pale, and I knew he didn't have long, my paltry attempts at stanching the wound ineffective for the amount of damage the infernabist had done to his insides.

Shit.

Starting to get desperate, I leaned my head back and bellowed at the top of my lungs. "Somebody help us! He's wounded!"

The sound of pounding hooves came not a moment later, and my shoulders nearly sagged with relief, but I couldn't move —he'd certainly bleed out if I did.

To my surprise, when I spotted the charging herd of centaurs heading our way, an older, gray-haired female led the pack, a furious expression deepening the lines on her weathered but still beautiful face.

"Flantian! You stupid, smug fool!"

The male beneath me grimaced. "Mother... You knew what I had to do."

She skidded to a stop inches from his downed flank, kneeling carefully to avoid his broken leg. She rummaged around in a bag at her waist, pulling out some sort of powder in a jar.

"You had to make the sacrifice *look* convincing. You didn't have to get gored and *actually die*." Her tone brooked no disagreement, but all her words did was confuse me further.

"Sacrifice? What the fuck are you talking about?"

She ignored my question, and so did Flantian. To be fair, though, his lips were turning blue, his skin ashen, and it didn't look like he had the breath left to argue.

"Slowly—very slowly—lift one hand at a time. Like this." She made a peeling motion in the air to illustrate. "I'm going to sprinkle this across the wound to seal it. The second he's not going to bleed out, we've got to move him to the hospital for a transfusion and probably surgery."

I did as she asked, watching with surprise as the fine, sandy-looking powder seemed to meld against the wound, *skin* spreading in its wake with magical speed.

When it was done, she nodded and pressed a kiss to the back of Flantian's limp hand, the only sign of tenderness she'd shown since galloping to his side.

The rest of the bigger, brawnier centaur males who'd followed her knelt down, efficiently tucking an oversized stretcher beneath their fallen comrade to carry him out of the forest. Only when they were moving did the elder healer turn to face me.

She grabbed my chin roughly, startling me into temporary quiescence as she inspected my scar. There was no judgment in her eyes, no revulsion, only interest. "Goddess bless." She looked up into a nearby tree. "The circle is complete." With nothing more than those puzzling words and a nod in my direction, she rose back to her hooves and galloped after her son.

When I finally looked up, Kane and Asithius were waiting with steely expressions.

THEY LED me from the forest in silence, and I didn't dare break it. I'd failed utterly, and I knew it.

But I felt no fury radiating from my high alpha, neither in person nor through the pack bonds. It was... acceptance.

I'd behaved honorably, and I knew he wouldn't have asked me to do otherwise, no matter what was on the line.

Perhaps, given the extenuating circumstances, they'd allow me a retrial? I would fight for it. If there was no winner, there could be no loser.

Right?

There had to be a way to salvage the situation. I'd been arguably closer to completing my task than Flantian; surely, that warranted a second try.

But as they led me to a circle of centaurs—both male and female, of varying ages, heights, and colorings—I suspected they were not excited to hear anything I had to say. This was the governing herd, I had no doubt. And we'd just instigated a challenge that had nearly gotten their champion killed. Might still get him killed, I mentally corrected—he'd been unconscious and pale last I'd seen him.

Asithius cleared his throat, joining the circle, and Kane followed suit, leaving me alone in the center. Naked, gore covered, and filthy—I'd never been more under the microscope in my life.

Still, I kept my chin high and dared any male or female to make me regret saving a life.

There was a beat of silence, and then a female centaur spoke without preamble. "Pass."

Another across the circle sounded bored as he said, "Pass," as well.

On and on it went, centaurs speaking a single word around me, with no context whatsoever. It was a singular chorus until there was no one left but Asithius and Kane. I turned slowly to face them.

Asithius also said, "Pass," with a nod, then gestured for Kane to speak.

"Lucien."

The bastard paused, letting me sweat as he stared around the circle. "You've passed the challenge. We won back the omega stone shard."

"What?" I blinked, so shocked, a pup could have bowled me over. "But I didn't... The infernabist escaped. I never completed the hunt."

At that, a grin spread slowly across Kane's face, like the sun rising on a hot summer morning, liquid ease and burning brightness all at once. "Your challenge was not, in fact, to hunt an infernabist for the feast. Your task was to choose well when your fellow champion was injured. And you did. Your swift actions and call for help saved Flantian's life and assured the centaurs that wolves will not act selfishly and throw away the other species as we come back into our own power. Besides, I hear those beasts taste as rotten as they smell." Kane wrinkled his nose.

Stunned didn't begin to encompass my feelings as he stepped forward, wrapping me in a hug and slapping me heartily on the back. When he pulled away, he gripped my shoulders, wearing an earnest expression. "Thank you. You acted with honor and were a *true* champion for wolves today. But we shouldn't linger. There's a she-wolf nearly beside herself with worry who needs to see with her own eyes that her mate is safe."

Olivia.

The second he mentioned her, nothing and no one else mattered.

He said I'd saved Flantian's life, won the challenge, and... she was waiting for me. I was ready to bolt, but I had no idea where she was.

"Come on. We'll go together." He clapped me on the back one more time and led the way.

TWENTY-FIVE

Olivia

I blinked back tears, a terrified hand pressed over my mouth as I watched Lucien do the honorable thing and help save Flantian's life. My tears started pouring when Flantiera arrived, clocked Lucien's scar, and then looked toward the nearby camera as if she were looking into my soul.

The circle is complete.

I felt the weight of those words in my bones. She'd helped me protect my mate, and my mate had, in turn, protected her son.

Our lives were a Goddess-blessed circle, one we all participated in every day without knowing. Flantiera hadn't known why the mágissa magic skipped her any more than I knew why it chose me, yet here we were. Connected.

It was a potent reminder that none of us were alone and that our actions impacted other magical races. In winning back the shard of the omega stone, we were one step closer to shaking the foundations of our modern, magical world. For *everyone.*

I wouldn't lose sight of that ever again. Not after today.

By the time Lucien was led onto the viewing platform, I was

sure I was a mess from crying, but the second I saw him, I didn't care.

Not about how I looked, not that he was covered in gore, not that we had an audience of hundreds.

I forced myself through the crowd as quickly as I could, dodging and darting between the large centaurs' bodies, narrowly missing getting my foot smashed by a hoof multiple times in the process.

But as soon as I broke free, I threw myself into his arms. His lips met mine in a bruising kiss, and before I realized what was happening, my hands were in his hair, and his hands were on my ass, lifting me off my feet. I wrapped my legs around his powerful waist, and a rowdy cheer startled us out of the kiss.

"Get it, girl!" Leigh's encouragement could be heard over the crowd, ever the troublemaker.

Lucien laughed, dropping his forehead to mine a little breathlessly. "I take it you're happy to see me again?"

"So fucking happy," I whispered. My cheeks blushed at the language I didn't usually use, but I didn't regret it. I hid my burning cheeks by burying my face against his neck, where his scent was strongest, and sucking it in as if I might never get another chance to embed it in my memory.

Our high alpha cleared his throat at Lucien's side, and finally, a tinge of embarrassment hit me. But Lucien wouldn't put me down when I squirmed, shushing me lightly and keeping me clutched tight even as we turned toward Kane.

"I'm sure you two would like some alone time, but it would be considered rude if all members of our pack didn't attend the welcome feast this evening. If you leave early, well, no one would blame you." He winked jovially, then strolled away toward the rest of the pack, where Brielle waited for him with open arms.

"Hot damn, I think our alpha just told us to duck out early and get naked." Lucien's voice was colored with repressed laughter, and I couldn't help it, I burst into giggles right along with him. It was absolutely, utterly absurd, but it was also exactly what we were going to do.

THE FEAST WAS ACTUALLY LOVELY, held in the largest of the open-air buildings where tables had been set up, each covered in a variety of food. They'd even made one table just for us carnivores, with nothing but roasted meat and fresh cheeses of every kind.

I only picked at the food, even though it was delicious. I couldn't bring myself to settle in, calm down after the long, treacherous day.

Lucien was safe at my side every single minute, but still, there was some part of me that needed reassurance that the blood drying on his bare chest wasn't his. I needed... more. I couldn't put my finger on what, but the restless urge rattled around under my skin just the same.

Within an hour, it seemed every centaur on the island had come by to slap Lucien's back or shake his hand. They were a blur of new faces and brightly colored coats, and honestly, I mostly tuned it out, focusing instead on the feel of Lucien's hand, warm and comforting in mine.

But when he stiffened at my side, hand gripping mine tightly before catching himself and loosening his grip, I turned to see who had walked up.

"Councilman Fortier," Lucien said, every part of him from his toes to his tone stiff as a rail.

"Councilman Vasilescu." The centaur—who I vaguely recognized now that Lucien had identified him as a member of the IGC—nodded in greeting, studying Lucien grimly as he towered over us, standing out from the rest because instead of Grecian-inspired clothing, he wore a pinstriped suit.

No, I corrected myself—he was studying Lucien's *scar* grimly. I was nearly overcome by the urge to insert myself between them, to block him from staring. Not that it would work when I was shorter than Lucien by a good bit, and they'd be able to see it over my head. Still, I knew how much that scar bothered him, and I didn't want him ogled like a zoo animal. I sidestepped closer, protectively wrapping my arm around Lucien's waist.

He hugged me back, and some of the building tension loosened just a smidge in my chest at his warmth.

"I didn't know you were here when we arrived." Lucien kept his tone light, even though his grip on my hip told me he wasn't entirely pleased to see a member of the IGC here.

"I wasn't. When Asithius called and told me of your pack's unusual request, well, I made it my business to be here."

I could feel the tension in Lucien's stance, but you'd never know it from his smooth-as-butter response. "Ah, well, I'm sorry you troubled yourself. This was pack business, not IGC business."

"So, it would seem. However, when a member of the council is abducted in broad daylight from the streets, the *whole* council takes that seriously. I'm here to get a report on what happened and find out if the target was you personally, your pack, or the council itself."

Shoot. It made sense, actually, that other council members would be concerned about the abduction, but I hadn't thought of that before with everything else going on. It was obvious to us why he'd been abducted, but they probably all thought they could be in danger too.

"We should speak privately, then, if you'd like the details. It does affect the rest of the council."

Councilman Fortier hesitated only a moment. "I'll leave you to your mate tonight, as you've had a trying evening. But before you leave in the morning, gather any members of your pack you'd like to join us, and we'll borrow one of Asithius's private rooms. And remember—officially? I never saw you."

Lucien nodded, turning and pulling me away from him without another word.

"You think it's not safe to talk here? Surely..." I was about to say Petró's name, then thought better of it. "Surely *they* don't have this much reach? It's so remote here."

Lucien spoke quietly as we weaved through the crowd, just enough for me to hear, but not the raucous celebrants around us. "His father had fingers in many pies, and his son is surely taking those connections over as quickly as possible. We don't know who is friend or foe in any supernatural circle on the planet."

Wow.

I'd been on the fringes of the pack's drama so far, and getting sucked straight into the middle of it was eye-opening. My birth pack had been small, Podunk, many would have said. This level of political drama and intrigue didn't make its way out to our part of backwater Arizona pretty much ever.

Granted, we also weren't getting kidnapped, hunted, or any of the rest back then either. There were benefits to small towns.

Lucien sidled up to Reed, whispered something to him, and Reed nodded, casting a glance around and spotting Kane and Gael. "I'll let them both know. We'll handle it in the morning, whatever comes of it." Reed slapped Lucien on the shoulder with a companionable grin. "You two sneaking out? I was thinking the same thing, personally." The look he gave Fiona was scorching, and in the past, it would have made me jealous.

But tonight? Tonight, I had my mate's hand in mine and a scorching fire of my own burning in my belly and demanding *more*. There was no room for jealousy. Just excitement and a new need that I was ready to explore.

"Yes, we're sneaking out. Cover us?" I directed the question to Fiona, who shot me a wink and a nod in response.

Lucien looked down at me with surprise, but when his nostrils flared, I knew he was scenting me, which just amped me up even more.

"Yeah, we're out. See you tomorrow." Lucien said to Reed, never breaking eye contact with me. The look in his eyes had morphed to delicious heat, and I knew he had picked up on what I was thinking. And while I wasn't experienced with men, the speed with which he moved us through the crowd to the exit told me he was fully on board.

Heck yes.

I followed him happily, his larger size acting as a buffer between my smaller frame and the huge centaurs. And when we broke out of the crowd into the empty courtyard, he didn't drop my hand. He turned back to look at me, wearing a panty-melting grin that promised trouble.

"You up for something a little bit wild tonight? I need to shake it all off."

Wild sounded intimidating in a way. But also... thrilling. My heart pounded as fast as a hummingbird's wings with exhilaration just at the suggestion. Being with Lucien made me feel like I was flying, and all we'd done was hold hands and kiss a little. What would sex with him be like?

I was ready to find out.

"Yes. Anything."

The grin stretched across his face, highlighting a dimple in his cheek that I wanted to kiss. "Excellent. Come on."

He picked up the pace to an easy jog, never letting go of my hand. To my surprise, we ran all the way back to our rooms. I wasn't sure what he had in mind, but I didn't think we'd just go back to our room.

When he slanted around and past the building, I knew I'd been correct. What I didn't expect was for him to run straight to the edge of the surf and start to peel off his pants.

My mouth went dry as he reached for the waistband, my

eyes riveted to his strong hands. He paused midmotion, but I didn't dare look away. "Olivia?"

I snapped my gaze up to his, cheeks heating at being caught staring so blatantly. "Yes?"

"Have you ever been skinny-dipping before?"

"Umm, no. Definitely not." I snagged my bottom lip between my teeth, and he stepped forward, closing the small space between us in record time, his thumb gently tugging my lip free.

"Don't be embarrassed. Never with me." The words were hot against the side of my neck, and when he pressed an open-mouthed kiss to my skin as punctuation, the heat I'd been feeling in my belly all night sank lower, flooding me with a new, delicious kind of longing.

I wrapped myself around him, melting as he wrapped his fingers into my hair, tilting my head back so he had full access to my neck.

It was vulnerable and erotic, and I couldn't hold back a needy whine as he nipped at my collarbone. My wolf wanted more than a nip; she wanted his bite and wasn't ashamed to whine if that was what it took to get it.

But he froze, bowing over me to rest his forehead against my shoulder. He shook under my hands, and when he finally lifted his head, his eyes were glowing and his fangs had dropped once again.

His wolf liked the whine. He wants to bite me.

It made me feel... *powerful.* It was new and exciting, and suddenly, I wanted him to finish what he'd started. I wanted to see him completely bare in the moonlight. I wanted to trace every line of his muscles, wanted him to see me too.

Riding the wave of confidence, I stepped back out of his arms and held eye contact as I reached down, grabbing the hem of my shirt. He was riveted as I slooowly peeled it up and over my head. I shook my hair free and tossed the shirt a few feet away up the beach before letting myself look back at him.

His expression was everything. Amazed, enthralled... worshipping. Just like that, all the anxiety I'd felt about our first time evaporated up to the clouds. I felt bold, I felt excited, but more, I felt desirable. And I never wanted him to stop looking at me exactly as he was right now.

Lucien hadn't moved, as if he were afraid that a single twitch would stop me. I reached down for the button of my pants, flicking it open with a satisfying pop.

He watched reverently as I kicked off my pants. But when I reached behind me for the clasp of my bra, he stepped forward.

"Let me."

His bare chest was warm against mine as he reached behind me, taking only a second to undo the hooks, then reached up to slide the straps down my arms.

He paused there, watching me intently as he slowly lowered the straps, sliding the thin fabric away, leaving us pressed together, and I finally closed my eyes, the sensations of our bare skin together for the first time absolutely blowing me away.

Lucien was strong and muscular—but his skin was soft, the light dusting of blonde hair scattered over his chest not detracting from the warmth of him, the way I craved to press myself tighter against him. I shuddered, tucking my nose to his shoulder as I wrapped myself tighter.

"You're so fucking beautiful," he said hoarsely, hugging me back. "And I'm the luckiest devil on the planet to get to experience all of this with you."

Warmth coiled inside me at his words, the subtle encouragement mixed with his awe. The bold person who'd taken me over had me lifting my head, grinning up at him. "You're not so bad yourself. Are you ready to go swimming?"

He chuckled darkly, the change in tone sending a new thrill

through me, and I found myself backing away as he stalked me, *hunting* me. But there was nowhere to hide.

I got a few steps away, and he paused as I turned my back and slowly peeled down my panties, looking back over my shoulder as I stood fully bare before him for the first time.

His eyes glowed, his erection tenting his pants very distractingly. But I had a plan, and I couldn't get sidetracked.

I tossed the balled-up undies toward him, grinning as he jumped to catch them before they could blow away, and then bolted at full speed for the surf.

If he wanted to hunt, I wasn't going to make it *easy* on him.

TWENTY-SIX

Lucien

The little minx. My jaw dropped as I watched her dive into the waves, wondering where my shy, easily embarrassed mate had gone and when she'd brought out her inner hellcat without me noticing.

I sure as fuck noticed now.

Making quick work of my pants, I took an extra second to tuck the panties into my pocket and toss the whole bundle a little way up the beach so that our things wouldn't get washed away as the tide rose. And then I dove in after her.

The water was comfortably balmy, darker cerulean under the moonlight than the daylight, shimmering like a completely different body of water from the playful aquamarine during the day. But it was perfect for this, and I watched with rising hunger as she popped up, red hair slicked back and bare breasts just hidden by the water.

The moon kissed every delicate inch of her I could see, painting her like a selkie out of the old myths. I charged through the shallows, diving under the water as soon as it was deep enough.

Powerful strokes cut the distance between us faster than she expected, and when I saw her legs were within reach, I took one last kick, wrapping my arms around her waist tightly before I exploded out of the water, bringing her up with me.

"Lucien!" My name was a surprised shriek on her damp lips, and I just grinned as she lightly smacked me on the shoulder for startling her.

"Olivia." I growled her name, my wolf close to the surface, pleased that we'd captured our pretty little mate so tidily. She smelled divine, and I knew I'd never forget the salty air mixed with her sweet peach perfume.

Tired of waiting, I captured her lips in a salt-tinged kiss, dropping a hand down to her hips, encouraging her to wrap her legs around my hips. She went easily, as engrossed in kissing me as I was her.

But when she felt my hard cock butt up against her pussy, she gasped, eyes flying open in surprise.

"Easy, hellcat," I murmured, pressing a gentler kiss to her lips, before trailing along her jaw. "We're in no rush, remember? Nice and slow until you're ready. We can just get used to each other for now." I stroked my thumb over her cheekbone and she relaxed in my grip, surprising me as she rocked against me instead of pulling herself back.

"What if I'm tired of slow?" The breathless question wreaked havoc on my control. I groaned, dropping my forehead to her shoulder.

What the fuck was a man supposed to say to that? I didn't want her to regret rushing her first time. But it was *her* first time, and if she was ready, well, no way in hell was I turning her down. I lifted my head.

"Then I'm your alpha. Tell me what you want, and it's yours."

She bit that bottom lip again, the only tell that she wasn't a hundred percent as brazen as she seemed. I resisted the urge to tug it free, take it between my own teeth.

"Touch me. Please."

God, she was cute. Sexy as hell, but cute that she thought she needed to say please.

"Mmm, I already am touching you." I squeezed her hips where I held her afloat. "You're going to have to be a little more specific to get what you want."

Her blush shone on her cheeks even in the moonlight. But instead of words, she reached down, snagging one of my hands and bringing it up to her breast.

I cupped the soft weight of her, and she groaned, going languid in my arms.

"You like that?"

"Mhmm."

I lightly circled her nipple with my thumb, teasing, avoiding the pebbled nub until she started to squirm.

"More, Lucien, I—" Her words broke on a gasp as I leaned down and sucked her nipple into my mouth, teasing it with my teeth, laving it with my tongue.

"Oh, Goddess, fuck!" She arched against me, fingertips digging into my shoulders as I worked her with my mouth, hands back on her hips to steady her as I moved back and forth between her breasts.

When she started to rock her hips against me with building urgency, I knew it was time to take her inside to our bed.

Our bed. The thought nearly struck me dumb, only instinct keeping me moving as I kept driving her higher.

I'd never had a shared bed, not once in my nearly four hundred years. I fucked and I left as a rule, and while Olivia and I had slept next to each other, we'd never had sex and then... stayed in bed.

It was a level of intimacy I didn't know what to do with, yet, strangely... I looked forward to waking up next to her, feeding her breakfast again.

The realization hit me like a physical blow, leaving me reeling. But right now, I had a needy mate in my arms, begging me for more.

I carried her out of the surf, squatting with her still in my arms to grab my pants with the keys to our room in the pocket.

All our other pack mates' rooms were still dark, the curtains drawn, and I was glad—I didn't want to share anything about this experience with anyone but her. It was all mine, all hers. My wolf was so on edge, he'd take another male's head off for even looking at her in this state.

She curled around me, lips on my shoulder and arms tight around my back as I quickly unlocked the front door and kicked it shut behind us.

The way she was restless in my arms, I knew she wanted more, and I was tempted to toss her right onto the bed. But she'd be uncomfortable in salt-sticky sheets, so I carried her to the bathroom first.

Flantian's blood had washed off me in the ocean, but a quick rinse for both of us and she'd enjoy this a lot more. She groaned happily as I backed her into the warm shower, leaning up to rinse her hair. Her breasts swayed with the motion of her arms, and I'd never seen a more perfect sight. I wanted her in my shower every day from now on, because I'd never get tired of watching her.

She kissed me when she finished rinsing, and I swapped our places so I could get the salt off myself too.

To my surprise, when I leaned back to run my hair under the water, she leaned forward, massaging my scalp with her strong fingers. It was a small thing, but knowing that my partner *cared* was... devastating.

She didn't want me for my wealth, my name, my looks like the many who came before her.

Olivia cared for me. Even with my scars, even when I'd treated her like an asshole. She still cared.

Suddenly, I had to get her out of this shower. I needed to be buried inside her with an intensity I couldn't explain. If I didn't take her soon, I was going to lose it.

I flicked off the shower, finally setting her on her feet so I could towel her off. Despite my hurry, I knelt in front of her to dry her legs, peppering kisses over her stomach, her thighs as I went.

She shivered, threading her fingers through my damp hair as I scooped her back up. I could tell she was lost to the moment, mindless with need as she traced my shoulders, lingering over my biceps as I laid her down on the fluffy comforter.

"Are you sure?" I made myself ask. No matter how badly I needed her, I meant it when I said we'd go at her pace.

"So sure. Please?" She reached for me, and I went into her arms like a starved man offered a feast. I worshipped her breasts again, pinning her wrists over her head as I kissed my way down her belly.

"Lucien? What are you— Oh!" She arched as I kissed her inner thigh, pushing her thighs wide to make room for my shoulders.

"So responsive. Are you still good?" I paused again, looking up at her from between her thighs, lips still skating against her tender skin.

"Y-yes." She was resolute, despite the tremor in her voice.

"I know it's new, but I promise I'm going to make it so good for you, hellcat. Do you trust me?"

"I do." The warmth in her eyes nearly slayed me. Her acceptance was a gift, and it was time to earn it.

"Hang on to the blankets if you need to."

"What?"

She gasped in surprise as I buried my face in her pussy, licking, stroking, spreading her wide with my thumbs as I traced every inch of her sweetness with my tongue. When I traced around her clit, she moaned, hips rocking against me, ready for more.

I sucked it between my lips, humming as I circled it with the tip of my tongue until she shattered into bliss, naughty fingers buried in my hair as she soaked my chin with her pleasure.

And I wouldn't have had it any other way.

"Oh my Goddess, Lucien, I— I—"

I rose above her, holding my weight on my palms so I didn't crush her. Her eyes were wild with need, her hair a damp strawberry halo around her. "Did you like that?"

"Like it? Holy shit. You're *incredible*." She cupped my jaw with her small hand, and I nuzzled into it, enjoying her praise, soaking in her happiness. My wolf was happy too. He preened at the praise, a warmth coming from him I hadn't felt in a long, long time.

"You're incredible, hellcat. Are you ready for more? Or do you want to be done for the night?" Feasting on her had somehow taken the edge off. I needed her more than oxygen, but if all she wanted was a snuggle, she'd get it. And I'd sleep with the scent of her arousal in my nose, and feast again in the morning, if she'd let me.

"I am *definitely* not done. I want you. All of you."

I took her lips in a searing kiss, her startled squeak at the taste of herself on my tongue melting into a sigh as I lifted her thighs, giving myself better access to that sweet pussy.

When my cock notched against her, she froze beneath me for the first time.

I pulled back from her lips, studying her. But before I could ask her if she was sure, she wrapped both arms around my neck, keeping me close.

"Yes. Just yes, okay?"

I nodded, slowly inching my way forward. She was soaked

and ready for me, but still the grip of her inner walls nearly stole my breath, and I'd barely moved.

"Hoooooly shit." Her eyes fell closed, but she didn't let me go. "The stretch is..." She shuddered, too lost in sensation to finish her sentence.

"Stay relaxed. Focus on the pleasure." I leaned in and kissed her neck, palming one breast and kneading it as I continued working my way in.

I stopped when I felt her tense beneath me.

"Hellcat?"

"Hmm?" She practically purred beneath me.

"Eyes on me, beautiful mate." Her gorgeous green eyes fluttered open as I snaked a hand between us, toying with her still-sensitive clit.

"It might hurt for a moment, and if you need me to stop, I will."

She shook her head, wrapping her heels around my hips in a clear message.

When she teetered on the edge, I withdrew, still strumming her with my fingers. Her expression changed the moment before she crashed over the edge, and I plunged deep, all the way to the hilt.

Her orgasm consumed her, and she arched, screaming my name as her walls gripped me.

"Don't stop, please, please!"

I ravaged her lips as we hunted our bliss together, chasing the stars in each other's arms.

TWENTY-SEVEN

Olivia

Two thoughts were warring for first place in my mind as I lay beneath Lucien, heart pounding in my chest after my *third* orgasm.

One: holy shit, that was incredible. *He* was incredible. I wanted to commit every single second of my first time to memory. He'd said it might hurt, but all I noticed was intense pleasure as he finally sheathed himself all the way inside me.

Two: I wasn't a virgin anymore. And I was so damn glad. Because if that was what I'd been missing out on... I never wanted to spend another day of my life missing out. I felt sexy and confident and... free, somehow. Like I was in on the secret. It was a little ridiculous, maybe.

But life-changing.

Lucien had shifted something in me tonight, on a cellular level. I couldn't describe it, but I could feel it—pounding in my rib cage right next to my heart, as if he'd left a little piece of himself behind, and I'd carry him with me always. I wondered if he felt the same way.

But in the aftermath, it felt too soon to ask, so I kept my wondering to myself.

He kissed me as he pulled out, promising to be right back as he went into the bathroom. I heard a faucet running, and a few moments later, he was back with a warm washcloth.

I felt stupidly embarrassed as he lifted one knee, then the other, exposing me again. But the warm cloth felt like heaven, and he was gentle as he took care of me, pressing a sweet kiss to the inside of my knee when he finished.

"Do you feel okay? Are you sore?" He was still perched on the edge of the bed, with an anxious expression I'd never seen before as he looked me over.

"A little, but in a good way. Kind of achy, like sore muscles, but like I want to do it all over again." I grinned. I couldn't hold it in.

Relief visibly washed over him, and he chuckled as he kissed my knee again. "Maybe in the morning, if you're a good girl. Tonight, you need to rest."

I shuddered as he walked back to the bathroom. Why was that so hot? I'd never thought anything of the whole *good girl* obsession, but when Lucien said it? Instant desire.

When he walked back out, I took a moment to finally appreciate every square inch of his masculine beauty. Before, when I first met him, he struck me as a Hollywood type. Always sharply dressed, blond hair perfectly slicked back. He reminded me of Leo DiCaprio, but wolfier.

Now? The scar gave him this rugged edge, and it somehow made him even better. Granted, I'd never tell him that, as I knew he was sensitive about it. But more than that, the physique he'd been hiding under those suits... His hair was rumpled from my fingertips, his abs flexing with every step he took, drawing my eyes down to the V at his hips that made my mouth go dry. And I'd never before spent the time to pick out my favorite body part on a man, but Lucien's thighs were just so powerful, they were top contenders. Every single inch of him was perfect.

I was a lucky lady.

He held out a hand for me, pulling me up as if I were weightless and devouring my lips in a soul-stealing kiss. Then he pulled back the covers, urging me under, and slid in next to me.

I wanted desperately to stay awake, to talk it all out, to make sure he'd enjoyed himself half as much as I had. But a jaw-cracking yawn broke free as soon as I was settled with his arm over my hips.

We were nearly nose to nose on the pillows, and I could see his lids drooping with exhaustion. But there was one thing I had to say before the morning.

"You got your mate marks." I trailed my fingertips over his pec, the red lines starting there and slashing down his side.

He blinked slowly at me before glancing down, surprised, as if he genuinely hadn't noticed them yet. "Yes, I did."

A flutter of anxiety danced across my skin. "They match mine." I let my fingertips wander to my own side, a few inches above where his forearm rested. I knew just where they were; I'd been staring at them every single day since they appeared in the bathroom mirror.

"Yours are better," he murmured, a half smirk forming on his lips. "Softer." His hand came up, cupping my hip with a little squeeze that sent the anxiety flying away as quickly as it had landed.

"So, you're okay with it?" I hated myself for asking, hated the insecurity I could hear in the question, but damn it, he'd been so hot and cold with me. Granted, tonight we were running hot, but I couldn't lie and say I wouldn't be scared to wake up and find him cold again.

He'd had plenty of sex; just because he'd blown my mind didn't mean this wasn't business as usual for him.

Oh Goddess. What if we woke up tomorrow and everything

went right back to normal, where everything was distant and polite, or just plain avoidant?

It would crush me. Apparently, my heart had a direct link to my vagina, because I was fully involved now, nothing held back.

Shit, that was not the plan.

Granted, the plan had mostly been to lose my virginity and get closer to my sexy alpha mate, but falling head over heels was *not* smart. Eventually, yes, of course; but not now. It was way too soon, and I was going to get myself hurt.

His brow furrowed, and between one heartbeat and the next, he rolled on top of me, warm skin and solid muscle pressing me into the mattress before I even realized what he was about to do. "What's wrong? You were blissed out not five seconds ago. What changed?"

Heat flooded my cheeks. Shoot. What was more embarrassing? Evading the question with something stupid or admitting I'd been worried I had more feelings than he did?

"I just... Umm."

"Hellcat..." The warning tone had words tumbling from my lips against my will. Not because he used an alpha bark, but because I wanted to please him.

Damn it.

"You weren't happy we were fated. What if you're not happy you got your marks? If this was just sex for you, then... I just need to be prepared. For tomorrow."

He nodded solemnly. "I see. Well, let me make it crystal clear for you."

I tensed, bracing myself for whatever he had to say next.

"In the morning, we're going to shower, and I'll feed you your breakfast. If you're not too sore and there aren't any interruptions, I might just push you up against the shower wall for round two." He dropped a kiss to my forehead that made me melt. "But whatever comes up after that, we'll figure it out.

Together," he added hastily, as if he was worried I hadn't caught that part. "Okay?"

"Okay." I was a lower rank, a nu, officially. But even so, I'd never been a girl who wanted to be dominated or to have to deal with alpha male toxicity. When Lucien was dominant, though? Whole different ball game. My wolf practically purred with happiness to be under him, the object of his full attention.

"Good. Now get some sleep, or else you'll be too tired for round two." He rolled over, but instead of lying beside me, he pulled me onto his chest, my cheek pressed against his chest, his hands on my back playing with the ends of my hair, our legs intertwined.

Within minutes, the steady sound of his heartbeat and the soft strokes on my hair lulled me into dreamless sleep.

SHOWER SEX WITH LUCIEN? Twelve out of ten. He'd lathered me up and then proceeded to get me dirty all over again, paying particular attention to my mate marks this time around, which he seemed shockingly possessive of. Nudity wasn't a big thing for wolves, but he'd adjusted my shirt as we walked out, making sure every single inch of them were covered. I definitely wasn't complaining as we walked out of our room midmorning, even though my stomach was rumbling.

No chef had shown up with a tray this time, but someone had left a note that the rest of the pack had gone in for breakfast with the centaurs. Apparently, they wanted more face time with us now that we'd passed their test.

It didn't take us long to find the breakfast buffet, partly because the scent of fresh bacon was a beacon, but also because of the racket. There was a huge crowd, and centaurs of all shapes and coat colors were milling around, practically queueing up to speak to our pack mates. They'd actually all spread out in groups of two or three, so after Lucien and I went through the line for our plates mounded with breakfast meat, eggs, and fresh chunks of feta, we found an empty spot and took it.

We weren't alone for long. It was a roulette wheel of centaurs, walking up to chat with us until they were shuffled out of the way by the next enthusiastic centaur. They wanted to know all sorts of things. How we'd met, where we were from, what was happening anywhere in the world but their island.

By the time our plates were nearly empty, it was very clear to me that they were starved for outside interaction. The days were gone where a creature as different as a centaur could roam freely without being exposed by human media.

My head spun by the time Gael slid into the seat on Lucien's other side. "It's time to meet with the herd leader and councilman. I'm taking the other women back to their rooms so they have time to pack, since we're leaving right after. Olivia, do you want to come along?"

I cast one glance at Lucien's face—the thunderclouds had settled in, his lack of excitement about having to share what had happened to him evident—and shook my head. "I don't have much to pack, so I'll stay with Luce."

"Sure thing." He nodded to me, slapped Lucien on the shoulder, and disappeared back into the crowd.

I saw our pack mates drifting together through the crowd, but in a moment, they were divvying up. Reed kissed Fiona on the cheek, letting her go with Gael, Galyna, and the rest of the females. To my surprise, Elodie and Kane stayed with him and walked our way.

"You don't need to go with Brielle and Leigh?" I asked Elodie quietly as she fell in beside me.

Her red lips twisted into a smirk. "You realize we're also watching *you*, right?" She gestured to my palm, the concealer I used to cover the omega seal starting to wear a bit thin after an open-air breakfast. It was warm out, and I'd have to be careful to keep the concealer in my pocket moving forward. I reflexively pressed it against my thigh, not wanting to start trouble.

"No, I didn't realize that. I'm not pregnant, so..."

She shook her head, expression suddenly intensely serious. "That doesn't matter. If word got out about *any* of you, you'd all be next on the chopping block. If they take out the sealed, there is no next generation. It's not the law, of course—but it's happened before."

An arctic chill shimmied its way down my spine, a new level of distress thrumming through my veins, leaving me colder than a glacier. It made a sick kind of sense that if omegas were so feared, the mothers would be an easier target.

Nip the problem in the bud before it began.

But I didn't have time to dwell on it, because we were stepping into a private office to speak with Councilman Fortier and Herd Leader Asithius.

When we entered the room, we were greeted with a short set of stairs leading to fancy office guest chairs on a raised platform, perfectly set so the average human would be at eye level with the centaurs they were meeting with.

I found it interesting that we hadn't been brought here the first day, but the second the door clicked shut behind Elodie and me, Fortier got down to business.

"Tell me everything." Fortier's tone brooked no argument, and I could tell Lucien was agitated by the order.

He waved me into a seat, but chose not to take one himself. Elodie leaned her hip on the back of my chair, watching everything with hawk-sharp attention to detail. After what she'd just told me, I was glad to have her there for more than just her friendship. Kane and Reed settled into chairs, watching it all play out in silence.

"I was downtown, walking through a parking lot to Bridgette."

Bridgette? A flash of irrational jealousy burned through my veins before I remembered. *Oh, the motorcycle.*

"Downtown near the council house?"

Lucien nodded, lips pursed with annoyance at the interruption. "Yes. As I was saying, I was in a parking lot. I'd just left the council for the day and was going to grab a bite to eat before heading home."

Lucien ran a hand through his freshly styled hair, and it was plain as ink on paper that he didn't want to continue. I wanted to hug him again, but didn't think he'd appreciate me drawing attention to his feelings in this kind of forum.

"Four guys jumped me. I managed to knock one out, and I was holding the second and third back easily enough. But while I was midshift, one of them snuck up from behind and stabbed me in the neck with something. I blacked out, woke up underground, human, naked, and in basically a dirt pit with a concrete floor. They chained me with magical cuffs, so I couldn't shift out of them." He absently rubbed a wrist, and my heart ached at the memory of the terrible burn wounds he'd had there.

He'd clearly tried to shift multiple times during his weeks of captivity. Between that and the wolfsbane, it was no wonder his connection with his wolf was damaged. The new realization hurt me to my soul, but I kept quiet, not wanting to drag this experience out for him. The physical wounds had healed; the mental and emotional ones? I wasn't so sure they had, but I *was* sure this play-by-play wasn't helping.

"After that, I got visits several times a day from Dominik, third-in-command of the Hungarian pack. I never saw Petró, but I heard him. He'd come every few days asking for an update. If I had confirmed the existence of an adult omega or had any lead on where the high alpha had 'scurried off to like a rat.'" His voice dripped with disgust, and I noticed Kane stiffen at the secondhand insult.

"So you believe it was pack targeted, not council targeted?" Fortier was all business, no emotion in his voice as he cut to his own concern, glossing over Lucien's pain and suffering.

"Yes, I do."

"Thank you. That's good to know." There was a lengthy pause while Fortier shifted on his hooves. "I want you to know that, given the circumstances, I'm still going to lodge a formal reprimand against the Hungarian pack—specifically citing both Dominik and Petró. Even if they weren't coming after you because of your council seat, we cannot and will not take attacks on the IGC lightly. Enforcers will be out looking for them, and when they're found, they will be brought to justice on your behalf." Fortier adjusted his tie. "This testimony in the presence of multiple witnesses is sufficient. No further testimony will be needed."

"Yeah? Well, you better pray you find them before I do, because next time I see either one of them, I'm going to kill the fuckers."

"Councilman Vasilescu!" Fortier snapped, face darkening with outrage. "It's highly inappropriate for a member of the Interspecies Governing Council to make blatant threats against a pack leader's life. I'm going to pretend I didn't hear that, but if you act outside the law, I will be forced to take action against you as well. And nobody wants that."

"You can pretend whatever helps you sleep at night, but I will have my revenge, whether you like it or not. There is *nothing* more important than making them pay."

His words made me feel hollow, cracked wide open and emptied out like a broken glass. I understood wanting payback for his torture. He was well within his rights to want them punished, and by wolf law, killed in a fair challenge. But to say that *nothing* was more important than revenge?

Where does that leave us?

Herd Leader Asithius cleared his throat, stepping forward

to defuse the situation, a carved wooden box in his hands. *The omega stone shard.* "You've earned this. But I implore you, use it wisely. All our fates may depend on it."

To my surprise, he pressed it into Lucien's hands, though Kane sat mere feet away. Lucien ducked his chin in acknowledgment, handling the box reverently. "We will. Thank you."

"Don't thank me. You earned it."

"And Flantian?" Lucien's shoulders tightened under his shirt, the movement so small, no one else probably noticed it.

"Recovering well, with his mother and his sister looming over him like Valkyries. He'll be fine."

Lucien nodded again. "Excellent."

"We should be going on our way." Kane stood gracefully, towering over the two centaurs as he leaned over to shake their hands. "We would appreciate your support with what's coming."

There was a pregnant pause, his words creating tension even without the explicit threat that hung over our heads.

Asithius finally spoke up. "While centaurs are lawfully neutral in interspecies conflicts, we will be watching your pack closely. I suspect the Goddess isn't done with you yet."

A few more handshakes, and we were done.

It was time to leave Nisí Mýthou, but I had absolutely no idea where we were heading next.

TWENTY-EIGHT

Lucien

Something was bothering Olivia. I'd noticed it in her silence while we'd thrown our few possessions into the speedboat, in the way she hadn't settled into my side on the ride, and in the way she looked drawn and tired now that we were boarding the private jet.

I'd worn her out last night, but she'd been happy and upbeat this morning at breakfast. No, this was something else.

And we were at least twelve hours away from enough privacy to find out what it was if we didn't want the whole pack listening in.

We'd settled into a pair of leather seats at the front of the jet, but our pack mates surrounded us, chattering happily about how we had two pieces, and that only left two to go, besides the one Shay and Dirge had gone to get from the fae realm. All except Samuel, who was still blessedly giving me and Olivia as wide a berth as possible in an enclosed space. It wasn't enough, but it was manageable.

Halfway there! was the mood, and I just wasn't feeling it. Going over my capture and torture this morning for Fortier had brought all my rage and desire for revenge burning back to the surface.

Was that what Olivia was reacting to? I cast a sideways glance her way, but at the moment, her head was bent as she read quietly on her phone. She was more empathetic than anyone I'd ever known, so it very well could be.

I sighed, kicking back in the seat as I thought it over. I knew I needed to get my shit together—but every time I thought I had, something brought it all back up as if it were yesterday.

"Hey, guys, I've got a heading for us," Reed called out from farther back in the jet.

Everyone turned or rose from their seats to see him better.

"I wasn't able to get in touch with Councilman Lug, but I just spoke with Xeor Blaise, a powerful warlock acquaintance in Las Vegas. He's hooked into the supernatural world well enough to keep tabs on pretty much everyone. He says the goblin leader was last seen in eastern Canada, near Toronto."

"Toronto? Don't goblins usually form colonies farther away from major population centers?" Leigh asked, the only person who still had her feet up.

"Yes, but he was sure of it. Frankly, that's good for us. The Hungarians won't start anything with enough humans around, not unless they want the entire supernatural world gunning for them for exposing the secret."

"Toronto it is, then." Brielle smiled, walking up the aisle to go tell the pilot.

"Any word on a phoenix?" I asked, worried about the fourth piece more than any of the others.

Reed grimaced, and I knew the answer. "No, not a peep. They're rare in every century, but it seems wolves aren't the only species in decline. There would usually be eight to ten alive at any given time, but Blaise wasn't aware of any he could direct us toward. He sends his apologies and promises to call again if he gets a lead."

I nodded. It was exactly as I'd suspected.

"I had no idea any of the species were so rare," Olivia said, worrying her bottom lip between her teeth as we settled back into our seats. I reached over and freed it with my thumb, earning me a fleeting smile.

Deciding to remind her of this morning, I leaned in and whispered, "I'm the only one who bites this lip now."

She shuddered, heat filling the depths of those green eyes. Damn, she was so responsive. If we weren't in the middle of a pack shitstorm, I'd have kept her in bed for a month, until we were so tangled up, we were ready to bond.

The realization struck me momentarily mute, but her expectant expression snapped me out of it.

"Each species has its own natural population set point. Humans are the only ones expanding like ants at this point, though vampires... They've had their ebbs and flows over the centuries. Phoenixes, though, are unique. One of the rarest species out there, except perhaps djinn, like Fiona." I shrugged. "No one really knows the why of it, but there are only ever a handful at any given time. They keep to themselves, because their feathers are potently magical, and they've been hunted over the years and held in captivity many times."

"Sentient magical beings, held in captivity for their *feathers*?" Olivia's horror was appropriate. What I'd learned in my IGC briefings was ugly. The council's enforcers were actively searching for any living phoenix, but it was feared they were either extinct or enslaved.

"Yes. Usually, the fear is that humans will discover us and experiment on us, but in this case, it's other magical races who want to amplify their own powers."

"Despicable." The little healer practically shook with anger, and I had to work not to find her cute in the moment. But damn it, she was objectively adorable, like a kitten squaring off against a mastiff, entirely certain she was going to take him.

"I agree. But hopefully, the IGC is wrong about the phoenixes, or we're going to be stuck."

She nodded, resigned, glancing back down at her phone.

"Go ahead, read. Relax a little. I'm sure as soon as we land, there won't be a quiet moment." I dropped a kiss on her forehead, and finally felt like I could exhale when she lifted the armrest between us and shifted so that our sides touched.

TWENTY-NINE

Olivia

B y the time we'd made several "throw the ODL off the scent" stops at various airports and then finally landed in Canada, it felt like we'd been on the jet for a month. In actuality, it was about a full day and a half of travel.

As we all exited the jet, the sun was setting over Toronto. But I didn't care because I was just so, so glad to be on solid ground again. It felt weird in the best possible way to be on pavement that wasn't moving under my feet.

There were black SUVs waiting, courtesy of Reed's endless business contacts, I had no doubt, and Lucien and I climbed into the back seat of one together.

We were all exhausted, so it was quiet as we drove to our temporary safe house, from which we'd look for the goblins. Lucien had arranged it from the air yesterday. There was a local witch who was willing to ward it as strongly as possible in exchange for a council member owing her coven a favor.

I tried not to let myself dwell on the fact that we weren't sure it would be enough to keep the ODL off us. The centaurs' special barrier had worked like a charm, but it took the might of their entire species to build and maintain that warding magic so that they had a safe haven.

Even once we found the goblins, not much was known about their powers or what kind of barrier we had. Basically, we all knew we were on borrowed time here, but we didn't have another choice. With no stone, we had no way to get the rest of the wolf packs to band together with us instead of against us because of the fear of omegas.

It didn't take us long to get to the safe house, and when we rolled to a stop, my jaw dropped. It was the most conspicuous home I could have imagined.

A candy-pink Victorian-style home with frosting-white trim, it had sharp peaks on the roof, wild landscaping with big, unnaturally threatening-looking plants all around it, and to top it all off, as the car doors opened, an eerie sense of intense foreboding washed over me. I wanted to run away and never set eyes on the place again.

Odd, given it looked like somebody's daughter had drawn it, probably with a rainbow unicorn in the stables out back.

It must have been the warding, and I took it as a good sign that we could already feel it from the street.

Hopefully, it would be enough.

The guys grabbed our minimal luggage, and by the time we were all on the sidewalk, a tall, thin witch was waiting for us on the front porch. Lucien held our bags in one hand and pulled me along to meet her with the other.

It was a great improvement from the early days, when he'd barely looked at me, let alone spoken to me—but just this once, I might have been fine to let him handle the witch alone. Granted, the utter terror that had rolled over me the second we stepped foot on the lawn probably had a lot to do with that.

"Inez. Thank you for meeting us on such short notice." Lucien spoke as if he wasn't feeling an ounce of what I was feeling, and I envied him his composure.

"Councilman Lucien. Our coven is *always* happy to help out the council. Please, do come inside so I can tailor the wards to your personal auras." She grinned, waving us all inside. But to me, it looked like she was starving, teeth sharp and threatening, and if we stepped foot across the threshold, she'd surely chop us up and put us into her evening stew.

I dragged my feet as Lucien stepped confidently through the door, but in the end, she didn't attack us as we came inside.

There *was* a large black cauldron bubbling in the fireplace, and I took a wary step away from it as soon as I noticed it. It made my skin crawl, and all I wanted was to run out the door. But quick as a flash, Inez darted around the room, plucking a hair from each of us before tossing the whole lot into the pot and stirring.

The house seemed to shudder around us, and then the pot belched a great cloud of green smoke from its belly, and everything went still.

"There. Is that better?" She turned and studied us.

Now that she'd mentioned it... yes. The terror and revulsion I'd been feeling had drained away, leaving nothing behind but my own emotions. She no longer seemed as if she wanted to toss us into her stewpot. So *freaking weird.*

"Yes, thank you." Lucien inclined his head politely. "So the house will admit only us?"

"It will admit all of you as well as the leadership of my coven. Which is me, Jarynda, and Kelley. We felt this was a matter best kept to the leadership instead of spread to the whole coven. Loose lips and all that." She mimed zipping her lips shut and throwing the key into the fire.

I jumped when it flared under the still-boiling pot.

"I've left instructions for you here on the mantel, but it's best that one or two of you memorize them, just in case. For every day you need continued protection, you'll need to throw a few ingredients into the cauldron and stir it three times clockwise. If a full week passes, I'll need to return to revive the spell. If I return in a week and you're not here, well, I'll assume our barter is complete and let you know when we need to cash in our favor."

Lucien maintained his smile, though I felt... annoyance? I wrinkled my eyebrows in concentration. It wasn't my own, but how was I feeling that?

Before I could figure it out, it faded away, and I shook it off. Whatever it was, it was gone now.

Kane stepped forward, extending a hand for her to shake. "We appreciate your help, Inez. But as Lucien mentioned over the phone, we'll need a bit of extra reassurance to ensure there are no issues."

The witch was tall, but still had to look up at the towering high alpha. "Yes, yes. He mentioned. Barbaric, you wolves." But still, she held up a palm and turned her head away.

Kane lifted her hand, pricking just her fingertip with one long, extended canine before releasing her. Oh, man. I'd never seen a blood bond before. My heartbeat sped as I watched.

"It's settled. Who has access to this home while under the current wards?"

"Inez, Jarynda, Kelley, and the wolves gathered here in this room." She rattled off the list as if she were bored.

"Truth. Are there any exceptions or loopholes to the protections?"

Inez hesitated, then shook her head. "None that I'm aware of, but it was a very potent spell, and it took all three of us to apply it to the home."

Kane frowned but soldiered on. "Truth. Do you swear a binding of silence—effective for your entire coven—as to our presence and purpose inside this safe house for the duration of our time here, plus fifty years?"

Her lips pursed into a pout, and she crossed her arms angrily over her chest. "I do."

"Thank you." Kane stepped back to the pack, casually looping his arm around Brielle's waist, as if he hadn't just permanently linked himself to the witch, absorbing a thread of her power through her blood.

The amount of power he must wield on a daily basis was mind-boggling to a weak nu like myself. I was comfortable with my wolf and my place in the pack, but I knew I was low on the totem pole, had been since my wolf presented in my late teens.

Inez stepped forward to shake Lucien's hand, so he dropped mine to shake it. The second he touched the witch, he gasped, staggering back, clutching his face, and dropping to his knees.

"Councilman, I swear that wasn't me! Nothing should be able to harm you inside the walls of this house, not even me!" The witch jerked back with her hands raised, as if the pack was about to turn on her.

Gael appeared at her side in an instant, escorting her out the front door and to the street as the rest of us crowded around Lucien—except Samuel, who bolted up the stairs to give Lucien space.

"Shit." He moaned, clutching his face as both Brielle and I dropped to our knees in front of him.

"What happened?" I asked, gently peeling one of his hands away from the scar. It looked the same as ever, though, and a frustrated helplessness filled me.

"My wolf reacted badly to me dropping your hand to touch another female. I think I'll be okay in a moment."

I blinked, surprised by that explanation.

Brielle, however, had her head in the game. "That is a really good observation, Lucien. It works with my theory that the pain is damage to your bond with your wolf, and if your wolf was angry about your actions because your bond with Olivia is still not complete, well..."

It strained their damaged bond.

Tears welled in my eyes. This all felt so impossible at times, and I was sick to death of being so damn helpless in my own life. All the power I'd felt at having sex for the first time was gone, withered to nothing in the face of this problem that I couldn't fix.

"If we completed our bond, do you think the pain would go away?" he asked, voice haggard. His shoulders were still slumped, and he didn't seem to have the energy to look up right now.

I froze in shock.

Now *that* I hadn't considered.

Brielle shrugged, looking just as frustrated as I felt. "Frankly, I don't know. That kind of power surge could heal the connection, or if it's too fragile, it could shatter it beyond repair. I had hoped your connection with your wolf would heal first, but it doesn't seem to be improving so far."

"No, it doesn't." I hated how defeated he sounded.

I might have been used to my weaknesses, but Lucien was an alpha. He was *not* used to being weak, ever. Angrily swiping away the tear trailing down my cheek, I remembered the little bottle of herbal paste I'd put together with Flantiera and pulled it from my bag with shaking hands.

"Here, let's try this again. It should help ease the pain."

The second my fingertips touched his brow, Lucien sighed, sagging in relief. "Just your touch makes him happier. Thank you."

I applied the paste carefully, kissing him on the unscarred brow before pulling back to cork it and stow it away. I watched as it flared green and then disappeared into the scar once again.

"The pain is already fading. Thank you." Lucien smiled, but it didn't reach his eyes, and he quickly looked away. A wash of shame that wasn't mine flooded my chest, and I barely held back my gasp.

Was I picking up on *Lucien's* emotions?

I didn't think that was possible before we'd bonded, but it was the only thing that made sense.

Gael came back inside, the sound of the door shutting behind him breaking up the crowd. Everyone began to disperse into different parts of the house, leaving only Brielle and me with Lucien in the foyer.

"I'll give you two a little space, but if you need me, I'll just be in the next room."

"Thank you, Bri," I murmured, not able to hold back my tears when I saw her compassionate expression.

"It's all going to work out. I really believe that." She hugged me tightly, then rose and quietly left us where we knelt.

"Do you want me to help you up, and we can go find our room? I'm sure a rest would help us both after all that flying."

He shook his head, shoving himself to his feet without touching me. "I think... I think I need a little space, if you don't mind."

"Oh. Okay. Of course." I felt numb as he walked away, watched as he took the stairs two at a time, all while I sat on the floor, alone with my tears and the silent echo of his shame in my chest.

THIRTY

Lucien

I was so fucking ashamed of myself, I couldn't breathe.

Last night, I'd collapsed in front of the whole pack again, and then to top it all off, I'd walked away and left my hurting mate alone on the floor. Then I followed the traces of Samuel's scent down the hallway and asked him to let me stay with him, hiding from my mate with my tail between my legs.

Samuel was a better man than I because he didn't even hesitate, just waved me inside without judgment. I *deserved* to be judged.

I was no better than the shitty father who'd haunted my nightmares last night, and that fact didn't sit well with me. At all.

My father was an abusive bastard, and I'd spent most of my younger years swearing I'd never be like him. When he'd died, I hadn't been sad.

And here I was, staring into a magically sparkling bathroom mirror with a gaudy purple frame, white-knuckle gripping the sink, dealing with the fact that I'd left my mate on the floor last night, crying.

The number of times I'd picked my mother off the floor looking just like that as a teen? Too many to count.

Granted, Olivia hadn't been down there because I'd hit her —I would *never* lay a finger on her that she didn't enjoy, and that I'd lost control and hurt her once, even by accident, would haunt me forever—but the look she'd given me as I walked away?

Déjà vu. She wore my mother's expression, the one painfully seared into my adolescent brain, and I was sick with it.

I hung my head, resisting the urge to roar out my disgust with myself. But if I did that, everyone would assume I'd gone off the deep end and attacked Samuel again, then bust down the door to separate us.

Because I was a risk. To Olivia, obviously. But to the whole damn pack too. Not only a risk—a fucking *liability*. Damaged.

When I first saw it, I thought the hideous scar on my face was the worst thing that could possibly come from my capture and torture. Fuck, the desire for revenge still burned like acid in my veins about that. But little did I know, it would open the door for me to hurt my mate.

All the anger, all the worry, all the shame built and built in my chest until it was a burning ball of desire for one single thing.

Revenge.

I wanted it more than anything. I wanted to slay the fuckers who did this to me. And I knew in my bones I wouldn't be happy again until their lifeblood ran between my fingers.

But what about Olivia? What happens to her when I go on a murderous rampage to get my revenge?

I didn't know, and it froze the air in my lungs, pulling me out of my burning frenzy just as swiftly as being dunked in a tank full of ice water.

My little hellcat. She trusted me, and I'd let her down *again*.

She was better off without my shit, I knew that. But would she let me go? Could I bear to leave her after tasting her sweetness?

No, no, I could not. And damn if she wasn't faithful, loyal. She seemed so shy, she'd fooled me at first. I thought that shy meant weak, but it didn't. She was the strongest person I knew, because where others broke, she bent.

She yielded, but she didn't let go. Her strength looked different from mine, but it was still strength.

There were plenty of ugly bastards in the world. The fact that I'd joined their numbers hurt no one but me.

Me being unhinged, with the full strength of an alpha wolf shifter?

Shit.

I could hurt people. Expose our secret to the *world*. My life would be forfeit, but would it even matter to me by the time I lost that much control?

That was a line I couldn't cross. And until I knew I *wouldn't* cross it ever again, knew that I had complete control over myself and my wolf, I had to keep my distance from Olivia.

I exhaled, the force of it lightly steaming the mirror, obscuring my scar. Almost as if I could pretend it wasn't there, like none of this had ever happened.

But it had. And I was at a crossroads. But there was only one decision I could make to keep her safe until I got my shit under control.

"Hey, Lucien, we're about to head out and start looking for goblins. You coming?"

I turned away from the mirror, toward Samuel's voice.

"Yeah, I'm coming." I swiped a hand through my unkempt hair and yanked the door open. "Where to first?"

SAMUEL and I paired up with Kane and Gael, while Reed, Fiona, Elodie, and Olivia formed the second team. Brielle, Galyna, and Leigh stayed in the house so that Brielle had the maximum amount of warding at all times.

It wasn't a perfect solution, but at this point, I didn't think there was one. I knew Olivia's group all loved her and would protect her, but that didn't stop the galling sensation that it should be *me* protecting her.

I couldn't, though. I had to sort out my own shit first.

The sad smile she gave me as the four of them left was burned into my brain, accusing me of being a shitty mate even though she hadn't said a word.

I'd asked for space, and she'd given it. Didn't mean I liked it, though.

"Is your head in the game?" Samuel's quiet question as the other two kissed their mates goodbye made me grind my back teeth. But it was fair. He let me crash; he earned a question.

"Yes. I'm fine."

He grunted, shooting me an incredulous look, but thankfully kept his opinions to himself.

The second Kane and Gael were ready, we strode out of the house and hit the sidewalk. Olivia's team had taken an SUV out to the nearest nature preserve because that seemed like the most logical place for goblins to hide in plain sight.

We were staying closer to the safe house, just in case the ODL showed up. So we were on foot, looking for any other supes who could point us toward some local goblin hangouts.

Four alpha wolves stalking down the sidewalk together weren't exactly inconspicuous, even in human form in neutral clothing, so we split up, Samuel and Kane heading left, while Gael and I went right.

Gael and I walked in silence for half an hour, nothing piquing our interest or our noses.

It was nice to move, though. *Space.* I'd wanted it. Now I had it, and it turned out being alone with my own thoughts wasn't great either.

Shocker.

"You wanna talk about it?" Gael eventually said as we turned down a side street with more houses squeezed closer together, his bored tone letting me know he wasn't thrilled about the idea. "You're brooding so loud, it's offensive."

"I haven't said a word."

"Yeah, loudly."

I snorted. I wasn't exactly close to Gael, but we had a mutual respect for each other. Was I missing an opportunity to get some perspective?

"You and Leigh had a rough time figuring things out." It wasn't a question, but I was at a loss for how to *ask* for help. Alphas didn't do that very often.

It was his turn to snort and shoot me an incredulous look. "You could say that. For a while there, I was pretty sure she was going to gut me with a rusty spoon."

Oddly, that made me feel better. "Good to know."

"Olivia doesn't seem like the type, though. She's a good egg. Which means you're the one fucking it up."

Right to the point.

"Yeah, I am."

The residential neighborhood was slowly turning commercial around us as we walked, cars whizzing by at faster speeds and more people out and about in business attire, darting into shops to complete a midmorning errand or grab a bagel sandwich.

"You going to elaborate?"

"I don't know what to tell you that you haven't seen me screw up firsthand. I keep messing up. We get a little better, take a step closer, then I fuck up again." I paused at the doorway of a paranormal shop, discreetly sniffing the air to see if there was any actual magic inside. Nope. I started walking again, and Gael stuck to my side. "She'd be better off without me, man."

He slapped a hand on my biceps, stopping me in my tracks. "Cut that shit out. This is the most pity-partying bullshit I've ever heard. Do you know how many males out there would *kill* for a mate? A fuck ton. And here you are with a good one, head so far up your own ass, you can't figure out how to lock things down before she wises up. Now listen—I'm not one to judge. Our path was rocky, but we didn't have it as good as you do."

I laughed bitterly, shaking my head. "You're insane if you think we've got it good."

"You've got mate marks. I spent *months* wanting Leigh, with not a damn sign that it was anything other than my imagination that she was mine. Then she got pregnant *without a heat* and still had fuck all to do with me. So you can take your self-pity and stuff it up your ass. I'm serious. You've got it *good*."

He turned and stormed down the sidewalk, picking up the pace so I had to jog to catch him like a bad rom-com hero.

"Look, I wasn't trying to insult you. You asked," I muttered a few minutes later, when the worst of his annoyance seemed to have faded. "Okay, that was an eye roll that Leigh would have been proud of, but I'm serious. Mate marks aren't the end-all, be-all."

"They could be. They're literally a sign from the Goddess herself."

I chewed on that for a few minutes, until Gael stopped, sniffing the air and pointing across the street. "You hungry? I could eat a horse. That one looks tasty." He pointed his thumb at a police horse down the street.

A woman walking the other way in a *Toronto is for Vegans* T-shirt shot us a dirty look at that. Pretty sure she mumbled something about *crass Americans* under her breath as she walked away. Joke was on her: we weren't Americans. And also, horse meat didn't taste good to a wolf. Mine preferred mutton, usually.

"Apparently, you've lost your native accent." I gave Gael a smartass grin, and he cussed me out in fluent Castilian Spanish as we crossed the road to the Chinese restaurant.

Four whole Peking ducks later, we hit the streets again. We passed a whole day searching fruitlessly for any sign of goblins, but still I couldn't get what he'd said off my mind.

When my head hit the pillow in Samuel's spare bed that night, the question remained.

Could it really be that simple?

THIRTY-ONE

Olivia

The days dragged by like sloths on Xanax. I'd lost count of how many it had been, but I knew it was enough that Inez the witch had needed to refresh our protective spells twice already, and we were on the way to a third. The good news was, the shielding spells seemed to be working, since the ODL hadn't pounced on us as long as Bri stayed inside.

The bad news was, I was sick to death of hiking the various patches of wilderness around Toronto, of the way my pack mates kept giving me little hugs and sad smiles, all of it. *Done*. And all the while, Lucien kept his distance, even while we lived under the same ugly pink roof. Again. It was downright insulting.

Infuriating was the word that came to mind.

Frankly? I was sick of it all. I wanted to light something on fire and watch it burn.

I scrubbed at an already clean plate with enough vigor, I was worried it might crack. But if I didn't get some kind of physical release for all the aggression that was building up inside me, I was going to go shout at my stubborn-ass mate, and that would only push him further away.

I dropped the plate into the empty side of the sink to be rinsed and braced myself on the edge of the counter, letting my head hang as I took a series of deep, slow breaths and tried to shake it off.

We were leaving in five minutes to go searching again, and I couldn't very well go out looking for trouble without having my head on straight. Someone would get hurt.

"Hey, girl." Elodie floated into the kitchen with the lithe grace of a dancer. "I'm feeling a little under the weather today, so I'm going to hang back."

I straightened up, narrowing my eyes at her. "Do you want me or Bri to check you out? I've got my herbalist kit. I'm sure between the two of us, we could get you feeling better in ten minutes flat."

She waved the offer away. "Nah. I just need a good day in bed and some trashy TV, and I'll be right as rain tomorrow. Promise."

Her smile was a little too bright for someone claiming to be ill. But you know what? I couldn't blame her for wanting to get out of what was starting to feel like the world's dullest vacation. Maybe tomorrow I should fake being sick and watch some trashy TV of my own. There would be fewer bug bites that way.

"All right. Feel better," I said with enough sarcasm to make my feelings on the matter clear.

"Oh, I will." She whistled as she strode out of the room, the picture of feminine health.

I quickly rinsed the last plate and put it aside to dry with a weary sigh. It could be worse. At least Fiona and Reed were good company, and they never made me feel like a third wheel.

I was lacing up my new tennis shoes when the others arrived to get going.

"Where to today?" I asked Reed, as he'd been meticulously mapping and tracking every area we'd checked so we didn't double up.

"Ah, new plan. We're going a little farther south, toward Niagara Falls. It's farther from Toronto, but we've pretty much covered every wild area around here and gotten not even a whiff of goblin activity. We've been focusing on less populated areas, but so far, we've got nothing. So... today, we're playing totally out of left field. Worst case scenario, we get more nothing."

I bobbed my head. Couldn't hurt, beyond some new blisters. "Sounds good to me. Elodie's taking a sick day, so we're down a man. Woman. Whatever, you know what I mean." I finished with my shoelaces and straightened. I really was going to play hooky tomorrow and stay in bed the whole day, eating cookies and watching reality TV. I'd definitely earned it.

He nodded, then shot a wary glance at Fiona before reaching up to fiddle with a shirt collar that wasn't there. Instead of his usual button-ups, he'd switched to outdoor gear to blend in better. "About that."

"You three ready to go?" Lucien stepped up to our group, giving me the same polite smile he would a stranger, making me want to punch him in the process.

"You're coming with us?"

"Yep. Kane told me Elodie wasn't feeling well, so..." He shrugged as if it was no big deal, and I *growled*.

I shocked myself in the process, but it was a downright decent growl.

Fiona's eyes widened, and she looped her arm through mine a second later. "We'll let the guys ride up front today. What do you say?"

"Good idea." The words were said between gritted teeth, and I couldn't stop myself from glowering at my obtuse mate.

Who was acting like *nothing was wrong*.

But before I could go off on him, Fiona dragged me out the door to our waiting SUV and pulled me into the back seat.

"Is this some kind of setup?" I turned to Fiona and snapped the second the door was hastily shut behind us.

"Okay, look, it's not a bad thing, I swear to God. Goddess?" She shook her head. "My point is, you're both *miserable*, and we've all been tiptoeing around both of you, and it's ridiculous. Me and the other girls might have been talking last night, and Elodie volunteered to hang back, so..."

I groaned, dropping my head back against the back of the seat. "So, you all decided to what, *Parent Trap* us like unsupervised children?"

"More or less. Please don't hate me. It was ninety-seven percent Leigh's idea, and she's scary pregnant right now."

I couldn't disagree there. Leigh had her own gravitational pull at this point, and she was shamelessly using it to get her way, as was the feminine tradition.

Before I could respond, though, the men climbed into the front seats, and we were on the road.

There was a conspicuous silence in the car as we made the drive south, but no one seemed eager to break it with idle chitchat. Eventually, Reed flipped on a jazz radio station, and the crooning of saxophones kept us company.

Eventually, we pulled up at a very touristy-looking visitor center, and I resisted a groan. This place was thrumming with people, and I could already tell this would be a fruitless day of tramping through—admittedly beautiful—woods in uncomfortable silence.

My anger at Luce was still simmering below the surface, and I slammed the SUV door just a little too hard. He arched an eyebrow at me but said nothing—his favorite party trick. His most *infuriating* party trick.

Reed rubbed his hands together, then pulled out a red marker and the paper atlas he'd been using to track our travels. "Okay, there are two main areas here, and I think we can safely split and cover the whole area today. Fi and I are going west, and I'd like you two to cover the eastern side of the park. It's going to be a little harder to get off the beaten track here, but as soon as you find a quiet area, get off the tourist trails and see what you find."

He glanced up, only to find stony stares in response. Their little trap had been effective enough thus far, but did they *really* expect Lucien and me to spend the entire day alone in the woods together without a buffer after two weeks of polite indifference and not start an international incident?

"Okay, then. When do you want us back here?" Lucien asked in an agreeable tone, shocking the socks off me. I snapped my gaze his way, but he looked completely unbothered.

"Let's do a check-in midafternoon. Say, three?"

Lucien nodded, accepting the bag of supplies from Fiona with a polite nod.

I was so sick of him being polite. Where was my virginity-stealing asshole who pushed things too far and didn't apologize to anyone for being exactly himself?

But I kept that question to myself as we branched off, stomping ahead onto the western trail in pointed silence. If he could ignore me, I could ignore him. It was as juvenile as could be, but frankly, if I said something to him right now, I'd regret it later.

Maybe.

Maybe I'd enjoy telling him off.

We did as Reed suggested, hiking along the marked trail for a while, until we naturally paced ourselves out of sight of any other hikers. Finding a good spot in the brush, we used a little bit of shifter speed to gain enough distance to be out of sight from anyone continuing along the main path.

That was when the quiet truly set in. There were nearly no forest sounds except the wind, because the small creatures all knew there were predators in the forest today. They could sense our wolves, even if the humans couldn't.

Underbrush tugged relentlessly at my pants and shoelaces, nearly tripping me a half dozen times before a moss-covered branch succeeded in sending me tumbling. I would have face-planted into a bush if Lucien hadn't grabbed me around the waist, stopping me midfall.

"Whoa, there. Do you want me to go first for a while?" He set me back on my feet and backed up as if the simple touch had burned him, though you'd never know it by his casual tone.

"Sure, why don't you go first, right over the nearest cliff." I was fuming, we were well and truly alone, and I was done hiding my feelings.

He blinked at me in shock, and I resisted the urge to scream out my frustration.

"Whatever. *Fine.* I'm staying in front, though." I turned and managed two furious stomps away before he snagged me by the arm, effortlessly turning me back his way.

"Please don't be mad at me." The expression he wore was sincere, but nearly a minute passed as I waited for more, which didn't come.

"That's it? You take my virginity, you have one attack—which I help you with, again—and then ice me out for *weeks*, and all you have to say for yourself is please don't be mad? Well, good news for you, bucko, I'm not mad. I'm fucking furious! We are *mates*. This isn't a faucet you can just turn on and off whenever it suits you! I deserve better than that, and if you're over me, at least have the balls to say so! To my face, preferably." I crossed my arms, staring him down and daring him to say something, anything. I was spoiling for a fight, and we weren't leaving these stupid woods without one.

"You're right. You're absolutely fucking right, and I'm sorry.

You deserve so much better." He wearily rubbed a hand over his face, and I lost some of my bluster.

When the tight smile and pretense fell away, he looked *exhausted*.

But I wasn't ready to let him off the hook yet, not after he pushed me away again, when I'd thought we were finally past the bullshit. So I waited, holding on to the very last scraps of my patience.

"I would understand if you wanted to walk away."

A stab of regret nailed me square in the chest, and I knew without a doubt it was *his*.

"You know what? *No.* If you want to be done with this relationship, you're going to have to look me in the eye and say the words. Say it. Right here, right now." I stepped forward, eating up all the space between us, our chests brushing as we breathed.

"I can't do that, hellcat." A single stroke of his fingertips over my hair, light as gossamer and a thousand times as devastating as anything he'd ever said to me, as he caressed the ends of my hair. "I don't have the strength to set you free. But if I hold on to you..." He shook his head sadly, and I saw the moment he closed himself back off, shutting me out, but this time, I wasn't having it.

"You know, for an alpha, you sure are a coward. What are you so damn afraid of? I'm not taking another step until you tell me everything. Because, Lucien, Goddess help me, I'm at the end of my rope here. I— I love you. I am actively *in love with you*. And I can't just flip a switch like you can. So tell me. What is so horrible that you'd push me away this time?" My chest was heaving—with anger, with short, panting breaths, with the unfairness of it all—but I couldn't stop it.

"I'm scared I'm going to hurt you."

There was no shout, no thunder, no heat behind the words.

Only deep, rending sadness that threatened to steal my breath from my lungs and leave me permanently desolate.

"What does that mean? Help me understand." I resisted the urge to reach forward, to lace our fingers together as if we were lovers. Right now, we weren't. Right now, we were on the edge of something, and frankly, I still wasn't sure if we were going to sail into the sunset or crash on the rocks, and my shaking hands showed it.

"My father was a politician. His job wasn't all that different from my current job with the IGC, actually." The wry twist of his lips told me he was deeply unsettled by that fact, but now that he'd started talking, no way was I interrupting.

"From the outside, our family was perfect. A fated couple with their two perfect children, high achievers in school, in athletics for me, and my sister, Lilly, was exceptional at the violin. But on the inside? We were rotten to the core. *He* was. Nothing we did was ever good enough. There was no degree of perfection that wouldn't make him snap the second we were alone behind closed doors."

And he thought he was turning into his father. Because of the episodes? I wasn't sure.

"I don't know if he hit my mother before I came along, all I know is that once I was big enough to get between them, he transferred the beatings to me. It was hell on earth, that house. And I didn't want any damn thing more than freedom. But it was the one thing I couldn't have."

His smile was bitter, then, as he rocked back on his heels and stared up at the treetops, the little bits of blue sky we could see through the leaves casting a dappled pattern over his face. Such a beautiful day for such a tragic story.

"Because you didn't want to leave your mother and sister?" I guessed, the deep sense of regret I now felt from him telling me this story didn't have a happy ending.

"Because I couldn't let him go back to hitting them. So I

237

stayed. But I was an angry kid by that point, and it pissed me off that I was stuck. More than that, it disgusted me that everyone we knew worshipped the ground he walked on. Like he was Zeus in the flesh, straight off Mount Olympus."

He laughed, the sound hollow. "One day, I came home from a day out with a few of my buddies. He'd come home early from work. He'd beaten the shit out of both of them. I found Lilliana hiding in a closet, still crying. He'd broken her favorite violin in a fit of rage. Her lip was bloody, and she was covered in welts. But he got away with it because we always healed so fast. He could beat me to a pulp at night, and every day, I woke up fit as a fiddle, ready to be trotted out like a show pony all over again."

"Goddess," I whispered, the mental image too awful to contemplate. I finally reached for his hand, unable to hold myself back anymore.

"The Goddess wasn't in that house."

I bit my lip, unwilling to argue that point. He'd obviously felt completely alone, with no one to turn to, and no way in hell was I going to invalidate that experience. But what did that have to do with us?

He shook his head, continuing with a different kind of regret in his voice. "I was so mad at myself. If I hadn't gone out, they'd have been safe. If I could just get a job, I could get them away from him once and for all."

He closed his eyes, and the dread in the pit of my stomach grew claws, sank them in deep.

"I got wind of a job two towns over. The pay was shit, but it came with a room over a tavern. I could give Mom and Lilly the bedroom, and sleep on the floor. We'd be safe. We could pack up while he was at work, and be gone before he knew where we went. The packs back then didn't care about abuse, so the Alpha would never step in. We were on our own, and it was the perfect opportunity. But I had to sneak out one night to get the owner to give me the job."

He paused, as if it was too painful to continue, the words lodged in his throat. "Lucien, it's okay—"

"No, it's not. Because when I snuck out, Lilly followed me. I didn't know it at the time. I'd shifted, carrying my clothes in my mouth so they wouldn't get messed up by the trip, and I could get there quicker. She was always a smart girl, smarter than me by a mile. She stayed downwind. When I heard the gunshot, I got this feeling that something was *wrong*. Our family bond was never healthy, but the darkness—"

A tear slid down his cheek, and I leaned forward, wrapping my arms around him as tightly as I could. His pain was so thick, it was choking me. And I hadn't lived it.

"It was a hunter. She was smaller, not an alpha like me. The hunter had been tracking me with his wolfsbane bullets, but caught her instead. The bastard left her there for the vultures."

"I'm so sorry, Lucien."

"I'm not done yet." The acid in his tone was enough to melt my bones. But I held him tighter. I probably should have run, but there was no way I was letting him go. Not now.

Not ever.

"I carried her body back home. I didn't know what else to do. My parents were awake, my mom frantic. She'd felt it in the bond, but didn't want to believe it. But when I lay her on the couch, my father lost it. He beat me to a pulp, and I let him. Didn't raise a fist to defend myself. The funeral was three days later. We laid her to rest in the family crypt, and by then, I was so numb, I couldn't even cry, not even for my baby sister. So numb, I didn't realize anything was wrong until my mother lay down over the coffin and didn't get back up."

I gasped, tears freely streaming down my cheeks at this point. "What happened?"

"Poison, taken right before the funeral. She couldn't bear to live in such an evil world anymore. The only blessing was that she took my bastard of a father with her through their bond."

THIRTY-TWO

Lucien

I finally drew up the courage to look at Olivia again, after pouring out the ugly truth of my past. Her cheeks were tearstained, her beautiful green eyes damp with more unshed tears.

"Don't cry, hellcat. I've done enough to you. You don't need to cry for me."

She shook her head, biting that sweet bottom lip. I tugged it free gently, soothing it over with the pad of my thumb.

"You're not done yet," she said, shocking me. I'd told her every ugly detail. What was left to say? I was broken, toxic, grown from bad seed. "That is all horrible. And I'm so incredibly sorry you went through that. But why does that mean you have to push me away? Because the one time you scratched me, that was an *accident*. That is *not* the same as intentionally abusing your wife and children for years."

I looked away again, unable to meet her gaze. Her beautiful, demanding gaze.

"Olivia, I—"

"Hellcat. My name is *hellcat* to you."

A ghostly wisp of joy filled me at her fire. "*Hellcat*," I

amended, squeezing her a little tighter, even though I was an ass for doing it. "I'm unstable. I've already hurt you once, and yes, it was an accident. But I'm not some well-adjusted mate ready to sweep you off your feet and give you the world. I'm angry. I want revenge. I can't go down that path and not hurt you. And my wolf? Fuck. Everything I touch is broken. Even the one thing a shifter takes for granted: a bond with their wolf. That may never get fixed. But there's one good decision that I can make right now, and that's to keep you safe, the way I couldn't keep Lilly safe. You reminded me of her, the day I first saw you. You don't look alike, but there's this *goodness* inside you that shines through."

She was already shaking her head, holding me at arm's length so she could stare me down when I tried to cup her cheek. "I don't accept that. I don't accept this absurd idea that you're going to break me. I'm tougher than I look. And your past doesn't have to define you. What your *father* did isn't your responsibility. You were a better man than him even at nineteen. You stayed, you protected the ones you loved. He wasn't one hundredth the man you are. And your sister's death was not your fault."

"If I'd protected them, they'd still be alive."

There it was, my ultimate wound. The wound that never healed, no matter how many centuries passed. No matter how much I drank, how much pussy I chased.

I was a failure. A devil, doomed from the start.

You might look like an angel, but you ruin everything you touch. You're no angel. You're a devil in an angel's disguise.

I closed my eyes as my father's voice echoed in my head, as crisp as if he stood at my side, looking down his nose at me right now. There was no way I was going to lose my hellcat the way I'd lost my mother and sister. I could feel it, the ghostly weight of Olivia's body, limp in my arms, just like Lilliana's. I could never let that future come to pass.

"Does that mean you're going to send me away? I told you before, and I meant it: I'm not leaving unless you tell me it's over. That you don't want me. When you look me in the eye and say you don't feel for me what I feel for you. That's what it's going to take, Lucien. And I'm not stepping aside for anything less."

I should. I should send her away, where she'd be safe.

"I can't do that. I'm not strong enough. I am going straight to the nine hells, but I'm too selfish to send you away, even if I can't have a bond with you."

One look, one hungry, desperate look, and then our lips crashed together, a wave of longing washing the pain away, just for a moment. I tangled my fingers in her silky hair and lost myself in the taste of her lips.

She was my angel, and I was her devil.

Maybe that was how it was always meant to be.

I backed her up to the nearest tree, cushioning the back of her head with a hand as I pressed in closer, lining us up perfectly as she ground her hips against mine. I was dying for another taste of her, and I didn't give a fuck if we were in the middle of the woods in broad daylight, I had to have her. Right here, right now. One last time.

But Olivia froze beneath me, frantic grasping turning to shoving, making me stagger back a step.

Good. She was coming to her senses.

Fresh pain lanced through my chest, but I welcomed it. I *deserved* it.

"Do you hear that?" she asked, fingers still twisted in the front of my T-shirt.

"Hear what?"

"Shh, listen." She pointed to her ear, then away into the forest.

Crunching underbrush.

We aren't alone.

I quickly pulled Olivia behind me, calling on my wolf for sharpened vision and hearing. He obliged begrudgingly to protect her. Within seconds, I'd pinpointed where the sounds were coming from. But when the two culprits walked into sight, my breath caught in my chest.

"Goblins," I whispered, low enough I knew the noisy pair wouldn't have heard me over the sound of their own crunching footsteps.

Olivia gripped the back of my shirt, her excitement palpable even as she remained still and silent.

They were short, probably around two and a half to three feet tall, with pale green skin and bright purple eyes. Darker green shocks of hair stuck out in many directions from their heads, and they conversed freely in Goble, their native language. Their clothes were ragged, seemingly handmade from scraps. The one on the left had a big red heart from an "I heart New York" T-shirt patched onto the seat of his—her?—pants.

Before I could decide what to do next, Olivia was past my shoulder, walking as noisily as she could in their general direction.

"Hellcat! What are you doing?" I hissed, forced to jump into motion to keep up with her.

"I'm alerting them to our presence in a nonthreatening way," she paused just long enough to whisper, then began to talk loudly as she walked again.

"This is such a beautiful area! I can't believe nobody lives here. Do you think we could settle near here, babe?"

Ahh. Casual approach. She elbowed me in the ribs when I didn't answer fast enough to suit her.

"I— Uh, sure. If that's what you want, *babe*."

An alarmed squeak came from the smaller goblin as it tugged on its friend's sleeve and wildly gestured in our direction as they exchanged rapid-fire Goble. I knew only a few pleasantries, and that was when it was spoken at a stately, dignified pace. This exchange was nothing one would call dignified.

Olivia giggled, and the sound lifted my spirits. "Excellent. I can definitely see us raising a whole litter of pups out here! So much green space for them to explore." She threw her arms wide and spun, the very picture of a carefree woman, and my heart ached at the fact that it was fake.

Fuck, I wanted the joy to be real. Just once in my life, I wanted the joy to be *real*.

We continued chatting about our fake moving plans as we slowly worked our way toward the pair, until finally, they had a decision to make.

The taller of the two stepped out from behind a bush, stopping us in our tracks. He—I could see now the small patches of facial hair that hadn't been visible at a distance—puffed out his chest, lifting his chin as he stared up at us.

"You cannot move here and raise your pups. This land is formally claimed by our goblin clan. Please leave."

Olivia wore a wide smile as she crouched down to be closer to his eye level. "Oh, my! Well, I am so sorry to intrude. My name is Olivia, and this is my mate, Lucien." She extended a hand, which the young—he was an adolescent, if I had to guess—goblin shook seriously. "Goblin clan, you say? Why, that sounds exciting! A few of our pack mates are also visiting the area, and since the land is already claimed, we will respect that and not encroach. But it *is* customary that the leaders meet if they're in the same area. Perhaps we could set something up between our pack alpha and your leader?"

"I am Tork, a scavenger for the clan. This is Wheelie, my girlfriend." He cast an appreciative glance over at the smaller female, who met it with a glare that *clearly* contradicted his assertion.

She cut in front of him, extending her own hand for Olivia

to shake, which she did. "*I am Wheelie, scavenger for my clan and a free woman.*" I nearly passed out when she turned her attention on me and winked, throwing in a salacious hip wiggle, even though I was three times her size.

"Well, it's been lovely to meet you both. If we wanted to bring our Alpha and pack mates back to meet you, where should we go? Oh, and when would your clan be open to receiving visitors?"

Tork and Wheelie broke into a verbal tussle in Goble, which Wheelie clearly won.

"You can return this evening. Seven o'human clock, two miles east of the visitor center. There's a footpath, but we will come and meet you," she said brightly, giving a little bow to each of us. "For now, we must go tell our clan to prepare a feast, for there are visitors!"

At that, they bolted, still arguing loudly as they zipped through the underbrush with speed, if not stealth.

"That just happened, right? We found them, and I'm not imagining it?" Olivia asked as she straightened, beaming up at me.

"Right. Looks like we better head back and make a call. We've got plans to make and goblins to befriend."

WE HIKED ALMOST BACK to the trailhead in contemplative silence, me leading the way to make it a little easier for my smaller mate coming behind me through the brush.

Her hand on my arm stopped me in my tracks.

"We didn't get to finish our conversation earlier, and I've been thinking this entire walk about what to say, because I don't want to belittle your feelings or any of the trauma you've been through. But..."

Tension I'd never experienced before radiated through my limbs as I waited for her to finish that one thought. "But?"

"I'm not scared of you. I don't think you're going to hurt me. I can handle your darkness if you'll give me a chance. But it's up to you. You've asked me if I trusted you, but now it's your turn to decide. Do you trust me?"

Her eyes shone in the soft afternoon light as she stared up at me. It felt like she could see into my soul without even trying. I ran a hand over her hair—she'd styled it in a thick, loose braid today, which was draped over one shoulder—tracing it down to the ends, which I twirled between my fingers as I thought.

She was right. I had asked her to trust me, over and over again. But was I returning that trust?

All I knew was that in the time I'd known her, she'd never once judged me or given me any reason to doubt her. But as a child of abuse, I didn't trust easily. I rarely trusted anyone besides my Alpha or maybe one or two pack mates.

But my little hellcat...

"Yes, I do."

She chuckled, swaying toward me and placing her small hand on my chest, which I felt like a brand through my shirt. "Why do you sound so surprised by that, you goose?"

"Because I am."

THIRTY-THREE

Olivia

The excitement was palpable in the safe house when we returned, the rest of the pack having heard the good news by phone that we'd found the goblins, finally.

"Man, if I'd known that taking a day off would get the job done so quickly, I'd have done it last week." Elodie stepped up, hugging me around the waist and spinning me around like a top until I begged for mercy.

"Fine, fine. Did you four have fun out there?" The question was innocent enough, but her primly arched eyebrow told me she wanted to know if their meddling between me and Lucien had been successful.

"We had some good conversations."

It was true. I wouldn't say that I was certain we were solid, but we were inching closer, hurdle by hurdle.

After what Lucien had shared with me, I suddenly no longer minded the slower pace. It was a miracle that he was even willing to try after what he'd been through.

My life growing up was no ice cream sundae, but at least I knew my father loved me unconditionally. My mother? Not so much. But there was no point thinking about her now; she'd abandoned me as an infant and never looked back.

"Excellent." The grin she shot me was wicked. "Well, I'm going to go finish my trashy TV until it's time to get going. I found a show where a whole bunch of different guys all vie for the one girl's attention. We've made it to the top four, and personally, I'm team *why choose*. It's just now starting to heat up, and who knows when we'll have a free afternoon again. Feel free to join us." One last wink, and she disappeared up the stairs.

"A shower and a little veg time sounds pretty damn good right now," Fiona said with a tired groan, kicking off her hiking boots and making her own way to the stairs. "You coming?" she asked.

I turned to face Lucien. "We'll talk again soon?"

The tender kiss he pressed to my lips was a promise, and I carried it upstairs with me like the treasure it was.

AFTER NO SMALL amount of disagreement—mostly between Bri and Kane—it was decided that the entire pack would go to meet the goblins and, hopefully, their leader.

True to their word, Tork and Wheelie were waiting exactly where they said they'd be when we arrived five minutes early to meet them. There was an older, sterner-looking female goblin with them who seemed significantly *less* excited to see us walk up the small path.

Lucien and I led the way, since we were somewhat familiar faces. We shook all three of their hands and quickly introduced them to the pack.

"And that's Galyna, Gael's sister."

"I am Batten. You have brought two warriors with you, and many alpha males, for a social expedition? Seems suss."

I blinked at the modern slang, surprised to hear it from an obviously mature goblin. "We were all traveling together, and it seemed rude to exclude anyone in our party."

"I see." She looked down her nose at us, an impressive feat given the difference in our relative heights. "Well, come along. The feast has been prepared, and our clan is waiting to greet you."

She strode off into the woods with impressive speed, but Tork and Wheelie dropped back to our sides. "We are very sorry about Batten. She is our lead scavenger, and she did *not* believe that we saved the clan from you two trying to populate our forest with small wolves. She is, as the humans say, suss-being," Wheelie whispered by way of explanation.

After that, we walked and chatted, but unease grew in my stomach with every step. Had I made a mistake by coming up with a nonthreatening cover story? They were such small beings, and I knew they were often treated poorly by other supernatural species. I just wanted to put them at ease, not make them suspicious.

My healer instincts rarely failed me, but this felt like a pretty large screwup based on the frequency with which Batten kept turning to glare at us. Suss-being, indeed.

The goblin city—Wrenchet, Tork told me it was called as we reached the perimeter—was far less grand than Nisí Mýthou, but it had the quaint sort of charm you might find in a small Midwestern town, only shorter. Goblins of many hair colors bustled about, all yelling and cartwheeling and carrying in things willy-nilly, or at least it seemed so to me.

But there was a general funneling happening toward the far end of the pint-sized city, and that was where Batten led us. Our pack spread out, each of us talking to any goblin brave enough to strike up a conversation.

We were midway through Wrenchet when a tiny goblin no higher than my knee in a fluffy purple dress darted into the stream of goblins, chasing a runaway ball. A larger goblin carrying a heavy tray of some round, baked sweets saw her coming, but couldn't stop his momentum in time to keep from bowling her over. He tried to dodge, but still she went flying, half his tray of pastries toppling heavily to the ground as well.

It didn't bode well for their taste that they sounded like rubber bullets as they landed.

"Button! Button!" A mother goblin raced after the tiny sprite, weaving more carefully through the foot traffic.

Little Button's tears were already welling in her big, lavender eyes as I left our party to kneel in front of her. "Hey, Button, is it?"

The little girl nodded, bottom lip trembling with a pitiful warning. Tears were imminent unless I pulled out some magic.

I spied a weed growing a little to our left, a sturdy thing despite the goblins trampling the area quite thoroughly. It was white and scrawny, but it was the only idea I had.

"Do you want to see a trick? It's really cool. I think you'd like it." I tried to sound aloof, not like I cared too much.

It worked; she was intrigued. Cautiously, she nodded.

"Watch this plant very closely now." I winked at her, then pressed my fingers into the earth around its base, closing my eyes to concentrate on the green tendrils of plant life I could faintly feel.

There. It only took a moment. I found the little weed and sent it warm thoughts of growth, of blooming. I fueled it with my own energy, visualizing a trickle of power from my fingertips directly into the roots.

A delighted gasp made me pull back and open my eyes.

"You grewed it so fast!" Her voice was little and squeaky and positively precious. She clapped her hands excitedly, scooching up onto her knees to coo at the flower as she looked closer.

Flowers, I should say. The plant had grown to half her

height and was positively bursting with new blooms. To my surprise, they were in a rainbow of colors, not just white.

The little goblin's mother finally made her way through the crowd, scooped her up, and gave her what sounded like a solid scolding in Goble.

When she turned my way, she bowed as if I were some kind of royalty. "Thank you for seeing to my Button. She is a very busy little girl. Always getting her pretty dresses dirty."

The edge of scorn in her voice saddened me. I'd been a little girl once who was always getting dirty in my garden. I couldn't imagine how different things would have been for me if my father had berated me for following my interests.

Focusing on Button, I leaned forward, whispering, "Me too, Button. Don't feel bad. Sometimes you have to get a little dirty to have a grand adventure. But stay with your mama, okay?"

Button giggled, all traces of tears gone as her mother carted her off, clutching a lavender bloom in her little green fist and thankfully no longer being scolded.

A strong, masculine hand appeared to help me up, and I took it, glancing up gratefully at Lucien as I dusted off my own knees. My pants were smudged, but they were dark, so hopefully no one would notice.

"You're very kind, you know that?"

"I try to be. I think the world could use a lot more kindness than it has right now." I shrugged, feeling the urge to blush even though it was a very safe compliment.

"Yeah, but other people *talk* about being kind. You're the real deal." He paused, stopping us both amid the stream of goblins. "It's a gift." He stroked his thumb over my cheek, looked like he was about to say something more, when I was bumped from behind and nearly knocked off my feet.

Harried squeaks in Goble were all I got by way of apology, making Lucien growl lightly as the offending goblin rushed out of reach.

"Come on, I've got to get you out of here, or they're going to carry you away like ants with a lollipop."

He wrapped his arm around me, letting out just enough of his alpha dominance that he thought I wouldn't notice.

But I definitely noticed the wide berth we received from our hosts for the rest of the walk, and the far-too-pleased smirk Lucien wore.

It was way sexier than it should have been.

THIRTY-FOUR

Lucien

A large clearing had been set with dozens of long trestle tables covered with patchwork tablecloths in preparation for our arrival. The far end of the clearing held a pair of firepits, each with a large hog spinning on a spit.

At least, I hoped it was a hog. After the infernabist fiasco with the centaurs, I'd be checking before I took my first bite.

It smelled like pork, anyway.

Before we made it through the teeming horde of goblins to find a seat at a table, Batten waved us over to the side.

"The feast will not be ready for a while yet. All visitors to our little haven must first meet with our wise elder. Come, she is waiting."

The winding side path was blessedly short—I'd had enough human hiking in the last two weeks to last me a lifetime—ending abruptly at a surprisingly large—well, tall—home.

It was as cobbled together as the rest, but the roof was high enough that a normal human could easily walk inside. A six-plus-foot alpha male? A little less easily.

"Wait here. I will let her know you've arrived." She

254

gestured to nearby Adirondack-style chairs, these crafted out of what appeared to be bent bicycle frames. The metal gleamed, though, and nothing stabbed me in the spleen as I sat.

It was surprisingly excellent craftsmanship, I noted as I studied the chair I sat in, looking slapdash only because of the choice of building materials.

I wasn't sure precisely what I'd expected from a goblin elder, but the small, sturdy crone before us wasn't it.

She had flowing lavender hair, with eyes that looked identical to the tiny Button, who Olivia had helped earlier. But the resemblance ended there. She had hunched shoulders, but a strong, wiry frame as if she'd done hard labor for much of her life, and time's stoop was her only allowance for her age.

She barely even had wrinkles, but her eyes... They held the wisdom of the ages.

For a long while, she merely stared at us, taking our measure, each one in turn. I knew without a doubt that she missed nothing as she slowly worked her way down the line, not bothering to introduce herself.

Satisfied or just finished, she spoke.

"I have heard many tales of you from the young ones of our clan, despite the fact that you've been with us such a short time. Which among you is the one who spoke to Tork and Wheelie this afternoon?"

Her voice was soft and whispery, like sheets of thin paper sliding together, but still commanding.

Olivia cleared her throat, took a half step forward. "I spoke first, ma'am. Myself and my mate." She nervously gestured to me. "I'm Olivia, by the way."

"Olivia. So, you are the one who wishes to populate our woods with little wolf pups? And with the scarred one. Interesting. You seem... soft for him. Too soft? Or just the softness he needs. Only time can tell."

Her gaze roved on quickly, settling squarely on Fiona next. "And you... You're no wolf at all, young one. What are you?"

Fiona hesitated, and the elder tsked. "Don't be shy, now, I'm not getting any more days on this rock. Spit it out."

"My ancestor was a djinn, ma'am," Fiona admitted, taking an anxious step closer to Reed, who looped his arm around her waist.

It stung a little that Olivia had so tidily kept her distance, but it was understandable.

The crone's eyebrows flew up. "My oh my. A djinn child. What is your element?"

"Uh, water? I think. It's kind of new. I didn't know until recently. But we are pretty sure it's water."

"A wonderful and dangerous talent, to be sure. Is that all? Djinn usually have... more. Not to be insulting."

"I sometimes have... visions." Fiona shrugged, saying no more.

The crone nodded slowly, considering. "Those who are unseen may see with clarity that which is unseen by others. That is an equally wonderful and dangerous talent."

Satisfied, she continued her slow way pacing down the line. When she reached Leigh, she arched an eyebrow at her swollen belly, but said nothing.

At Kane, however, she paused, scowling.

"State your name, boy, and your title as well."

I held back a growl at the high alpha being called *boy*, but to the ancient goblin before us, he probably was just a boy. She clearly cared nothing for offending us.

Perhaps it was a test.

"Kane, son of Kosta, son of Konstantin, high alpha of the nine great packs." Kane stood tall, unflinching.

But so did she, despite barely coming to his midthigh. She craned her neck to look up at him and nodded, gaze sliding over to the diminutive Brielle.

"And you?"

"Brielle, ma'am. I'm a doctor." Brielle smiled, none of the nerves the rest of us seemed to be feeling evident in her face. "And the high alpha's mate."

The crone tapped her chin, then strolled back to stand between Olivia and me. "You two have lied to our young scavengers. That much is clear, traveling with the high alpha of your kind as if this were some great camping adventure. The only question is, why are you really here, and do you mean us harm?"

"Oh, gosh, no! I mean, yes, it was a small fib. They looked so young, and we'd been looking for goblins for weeks, and I was determined not to scare them off. We just wanted to meet you —" Olivia's nervous ramble was cut off midstream by a sharply raised hand.

"Ah-ah. Watch your tongue. And think very carefully about telling any more lies. You might have fooled the likes of Tork— he's a bit simple—but you will not fool me."

Olivia cast me a helpless glance, so I stepped forward, wrapping an arm around her shoulders.

"I can assure you, no harm is intended by our pack. Yes, we are traveling with the high alpha pair and his top men, but we are not here to cause you trouble. We seek the return of something that belongs to us that we were told has been held by the goblins for... some centuries."

Her face paled. "And you seek to take the stone by force? You'll not succeed. It's not here, and if you raze every clan dwelling to ash and murder every innocent under my protection, you'll only gain blood on your hands."

I was surprised when the usually hotheaded Leigh stepped forward, none of her usual piss and vinegar on display. "Listen, I get that Olivia told a white lie to get us here. But I promise you, we're not here to hurt your people. Okay? We're trying to protect our *own* people. I get the feeling you know what Brielle is. What my daughter is." She rested a hand on her belly, a sorrowful expression the only sign that it hurt her to admit.

"And if we don't get that stone—all of it—and soon? There's an entire department of the Interspecies Governing Council that's going to try to rip my baby out of my arms and kill her. I can't let that happen." Her chin jutted up, the fire in her eyes leaving no room for argument as it burned up the sorrow from before.

The crone was silent for a long, long time. So long that if I hadn't already observed that she was whip-smart, I'd have thought her mind had wandered.

"Sympathetic as I am to your plight, you don't know what you ask. You mean us no harm? The last time that stone was held by a wolf, whole clans were destroyed, bloodlines gone, heritages erased, for naught but petty gain. So I say this. You came under the guise of friendship. My people have prepared you a feast fit for any king. You may stay and enjoy our hospitality, and then you will leave. If you truly mean us no harm, you will accept this." She waved her hand and turned, walking away without a glance back.

Batten—who had been so silent this entire time I'd nearly forgotten she'd led us here—cleared her throat, breaking the heavy air of failure permeating the clearing.

"Right this way. The feast is prepared, and the younglings grow overexcited. Word has spread about your way with plants, green witch."

Olivia blanched and shot me an anxious glance. I gave her a reassuring squeeze and followed.

There was nothing we could do for now, but wait and hope for a second chance. My wolf had detected no lies when the crone had spoken; the stone was not here, but I had no doubt that she knew where it was.

And with the steel in her spine? She wouldn't tell us where it was unless she wanted to.

But how the fuck did we make her want to?

THIRTY-FIVE

Olivia

I was so furious with myself, I could scream. One little mistruth had felt so innocent, a simple introduction, nothing more.

The fact that the goblin elder was now refusing us the one thing we needed to save basically all of us?

Forget screaming, I wanted to have a cry. A good, long, hard one. With a tear-jerker movie and ice cream and my favorite blankets that were softer than butter piled around me in a great big nest.

But I couldn't have any of that—hadn't had any of that in a long time. I had to keep my shit together and try to fix my screwup. That was my responsibility since I'd messed this up so royally.

And to do that, I had to get my head back in the game.

We were ushered to a pair of larger tables, clearly specially made with taller visitors in mind, though the table was already dotted with goblins, all of them excited to be seated with the visitors.

I paused a few feet away, hesitating as I struggled to pick a spot to sit, when one of the younger goblins stood on the bench, waving his arm madly. "Witch, witch! Sit next to me!"

Fiona arched an eyebrow my way but didn't comment as she and Reed were waved toward the other end of the long picnic-style table.

"I can scent your stress. It's all going to work out," Lucien leaned in and whispered, his lips nothing more than a hint of a caress against my skin, but it still made me quiver.

His large hand spanned the small of my back as we walked the last few feet to the table, and he waited until I was seated directly across from the goblin who'd hailed me before sitting at my side.

In the beginning, I'd never have guessed what a gentleman he could be, but I was learning more and more about him as time went on. And the more I learned, the more there was to love, no matter how hard I tried to rein in my heart.

"Welcome to Wrenchet. Have you enjoyed your visit so far, witch?" The little guy practically bounced in his seat as he spoke, as if the enthusiasm was trying to vibrate its way right out of him. His hair was short, spiky, and neon green, instead of the more common lavender and darker green tones the rest of the clan were sporting. He reminded me of the little naked dolls with the crazy hair I'd had as a kid, except his skin was also light green.

"You can call me Olivia," I said, smiling warmly at his enthusiasm. "What's your name?"

"I am the Grand Inventor Rivetsky!" He executed a twirl and a bow, grinning up at us with an expectant tilt to his chin.

"Well, we are very honored to be seated with such an important goblin for this feast," Lucien said, cutting in smoothly and smiling.

"Indeed. I am nearly famous making." Rivetsky's chest puffed proudly as he resumed sitting, just in time for the... unique dishes to be brought to our table. Unlike the centaur's stately spreads, the goblins worked in swarms, four or more of them carrying each handmade tray, chattering—sometimes fighting—as they loaded the table slap full with steaming food.

Some of it was familiar—I was sure I spotted a tray of fried chicken at the other end of the table that looked amazing—but most of it was just plain interesting.

We weren't given time to overthink about what to choose, though. The second the table was too full to hold another tray, the servers began plopping food onto our plates with their spoons. Sometimes they told us the name of the dish, sometimes they didn't.

By the time they'd all swarmed away from our long table off to the next, the copious mound of food piled on my oval, Thanksgiving-sized plate was actually overflowing a bit onto the table.

Steeling myself to eat whatever I'd been served with a gracious smile, I lifted my fork. "I hope you won't be offended if I don't clean my plate. I'm a lower rank than most of the others, and I often have a small appetite."

Rivetsky beamed. "It is our great honor to feed you full and have excess."

His enthusiasm was catching. While the goblins were all a little odd by wolf standards, I'd never met a more genuine supernatural race, or one more open and welcoming. The centaurs had rolled out the red carpet, but the goblins?

They extended *friendship* as easily as breathing. It was a wonderful surprise, as were most of the strange-looking foods on my plate.

"Olivia-witch, if you don't mind an inventor's curiosity, what else can you do with your witch magic?" Rivetsky saved the question until I was nearly a quarter of the way through some sort of sweet-potato mash with crunchy nuts mixed through it.

"Well... this is all pretty new to me, but so far, I can identify plant species and their uses. A mentor I met recently told me I could identify poisons and their antidotes, as well." I shrugged, not sure what else to say.

He nodded gravely, as if this was the most serious news he'd heard in a week. Lucien squeezed my knee supportively under the table, then traced his fingers up my inner thigh, causing me to clench my legs together and resist the urge to swat him away. I was trying to be *friendly* here, and the shameless alpha was distracting me.

Small circles over my inner thigh, trailing lazily up and down over my thin hiking pants as if there wasn't a single other thing happening.

"You also make them grow, no?"

Lucien inched his way closer to my pussy, and I let out an unintended squeak, dropping my hand over his and yanking his questing fingers back to my knee as I scrambled for an answer. "Yes! Yes. Umm, you're right. I can make an existing plant grow faster than usual as well."

"Would you consider visiting our gardens? Some of our crops have not done well this year, and our stores run short. I have been inventing and inventing, but nothing makes our crops more plentiful."

There were small creases around his eyes when he looked down at his plate, as if he was truly distressed, and suddenly, I felt *incredibly* guilty and humbled that we were eating up their limited food stores. I made a mental note to make sure the pack sent them gifts of food to replace all they'd shared, once things settled down and it was safe to do so.

"It would be my *honor* to be given a tour of Wrenchet's gardens with their most famous inventor. I don't know a thing about building, but perhaps I can sense what the plants need, and you can come up with a way to provide it? I think we'd make an excellent team."

His grin stretched wide, and he was once more bouncing in the seat. Lucien's fingers began to wander again, and I shot him a warning look, but he just grinned at me shamelessly, as if daring me to complain in front of our goblin hosts.

Two can play at that game, alpha of mine.

I left his hand to roam and leaned in closer, placing my own hand on his inner thigh and squeezing. He froze as if stunned I'd been willing to fight fire with fire, and suddenly, I was the one smug as I trailed my fingertips up his muscular thigh, stopping just shy of where he wanted me to caress. His scent sharpened, the heady aroma of warm almonds intensifying in the air around us as his own interest was piqued.

Take that, I thought as I moved his hand from my leg to his own.

Before our secret repartee could escalate to an inappropriate level, a burst of unease hit me square in the chest.

Lucien picked up on it immediately, his lascivious grin turning to concern in half a second flat. "Hellcat? What's wrong? What happened?"

His hands were on my shoulders, running down my arms as if he could spot a physical injury.

"I don't know. I just got this intense feeling that something's very wrong. I don't know where it's coming from."

"Green witch." Rivetsky breathed the words with awe, staring at me as if I were a circus freak.

"No, I don't think it's from the plants, although—"

A shock wave shook the clearing, goblins screaming as the platters and glasses on the tables shook as if there was an earthquake.

Lucien's arms locked around me before I registered what was happening, hauling me out of the seat and toward the rest of the pack with alpha wolf speed. We formed up in a loose circle, goblins screaming and weaving between us as they bolted for the trees in every direction.

"What's happening?" Lucien asked, his wolf's influence making his words sharp, like a bark. A second impact rocked us, the ground trembling beneath our feet so violently, I had to hang on to Lucien's arm to stay upright.

"Attaaaaack on the barrier! Battle stations!" a stout goblin screamed, running in the direction the second percussion had come from.

"What are the chances it's unrelated to our visit?" Leigh asked, wincing and holding her belly.

"Zero. It's got to be the ODL," Gael answered her, eyes piercing as they glowed toward the center of Wrenchet, almost as if he could see the attackers despite the obstacles in the way. "We've got to get the females to safety. Once we're in the air again, they'll be safe."

"No! We can't just abandon the goblins after we dropped trouble on their doorstep," I argued, immediately regretting it when all those alpha-dominant eyes landed on me.

"She's right." Kane shocked the hell out of me by agreeing. "If we have any chance of proving to the goblins we aren't the same as our ancestors, we've got to stay and help them. They're not as equipped as the Kodiak bears were to fight off an attack of this magnitude."

Relief flooded me, even as fear clouded my thoughts. I wasn't excited to fight, not by a mile, but it was the right thing to do.

"So what do we do?" Reed asked. "It's chaos."

And it was. Some goblins were running toward the fray, but most were still screaming and hightailing it toward the relative safety of the forest.

"Batten!" Lucien half roared, snagging our guide's attention from a little distance away. She turned and spotted us, anger tightening her features as she scooped up the goblin child she'd been directing and ran our way, dodging her clan mates every step of the way.

"Just go! You don't need my permission." She threw up a hand in disgust and made to turn away.

"Wait! We're staying to help. Where is everyone going?" I grabbed her shoulder, then quickly snatched my hand away when she glared at me.

"The fighters are gathering the catapults. The rest... They need to go to the caves, but most are too terrified to think straight."

"Where are the caves? We'll help you get everyone to safety," I offered, my healer instincts kicking in as I noticed the sheer number of panicked children running *into* danger.

"The women can help get people to safety. The men will help the fighters." Kane turned to Elodie and Galyna with a thunderous expression that promised trouble. "I am entrusting you with my mate's life. If a single hair on her head, or any female under my protection, is harmed—"

"We will protect them with our lives, High Alpha," Galyna said, drawing her sword and saluting.

Lucien turned to me, his face a mask of torture. "I don't want to leave you. You could get hurt or killed if the ODL is really here."

I cupped his cheek in my hand and let my wolf shine through my eyes, trusting her strength to speak to his. "We're all going to be just fine, and they deserve an ass kicking for hunting us when we've done nothing wrong."

He bared his teeth in agreement. "If you're sure. If anything changes, promise me you'll tell one of the others to call for me with their bond."

Despite the chaos all around us, his sincerity melted something inside me that had been frozen from his avoidance the last two weeks. He cared, he just didn't know how to show it. Didn't feel like he deserved to show it.

"I promise."

He threaded his fingers through my hair and captured my lips in a domineering kiss that left my knees jelly and my thoughts scattered.

When he stepped away and started shucking off his clothes so he could shift, my brain whirred back into working order. We had a crisis to manage and kids to save. The other mates had also said their farewells, and Batten had turned away, pointing and giving orders to every goblin who ran past.

"Batten, what do you need?" I stepped up beside her, the rest of the pack females forming into a semicircle around her, with Galyna and Elodie bracketing us, butterfly swords in hand.

Before she could answer me, though, a wave of alpha dominance washed over the clearing with so much power, it knocked me to my knees in the dirt.

No, not just me... *Every creature save Brielle.*

I looked back in the direction it had come from to see a large midnight wolf standing head and shoulders above the rest, his bright green eyes glowing with unfettered rage as the rest of his pack mates shifted. As one, the males ran toward the battle, as fluid as water in a stream, but a thousand times more deadly.

For the first time since I'd been with the pack, the high alpha had shifted. And nothing but death followed in his wake.

THIRTY-SIX

Lucien

I followed closely behind Kane as we wove through Wrenchet, goblins screeching so loudly, it hurt my wolf's delicate ears. It was nothing compared to the third explosion, which rocked the ground beneath our paws and shook the foundations of the handmade buildings we ran between.

It wasn't hard to find the source of the battle.

A warlock and a lesser fae stood a few feet back from the edge of the city, the former hurling fireballs as if it was nothing, the latter shooting magical attacks that hit with the force of a bomb, blowing trees out of the ground by their roots, and sending them flying.

They weren't alone, though. At least thirty enforcers were behind them, wearing magically enhanced body armor, and that was only what we could see between the trees. There was no telling how many they'd actually brought.

It was crystal clear that they hadn't come to capture or question us. They'd come to wipe us off the map. But good luck to them, because Kane's power... I hadn't noticed it when he was in human form, but now that he'd shifted, it had multiplied.

Since Brielle's omega powers had been unlocked and her curse removed, he'd clearly leveled up.

Focus on the magic users first. The rest will do less harm individually.

Kane's order came through the pack bond, and we arrowed toward the two out front who were hurling mass destruction as if it was any other Tuesday.

As soon as the enforcers saw us, they surged forward, half surrounding their magic users, while the other half ran at top speed toward us.

We were outnumbered and out-magicked, but we fanned out into an arrowhead shape with Kane at the tip. I lunged and tore my way into the enforcers, my wolf relishing the gore as we found targets not protected by their armor.

Many shifted, mostly big cats, but there were at least two bears in the mix, swiping with their giant, razor-sharp claws.

I can't say if I killed or only disabled my opponents as we cut our way through the horde. But Kane was relentless, pushing toward the magic users with single-minded focus. We'd reached their outer ring of protectors when we finally ground to a halt.

Samuel and I fought back to back, each of us fending off blows both magical and physical from either side.

That was when Kane released his high alpha power.

I felt the sucking sensation in my chest a second before he unleashed it, and the impact was devastating. Our pack was unharmed, but our opponents?

All but the strongest within a hundred yards were blown back or pinned down as we bounded over and through them.

It was the break we needed to get to the fae, and he knew it. His eyes grew wide, terror filling them before he flashed out of existence, abandoning his comrades in a blatant act of self-preservation.

The warlock realized a second too late what had happened,

hurling a fireball our way as he attempted to run, his long black and silver robes flapping behind him.

I was far enough to the side of our formation that I only felt the heat, but pain seared the pack bond, and I knew at least one of my brothers had been hit. Despite the injury, the rest of us couldn't stop, couldn't falter, or else the warlock would send another fireball hurtling our way.

We circled the warlock like sharks, nipping and harassing his personal shields, attacking from too many directions for him to block us all at once. Sweat began to roll down his face, his pointed velvet hat knocked askew by his efforts to keep us at bay.

One of Kane's lunges broke through, and he sank his fangs into the warlock's thigh.

I saw the opening before I even realized I had lunged. I leapt for his throat, fangs and claws extended.

His blood was hot and sour on my tongue. The unfamiliar tang of magic zipped through me as I rode his body to the ground, shaking the life out of him with all my might.

By the time we hit the ground, his head was gone, his magic fizzled out like a candle in a hurricane. His hat rolled away, disappearing in a poof a few seconds later.

But the rest of the enforcers had recovered from Kane's blow, and the fight wasn't over. With the most immediate, deadly threat eliminated, we ran back to where Gael had fallen, forming a protective circle around our wounded pack mate as we fought off the endless horde of attackers.

More and more of them poured from the forest, and bodies began to pile around us as blood soaked the earth.

My humanity waned as the wolf's rage grew as high as the pile of enemies we'd slain, my control on him thready at best. Time grew warped by the battle. All that remained was blood and death and the next attacker who dared defy us.

THIRTY-SEVEN

Olivia

I lost count of how many trips we'd made to and from the caves, carrying children through the dark and helping the elderly, until Leigh screamed, clutching her chest and falling into the leaf litter like she'd been shot.

Brielle shouted her name in panic, both of us racing to our fallen pack mate's side.

"What's wrong? What hurts?"

"It's Gael," Leigh sobbed, clutching her right shoulder. "He's been hit. I don't— I don't know if he's going to survive." Her words were broken between the fountain of tears she cried as she clutched her own shoulder as if she'd been the one who was hit. "His thoughts are scattered. I can't tell what's happening."

Brielle looked up at me with a determined expression that told me she was about to do something the high alpha wouldn't approve of if I didn't stop her.

"I'll go," I blurted, cutting her off at the pass. "I'm not as skilled as you, but I can triage, and maybe Elodie can help me carry him back here for you to heal?" I looked up to where she stood at my shoulder for confirmation.

"It would be faster if I went myself. I could heal him and then get back here."

"No," Galyna said. "The high alpha gave me a direct order not to let you near the fight. If they catch sight of you, you're dead, and so is he through your bond. The packs can't survive losing another high alpha. They'll be fractured. Don't put that on me."

Brielle grimaced, holding Leigh in her lap as she cried. "I refuse to let my best friend, her mate, and their baby die for want of medical care that I can provide. Bring him to me as fast as you can. If he takes a turn, I am coming." Brielle was all high alpha mate as she issued the order to me and Elodie.

Lightning cracked nearby, striking a tree and sending shards flying through the air in every direction.

I snapped my gaze around to Fiona, who was fully shifted into her djinn form, amber eyes molten with simmering power. "I'm coming with you."

"We don't have time to waste. Let's go." Elodie was off at a full run, sheathing her sword only for speed. I barely kept up with her in human form, but I ran as fast as I could, calling on my wolf for strength when my lungs began to burn and my thighs felt like lead.

But as fast as we ran, Wrenchet was already burning, the flames licking hungrily at the velvet night air. Smoke clogged my lungs as unnatural fire hopped from building to building, consuming them with scalding heat that buffeted us even as we ran past at a distance.

"Can you do anything about that?" I gasped out the question to Fiona, who looked askance at the rampant inferno.

"Yes, but not until after we get Gael. He has to come first."

I nodded, and we ran faster, roars and screeches of violent battle hitting us now that we were closer.

Anxiety was just more fuel to run faster, worry that Lucien

or any of our pack mates would be next urging me on when I wanted to collapse.

When Elodie swore and skidded to a stop, I nearly ran into her. I dropped my hands to my knees and breathed hard as she surveyed the fight.

"I think they're over there, in the middle of that knot of attackers. The goblins are trying to get to them, but they're outgunned compared to the enforcers." She pointed to a ring of attackers, so numerous they might as well have been ants on an ant hill, the crowd visible through the darkness with my wolf's superior vision aiding me.

"Why aren't they breaking away so they've got backup?" Fiona asked, her breath coming back faster than mine.

"Because that's where Gael fell," I said, finally able to catch my breath enough to answer as Elodie drew her sword.

"Stay behind me. They don't need any distractions, and if either of you gets hurt, they might all fall." Her grave words made me glad Lucien and I hadn't bonded. Even if something happened to me, he'd be okay.

It was a small comfort as we stared down a slavering horde.

"Fuck that," Fiona said, raising her hands and closing her eyes. "Just give me a moment."

I looked up, expecting to see thunderclouds scudding into view overhead, but instead of rain, the ghastly howl of a tornado filled the clearing.

"Fi, how good is your control over that thing?" I asked as a towering funnel cloud ripped into the clearing, snatching massive trees up by the roots and plucking enforcers up as if they were dolls before they realized what was happening.

"Good enough for government work, as my father would say." She gritted her teeth as she held the storm, breaking a path to our males.

"Let's go," Elodie hissed, taking off at a jog now that the tornado had enforcers running for their lives.

She slashed with her sword like a dancer, gracefully light on her feet even as she delivered death to every enemy we passed.

Despite the fray, no one got close enough to touch me without Elodie's sword lopping something off their body.

She sang as she whirled, and within minutes, the three of us made it to our pack.

The second I saw Gael, naked and wounded in the middle of their circle, I shoved past Elodie, between two sleek, blood-soaked wolf bodies, to where he lay. My own exhaustion from the never-ending night was forgotten as I scanned him for injuries.

He was scorched from his jaw to his hip, second- and third-degree burns already blistering and peeling sickeningly down his right side. He groaned in pain as the fight raged around him, and as soon as I touched his unburnt cheek, I knew he didn't have time to be carried back to Brielle. If his wounds were this bad *after* he'd already shifted... *Fuck.*

But what could I do? The ground around us was trampled, devoid of plant life that I could use as medicine.

Elodie squatted as if to lift him.

"No! Don't touch him. He's not well enough to be moved, and he doesn't have time to go back." I left my hand on his unburnt cheek, desperation making me dig my fingers into the earth, searching for any wisp of power, any help that was available to me.

I remembered Flantiera's words, and I called the little green wisps of power with all my might, envisioning them flowing through my fingertips, forming a healing cocoon around Gael.

Heal him, I demanded, even as my own energy waned with alarming speed. I'd barely used my powers at all, let alone for something of this magnitude. I wasn't sure how long I could keep it up, but I just needed him to survive until we could get to Brielle. That was it. After that, I could collapse. *Help me,* I pleaded with my wolf.

"Holy shit," Elodie whispered, and my eyes fluttered open.

Just as I'd envisioned, he was encased in a luminous green bubble of energy, his breathing already less labored and more even, the lightest burns along the edges stable, receding.

"We need to go. I can't hold the power long." My words were slurred, and I knew my time of acting as his life support was limited.

Thankfully, Elodie didn't waste time. She and Fiona—who'd released her tornado at some point—squatted and grabbed him under his shoulders.

I winced as he groaned, knowing how much his burned flesh would hurt as they carried him, but seeing no other choice. He needed more than I could do for him here.

A human hand on the back of my neck froze me in place, until I heard Lucien's familiar voice. "Olivia? What the fuck are you doing out here?" He dropped to his knees in front of me, cupping my face in his larger hands, and I nearly wept as I leaned against him, too tired to hold myself upright and keep the energy flowing that was keeping Gael stable.

"We had to get Gael. Leigh felt it when he got hit. Brielle couldn't risk it, so—"

"You are *not* expendable!" he roared, eyes flickering to his wolf's orange as he stared into my own. "Do you hear me? Don't you ever pull shit like this again. You could have been killed." He wrapped me in his arms, hauling me against his chest. I went without resistance, basking in the glow of his anger even as I held the healing energy around Gael.

Because he was angry for me.

He cared. He *cared*, and in my exhausted state, it made me want to sob with relief. But I couldn't do that. My pack mates were depending on me—Leigh and her daughter were back in the caves, depending on me.

"We have to get him back to Brielle, and you have to keep

fighting. I'll be okay. Thank you." I pressed a kiss to his lips, salty with the tears I hadn't realized had escaped.

He looked to the circle he'd left and back to me with agony written across his features. He needed to be there for the pack, but he didn't want me to leave.

"I'm strong enough to do this, and so are you. Our pack is counting on us."

He dropped his forehead to mine, letting his eyes fall closed for only a second. "You're stronger than I ever gave you credit for, and I don't know how I ever failed to see that. Let's go."

Lucien stood, pulling me to my feet and steadying me as I swayed.

"I'll keep her safe, Alpha," Elodie promised, Gael's arm looped over one shoulder, with her sword still in her left hand.

"I dare any of these fuckers to mess with us," Fiona snarled, holding Gael up from his other side. Lightning popped a dozen yards away, blowing a tiger shifter who'd been heading for Reed's wolf to pieces before he could make it.

Her djinn was a little bloodthirsty, but, given the circumstances... who could blame her?

"Go." He kissed me on the lips one more time and stepped back, retaking his wolf form in one smooth motion and shouldering his way back in to help with the fight.

"Ready?" Elodie asked me, not missing that I was depleted, the green energy around Gael already beginning to flicker.

"Yes. I'll keep up." I would, no matter what. I willed the green light to focus on his vital organs as we made our way out of the battle.

To my surprise, Lucien and Reed broke away from the group, bracketing us as we worked our way toward the city.

When we were free of the melee, they turned, standing guard between us and any pursuers.

We only made it another block before I had to stop.

"I'm sorry, I can't keep going. I'm about to lose the power.

You need to run. Get him to Brielle." I finally broke, letting my desperation show, and Elodie flew into action.

"Stay with her, Fiona, and fry anybody who even looks at you funny." Elodie scooped Gael into her arms and, with impressive speed, sprinted back toward the caves.

I felt it when the thread of power snapped out of my hold, the edges of the world around me going soft and fuzzy black, closing me up until all was darkness.

THIRTY-EIGHT

Lucien

There just weren't enough of us. The enforcers were relentless, and no matter how many we killed, more kept pouring out of the woods. It had to be another magic user, someone in the forest, flashing reinforcements here from one of the ODL bases.

If that were the case, the stream of enforcers would never end until we'd been crushed under the ODL's boots. Something had to change, and *fast*, or we were going to lose. Sheer fatigue was going to start taking us down eventually.

Making a snap decision now that the girls were safely out of sight within the deserted, burning goblin city, I barked at Reed to get his attention, and then ran into the fray.

He stayed on my heels, the pair of us weaving at top speed through the oncoming fighters toward the forest.

It was like swimming upstream, and our path wasn't without skirmishes, but we made pretty good time, dodging and leaving enemies at our back using our superior speed.

Only the vampires were really an obstacle, but their general youth and solitary nature helped us take them out. Older, more powerful vampires didn't join the ODL.

I was panting, sides heaving, when we finally broke through the stream of attackers into the silent forest. I paused, listening, trying to expand my senses far enough to pick up the telltale tingle of magic.

For several long minutes, there was nothing.

Frustration built as we waited, and I heard Reed shifting on his feet at my side, clearly not understanding why we'd abandoned our pack to stand around in the empty trees.

But then I felt it. It struck faster than lightning, the tingling electricity, the crisp scent of ozone off to the right.

Bingo, bitches.

I took off at a full run, Reed getting the picture now that he'd felt what I felt. The scent of ozone grew stronger, making my wolf want to sneeze as we cut through the forest. Within a minute, we could hear the thundering racket of reinforcements running away from the spot, and I knew if we didn't hurry, the magic user would be gone again, out of reach.

Our only hope was a refractory period, where he couldn't flash away before we could take him down. I dug deep, pulling out all the stops and urging my wolf forward, forward—and he gave it his all. It was the first time I'd felt truly in sync with my wolf since before the torture. Maybe for *years*. We practically flew, paws barely touching the earth, single-minded focus on taking out the one who kept bringing more forces to attack our pack, endanger our mate.

Our mate.

My wolf's pleasure at merely the thought of Olivia was breathtaking. It was the first time I'd seen her through his eyes, and in that one moment of clarity, I understood more than I had time to process in the middle of a battle.

I understand now, I told the wolf, and a sense of well-being flooded me, as if something were trying to knit itself back together.

The bond?

I didn't know.

But at that moment, we closed the distance, and the same fucking lesser fae that had been in the clearing earlier stood, looking bored after having dropped off no fewer than a dozen reinforcements in one go.

He noticed us a second too late. I was already in the air, arrowing toward his groin as Reed went high, aiming for his throat. His barriers went up just in time, diverting me from making contact with less than an inch of margin between his family jewels and my razor-sharp canines.

We couldn't stop, couldn't give him time to recharge, though, or this would all be for naught. He'd change where he returned, and we'd be even worse off than we were now. I hit the ground and circled tightly, continuing to charge and snap, Reed and I working as one as we sought a break in his personal protections.

I could feel time ticking past, knew we were about to lose him, when the same magical tingle zapped over me like electricity.

The scent of ozone was so close by, it burned my nostrils, and this time, I did sneeze.

Defeat. I froze in place. We'd fucked it up, and he'd gone.

Except, the lesser fae was still in front of me, his face etched with awe as he looked behind us, over my shoulder.

Shit, he has backup!

I spun, not wanting to leave my and Reed's flanks exposed to another attack—but what I saw had me stopping in awe of my own.

A glow as bright as a star, in faerie form. I couldn't look at it dead-on, the light too bright for my wolf even with a squint. But the sheer magnitude of *power* emanating from the fae was undeniable.

The light faded quickly, and things hit me in waves. Two beings, one with wings, one without.

The winged creature was a greater fae, easily powerful enough to wipe the lesser fae we'd been fighting off the map with a snap.

But as the light faded, my shock only grew.

The greater, winged fae standing in the clearing *was Shay*.

THIRTY-NINE

Lucien

Winged Shay glanced briefly at me and Reed, a half smile the only acknowledgment that she recognized our wolves, before turning the full force of her gaze on the lesser fae behind us.

He started begging and backing away before she even said a word. "Please, no! I don't want to go back. I can't ever go back!"

"The queen would like to see you, Narshall. We both know we can't defy the queen's orders, don't we?" Shay's voice was calm and even as she raised her right hand. A simple snap—nothing more—and the other fae winked out of existence, leaving nothing but sharp ozone and fur-tingling power behind.

Dirge stepped toward us, concern etched into the familiar lines of his face. "Where is the rest of the pack? We came as quickly as we could."

Reed yipped, and we both took off back in the direction of the raging battle, knowing they'd follow. And follow they did. As we tore through the ODL enforcers from behind, cutting through them with fang and claw and renewed might, Dirge shifted to run with us, and Shay flew behind, sending bright white jets of power and blasting anyone who dared try to attack us from the sides.

After the endless time warp that was a battle to the death, the field fell eerily silent faster than seemed possible as the sun rose to beat down on us. We met the other pack males in the middle, surprised to see the goblin warriors in simple leather armor, trailing behind with chests puffed up practically to their ears.

We all shifted back, exhaustion filling me from top to toe as I stood swaying on my human feet once more.

Everyone began to talk at once—most asking Shay how the fuck she'd gotten *wings*—but there was only one woman on my mind, and wanting to see her again was like an itch I had to scratch.

"I need to go check on Olivia," I announced to no one in particular, then set off across the body-strewn battlefield. Objectively, there were fewer than expected because the vampires turned to ash after the sun rose on their dead bodies. But still, it was gory. The goblin warriors who'd grown bored with admiring the fae-wolf and the high alpha had already begun dragging the bodies toward the end of the clearing, working in teams as they did with everything.

I wasn't far into the city when I realized I had no idea where the caves were that the women had hidden in. Luckily, as I paused amid the steaming rubble of fireball-damaged houses, Kane appeared at my side like a ghost.

That, or I was just so exhausted from battling all night and into the morning, I hadn't heard him approach.

"Brielle sent me a map." He tapped his temple, and not for the first time today, I was jealous of the other mated pair's mental connection. Slowly, a mate bond was becoming a *good thing* in my mind, and frankly, I never saw that coming. But here I was, and I couldn't deny how appealing it sounded to have my hellcat in my head, her wolf tethered in my chest where I could always feel her. "Come on." He smiled, gore-spattered face and exhaustion not dimming his excitement at getting back to his female, and it was just another tick in the *pro* column for a mate.

"Do you think the ODL will strike again before we can get out of here?" I asked, the question dogging my every step.

He shook his head, a thoughtful expression telling me he took the question seriously. "This was a major setback. I have no doubt they'll come after us again, but I don't think it will be immediate. They know now what we're capable of, and they'll be more prepared next time."

It was grim but accurate. After that, we walked in silence for several minutes, until a more personal question occurred to me. "Kane, if you don't mind me asking... How did you know it was the right thing to complete your bond with Brielle? She had health issues, right?"

He nodded gravely, shadows crossing his face as if he were reliving those early days and didn't like it much. "She was tainted with the curse that hid her omega powers, the same curse that killed her mother, and didn't want to bond with me because she knew if we did, it would kill me too."

"Wow. So *she* was the one refusing the mating?"

"Not at first. At first, I thought she was too weak to be an alpha mate. I was wrong. Her strength isn't like mine. It's softer, but no less made of steel. If she hadn't been in danger of being kidnapped or targeted today—and as a result, I asked her to stay back—she would have been on that battlefield at my shoulder, without question."

I pondered that as we left the city, meandering through the woods. There wasn't a path, per se, but there was trampled foliage where many small feet had tread recently, and it was easy to spot in the daylight. I made a mental note to mention that to Rivetsky, that they needed a more discreet way to access their cave safe house so attackers couldn't follow them in the future.

"What if I hurt her?" The question was humiliating, but I had to ask it. I was leaning toward falling headfirst into this relationship, but if I hurt her... it would kill me.

I could not be my father.

I *refused* to be my father.

"You will hurt her. Not on purpose, or you'll be dealing with me—but it's almost a guarantee that you'll fuck it up."

What a vote of confidence.

"Do you know how I know?"

I grimaced, not excited to ask which of my failings made him so certain I would be an awful mate. Eventually, I shook my head.

"Because I fuck it up all the time."

I stopped dead in the middle of the path. "What?"

He turned toward me, laughing as he slapped me on the shoulder as if we were two old friends and not the high alpha and his subject. "You think I'm perfect? I'm just as damaged as the rest of you. Burying my parents before their time was not something I'd wish on my worst enemy, let alone figuring out a new mate bond and taking over as high alpha at the same time. That's all before the part where half the world wants to murder my mate. I fuck up constantly. But she forgives me. And whenever I make a mistake, I just do my best not to do that thing again."

Holy shit.

It sounded so simple. But was that really possible? The only relationship I'd ever seen up close was my abusive father and my mother, who was just trying to survive him.

"And that works?"

Kane laughed again, throwing his head back this time and squeezing my shoulder. We started to walk again before he answered. "I'm not saying it's all roses. But, yeah. I put her first.

I love her more than my own life. If I wrong her? I do whatever it takes to fix it and make things right again. I can't tell you how many foot rubs and apologies I've delivered in the past few months. But she can feel what I feel. She knows what I meant and that the apology is sincere. Once that bond is sealed... things get both simpler and more complicated."

"It sounds really fucking complicated."

A small, knowing smile. "The best things in life are. You feel up to a run? We're not far now."

"I'm ready."

And I was.

FORTY

Olivia

I woke up on a small cot, staring up at a rocky, natural ceiling. It took me a hot minute to figure out where I was and how I'd gotten there, but when Fiona's no-longer-blue face appeared above me, it all came back to me.

"Hey, bestie! You were out for the walk back to the caves. But good news! Gael's gonna make it. I'm pretty sure that as soon as you're semiupright again, Leigh is going to pounce on you and never let go. I convinced her that would be rude to do while you were still unconscious."

"Thank you." The words were a bit croaky, and a second later, a little tin cup appeared, condensation on the sides letting me know whatever was inside was really, really cold. And I wanted it so badly, I shoved myself upright in one motion.

The room spun, and I instantly regretted it. But Elodie was there like magic, propping me up with her ridiculous maiden strength, and after a moment, it passed. I chugged the entire cup of icy cold water and held it out for another.

As it turned out, wielding magic was ridiculously draining. I didn't know how Bri managed to make it look so easy.

True to her word, the second Fiona backed away to refill my

cup, Leigh was at my side, sobbing and hugging me with crushing force of her own.

"Oh my Goddess, I don't even have the words to tell you how grateful I am. Brielle says you saved his life. Whatever magical rabbit you pulled out of the hat reversed the worst of the damage and kept him stabilized until Elodie could run him here. He's going to need a few weeks of healing and rest, but he's going to live to see our daughter's birth. Really, you saved her too. All of us." Leigh sobbed on my shoulder, and I patted her back, an intense gratitude filling me as we rocked together.

That was how the men found us. Their bulk easily filled the goblin-made doorway to this little pocket of the cave.

"Is everything okay? Brielle told me Gael had stabilized..." Kane glanced sideways, walking up with Lucien.

Elodie intercepted him with answers as Leigh pulled back, sending me an apologetic look as she wiped away her tears, then followed them over to Gael's bedside.

That left just me and Lucien.

His stare was hot enough to burn right through me, a wild-fire of emotion contained in those glowing orange eyes, and at the moment, I was ready to let it consume me whole.

He didn't speak, just knelt at the foot of my cot, taking my hand.

"Olivia, my hellcat," he added with a grin, stroking his thumb over the back of my hand. "I'm not sure I'll ever be deserving of you. Your light shines brighter than anything I've ever seen before. You're kind and caring, smart, and painfully gorgeous. I've got it on good authority that I'm going to keep screwing up, probably for the rest of our lives. But I promise you, if you give me the chance, I'll always make it up to you. I'll learn, for you."

"Luce, what are you saying?" I asked, a tremor rolling through my body as he continued to speak.

"I'm asking if you'll bond with me. I'll do whatever it takes to be the man you deserve, and—"

I leaned forward, cutting off his words with a breath-stealing kiss.

He threaded filthy fingers into my hair, tilting my chin and driving us deeper, tasting, loving, promising without words. When I finally pulled back, I rested my forehead against his. "Yes. Yes, I'll bond with you."

If I lived to be ten thousand, there would never be a sight better than his dirty, battle-smudged face with that wolfish grin, as if I'd just promised him the moon.

He looked at me like I was important, as if to him I was the moon, and the stars, and the whole damn sky.

FORTY-ONE

Olivia

C heers erupted from our pack mates, bouncing off the
walls of the small cave, and we separated, laughing.
Goddess, it felt good to laugh after how terrible a night it had
been. Though, by now, it was probably tomorrow.

The sound of a throat clearing repeatedly interrupted the
well-wishes from our pack mates, and we all turned to see
Batten, our goblin host, standing in the doorway.

It looked much less ridiculous with an occupant whose size
it was intended for.

"Please come with me."

Without another word, she turned on her heel and walked
into the pathway.

After a quick shuffle, those of us who were able followed
her out of the cave, back into the woods. The breaking dawn
was comforting after the long night of fear. Almost as if the sun
were saying, *See? You survived.*

Questions raced through my mind, but when we entered
the elder goblin's yard, they all vanished. Was she going to boot
us out for bringing trouble to their doorstep?

We'd done our best to help, but there had been serious

damage to their city, and I'd seen goblin bodies mixed in with the attackers. They'd lost friends and loved ones.

I swallowed hard, my eyes going misty as I stared at my shoes.

Everything about this had been messed up from the start. And while we'd all been joyous at surviving the battle, we were nowhere near completing the war. Without the goblins' piece, it wouldn't matter if we got the other four. The ODL would keep coming, and without the combined might of the packs fighting with us... It was a dark, dark future.

Batten helped the goblin elder down her front steps, lending her an arm for leaning as she crossed the distance between us.

This time, Batten also ran back inside and retrieved a chair for her.

As soon as she was settled, she began to speak. "I have had many interesting reports of all the things that have transpired since your arrival yesterday." Her fingers were steepled just under her chin as she gazed blandly at us, as if she was waiting for one of us to wax eloquent about the battle.

I didn't have a scrap of eloquence inside me, only exhaustion.

"It was a long night," Lucien said quietly, a stony press to his lips. "I'm sure you heard many a tale, most of them sad."

She nodded slowly, seeming to absorb his words one by one.

"Indeed, many of the reports were sad, as you say. Homes and businesses burned. Children terrified, nearly trampled. One young boy is still lost. Did you know that? His mother is beside herself."

I gasped, pressing my fingertips to my lips to silence my fear. *They must be so scared.*

Reed stepped forward, brows furrowed. "Our wolves' greater sense of smell should be able to find him quickly. If the parents have an article of clothing, we can shift and help you find him."

The elder inclined her head in his direction, thoughtful. After a long moment, she gestured to Batten. "Take him to the mother. Let them find the boy now, before he wanders into human territory and greater trouble."

Reed and Samuel both split off to follow Batten, jogging away into the woods without a backward glance.

It was Kane's turn to awkwardly clear his throat. "I know it doesn't put things back to rights, elder, but Pack Blackwater has the means to help repair what was damaged. I will see to it that all damage to your clan is repaid to the best of our ability."

"And the lives lost?" She arched one thin, white eyebrow accusingly.

It was amazing that a two-and-a-half-foot-tall goblin grandma could make the high alpha—whose power could flatten a field of attackers—look like a chastised schoolboy. But look abashed, he did.

"Elder, there is no right answer here. Money cannot replace the lives stolen by this brutal attack. I won't diminish their bravery or sacrifice by pretending it will. However, I will compensate each family for the loved one lost, so that no one they left behind struggles to survive. It's only right."

The elder nodded again, and my anxiety grew.

This was it, the part where she kicked us out and spat after us, like we were rodents she couldn't wait to be rid of. My eyes fell closed, and I leaned into Lucien's shoulder, bracing for the blow.

"Well, then. There's something I need to give you before you take your leave."

My eyes snapped back open, confusion filling me.

She pulled a thin sheet of parchment from her pocket, which appeared to be hundreds of years old.

Kane stepped forward, accepting the paper without question. He carefully unrolled it, then looked back up at the elder in shock. "The map to the omega stone fragment?"

For the first time since we'd met her, the old crone laughed. "You should see your face, boy. The whole lot of you look like a feather could take out the entire pack." She slapped her knee, then grew more serious. "What I said was true. I did hear many sad tales of the evening's events. But that wasn't all I heard."

She waved a hand forward, and a large group of goblins stepped into sight, from where I hadn't even sensed them hiding out in the woods.

I must really be exhausted to not have noticed that many magical beings so close by. I thought ruefully.

"Ever since the battle ended, my people have been showing up on my doorstep, bending my ear with countless tales of your pack's tireless determination to protect our clan from the ODL scum who care not for innocent life."

With that, she shook her head, disgust plain on her wizened features.

"You are not your ancestors. You are better. Don't forget it, and don't let the power make you forget what truly matters."

With that, she shoved slowly to her feet, waving one of her people forward. Two of them raced ahead, taking hold of her arms and supporting her as she walked the short distance to her steps.

To my surprise, though, a third goblin, who I recognized, ran forward.

"Rivetsky?" I asked, ninety percent sure it was him beneath the layer of grime hiding his neon hair.

"It is I! Grand Inventor Rivetsky!" He bowed with a flourish. "I am here to remind you of your promise to visit our gardens."

"Oh. Right." Exhaustion weighed heavy on every limb, but a promise was a promise, and I truly wanted to help these quirky, intelligent beings.

"Do not fret. First, I will lead you to our guest quarters,

where you may wash and rest. Mighty heroes deserve mighty rewards, after all. Besides, I have had many ideas about great battle machines that may aid in our defense in the future, and I wish to discuss this with your pack mates while you tour the gardens. While we think it is unlikely there will be another world breaking like the omega wars, a prepared goblin is a wealthy goblin."

With a twinkle in his eye and his chest puffed to the max, Rivetsky led us out of the woods and back to the safe caves.

FORTY-TWO

Lucien

It took us many long days to repair as much of the damage to the city of Wrenchet, and for Olivia to pour her still-recovering powers safely into their gardens. The full moon came and went as we all worked like dogs, other than a brief trip to renew our safe house wards, and we fell into our borrowed beds exhausted each night.

Brielle, Leigh, and Fiona all helped man the infirmaries, healing as many goblins as possible while the rest of us worked at our various tasks.

It was still unnerving to see Shay use *visible* bolts of white light to lift things ten times her body size, but she got shit done quickly, and we all appreciated that.

But finally, finally, it was time to leave.

A massive crowd of goblins teemed before us, excited and sad to send us off. Reed made a pretty speech about how much we appreciated their hospitality, and I wouldn't lie and say my mind didn't wander.

I was already on to the next steps, and where the fuck to find the last piece. Presuming Shay and Dirge had returned successful, a fact no one had brought up while we were repairing Wrenchet.

When Batten sidled up next to me, I didn't think anything of it. She had hovered around us like an accusing fly for our entire stay, as if at any moment we might turn on them, now that the crone had given us what we came for.

Little did she know, loyalty ran deep with this pack.

When I looked down, though, she was staring directly at me. "Everything okay?" I murmured, not wanting to detract from Reed's talk to the feisty crowd.

She nodded, solemn, considering. "You lack a wise one, but perhaps honor is enough. And you have behaved with honor to our people."

"Thank you?"

She snorted, rolling her eyes. "Many underestimate goblins. We are small, and we look different, and many of us are unserious, as you well know by now."

It was my turn to snort. "Yeah."

"But those beings overlook our greatest strength. Community. We are many, and we are spread over the world as easily as grass seeds on the wind."

I nodded, unsure where she was going with this little visit.

"There are no living phoenixes currently in the world. The New York clan reported the only one remaining—she was hiding in plain sight as a socialite—disappeared last Christmas, presumed dead by the police."

Fuck.

"Do not despair, silly wolf. Much like we do not store our valuables in our cities, the phoenixes of old would not have left their prized possessions just *anywhere*. Turn back the pages of time and go to the history. Where did they store their valuables then?" To my surprise, she patted me on the hand, as if she approved. "You are a smart, silly wolf. You will find it."

With that, she turned and walked away, leaving me to puzzle over everything she'd said.

BY THE TIME we'd made it back to our safe house, the mood had lifted. The goblin piece was nearby, as best as we could tell, hidden behind Niagara Falls. And I hadn't stopped thinking about the clue that Batten had given me, about where phoenixes had hidden things *back then*.

The second the door shut behind us, though, all attention turned to Shay and Dirge.

"Well, we have a lot to catch up on." Leigh, as usual, wasn't afraid to get the party started. She had settled the still-recovering Gael onto the couch and immediately turned toward her friend. "Can you fill in some gaps for us?"

Shay and Dirge shared a loaded look, and then Dirge pulled a small, glowing pouch from a pocket, shaking out the smallest glowing shard we'd seen yet into his palm.

A cheer went up, the females hugging and the males slapping each other on the backs.

"Okay, so, that's three. We know where the goblin's piece is, and we can get that before we leave. All that leaves is the phoenix piece," Reed summarized, right back to business.

"I think I know where it might be."

My announcement was met by all heads turning my way, even Gael, who looked close to dozing off over there.

"You've been holding out on us?" Olivia said, poking me lightly in the ribs with her elbow as she grinned up at me.

"No, actually. Batten gave me a hint before we left. She said there are no living phoenixes, per the goblin network. Even if a new phoenix has been born, they're probably not old enough yet to be of any help."

"Failing to see the good news here," Leigh grumbled under her breath, but our shifter hearing still picked it up.

"The hint was to not worry about who was alive right now, and think about where they would have hidden the piece back then. 'Turn back the pages of time,' specifically."

The confusion on everyone's faces led me to continue.

"Egypt, guys. The phoenixes' ancestral home was Egypt. I believe that's where their nesting grounds were originally."

Everyone began talking at once. Eventually, Olivia clapped twice, surprising me as everyone's fractured conversations ground to a halt.

She blushed when I looked down, blinking in surprise. "I was an assistant teacher at a preschool. Sometimes you need a little clap to get people to focus. So, if we have two pieces, do we split up? Gael isn't ready to go hiking off to the falls or tramping through the desert in Egypt."

Ever the healer, thinking of others' needs first before her own. I slid my arm around her waist and pulled her in close to my side, dropping a kiss on the top of her head and stealing a whiff of her delicious scent.

My wolf rumbled happily in my chest, enjoying this new phase where our bond was coming as soon as the moon was right, and we were safe.

"As much as I hate to split the pack further, I agree. Gael and Leigh need time to rest and heal." Kane scanned the group, calculating.

Elodie spoke up. "Head Priestess Marciana called me yesterday. The last few watchers the ODL left at the enclave finally gave up and left after the battle, since they had hard evidence you weren't there. They should be perfectly fine to go back, take some R&R. Actually... Brielle could go back, also. Where she's safely behind the barrier."

While most of the pack would take that as good news— having a safe haven was good; there was no arguing that even if it was temporary at best—I found it concerning. If we didn't know where the ODL were, we wouldn't know where to watch for the next strike.

We need to get the fuck out of Canada. Tension radiated through me as the mounting risk of every minute we stayed here seemed to pile like boulders right onto my shoulders. Olivia wasn't safe here. And as her mate, it was my job to keep her safe.

A whole new wave of inadequacy threatened to swamp me. I didn't know shit about protecting a female. The only one who'd ever depended on me was gone.

Not a good track record.

Olivia frowned up at me in confusion as if she could tell something was bothering me, and I quickly forced a smile. I didn't want her to worry about her safety or about our relationship. We'd had enough ups and downs. It was time to move *forward*.

"If one of the pieces is behind a waterfall, I could probably help with that," Fiona offered, wiggling her fingers and making thunder rumble overhead. "I can manipulate the water if needed, make it a little easier to get where we're going safely. Reed can protect me, and we can bring it back to the enclave after we get it."

"But you can't go alone. We don't want anyone to be alone, not with the ODL regrouping, and Goddess knows what the Hungarians are up to right now." Brielle shuddered, looking up at Kane with tortured eyes.

"I'll go with them," Samuel said, sharing a respectful nod with Reed and Fiona. "I was going to head back to Alaska, but I don't have anything back home more pressing than this."

"If the three of you are willing to go, I can't be too proud to accept the offer. But I think one of the maidens needs to go with you. Fiona needs protection, as do all the marked females," Kane said solemnly.

"So, is everyone else going to Egypt?" I asked, scanning the much-larger group of remaining pack mates.

Kane was already shaking his head. Arguments ensued, my impatience growing by the second, but in the end, it was agreed that we'd split into three groups.

The first group would get the piece here in Canada. Galyna would go with them to protect Fiona from any more issues with the ODL and, I quote, "To avoid sand in her fucking boots."

The second group consisted of me, Olivia, Shay, and Dirge, heading to Egypt. After some disagreement, it was agreed that Oli was safe enough with both her mate and a full-powered greater fae at her back.

Elodie would stay with Brielle, Kane, Leigh, and Gael. We'd all be meeting back at the enclave as soon as it was safe, but no later than the day before the full moon, for our bonding ceremony.

The group was just about to disperse for a night of solid rest before we split up when a thought occurred to me. "How are we going to get to Egypt? The pack jet should probably stay here, in case most of the pack needs to get to the enclave quickly."

Shay snorted, throwing an arm around Oli's shoulders as she smirked at me like I was missing something obvious.

It was Dirge who finally filled me in. "How do you feel about light travel?"

Shit.

We were gonna get flashed across the world by a fae. My groan had everyone laughing.

FORTY-THREE

Olivia

The next morning dawned like any other, except I woke up in the arms of my mate, content. It was a beautifully mundane experience, and I wanted ten thousand more exactly like it.

He kissed me good morning before he climbed out of bed, and I was a woman obsessed.

Only partly with watching his bare ass flex as he crossed the room, disappearing into the bathroom. The bigger part was just the feeling of us being solid for the first time. Sure, we'd had sex and it was mind-blowing—but in this moment, it felt like we were on real, solid ground.

There was a comfort in it, in him, that I had never experienced before.

My dad had been my world growing up, but it wasn't the same, the way a little girl put her daddy on a pedestal compared to the love of mates. Lucien completed me in ways I hadn't realized were incomplete before.

I kept my thoughts to myself as we got ready for our journey, packing our few belongings into backpacks. The hiking boots, unfortunately, got to come along, but hopefully, this time, it would be quicker to find what we were looking for. The phoenixes weren't there, and they weren't actively hiding from us.

Within an hour, we'd loaded up, had breakfast, and shared hugs with the pack as everyone parted ways. All that was left to do was step onto the lawn with Shay and Dirge.

My stomach flipped with curiosity and anxiety in equal measure as she asked us all to touch her arm.

"Everybody ready for the ride of a lifetime?" she asked, grinning from ear to ear as she looked from me to Lucien, then Dirge.

"Not at all," Lucien grumbled, but he closed his eyes in easy acceptance anyway.

"Is it scary?" I asked, even though I'd meant to keep my trepidations to myself.

"Not for the fae, it's not. Just... don't let go." Shay winked, and then, before I could ask a follow-up question, everything around us turned to light.

Solid objects bled into streaks of color, making me think my eyes were playing tricks on me for a split second.

Then my stomach kicked into gear, vicious nausea, as if the force was trying to rip my stomach out through my throat. A hiss escaped my lips as the world faded to nothing but white, and time lost all meaning.

After what felt like both a thousand years and a single blink, my feet hit semisolid earth, and our new surroundings came into focus.

Well, they would have if I hadn't bent over and puked up my breakfast into the sand.

Lucien was there, holding my hair back and whispering soothing words. To my surprise, when I'd finished, he handed me a real cloth hanky, with baby blue initials monogrammed in one scallop-edged corner. *LVJ*, the V very grand and curlicued in the middle.

I cleaned myself up, then gave him a regretful smile. "That was too fancy for cleanup duty."

His smile was tinged with sadness. "Just a memento, nothing that can't be laundered."

Before I could ask who it was a memento from—I'd assumed the initials were his, Lucien J. Vasilescu—Dirge was ready to get moving.

I'll ask him later.

"So, where are we going?" I asked instead, seeing nothing before us but empty sand. "Because civilization appears to be behind us."

Shay laughed quietly. "Phoenixes are solitary creatures, mostly. They would have built their nesting grounds well away from any human populations."

"Ahh." I tripped over the sand, one of the waves higher than I'd realized as we trudged along. "In that case, I don't think we packed enough water." I only had two bottles in the drink pockets of my pack, and that was just because it was sometimes inconvenient to find when you were traveling. When they said we were going to Egypt, I envisioned *modern* Egypt.

"My pack and Dirge's pack are both full," Lucien said, hiking easily at my side, unaffected by the massive amount of weight his pack must have been holding. "Reed worked with a local magical historian last night and, one obscenely large bank deposit later, said this was the direction to go if we were interested in phoenix history. Supposedly, it's walkable if you're willing to spend the whole day in the desert."

"But don't worry, if we get in bad shape, I can always flash us somewhere safe," Shay added.

I nodded, thinking about that. "You came back with a lot more than just a piece of the stone. What happened?"

The question hung in empty air for long enough that I started to wonder if I'd offended her.

"The fae queen... required us to complete challenges in order to get the piece."

"The fae queen and the centaurs clearly swapped notes," Lucien muttered under his breath.

Dirge snorted, but Shay just continued as if he hadn't spoken. "One of them was to take my true form. I thought she meant wolf, but, uh, apparently I've got more forms than I realized. It's harder to call on it outside the realm, but flying is worth it."

Her apparent joy at her transformation made me happy. We'd all been through so much in the past few months, she deserved a cool new power.

"So, you can fly, shoot beams of light, and flash. Anything else?" Lucien asked.

"That's not enough? Sheesh, you people aren't easily impressed."

"I'm plenty impressed, just making sure we didn't miss anything."

"Nope," she responded, popping the p. "Oh, there was one more thing. Time is different between the realms. When we came back, I was surprised so little time had passed. Being in the fae court is... overwhelming. It gets hard to keep track of how long you've been there, and there's no modern technology, and any tech you bring doesn't work. So we didn't know if we'd been gone too long."

Weird. I was so used to having a phone in my pocket, readily available for any little question—well, mundane question. For magical questions, you still had to visit the pack library—it was odd to think about a society with *no* technology.

Granted, fae had wings. Fair trade.

We walked, and we walked, and we walked.

Sweat slid down my face at an alarming rate, and by the

time the sun finally thought about setting, my water bottles were both drained, and we'd had to tap the water the males carried.

The sun was only two fingers from kissing the top of the sand dunes when Shay froze.

"Do any of you see that... blur?" She pointed off to the left, and to be honest, my eyes were so gritty, I couldn't tell if there was anything out of the ordinary.

But after a second, Lucien did. "Right there. There's something blurring the horizon."

"I think that's it. We found it, guys!" I didn't know how she still had the energy for the happy little hop-skip she did or how she sped up as we closed the distance between us and the blur.

It wasn't until we were much closer that I saw it, but when I did, it was obvious. A massive rectangular shape, see-through but clearly something, altering the shape of the horizon just slightly. It was big enough to hide three cruise ships, but disguised enough to make a human write it off as a mirage, a trick of the heat.

But not a wolf looking for a phoenix nesting ground.

Twilight had fallen as we stepped through the barrier, and I braced myself for the unpleasant twang I'd grown accustomed to with magical barriers. But it never came.

It wasn't even an itch, just a gentle brush over my skin. Once we were through, though, everything became clear.

And sorrow was my instant companion.

What once had been teeming with life was completely barren.

The structure was beautiful, but there was an *emptiness* to it that felt wrong. It looked like an ancient temple. Tall pillars of sandstone supported the long, tiered, rectangular structure. We were staring at a ramp up to the first tier of open gardens, where palm trees swayed in the breeze, the soft grassy areas stretching between them inviting in the waning evening light.

The second level of the temple was also open, but the top level was walled, hiding whatever lay inside.

But besides the plants, there wasn't a living soul besides the four of us. And I had a feeling there hadn't been, for a long, long time.

"Do you guys see nests anywhere?" I asked, eyeing the tops of the palms skeptically. I'd never seen a phoenix, but surely their nests wouldn't be in the top of any old palm tree.

Medemia Argun. The magic was almost annoyed at my dismissal of the trees, apparently a rarer species of palm, recently thought to be extinct.

Sorry, I thought back, feeling a ripple of acceptance in the green tendrils I could now feel, since I was paying attention.

We climbed the ramp to the first tier in hallowed silence, as if all of us sensed the ground we walked upon was sacred. But the farther we walked—the temple was enormous—the more certain I became that this garden wasn't where the nests were. There certainly weren't any stone shards lying around, besides the occasional chip of sandstone.

Night had fallen by the time we finished searching the first tier. We paused at the ramp to the second tier of three.

"Should we split up?" Lucien asked, glancing down at me and then frowning. "Or are we going to find a comfortable spot and break for the night?"

"I can search a little longer." I appreciated his concern, but the sooner we found the shard, the sooner this would be behind us.

I doubted it would take Fiona and Reed more than a day to get the shard from where the goblins had stored it, which meant we were officially the last holdup.

"If you get tired, we'll rest." He squeezed my hand where our fingers were joined, dropping a kiss on the back of my knuckles, not minding the bits of sand and sweat that had accumulated there on our journey.

"Deal."

The second tier was just as large, though quicker to search, because instead of long gardens, it was all stone and still, rectangular pools. By the time we'd crossed it, we were all ready to break for the evening.

After a quick dip in one of the shallow pools to wash off the worst of the day, we shifted into our wolf forms and found a comfy spot in the gardens below to curl up. With the stars shining brightly and the desert winds blowing through the palms above us, we slept.

MORNING LIGHT and the promise of beef jerky got us moving quickly the next morning. But when we climbed the ramp to the third and final tier, our search came to an abrupt halt. The massive stone doors—this was the only tier with walls—were either locked or stuck.

No amount of alpha muscle or fae magical encouragement could budge them. There was a walkway around the outside, and so we split up into pairs to see if we could find another way inside.

"This place is enormous. I didn't think phoenixes were that large," I mused aloud as Lucien and I strolled around the first corner.

"I don't think they were, but based on when and where this was built... grand design was the style."

I nodded, thinking of the Egyptian pyramids so many people traveled to see each year. My mind wandered a bit as we walked, studying each nook and cranny, but finding nothing yet that would give a clue as to how to get inside.

We stopped at an archway, feeling around the cracks to see if there were any hidden levers or buttons. "I sense more plants in there, but nothing else. It would be nice if that could extend to other things, wouldn't it?"

Lucien gave me a sideways glance. "Your herbalist powers have grown a lot lately. I've never seen anything like what you did for Gael."

I paused my search, studying him. "Does that bother you? I know it's strange for a wolf. Granted..." I held up my palm, not glowing this far from Kane and Brielle. "It's not that things are particularly normal for us on any level."

He shook his head, giving up his own search to wrap me in a hug. "I think it's part of who you are, and that's perfect. It does make me nervous that we don't understand it all, though. Reed told me that you exhausted yourself to the point you passed out."

"Fiona ratted me out." I squinted off into the distance, as if she could feel my displeasure from another continent.

"I'm more wondering why *you* didn't tell me."

Guilt reared up at the words, even though they weren't accusing. "I didn't want you to worry. I also had no idea I could do that. I was just desperate to save a pack mate."

He brushed my hair away from my forehead, shaking his head slightly at me. "You're the most selfless person I've ever met. And while I don't want to change a single thing about you, I worry sometimes that you'll give too much one day at your own expense. And I can't bear to see you hurt again."

I pondered his words, stroking his back as I listened to his heartbeat under my cheek.

"I can't promise you that I'll stop helping people. But I *will* try not to hurt myself in the process."

He nodded, seeming satisfied with that. "Ready to keep going?"

I groaned. "It's so hot. Would it be terrible if we took a break?"

His lips twisted in a devious smirk. "The kind of break

where we hydrate, or the kind where I press you up against this wall and make you coat my chin with your sweet honey?"

I gasped as he stepped forward and pressed me up against the archway, nuzzling his face into the crook of my neck and peppering the area with teasing nips.

When I arched and moaned under his touch, they quickly got less teasing. He moved to pull away, but I dragged him back in against my chest, heart pounding as I considered what to say.

I wasn't good at any of this, not yet. But I wanted to learn.

I want him to teach me.

"Yes."

He arched one eyebrow, cupping the back of my neck with his hand, making me shudder as he leaned in close, his breath brushing against my ear. "Be a good girl and keep your hands against the wall. Don't move unless I tell you to."

"Okay," I answered breathlessly, pressing my palms back against the smooth stones at my sides.

He knelt in front of me, and before I knew it, my pants were sliding down to my ankles, and his warm hands were skimming my outer thighs. My underwear was quick to follow, and his mouth was on my skin, warm and teasing, as he urged my legs wider, trailing kisses up my inner thigh.

It felt vulnerable, exposed, but when he gazed up at me with molten heat in his amber eyes and latched on to my pussy, all thoughts of anything but pleasure fled.

Lucien was a master with his tongue, driving me to the edge in record time with skillful strokes and swirls, and when he inserted first one finger, then another, I fell over the edge, clamping around his fingers as I muffled my cries against my palm.

He stood, slowly easing his fingers out of me as he leaned in, bracketing me against the wall as I caught my breath. "You come apart like a masterpiece. I'll never get tired of watching you, hellcat." He wove his fingers into my hair, tilting my head back for a kiss, tinged with the taste of myself on his lips.

I wrapped myself around him, enjoying the feel of his hard muscles and wanting *more*, but we both froze at the sound of stones scraping behind us.

And then he was in motion, moving me back, helping me put my pants and panties back in place.

Because somehow, we'd accidentally opened a door into the phoenix temple.

FORTY-FOUR

Lucien

As soon as Olivia was put back together—like fuck was I sharing a single glimpse of her looking like that with anyone but me—we called Shay and Dirge. They came jogging around the corner nearly ten minutes later, due to the sheer size of the temple.

Dirge slapped me on the back with a grin. "How'd you two get it open?"

"Don't ask."

He laughed, his keen eyes not missing Olivia's rosy cheeks and slightly mussed ponytail. "Wouldn't dream of it." The wink he shot me would have made my hackles rise, except he walked around and slid his arm around his own mate, dropping a kiss on top of her head.

Dirge was a wolf content, *whole*, and I craved that feeling with every fiber of my being.

But at the same time, I didn't hate where we were either. It was nice to learn her slowly, in waves. To take our time and wait for the moon. For the first time in my life, it felt like time was on my side. And after getting captured and tortured, that was a luxury I thought I'd never experience again.

Time with my mate, time to grow this fledgling relationship into something sturdier, something lasting.

I was excited for our future. There were challenges ahead, but Olivia and I could face them *together*.

What we'd found was a rare, precious thing. And I didn't intend to squander a moment of our future.

I slid my hand back into hers, and we led the way into the temple's top level.

It was dim but not dark inside, though I couldn't immediately spot the source of light. The archway we walked through led us into a hallway, stone walls on either side of us funneling us toward the middle of the building.

Building wasn't quite the word for it, but that was all I had that fit. It felt like a maze, the walls taller than usual and closing in on the hallway.

Hieroglyphics lined the walls, but these weren't your usual Egyptian drawings. No, these were of great, fiery birds, with humans worshipping at their feet.

As we walked, the entire life cycle of a phoenix played out on the walls, and I found myself slowing down to take in the details and absorb the beauty. Olivia was by my side, quietly taking it all in right along with me.

"Guys, look at this one." Shay's voice was reverent from a little farther down. I hadn't even noticed them stepping down a side hall, but the hieroglyph she pointed to was of a great, jewel-toned nest, a gleaming golden egg sitting in the middle. "I think we're close. As far as I can tell, the center of the ceiling is just over there. But the path splits on that branch. Something about this place, though... I don't think we should separate again."

She shuddered, and my wolf went on high alert. Her fae senses could pick up different magics than I could with my wolf's keen senses, and while I only felt or scented inert stone around us… "Olivia, didn't you say you sensed living plants inside?"

My mate nodded hesitantly. "I still do, but they could be in these rooms. It's hard to say. I'm still not great at judging distance."

"The fact that you were able to take brand-new power and save Gael's life in the middle of a battle was incredible. Normally, that kind of skill would take *years* of practice, especially based on what we learned about new powers in the fae court." Shay pointed over her shoulder to where her wings would be in her full form. "It's okay if it doesn't all come to you at once."

Olivia nodded, seeming pleased by the praise.

Does my mate have a praise kink? Food for thought.

We continued walking, arriving at the fork in the hallway slash maze. There were no scents for our wolves to follow, no footsteps left after this place had been so long unattended. It was a toss-up.

"As long as we stay within earshot, we can go a little ways down each and see if one way looks more promising than the other. Neither path goes straight to the center." Dirge pointed overhead, then followed the line down from the middle of the ceiling toward a spot off in the distance. "We'll take right, and we'll both walk for"—he checked his watch—"five minutes before turning around and deciding which path we want to take."

"I'd say we'll call, but my phone is a brick in here." Olivia frowned as she held up her cell.

"Good old-fashioned way it is, then. No biggie." Shay's smile was tight and not at all believable.

"Five minutes." I nodded at Dirge, checked my watch, and then Olivia and I turned left.

The hallway we'd chosen was plain. No paint adorned the walls, there were no doorways, and no additional lights that we could see. We *did* walk under a skylight way up above, though, so at least the question of where the light was coming from was answered.

"We definitely won't be hanging out in here after dark. This place gives me the creeps."

Oli laughed, the sound far too musical for our surroundings. "Really? I think it's amazing. I feel like a real-life Indiana. Going on archaeological adventures, but without all the spiderwebs."

I snorted. "You can always see the bright side, can't you?"

"It's one of my many talents, actually." She turned and shot me a saucy look over her shoulder, when all the hair on the back of my neck stood up.

"Hellcat, something's—"

The ground gave out beneath us, and then we were falling.

I WOKE TO WHIMPERING. My eyes were blurry, and I blinked a few times, only to realize that it was dust floating in the air making the light from above filter through the grime. Scratch that, *way the hell above.*

I didn't know how far we'd fallen, but I had the sense we were deep, deep under this temple.

Another whimper snapped my focus back to the present.

"Olivia?" I kept my voice calm, scanning the rubble-filled space with my heart thundering at top speed, not at all calm. When she didn't answer, I yelled her name.

"Here. I'm over here."

Her voice was small, terrified, shaking, and in the two-point-five seconds it took me to scale the pile of broken rock between us, one million terrifying scenarios of her being hurt and maimed flashed through my mind. Every last one would haunt my nightmares, I knew that like I knew I needed oxygen.

She was huddled on the floor, dirt dulling her fiery hair's shine, and my nose picked up the coppery tang of blood in the air.

"Where are you hurt? How bad is it?"

I didn't mean to bark at her, but my wolf was scratching and clawing for release. He needed to protect her, no matter that the foe was gravity and time.

When she didn't answer, I dropped to my knees, nearly sighing with relief when I saw the grazes on her palms, a few small nicks on her shins.

Not life-threatening. Not maimed. Not dying.

I took my first full inhalation since coming to and held her to my chest, looking around for an escape route. My eyes were starting to adjust with help from my wolf, and I could see the grayscale outline of a small room. An empty bench lined one wall, and it looked like there was an outline of a doorway, unfortunately *behind* the pile of flooring stones we'd fallen through.

"It's going to be okay. I can see a door over there. We must have just found a weak spot in the floor." I chafed her arms with my hands, but she didn't respond. "Hellcat? Olivia?" I resisted the urge to shake her, in case she had a concussion or something that her shifter healing was still battling. "Can you tell me where it hurts? Anything, little mate."

"Too-oo small. Don't like tight spaces."

Shit. "You're claustrophobic?"

She nodded, finally looking up at me, her face white as a sheet. She was pale normally, but this was as if all the blood had drained from her face and she was about to pass out.

"I'm going to get you out of here, okay? I promise it's going to be fine. But I've got to get you out of the way so I can move the rocks." I scooped her off the ground, her terrified tremors making me move faster. To my relief, there was a dusty but solid chair in the corner of the room. When I tried to set her down, though, she clung to my shirt.

"Please don't leave me," she begged in a distressed whisper.

My wolf was not happy. Frankly, the man wasn't too happy either. I was pretty sure I had a goose egg on the back of my skull from that landing.

"Shhh. I'm never leaving you again, hellcat. You're *mine*. You know that? As soon as the full moon is here, I'm going to leave my bite on this beautiful skin. Where do you think you want it?"

It was not at all the appropriate time to choose where we wanted our bites, but I hoped the topic might distract her.

I had less than zero experience dealing with claustrophobia, so I was shooting from the hip.

"I would be happy..." She shuddered, trying to focus on something besides the fear that held her in its tightly clenched fist. "I would be happy to wear your bite anywhere."

Her voice rose at the end, determination as she tried to rise out of it.

"That's because you're such a good mate. You know that? The Goddess made a mistake giving somebody as perfect as you to somebody as busted up as I am, but we're absolutely not going to tell her that, okay? Because now that I've seen what life is like with you? I can't go back. I'm addicted." I smiled, stroking her cheek and holding her gaze.

She seemed to draw strength from the words, from my steadiness. After a moment, she shook her head. "I'm far from perfect, Luce. And I'm not sure I'll really believe you're mine until the bite is on my neck to prove it." She fingered the area above her collarbone, and I leaned down to kiss it.

"Believe it, hellcat. You've been claimed by an alpha, and alphas don't ever let go."

"It didn't stop my mother." I almost didn't catch her whisper, and confusion filled me at her words.

"What do you mean?"

She shook her head, closing her eyes, and I felt her panic start to descend again, her scent acrid with the weight of it.

Shit.

I had to change tactics, and *quick.*

"You told me you sensed plants in here before. Are there any close by?"

She squinched up her eyebrows, concentrating. "I'm not sure. It's hard to tell. The power doesn't want to talk."

"Yeah? I bet you could find out what's around. Why don't you close your eyes and focus on that? You tell me every single plant you can reach in the area. I want every name."

She closed her eyes immediately, and my wolf rumbled his pleasure at her submission. *Wolves are so damn predictable.*

"Every plant, you promise me?" I dropped a kiss on her forehead.

"The palms from outside are annoyed at us again."

I chuckled, letting go of my grip on her jaw, slowly backing away at first, then more quickly turning toward the pile that stood between us and freedom. "Again? What did we do to the bastards to piss 'em off the first time?"

"I called them *average* palm trees. Apparently, they're quite rare."

"Who knew trees could be uppity," I huffed, moving chunks of rock at top speed, piling them in the far corner, where there was no chance they could roll and hit my girl.

"Very uppity. There are also water lilies. I love lilies. Their scent is so sweet. It reminds me of summer."

The way my heart clenched at the reference to lilies, I nearly faltered in my task. But then I remembered that Lilly was long gone, and Olivia needed me right now.

I'm going to fail her.

I shook it off and kept working, urging Olivia on any time she slowed in reciting the various plants. I could tell she was good and into it when she started telling me their scientific names a few minutes in.

"Oh shit, Dirge, I think they're in that hole!" Shay's voice rang out overhead, and I froze, looking up, finally gauging how incredibly far we'd fallen. It was a miracle we hadn't both broken all our bones. I eyed the dangling roof material overhead, realizing the ancient leather had probably saved our lives.

"Stay back from the edge! If more rocks fall, we don't have any cover!" I shouted, chucking the rock I was still holding to the corner and bracing myself over Olivia.

"We won't come any closer. Are you injured?" Dirge shouted down, the sound getting swallowed up by the vast chasm of space between us.

"Just bumps and bruises. There's a door in this room, and we're nearly out."

"That's good, because the other path was a dead end. If we can't get past here, I'm not sure we can make it any deeper into the temple."

"We've got a door. Now we just have to figure a way back out."

"We'll keep looking from the outside. Do you have a flashlight?"

"Yeah, in my pack," Olivia supplied, not yelling. Her eyes were still screwed tightly shut, her knuckles bone white where she gripped the seat of her chair.

"We're good."

As long as we weren't trapped. *Please, Goddess, don't let us be trapped.*

FORTY-FIVE

Olivia

"Okay, mate, you can open your eyes." Lucien's tone was cool and soothing, and I knew I was safe with him, but still, the terror was there, clenching my heart to dust.

I shook my head.

"Not ready yet?"

Another shake.

He chuckled. And then I gasped and grabbed on to his T-shirt when he scooped me out of the chair without another word. I kept my eyes screwed tightly shut, not wanting to see the pit of despair we were in.

But as he carried me, the air around us... changed. We'd taken only a few steps—less than ten?—before he paused, inhaling deeply.

That was when it hit me.

Fresh air.

My eyes flew open, and what I saw was beyond my wildest imaginings of what I thought we'd find inside this dusty old temple.

It was *life*. Vibrant, bold growth was everywhere I looked. Plants I had no names for buzzed against my senses, caressing my energy with excited tendrils from every direction. We were still underground—but we were far, *far* below the stone ceiling above us. It had to be at least a hundred-plus feet of open space.

The air was crisp and cool, scented with the exotic perfumes of big, pink flowers that bloomed a few feet away, thick vines tangled overhead, between ancient trees I had no name for.

"Can you put me down, please?" I asked, patting Lucien on the shoulder as I continued gawking in wonder.

He set me on my feet, and I walked across the spongy earth to rest my hand on the nearest tree.

Its energy was a gentle green glow in my mind's eye, the quiet hum of a long, protected life. It had stood here for centuries, magically renewed by this place of power for the phoenix people.

As soon as I thought of the phoenixes, an image flashed into my mind. From the tree, I thought. It was two great, fiery birds swooping and dancing in the air overhead, their power-ful, triumphant cry as they clashed together and plummeted toward the earth shattering the vision, but leaving me breath-less nonetheless.

"What do you think this is?" Lucien asked, gesturing to the wide expanse of untouched nature that defied all the odds.

"I think... it was their mating grounds. A protected area where they could fly free and have a little section of paradise to bring their young into the world."

He nodded, glancing back the way we came. "I think you're right. Look."

I followed where he was pointing, grinning as I saw a scene similar to what I'd just been given by the tree, painted on the wall in stunning color. Phoenixes in a rainbow of fiery reds and oranges swooped across the walls, some locked together and tumbling, some sitting on great jeweled nests, and others just flying free for the joy of it. You could see it in every upturned line and sweeping curve.

Joy, freedom, power.

But sadness washed over me as I turned back around. There was none of that now, only an empty sanctuary, untouched for seemingly hundreds of years. Where had all the phoenixes *gone*? They couldn't die without regenerating, as far as the lore went. So why had they abandoned their ancestral home?

It was a mystery I wouldn't be able to solve.

"Do you see any way back up?" I asked, realizing that while this place was wondrous, it wasn't built for wolves. While I had no doubt there was a fresh water source hidden here somewhere, there was no prey here to hunt. Even if we'd found the nesting grounds, with no way out... we couldn't return the omega stone piece to our pack.

"No, but it looks like this cavern is significantly larger than the temple structure up above. Look there." He pointed upward this time, and I saw the precise corner cut into the ceiling above us, a massive support pillar of stone stretching down to the ground below. Turning, I spotted the other three. There were also great, burning sconces that provided flickering light to the underground area, though it defied all logic that they were still burning after being so long untended.

"You're right. Those are clearly the temple corners overhead. So did they just... fly down here? Or... Oh, look!" Dead in the center of paradise, a twisting stairway to the surface.

The room we'd fallen into was part of a small building, tucked into the foliage and hiding human—or, perhaps, shifted phoenix—amenities. Beds, washing chambers, storage bins. Nothing fancy, though it probably was by ancient standards.

In hindsight, I suppose it was better we'd fallen where we had than getting impaled on a tree limb.

Lucien and I strolled through the mating grounds, looking

high and low for any sign of a nest, stopping at any small buildings to check the storage areas for signs of the stone shard, but
we found nothing.

More than that, as beautiful as the underground paradise
was, there was no sign of anything resembling the jeweled nests
we'd seen in the paintings.

When we finally reached the staircase, I was relieved to find
it was magically hewn from sturdy stone and still looked brand-
new, spiraling up the long distance into the temple overhead.
But it didn't only offer us freedom. It also spiraled down into
complete darkness below.

Anxiety filled me at the thought of going farther down,
back into close, dark spaces. I was shaking my head and
backing away before I even realized what I was doing.

"Hey, it's okay. If you don't want to go down, I can go. You
can start climbing, and I'll meet you at the top with Shay and
Dirge." Lucien chafed my arms lightly, not pressuring me in the
slightest. Despite my fear, though, my wolf revolted at the idea
of leaving our mate alone down here.

"You can go first. But I'm coming with you." I lifted my chin
and swallowed hard as I said it, my stomach flipping like a
pancake at the idea, but I meant it.

"Brave mate," he murmured, kissing me slowly, reminding
me of how he'd made me come apart just a little while before.
Still, that taste made me want more.

But he was right.

I was brave. I could do hard things.

Goddess, help me.

"Should we tell Shay and Dirge before we go down?" I
asked, glancing up at the damaged spot in the ceiling from
which we'd fallen.

"I would love to, but our phones still aren't working, and
they're back outside, trying to find an alternate way in. I think

our best bet is to find what we came for and get back to the surface as quickly as we can."

"Okay, then, let's do it."

If we waited much longer, I might lose my nerve.

One more kiss, and Lucien started climbing down the spiral staircase. I sucked in a deep breath through my nose and followed him into the darkness.

I focused on the light filtering in from the stairwell, not daring to let myself look down or think about the fact that the ground was swallowing me up with every step.

Still, by the time Lucien's footsteps stopped, my breathing was rapid, and my heart was pounding as if I'd just run a marathon instead of descending the stairs for a few minutes.

The staircase had taken us several stories down, the light small overhead. I just kept my focus on it as I reached the bottom stair and waited.

"Hang on. There's a torch here and what looks like a lantern. The room is pretty big." He kept talking as he worked, and within a few moments, he had lit the torch and was touching it to the bowl-style lantern he'd found. But the fire didn't stay in the bowl; it raced along the walls, where troughs of oil surrounded the room and ignited, casting their dancing light into the room.

Finally, I exhaled.

This room was at least as large as the temple itself, but now that it was lit, shock filled me.

It was made of the same stone, sure. But that was where the similarities ended. Gold and treasure were stacked higher than my head, in great mounds all throughout the room.

"Holy shit," Lucien murmured, taking my hand in his free one as we gazed around at the massive hoard of treasure together and began to walk deeper.

"I think this is more gold than Fort Knox." Everywhere I looked, there was some kind of treasure. Coins, bars, jewelry, and jeweled goblets that looked like they belonged on King Arthur's round table.

"Is that... the Florentine Diamond?" Lucien paused next to one of the mounds, pointing at an enormous, glittering diamond two-thirds of the way up the pile.

"I've never heard of it."

"That's because it was stolen over a hundred years ago, and it's been missing ever since." He shook his head, but we kept walking.

"We probably shouldn't touch anything, just in case." Maybe it was superstitious of me, but you didn't mess with the dead or the sacred, and this place *felt* like hallowed ground. Almost as if the spirits of the phoenixes were still here, guarding it, watching us.

"I agree. We're not here to get rich. We're here to save our people." I didn't miss the way his gaze dropped to my palm, the way he seemed to swallow the unspoken *you*.

They lay heavy in the space between us, all those unspoken things. Like how he felt about me. I'd told him I loved him, and even though he'd asked me to bond with him, he hadn't told me he loved me. I thought he did, but what if I was just reading into things more than what he actually felt?

"Hellcat, look there." He pointed up at a taller mound, a giant, sapphire nest sitting atop it. "We found the nesting grounds."

"Yes, we did. The question is, how do we find a single piece of the omega stone in this hoard without disturbing anything?" This was way more than finding a needle in a haystack; this was a single piece of treasure in a hoard any dragon would be proud of.

"I have no idea. I guess we just start looking." He shrugged, and we walked deeper.

We looked high and low in the mounds, careful not to

touch anything, in case they all came tumbling down. Or we set off some kind of ancient alarm system that would fry us.

You know, either or.

"All the nests so far have been empty." I hadn't put much weight on the first one, because, well, we'd known the phoenixes were always rare. But I'd counted four so far, and not a single egg. It looked like we were about halfway through the room, and those weren't good odds.

Was the entire species really gone? It was a depressing thought. So many species were in decline, and I knew the omega wars had been deadly, but wiping an entire magical race from the planet was a new level of horrible I couldn't stand to think about, as we stood here in the midst of the amazing things they'd created.

But it wasn't just phoenixes. We were *all* in decline because we couldn't stop fighting and let each other exist. It made me wonder what would happen once we did complete the stone and Brielle's powers extended to all the wolf packs in the world. Our numbers would increase again, but would the new power tip us back in the wrong direction or right the scales?

All told, there were eight nests, each formed from a single, large gemstone into a bowl-like nest shape.

From the ground, they all looked empty.

At the very end of the rectangular space sat a single chest made of wood and iron. It looked old and, other than its age making it rare, relatively worthless.

"That doesn't blend in with everything else, don't you think?" I pointed it out to Lucien, who was studying a mound a few feet away, topped with a fiery ruby nest.

"Not at all. I think we're going to have to check it. I was hoping we'd see the piece lying somewhere so we could take it and go, but this all seems to be unmagical, just valuable."

I nodded, agreeing with his assessment.

"I'll do it," I offered, ascending the eight steps to the elevated platform where the chest sat, completely alone.

"Go slow, just in case." He was right behind me, ready to spring into action if anything went wrong.

But when I hesitantly placed my hand on the heavy iron clasp, nothing happened. No magical zing, just inert metal.

I lifted the clasp, and it moved with ease, as if it were freshly oiled. The lid of the chest was heavier, and it took some effort to lift. Once it locked open, I looked down, and it took a moment for my brain to process what I was seeing.

There it was, the final shard of celestine, glowing softly from the side of the chest. There were also two feathers, gleaming and long, the golden tips wispy and curved against the ancient wood of the box. Beneath it all... was ash.

Soft gray and dull, it lined the entire bottom, and I felt sick to my stomach.

The lore said that phoenixes burned up when they died, and then regenerated from those ashes. But these hadn't.

Whatever had happened, these ashes had stayed dead.

I leaned down carefully to lift the last stone shard our pack needed, moving slowly so as not to touch or disturb the ash beneath it. A single tear rolled off my cheek and landed in the ash as I lifted the piece free.

When I turned and showed Lucien the fragment, his eyes lit with a smile, until he saw my face. "What's wrong? We found it! We can get out of here and finally put this rock back together." He wrapped me up in a hug, and I accepted the comfort but couldn't shake the sadness.

"There are ashes in that box."

He froze, not letting me go. When he slowly pulled back, his expression was thoughtful. "They might not be gone, not forever. Things are changing by the minute. Magic is nuanced, and balance shifts over time. Maybe when the rest of the super-natural world comes back into balance, they will too."

Lucien wiped my tears away with his thumbs, holding me, giving me the time I needed to grieve all that was lost from the decline of this magnificent species.

When the tears stopped, I wiped my eyes, pocketed the omega stone shard, and looked out over the nesting grounds. And when my gaze landed on the ruby nest, I nearly burst into tears all over again.

There's an egg inside.

Golden and delicate, I could see a hint of flame, as if the pattern was etched into the shell. One tiny, fragile egg.

But there was still hope for the phoenixes.

Maybe, just maybe, there was hope for us all.

FORTY-SIX

Lucien

It took the rest of the day and half the night to figure out how to get out of the temple. Partly because it was a fuck ton of stairs, and even werewolf muscles were burning by the time we made it back to solid ground, but more than that, the inside of the temple was one big maze.

When we finally stumbled out into the desert night air to our waiting pack mates, we were all exhausted.

We spent another night in the sanctuary, where it was cooler and there was water, grateful to be aboveground, no matter how beautiful the underground sanctuary had been.

The next morning, we stepped back into the waiting desert sands, and our phones magically began working again by the time we'd hiked for two hours. As soon as we had a signal, I called Kane.

"Speak."

"Alpha, it's us. We found the shard."

"Lucien. Everyone is safe?"

"Yes, we're all fine. A few bumps and bruises, but those have mostly healed." I rubbed idly at the knot that had shrunk significantly but still lingered on the back of my head. My healing still wasn't back to full speed, probably another effect of my damaged bond.

"Excellent. Reed and his party retrieved the goblin piece as well. We're all on the jet, flying back toward the enclave. Priestess Marciana confirmed it was still clear, and we all agreed that the enclave was the best place to try to reassemble the stone."

I nodded, glancing around at everyone. "Do you want us to meet you there?"

"Yes. Meet us at the airstrip, and we'll make a plan of approach. I want to be cautious, just in case Varga's watchers are still in the area."

"Will do."

We disconnected the call, and I filled everyone in on what Kane had shared.

"So, back to Romania. Can't say I'll miss the sand," Dirge said, his sarcasm thick enough to survive a chain saw as he lifted a booted foot and sand rained down from it like a miniature waterfall.

"Me either," Olivia agreed, though she hadn't voiced a word of complaint this entire trip. She was tougher than I'd given her credit for early on. She didn't let fear stop her, and she loved deeply, no matter the cost to herself.

She was a worthy mate. And I was damn lucky to have her.

I wrapped an arm around her shoulders and kissed her on the head. She looked up at me quizzically but didn't comment.

"All right. Who's ready to go now?"

I repressed a groan. Flashing sucked, but hiking all day through the desert wasn't exactly fun either. "Let's get it over with."

Shay grinned, sticking out her arm for everyone to hold on.

"Three... two... one."

The desert warped around us, bleeding out of existence.

THE LANDING in Romania was a little easier than the first time. Olivia was green around the gills but didn't get sick, at least.

We had the better part of a day to waste, so we spent it quietly at an inn in the little town nearby, keeping our eyes open but not seeing any of Petró's pack or anyone wearing an ODL uniform.

It was after dark when the others landed, so they joined us at the inn. We all slept, and just before dawn, it was time to make our way back to the enclave. The plan we'd established last night was simple. Gael, Leigh, and Galyna would leave an hour after us and drive right up to the front gates. They were our cover, since Gael was a prince and Leigh was pregnant. Kane and Brielle would hide in the back of the SUV, out of sight, until we could race them straight through the front gates.

Meanwhile, the rest of us would take the longer, bumpier back way, splitting off on foot once we were about thirty minutes out, to sound the alarm in case of danger.

I didn't like that Olivia was going to be out in the woods, possibly in danger, but she'd insisted on sticking with me. I drove our SUV, Olivia in the front passenger seat. By the time we'd made it onto the interstate, the rest of our team was asleep in the back seats, snoring softly.

Olivia was chipper, though, happy to be awake and sipping coffee as the sun made its appearance over the mountains.

"I've been meaning to ask you something," I said softly, not wanting to wake the others.

"Oh yeah? What's that?" She was still looking out the window, enjoying the view, and it made me second-guess interrupting her happiness with what seemed to be a sore subject, but it had been lurking in the back of my mind ever since she'd mentioned it, and we still had several hours of driving ahead of us.

"What happened with your mom?"

She went still, then slowly set her coffee cup down in the cup holder. "Oh."

"Yeah, you mentioned something about her, but that wasn't a good time to discuss it. And it made me realize that I still don't know anything about your family or your home pack. But I'd like to, before we bond. I'd like to know everything about you eventually." I smiled over at her, and she returned it, but it didn't reach her eyes.

As I'd suspected, something was very wrong in Olivia's past to make her react that way.

"It's not a happy story, but you're right, you should know."

I hated how unhappy she sounded, but I didn't want to interrupt her. I needed to give her the space to share.

"I'm originally from Arizona. My parents weren't fated mates. My mom is an alpha—not the Canyon pack Alpha, but she was the pack's third—and my father is a nu, like me. Their pairing was... unusual, by a long stretch. But he's a kind man, and he worked for the pack Alpha, so they saw each other often. From what he told me, one thing led to another, and when she went into heat without a mate, for some reason, she picked him to spend it with. I was born a few months later, and they tried to make the relationship work for my sake. But my mother was unhappy. Her wolf wouldn't accept a weaker male, and she always had one foot out the door."

Olivia's voice grew distant as she told the story, as if she had left me and was back there in Arizona. "I was five when she found her fated mate. Another alpha, from a pack in Oklahoma."

She paused, and I tried to brace myself for what was coming. Whatever it was, it had clearly hurt her, but I had to listen and keep my feelings about it to myself, no matter how much I wanted to fly to Oklahoma and skin her mother for hurting my hellcat.

"It's okay. Take your time."

"Thanks, but there's not much left to the story, honestly. She fell madly in love with him and his power. He took one look at me and wanted nothing to do with a weak shifter pup from another male. So, she packed her things and left me with my father. Never looked back, or called, or wrote. It was just me and Dad for a very long time. He did his best to be mom and dad, but it was hard on him."

"I bet. I can't imagine raising a daughter completely alone. Did your pack mates help?"

She drummed her fingers on the windowsill, then caught herself and dropped her hand back into her lap. "Here and there. But when my gifts started appearing in my late teens... they wanted me gone. My dad was the only reason I stayed. It might not have been perfect, but he loved me more than anything."

"Loved?" My heart sank, and I braced myself for the news of his death.

"He still loves me. I shouldn't have said it that way. But after he met Tanya... well, I came second. That's how it is with fated mates. She wasn't thrilled he already had a child either, but she tried to hide it for both of our sakes. But it wasn't easy. Tanya was my mom's younger sister. And every time she looked at me, it reminded her that my father had been with her sister first."

"Holy shit." I bit my tongue, not having meant to let the expletive slip out. "Sorry, go on."

"It's okay. It's... shocking. The pack had a field day with it when the news first got out. Anyway, I was seventeen when they bonded, and as soon as I turned eighteen, I started studying herbalism. I knew that it was a useful skill that could get me into almost any pack, and the second I finished my course, I started looking for new packs. Johnson City needed a healer after Brielle left, and... well, you know what happened, after that." She shrugged like it was nothing.

But it wasn't nothing. It was a lifetime of pain and rejection from the people who were supposed to love you the most.

Suddenly, the fact that she was even still willing to be in the same vehicle as me after the way I'd treated her at first felt like a real, Goddess-blessed miracle.

"Did you ever talk to your father about how you felt?"

She shook her head, looking away again. "I couldn't bear to bring him more pain after how happy she made him. It was just... better for everyone, this way."

Selfless to a fault. It made me even more determined to protect her from those she couldn't protect herself from. "I'm sorry you went through all of that. But I can promise you one thing. I'm never going to send you away. You're mine. I meant it before when I said that once an alpha latches on to something he wants, he never lets go. And I want you, Olivia. With every fiber of my being. I choose you." I twined our fingers together on the console, lifting her knuckles to my lips and pressing a tender kiss there.

Her lower lip trembled, and I was tempted to pull the damn SUV over and drag her into my lap.

"But do you love me?"

The question floored me. Did I love her?

As crazy as it sounded, I was scared to even *think* yes, let alone say it. The last person I'd let myself love unequivocally had been brutally murdered and taken from me. Loving Olivia felt more terrifying than anything else I'd ever done in my life.

"It's okay. You don't have to say it," she whispered, turning her face away. Her sorrow filled the car, her scent turning dark and deep, a veritable ocean of pain.

And still, I said nothing.

It was like I couldn't get the words out, even as her silent tears carved the heart right out of my chest. I had to say something, *do something*, but how?

Admitting I loved her was like a giant, blinking sign to the universe to come and steal her out of my life.

"Olivia, I care about you more than anyone else in my life. It's not that I don't. You *know* I do."

"Please, don't. I don't want you to try to fix it, okay? It's all still new. I get that. I'm a grown-ass woman. I can handle the truth." She scrubbed at her cheeks, trying to erase the evidence of her pain, but even when her skin was once more dry and her eyes no longer glassy, I knew.

I knew I'd hurt her.

Knew it wasn't good enough. But if I tried to argue now, she wouldn't believe me.

Fucking hell.

We hit the dirt road a few minutes later, and our back seat passengers woke. They were quiet, probably sensing the tension in the front seat, and too polite to call us on it.

I wished one of them would call me on it. Help me work my way through the messed-up shit rattling around in my brain. Or maybe I just needed another big, angry alpha to spar with until I was so exhausted, I couldn't stand. So the walls could finally come down.

Gael was always down for a good session of torture by sparring ring, but unfortunately, he was a bit occupied at the moment.

And I had to get my head in the game. I tried to clear my thoughts, but by the time we reached the designated stopping point, I was no better off. It was an endless circle in my head of *can't hurt her, have to keep her safe*. And loving her wasn't safe.

We all piled out of the SUV, quiet as we hit the ground, already scenting the air and looking for enemies.

The breeze was untainted by strangers' scents, but that didn't mean all was clear just yet. We fanned out in pairs, and

Olivia and I went straight up the mountain toward the enclave. It was the most direct path, so if shit hit the fan, I could get her to safety more quickly.

Not that she wanted to be alone with me. And because we were scouting, we had to stay silent. Though it was probably for the best; I didn't have anything intelligent to say right now. I needed to explain why I'd hesitated. I knew that. But was giving her time to process considerate or cowardly?

The longer we walked, the more I leaned toward cowardly.

"I'm sorry," I whispered, not willing to risk more than that. She cut her eyes the other direction, clearly not even willing to *look* at me at the moment.

Frustration filled me. "Hellcat—"

She waved her hand down low, cutting me off, and my wolf went on high alert as she focused off into the distance, uphill from where we stood and a little to the right.

Movement. We're not alone.

FORTY-SEVEN

Olivia

Lucien grabbed me by the shoulders and pulled me behind him, gesturing for me to crouch down, stay hidden. I did as he asked, not wanting to distract him or draw unwanted attention to our position.

I wasn't sure what I'd seen up the hill—only a flash of dark blue, gone too quickly for me to process. Lucien was an alpha, though, with sharper senses. Hopefully, he'd sense that it was just one of the maidens, out for a midday stroll.

Surely that was all it was. We'd been gone from the enclave for weeks; anyone who would just sit around here and wait for that long needed to find something better to do with their lives.

Everything burst into motion at once. Gray wolves barreled down the hill toward us, weaving between the trees at top speed. Too many to count.

I held out hope for one second that they were friendly, and then their scents hit me like a tsunami. *Strangers!* my wolf shouted in my mind, clawing for freedom.

I let her have it, terrified as she burst from my skin. But Lucien was faster, and by the time my paws hit the ground, he'd already shifted and darted forward, meeting the intruders a dozen feet from me. Trying to protect me even now, when we were sorely outnumbered.

But there were too many of them, and he was *alone*. I was a terrible fighter, but the least I could do was guard one of his flanks so the wolves couldn't attack him from that side. Our allies were nearby; surely they'd hear the scuffle and come running to help any minute, or feel the attack through Lucien's pack bond. We just had to hang on until then.

With a plan in mind, my wolf charged forward, snarling and snapping at anyone who came too close to Lucien's flank. But as more and more wolves surrounded us and no help appeared on the horizon, they pressed in closer, their attacks more vicious with more pack mates behind them. One of them grabbed my back leg, snapping it between his teeth.

I couldn't hold back a howl of pain, and Lucien's wolf roared his fury as he turned and ripped out my attacker's throat.

Even though his lifeless jaws dropped from my leg, it was too late. My leg was broken, dangling uselessly. The break meant I could no longer dodge attacks effectively, and Lucien couldn't protect both of us from an entire pack alone. Where the hell was everyone else?

Howls lit up the woods in every direction, and that was the moment it sank in.

Help wasn't coming because *they were all fighting for their lives too*. We'd been ambushed by the Hungarian pack.

My movements were slow, and Lucien, Goddess, he fought for me like a wolf possessed by a thousand and one demons. More wolves fell between his teeth than I could count.

But I was drifting, pain and my injury slowing me down, and more and more gashes were ripped into my sides as Lucien slowly lost the war. My blood puddled beneath me, and my healer instincts kicked in.

This had to end before someone gutted me or ripped out

my throat. They were content to toy with and torture me now, but for how long? Lucien's wolf cut them down with startling ferocity, and eventually, they'd stop playing games.

Three short, sharp barks, and the wolves surrounding us fell back, forming up in a closed circle. There was no escape, but they weren't actively attacking.

I swayed on my feet, the blood loss really starting to get me. *Drip, drip, drip.*

My life force, draining away faster than my wolf could close the wounds, though she was trying. I needed to shift back to help the healing speed up, but as I stared out at the males circling us, I knew that was a bad idea.

So many of their eyes were on *me,* and it confused me. My thoughts floated slowly to the mark on my palm, and it suddenly made sense. That was why they'd been distracted enough for Lucien to take them out. My scent...

They didn't want me dead. They wanted me too weak to fight, and the realization was horrifying.

I whimpered, and Lucien pressed himself to my side, snarling defiantly at the males who would snatch me away from him. But before he could charge again, the circle parted.

Petró *Fucking* Varga himself, Alpha of the Hungarian wolves pack that he'd set on us like we were prey.

"What do we have here but a little escapee and... his latest piece of ass?" Varga turned, directing the question at the two men over his shoulder, also walking in human form. I didn't recognize them, but when Lucien saw them, he snarled, surging forward so fast, I nearly collapsed into the dirt from the loss of his support.

He realized that and came back, propping me up with his shoulder, even though he continued glaring at one of the two followers. One was tall, broad, and proud. The other was shorter, but, more than that, crueler. From his glare to the way he carried himself, hatred practically oozed from his pores.

338

"Nah, this fucker doesn't keep a bitch for more than four hours. He wears 'em out and lets 'em go. Apparently, they like it like that. Understandable these days, given..." The awful man pointed to his face, clearly mocking Lucien's scar, and that made *me* want to lunge, rip his throat out for daring to mock my mate.

Was this the man who'd tortured him?

I cocked my head and looked at Lucien, studying his lupine features, and thought it must be. His single-minded focus on the man was personal.

Even so, I wasn't expecting Lucien to shift back to human form, right there in the middle of all those enemies.

"This is just like you, Petró. Too cowardly to fight your own battles, so you send others to do it for you. Get a good look." He waved to his scar, turning his face from side to side so all gathered could see it. "This is what happens when Petró Varga lets his bastard brother get hold of you. Well, I say, if you're going to lead a pack, you need to be man enough to do your own dirty work."

Petró scoffed, but I saw the way he looked around at the gathered wolves, the way they all shuffled on their feet, ears perked up as they took in the accusation. "I do my own dirty work. You just weren't important enough to bother with."

Howls that felt like jeers went up all around us, and answering calls echoed eerily from all over the woods, reminding me of our pack mates fighting their own battles. *Goddess save us all.*

My vision was growing hazy around the edges, and I blinked rapidly to clear it. A few more minutes, and I wouldn't be able to hold my shift anymore. My injuries should all close up and stop the blood loss as soon as I was back in my skin, but then I'd be a naked invitation to any of these shifters.

Hang on, please hang on, I begged my wolf, and to her credit, she snarled and fought back against the exhaustion. She drew strength from Lucien's wolf, I was sure of it. Otherwise, I'd already be shifted to human and unconscious.

"I'm *so* glad to hear you say that," Lucien said with a vicious imitation of a smile. "Because I challenge you, Petró Varga, the Alpha of the Hungarian pack."

The clearing fell silent, every wolf attuned to the challenge.

Varga only had two choices, really. Accept the challenge and fight Lucien to the death, or step down and cede control of his father's pack to an outsider.

There was only one acceptable choice.

"I accept your challenge. And I will piss on your corpse and then fuck your sidepiece right next to it in the dirt when I'm done with you."

Lucien smiled a deadly smile that sent chills down my spine. "You can try."

Fear filled my heart as my limbs started to shake. I had to leave the circle before the fight started, but the second I did, I was going to lose my shift. I backed away from Varga and then stopped, realizing there was nowhere safe for me to go while Lucien was occupied.

The second I moved, though, he was there, holding me up. "It's going to be okay, Olivia. Once I win, I'm in control, and I can call off this attack. It's the only way. I won't let anything happen to you, I promise. Be strong for me, hellcat, okay?" he leaned down and whispered, my sensitive hearing picking up the promises easily in this form.

I whimpered as I dipped my muzzle in a nod, but I had to try.

Lucien straightened, turning back to the gathered wolves. "I want your personal guarantee that no matter the outcome of this fight, you'll protect my pack mate. This fight isn't for females, and she shouldn't suffer for being in the wrong place at the wrong time."

It stung to hear him call me his pack mate instead of his

mate, mate. But it was probably wise. If they knew what I was to him… they wouldn't take it easier on me. To my surprise, it wasn't Varga who answered. It was the taller man behind him.

"I swear on my honor that no further harm shall come to this female by the hands of my pack this day. And on my honor as second of the Hungarian Pack, there will be no interference." The man nodded gravely, then waved me over. The wolves between us stepped aside, clearly accepting his word as law too, which meant he had to be well respected by his pack.

Lucien picked me up carefully and carried me to the man's side, kissing the top of my muzzle before setting me down, turning back, and stepping into the ring of bloodthirsty shifters.

He was bruised and scraped and bloody, but even naked and wounded, he held himself proudly, like the Lucien I met the first time, who had the whole world in the palm of his hand.

The man at my side watched me with a frown, instead of the fight. He squatted at my side, making it easier for me to take in his dark, handsome features up close. He was a stunning alpha, but I felt no attraction. "My name is Valens, little female. Are you close to your heat? Your scent… It will be a struggle to keep the others away from you, but I have given my word. I will guard you as I guard my own sister."

I shook my head no, the best I could manage, and tucked his name away for later. I wanted to ask Lucien why he trusted this stranger, though it seemed he'd made the best choice available.

Petró had already shucked off most of his clothing. Lucien stood with his arms crossed, staring at his torturer.

He pointed at the cruel man, a deadly promise in his eyes. "You're next after I take out your piss-poor Alpha."

I scented the fury rolling off the other male, and resisted the urge to cower away. Only the fact that it hurt to breathe, let alone move, kept me still. Doing my best to ignore it all, I focused on Lucien, willing him to win with every last scrap of rapidly waning energy in my body.

The two males in the center of the ring shifted, and the last sight I saw as my own shift overtook me was Lucien barreling into Petró, taking him down to the ground.

FORTY-EIGHT

Lucien

———

My focus should have been single-minded as I barreled into Varga, but I couldn't stop fantasizing about ripping Dominik limb from limb. The fucker who ruined my life was *right there*, and I was going to get my revenge if it killed me.

Petró rolled underneath me, scrambling to get away now that I'd gone in broadside and taken him unaware.

He succeeded, but not before I managed to tear into his shoulder, leaving a gaping wound that should start to slow him down.

A smarter wolf might have been worried; he was fresh as a daisy after letting his lackeys wear me down. But I wasn't. Pure hatred flowed through my veins, and neither my wolf nor I felt the least bit tired.

Worried about Olivia, yes, but I couldn't let my brain go there in the middle of the battle. I needed to end this threat, then the next one in Dominik, and then get her to Brielle. That was it, that was the best I could do. After that, I had to hope that word spread quickly through their pack bond that this shit stain of a shifter was dead, and they all ran with their tails between their legs.

Petró spun and leapt at my flank, and I had to stop thinking and fight. He was a better fighter than I gave him credit for, and for several minutes, we circled and traded blows, a swipe with claws here, a tearing bite there. But eventually, he started to show his lack of stamina in small ways. Missing opportunities to attack because he was still recovering from the last blow. Choosing to walk instead of run.

He was flagging. Petró didn't have the burning need for revenge in him that I did, and it showed. I executed a series of feints, slipping past his defenses and landing a crushing bite to his tail.

It wasn't deadly, but it *was* horribly painful and degrading to an alpha. A broken tail was a sign that he was too weak to defend himself, that his *pride* had been insulted. That made him angry, and I knew I'd hit the mark.

A tired, insulted shifter wouldn't think logically. He was out for blood, and that would give me my opening to end it.

He charged me head-on, jaws wide as he went for my throat. But I saw it coming a mile away and dove down, twisting my body as I skidded beneath him. He soared over me harmlessly, but I didn't miss.

I clamped on to his bottom jaw, my momentum snapping it as I dragged it with me in the opposite direction. His howl of pain rang through the forest, and I knew I had won.

I leapt on his back, biting for his spinal cord as I bore him down to the ground beneath me. I paused, teeth primed for the kill as one of his more loyal pack mates dove toward me in a lawless, last-ditch effort to save his Alpha.

He never made it to me.

Petró's second, Valens, dove over the circle of wolves, collaring the imbecile and dragging him back out of the ring.

Petró Varga's life ended as he deserved: defeated and in the dirt.

Not a wolf dared howl to mourn his passing as they looked on, watching me shake their leader into the afterlife like a rag doll.

I was tempted to piss on his body as he had threatened to do to me, but I didn't want to stoop to his level. It had been a clean fight, and he'd lost. The driving force behind all these attacks was gone, and there was only one threat remaining.

I looked up, the red haze of battle still clouding my vision as I searched for Dominik. But he wasn't where I left him.

For one second, I thought the coward had run. But when I spotted him, the reality was much, much worse.

A naked, human Olivia was in his arms, her back pressed against his chest, his claw-tipped hand clamped over her mouth to keep her from screaming out and getting my attention.

Valens stood furiously a few feet away, eyes glowing with rage at his own pack mate.

"Put the girl down, Dominik," he barked, but Petró's bastard cousin didn't flinch. The sick son of a bitch grinned.

"I don't think I will, Valens. You see, the second I put this little hottie down, he's going to charge me and rip my throat out like he did my cousin. And while you stand on honor, I don't. In my world, winning is staying alive."

I shifted effortlessly, and once again, I stood as a man. "Your hands are on my mate, Dominik. If what you'd already done wasn't enough, this alone would seal your death warrant. Put her down unharmed, or I'll make what you did to me look like a baby's first art project."

He laughed, head thrown back and shoulders shaking. His gaze was demented when it met mine again. "You really haven't figured it out, have you?" He shook his head. "You'll never be like me, Lucien. Your threats are just petty tantrums. Mine? They're real."

I watched in slow motion as his other clawed hand came to Olivia's throat, resting just above her breastbone. As she struggled weakly, all five claws sank into her pale, perfect skin and ripped straight down to her navel. I was moving, my body and brain disconnected by the horror as she fell, her blood running like a river that I knew was too much.

I dove to catch her head and shoulders, Dominik forgotten as I cradled my mate in my arms. Her eyes were wide with shock, her soft red hair a halo around her rapidly paling face.

"Olivia, no," I sobbed, tears falling freely as her lips began to turn blue. "Don't leave me, please!" I brushed my thumbs over her cheekbones as I begged, a man in torment. Glancing down at her wounds only confirmed what I didn't want to know in my chest. There was no surviving it, not even for a wolf. She was going to die in my arms, and I didn't have her skills to stop it.

When it really mattered, I was completely, utterly helpless.

Her cold, shaking hand pressed against my cheek, and I cupped it, savoring every last moment even as my wolf demanded that I do *something, anything.*

She knew. The look in her eyes was acceptance, not fear. She wet her lips with her tongue, tried and failed to speak.

I leaned down, closer, so I could hear whatever she was trying to say.

"I'm... sorry. I wanted to be yours. More than anything, I wanted to be yours." My heart shattered into a million pieces. Her dying words. *She wanted to be mine.*

Her hand fell from my cheek, and something feral and wild came over me, something uncontrollable. I didn't want her to die. I *couldn't let her* slip away. She *was* mine, and I was nothing without her light, nothing but darkness and pain. And if she was going to die, I was going to go with her into the afterlife. Without her light, my life meant nothing.

I held her to my lips and sank my teeth into her throat, right where she'd wanted.

Her pulse was weak, her heart barely stuttering, but I held on for us both.

Take me instead! I demanded, taunting the Goddess herself. It was enough.

The moment our bond snapped partially into place, Olivia's pain radiated through my body, and I fell at her side, still cradling her to my chest.

"I'm so sorry, hellcat." The words were nothing but a rasp of pain as the cold she felt sucked me under with her. "You deserved so much better. And I'm sorry. I love you."

Her blood bathed me as the light faded around us.

I leaned into the abyss, arms wide open as I welcomed the end.

FORTY-NINE

Olivia

Something was very, very wrong. Everything had faded, my body had gone cold and numb, and I knew it was shutting down. The wounds were too grave for my brain to process the pain, so it shut off. Protecting me at the end, a simple mercy of biology.

Lucien had told me he loved me, finally, and then everything had gone cold. But someone was *burning me*. My neck felt like someone held a torch to it, and I just wanted it to end.

I thought dying would be less painful, not more. But the burn only increased, and I tried to scream, but no sound came out. Desperate, I clawed the ground, longing for the cool earth to stop it.

Help me! I cried out, and Mother Earth answered my call.

Cool, green, and lovely, the plants around me answered my call. The burn in my neck wasn't extinguished, but I felt myself being wrapped in light, in power, in peace.

And sleep overtook me.

FIFTY

Lucien

M y eyes cracked open, and the world was green. Or rather, the *afterlife* was green. Right?

I tried to sit up and couldn't. *Olivia*.

She was still in my arms, our bodies sticky with blood, and horror filled me. Had I not died with her? That wasn't possible. I'd bitten her while her heart still beat. I'd *felt* the bond.

Panicked, my eyes flew up, and that was when I saw it.

A bower of flowers, vines, and stems interwoven around us like a living funeral pyre. Between it all, a thick green glow, her power pulsating with life as it cocooned us.

"Olivia? Hellcat, can you hear me?" I fumbled as I felt for her pulse, and nearly wept when I felt it. It was faint, but steady.

We were alive.

I'd bitten her, and somehow, we were alive.

I wept as I held her, unashamed of my tears. I would never be anything but grateful for any moment this woman spent in my arms, ever again.

She was my personal miracle, my light, my everything.

"Lucien?" My name was slurred on her lips, and still it was the best sound I'd ever heard in my whole, long, miserable life.

"I'm here, my love. I'm here."

"My neck hurts."

That was not what I expected her to say, and suddenly, I was very, very aware that I'd bonded us—partially—without her consent.

"I-I bit you."

"You what?" Her shock was genuine, and I soldiered on.

"You were dying. Your heart was barely beating, and I didn't want to go on without you. So I bit you so we'd be bonded, and I could go with you into the afterlife. I'm sorry. I know you should have consented, but I couldn't— I just couldn't let you go."

Her fingertips brushed my cheek, settled over my lips. "It's okay. I couldn't bear to live without you either. You love me? Truly?"

"More than I've ever loved anyone." It was a terrifying truth.

I loved and missed my sister, my sweet Lilliana. Her face was a distant memory now, after all these years, but still I loved her.

But Olivia... She held the other half of my soul. And every day I spent with her, I became a better man. And I loved her dearly, even if I'd lied to myself before.

It hadn't saved her.

Pretending she wasn't my everything *hadn't saved her*. She had saved us both. With her own beautiful, gentle power.

I closed my eyes and held her close, thanking the Goddess and every star in the sky that my mate was a quiet badass and I got another chance with her that I didn't deserve.

"OLIVIA!" A panicked voice startled us sometime later. "Oh my Goddess. How long has she been in there?" Elodie, on closer inspection.

"A while." *Valens.*

"Can you hear me?"

"Yes," I called back, trying not to disturb Olivia, who was sleeping on my chest. She stirred anyway, blinking up at me sleepily.

"Holy shit, they're both in there? Why are you all just standing here!"

Their voices got farther away, too far to hear the conversation, and then Elodie returned a few minutes later. "Are you guys okay? What happened, and can you come out? Things are... weird out here."

I looked down at Olivia. "I don't know if you're healed enough to come out yet. Are you?"

She frowned, considering. "I feel tired, but I think all my external wounds are gone? She lifted herself up with shaky limbs, and to my amazement, every mark she'd had before was gone, her skin healed cleanly.

"Can you let the power go safely? Or should we wait for Brielle?" I didn't give a fuck what was happening outside our cocoon, as long as Olivia was safe.

"I think I just need clothes. And a nap. And food. I'm *starving.*" Her stomach rumbled, and I chuckled.

"You need energy after all that wound repair."

"Probably, yes." She blushed pink, finally realizing that we were both fully naked and pressed together like sardines.

"Hello? Did you pass out again?" The sound of leaves rustling reached us, and Elodie yelped as if something had zapped her.

"Hang on," Olivia called, and then wrinkled her nose as she concentrated. The flowery bower covering us peeled back, and the green web of light slowly faded back into the earth, the calm, cool sensation I'd felt inside it leaving, replaced with the scent of blood and strange wolves.

Although... they didn't *feel* as strange anymore. Something to figure out later, after I'd taken care of my mate.

Elodie's face appeared overhead, and her eyes went wide as she took in the mess the two of us were in. Blood, tacky and crusted, from my many attackers, covered my body, and Olivia was no better off.

"Thank fuck," Elodie muttered, leaning down a hand and helping Olivia off me. A moment later, she extended a hand down for me, and I took it—after what I'd just been through, I wasn't too proud.

The moment I was upright, I nearly fell back down.

More than a hundred naked shifters knelt in a perfect circle all around us. At the front of them all, Valens had his knee on Dominik's neck.

"What happened?" I asked Elodie, who stared at them all as if they were a sideshow spectacle and not a threat.

"You tell me. Samuel and I were fighting our asses off, when they all froze and started running this direction. We knew something was up, so we followed. We found... this." She gestured back into the woods, where the Hungarian males all waited, kneeling.

"Alpha Vasilescu, if I may?" Valens asked, though he didn't rise or let his gaze wander above my chest.

He was a powerful alpha in his own right, most likely the new leader of the Hungarians, assuming they accepted him after I killed Dominik for what he'd done to Olivia.

"Yes, but don't let him go. We have unfinished business." My wolf's growl lined the last word, his own desire to finish the one who'd dared harm our mate simmering close to the surface.

"We kneel in honor of our new Alpha."

I blinked, waiting for more. I glanced over at first Olivia, then Elodie, and Samuel, but they all seemed as confused as I was.

"Who is your new Alpha?" I asked.

"You, sire. You defeated Petró Varga in a fair fight. By pack law, you are the new Alpha of the Hungarian pack. We kneel at your command."

Well, fuck me sideways and call it a love story.

I'd assumed when Petró died, they'd all run. I did *not* consider the consequences of becoming accidental Alpha to a pack of bloodthirsty strangers.

I finally looked out over the sea of waiting shifters, mind reeling as I tried to figure out what to do now. Before I could, though, Kane, Dirge, and a fuck ton of warrior maidens with their butterfly swords in hand swarmed into the woods, surrounding us.

Kane strode through the men, and they all flinched back as his unchecked dominance steamrolled over them, pressing them farther down as he walked past.

He stepped up to my side, blanching slightly at the amount of blood covering both Olivia and me, but he covered it quickly.

"Did I just hear what I think I heard?" he murmured, the question only for me.

"Yes, High Alpha. I don't know what to do. I have no idea how to be a pack Alpha."

Kane snorted, giving me an incredulous look. "No one does on their first day. You just do it, and over time, you get better."

"You're saying I should *accept*?" There was no way. We had too much work to do; I couldn't step aside from the pack—taking Olivia with me—in the middle of what was about to be a war.

"I'm saying you already are the Alpha. Do you see the way they waited for you, even when you were on the ground? That is respect. If a hated Alpha falls low, a stronger one comes behind to replace him. When you were laid low, they waited for you. They need a good, honest leader. We both know Petró is not that. Look out, look at their faces. They didn't want this battle. They fought for loyalty, and that doesn't make them bad men."

I did as he suggested, studying face after face. I saw defeat, regret, and shame. Over and over again. Felt it in my chest, actually, echoing through... a new pack bond.

"Did I get kicked out of Pack Blackwater?" I asked, dismayed.

Kane snorted. "Only temporarily. When you became Alpha of a new pack, your own pack bond snapped into place. Once you reswear your fealty to me, our bond will reconnect seamlessly." He patted me on the back as if we were old buddies talking about the latest rugby game, not the fate of an entire pack.

"I'm not sure I can do it. Olivia's safety is the most important thing." I glanced over his shoulder at my beautiful mate, not liking how pale she was, leaning against Elodie's shoulder.

"I can't force you to take the pack. But I will say this—I could use a strong ally at my back instead of another enemy at my gates. Given the circumstances, I'm sure we could get a pair of maidens assigned specifically to Olivia, at least until you felt comfortable with your pack power structure and knew and trusted everyone. And I wouldn't be surprised if a few of our other pack mates would be happy to come along and help you rebuild."

I looked over again at the women, and Elodie rolled her eyes. "I volunteer. Obviously." She grinned down at Olivia, giving her a squeeze around the shoulders. "Besties have to stick together."

"Okay. I'll do it. There's a war coming, and we'd be stupid to throw away a whole pack's worth of potential allies."

"Good man. How do you want to deal with the cousin?" He eyed the sniveling mess under Valens's knee.

"I don't want to deal with him at all. I want him dead."

Kane nodded, agreeing. "So give the order, Alpha. Take control of your pack."

I stalked forward, stopping just a few feet away from Valens and Dominik, who'd pissed himself like a puppy.

"Valens, will you accept the position as my second?"

"Yes, Alpha Vasilescu." He bowed low, the movement graceful despite his awkward hold on the other male.

"You let me escape when he had been torturing me under your previous Alpha's orders. Why?"

It had taken me a moment to place him, but I remembered now. I'd seen him in the Jeep's rearview mirror, holding back the other shifter who wanted to chase us down.

"Torture isn't honorable, sir. It was wrong, what they did to you." This time, he let his gaze rise to my face.

As I sensed, he was an honorable male. The kind I'd want to have my back. "Then stand him up. He nearly killed my mate, and no one who harms a hair on her head gets to live to see tomorrow."

"You'll regret it!" Dominik gasped as Valens's knee was removed from his neck, and he was dragged to his feet. "We were just pawns. You'll see! This isn't the end, and you're all going to die. You'll never stop what's coming for you now!"

I ripped Dominik's throat out, his screams reduced to gurgles, and then, blessed silence.

It was finally over.

FIFTY-ONE

Olivia

T*hree weeks later*

REBUILDING A SAD, broken pack was no easy feat even in the best of circumstances. It felt like no time at all and also an eternity since Lucien had become the new Alpha of the Hungarian pack, and every single day was fraught with new difficulties. Petró Varga and his father had been terrible leaders. They hadn't cared about their people, and it showed in every facet of the pack's life.

We'd been staying in their pack mansion, since that was what was available, and every single day, it just grossed me out a little more. Their pack lived in poverty while the Vargas had lorded insane wealth over them. It made me furious, but at least things were starting to slowly work toward equilibrium with Lucien at the helm. In time, we would build these wolves into a happy, healthy pack.

Tonight, though, wasn't about the pack. Tonight was the full moon, and it was about Lucien and me finally completing our mate bond before the Goddess and our friends.

We were gathering soon. Our closest pack mates, maidens, and a few top members of the new Hungarian pack had been invited.

Right this minute, Elodie and Fiona were putting the finishing touches on my hair in the beautiful bridal suite in Hungary, near the pack's mating grounds.

"I think it looks good," Elodie said, shooting me a smile. She wore her formal maiden's robes, the ones that made her look like a Greek goddess.

"Good isn't what we're after for a bonding ceremony. We're after 'make him mad anyone else even gets to *look* at her because she's so fuckable.'" Fiona shot me a naughty wink.

Elodie snorted. "I don't think that's a word."

Fiona grinned. "It is when your mate is an insatiable wolf shifter with zero refractory period. Trust me, he's fuckable. And with one more little zhuzh—so is our sweet Olivia." She pushed a small, white ranunculus bloom into my updo, and nodded. "Perfection. If he doesn't swallow his tongue, I don't know a damn thing about what an alpha wants."

I laughed, because what else could I do?

They'd done an excellent job prepping me for the night, and when I walked out to see the rest of the Blackwater pack females there, I nearly burst into tears and ruined all their efforts.

Brielle, Shay, and Leigh waited just outside the doors, and they passed me between them for hugs and congratulations. I wasn't sure they'd be able to sneak away from the Maiden's Enclave for this, and the fact that they'd traveled all the way to *my* new pack lands to be here... well, it was the cherry on top of the perfect evening plans. I could even sense the very, very heavy shielding spell Brielle had used to mask her travels for the occasion.

By the time we were done, the moon hung in position overhead, and it was time. But I had one more question before I walked down the aisle.

"Any luck on getting the stone back together?" I asked Brielle in a hushed whisper, even though there was no one else in sight. We couldn't be too careful since we were still getting to know who we could trust.

Her expression told me everything before she even answered. "No. We're missing something, I just know it. But don't worry about that tonight. It's been a long few weeks for all of us, and tonight, we're celebrating. Let it all go and just focus on you and your mate."

"You're right. I was just hoping... I guess I was hoping for good news."

She sighed. "I know, and I love that you care so much. I know we're going to figure it out. The Goddess wouldn't give us such a great gift and then not make a way for us to use it."

Her face grew desolate, but she quickly covered it with a smile. I knew that meant bad news. They'd been looking into the pack records, digging for proof of what Dominik had claimed, that the Hungarian pack were just pawns in a larger game. I hadn't heard any definitive answer yet on who was pulling the strings, but it didn't look good.

I decided not to ask, not tonight.

Tonight was about love.

I blew out a breath and accepted my bouquet from Shay. I'd grown the flowers myself and shaped them into a bouquet using my powers. They were actually all still alive, and I was going to plant them in my little garden tomorrow, a permanent reminder of this night, behind our new home.

"One last thing," Brielle said, pausing, her gaze roaming down my body as if she were inspecting the dress. "Show me your feet."

"Uh, what?" I asked, but picked up the hem of my dress

anyway and stuck out my foot. I wore simple ballet slippers, the green ribbon matching the dress.

"Knew it! Take 'em off. It's pack tradition. You have to be barefoot, something about better access to the earth's magic."

"I'm not sure I can get back down there with my dress zipped. Elodie had to help me tie them on."

"I'm not getting down there, that's for sure." Leigh grinned at me and rubbed her *very* pregnant belly. "I might pop."

"Hush, now. My niece isn't ready to come out for a little while yet." Bri shot her a look and dropped down to help Elodie untie my slippers so I could slip them off. "There. Now you're absolutely perfect."

"You three better go get in your seats. The Hungarians were *not* playing about getting there early."

Shay growled, eyes narrowing as visible white light buzzed up her forearms. The three of them turned and hustled away, leaving us to come more slowly.

"My money's on Shay and the pregnant wolf," Fiona quipped, looping her arm with mine. Elodie did the same on the other side, and the three of us walked down the path after the others.

The Hungarian pack's mating grounds were beautiful, surrounded by flowering cherry plums. They wouldn't normally be blooming this time of year, but I'd snuck down here earlier today to give them a little encouragement.

Tonight, they were dripping with twinkle lights, lighting the pink blooms beautifully. I could just barely see them from the head of the path, and already, my heart was overflowing.

"This is where we leave you, chickadee," Fiona said, squeezing the breath out of me with a hug. "We'll see you by the flower mound."

"See you soon," I murmured, a sudden flight of butterflies taking wing in my stomach. And then they were gone, walking down the aisle with their ceremonial items.

A few moments that felt like an eternity later, I heard the music that was my cue to head down the aisle.

Touching Lucien's mark at the base of my throat to steady myself, I took my first step toward the rest of my life.

FIFTY-TWO

Lucien

I was completely fine until I saw Elodie and Fiona walking down the aisle toward where I stood on the ceremonial flower mound. I glanced over at Kane, who just grinned at me as if I was a lovesick fool.

To be fair, I was. And I was willing to tell anyone who asked how much I loved the woman about to walk down the aisle to finally seal our bond.

The last two weeks had been torture. I wanted to complete our bond the second she felt well enough, but she wanted to wait for the full moon.

I couldn't deny her anything she wanted, and if that was a traditional bonding, well, it was hers. So we'd done it up big, and I think it ended up being a good thing. The pack females were really into it, and it seemed to have helped everyone rally around us as their new Alpha pair.

That was still strange, but I was dealing. Having Valens's support had been a big help. He was sitting in the front row, next to his little sister, Vee. She was the one exception to the rule about everyone rallying around us. She'd been sullen and avoidant, and Olivia and I had both given her space.

Petró had been her fiancé. I couldn't blame her for being mad at the man who'd killed him and taken his place.

But then I caught my first glimpse of Olivia, and all thoughts of pack politics flew out of my head as if they'd never been there.

She was the most beautiful creature I'd ever laid eyes on, bar none. Her red hair was swept up off her neck in a graceful twist, dotted with little white flowers. The dress she wore was green, just like her magic, and it fit her beautifully. The off-the-shoulder top dipped dangerously low, displaying more than a hint of her creamy breasts, cinching in at her waist, and then flaring out into a large, sparkling green skirt that skimmed over the flower petal walkway. Every step she took, a hint of bare thigh flashed at me from between the flowing layers of her skirt, making me want to growl at every other male in attendance for daring to look at her beauty.

But her smile? Her smile alone was radiant enough to steal the show.

Stunning didn't begin to describe her, and I wanted every single detail etched into my brain for the rest of my life. I would never forget the way she looked at me right now.

She made good time up the walkway, but still, I was impatient.

This was the first day we'd been apart since her accident, and missing her was a constant itch under my skin. I needed her presence on a visceral level, and when I broke tradition and closed the distance between us, she just smiled, opening her arms for me. When I scooped her up and carried her the rest of the way, her heavy gown draped over my arm, she kissed me on the cheek and rested her head on my shoulder.

Mine.

The claim was a happy thrum in my chest, my wolf's contentment that we were finally getting to bond undeniable. I hadn't had another scar attack since I'd bitten her, and I knew my connection with my wolf had healed significantly since I stopped fighting the truth.

Olivia and I belonged together.

I hoped tonight, when we sealed the bond, we could also put the issues with my wolf behind us permanently.

Kane cleared his throat, reminding me I needed to set her back on her feet so the ceremony could continue. Reluctantly, I did. But I didn't let go of her hands.

The small connection helped center me, kept me in the moment as the ceremony began.

Reed stepped up first with a single sheet of paper. Normally, he'd just lay it at our feet and say the ceremonial blessing. He paused, though, for a moment, holding it up so we could see it. *The deed to a hundred-hectare nature preserve, right here in Hungary.* "For prosperity," he said, before squeezing my shoulder.

It was perfect for Olivia, with her mágissa talents. Untouched, raw nature, whenever she needed it.

Next was Fiona's turn.

"For fertility," she said, dropping to her knees between us and sprinkling scented water from a jar on our bare feet and ankles. Fiona rose gracefully, then dropped a kiss on Olivia's cheek before resuming her proud stance behind her.

Elodie came next, grinning from ear to ear. "For passion." I couldn't hear what she whispered to Olivia as she dabbed the lovelace aphrodisiac perfume behind her ears, but it sent a delicious blush crawling up her neck that I wanted to trace with my lips.

Kane was the last one, holding our rings. He pressed the larger of the pair into Olivia's hand and then her daintier band into mine. "For eternity."

My hand shook as I held it up for Olivia to slide the band on my finger. Hers were rock steady as I slid her own diamond ring into place. I leaned forward and kissed her knuckle below the ring, and I knew my wolf shone through my eyes as I looked up at her.

"Mine." It was a promise, and when she shuddered, the heat in her gaze lit the same fire in me. This ceremony needed to end, and fast. I needed to wear my female's bite. No more waiting.

Kane almost looked apologetic as he spoke again, interrupting the intense moment. "It's customary for the male to offer a gift to his mate, to prove that he can protect and provide for her. But more than that, that he *cares* for her. Lucien, are you prepared to offer Olivia a mating gift to show you're worthy of her love?"

I nodded, rocking back on my heels as nerves hit me square in the jaw for the first time since I'd seen her. What if she didn't like it? I'd been working on it every spare minute since we'd arrived at our new pack lands. I blew out a breath, knowing I needed to just get it out.

"I'd like to take you there and show you, if that's okay?"

"Of course." She smiled, looking confused.

"I promise it'll be worth it."

She nodded, and we both turned to Kane, waiting for his blessing.

"Okay, then. If you accept, there's only one thing left. Lucien and Olivia, we gather here under the Goddess's moon to bind you two together as mates. It is a lifelong bond, unbreakable, even in death."

Olivia squeezed my fingers when he said that part. We both knew that death wasn't strong enough to break us. I lifted her hand, pressing it to my face and holding it there, needing more of her.

"The bond between mates is completed with a bite. It is customary for this to be done privately and must be completed before the moon sinks from the night sky. In the eyes of the

Goddess and these witnesses, I bless this joining. Go forth and claim your mate."

I had her off her feet and in my arms before the small crowd even thought to cheer, and within a second, their cheers turned to laughter as I spun in a circle for the sheer joy of it.

She was mine, finally.

FIFTY-THREE

Olivia

Lucien carried me past the small group of witnesses for our bonding ceremony, and I couldn't stop grinning. I'd never been so happy, even though I *was* curious what gift he'd picked for me that he couldn't bring to the ceremony.

Right now, it didn't matter. We were bonded, and all that was left was for me to give him his bite. I was so ready. The emotions I'd been picking up from him had only grown stronger since he'd bitten me, and I had a feeling that as soon as I bit him, we'd get our mental connection.

That was the only gift I wanted, truly.

To my surprise, he carried me right through the center of the pack lands, away from the beautiful flowering trees, and... away from the bonding house.

"Where are we going?" I finally asked as he carried me straight through the center of our pack's housing and out into the forest again.

He didn't answer right away, but just as I began to see lights in the forest, he said, "Our new home."

I gasped as it came into sight, and tears sprang to my eyes as I took it all in.

It was the perfect little cottage, made of stone, with happy little windows to look out over the giant, empty garden beds waiting for me to fill them on either side of the front door.

"Do you like it?"

I was surprised to hear the worry in his tone, because this... was more than I'd dared dream of. I glanced up, holding his face between my hands and looking him right in the eye so he'd know I meant it. "It's absolutely perfect. I love it. And I love you."

He pressed a kiss to my lips that was tender and sweet, but it just stoked my desire for more. I needed him, right now. No more waiting, no more separation. I made an impatient sound in the back of my throat, and that was all the permission he needed.

Lucien carried me over the threshold, right as it started to rain, the gentle droplets kissing my skin like a benediction from the Goddess herself.

I didn't pull back from the kiss as he carried me to our new bedroom. When he sat me down on the edge of the bed, I finally looked around. It was perfect. Honey-colored wood flooring, floor-to-ceiling windows, and a sliding glass door that looked out into a massive, freshly planted garden. There was even a little gazebo in the back that I couldn't wait to spend my afternoons reading in. Surrounding it all was a high stone wall that matched the house, giving us privacy and space from our new duties.

"I don't know how you knew, but this is... exactly what we needed."

He climbed on the bed behind me, wrapping me in his arms, and I relished the feeling of safety and joy and love it gave me, being there in his arms. Surrounded. Protected. Cherished.

With Lucien, I was all of those things. But the need

pounding through my veins wouldn't be denied, and I turned in his arms.

"Luce?"

"Hmm," he murmured, a contented rumble in his chest making me shudder.

"This is beautiful, and I'm so grateful for all the thought and work you put into making this place amazing for us, but..." I felt the blush creeping up my neck, and he arched an eyebrow.

"Use your words, hellcat. What do you need?"

"I need you to fuck me. Right now. Or I'm going to explode out of my skin."

He growled, the sound rumbling through our bodies everywhere they touched and lighting up every nerve in my body.

"Careful, now." He threaded his fingers in my hair, pulling my head back and baring my neck for his hungry gaze. "If you keep talking like that, you might get more than you bargained for."

Breathless, I looked him in the eye, drawing on all my courage, all my desire. "Good."

His eyes burned as his hands skimmed over the bare skin left exposed by my dress, his hands reaching the zipper and tearing.

The fabric gave way like tissue paper under his strength, and I felt cool air on my exposed backside, down the tops of my thighs.

"Off," he demanded, urging the already-low straps down, baring my breasts to the chilly air. They weren't cold for long, because his mouth was on me as he pressed me back into the bed, worshipping my breasts with finesse with his lips and tongue. His hands made quick work of my dress, leaving me bare for his attention.

He didn't waste time, his fingers going to my aching core, and, finding me dripping and needy, he plunged two fingers in, curling them up to my G-spot as I adjusted to the sudden intrusion. And what a glorious intrusion it was, making me arch and bow under the force of pleasure flooding through my veins. He drove into me hard and fast, urged on by my cries of pleasure. But when his eyes began to glow and his fangs descended, everything changed. Intensified.

He dropped his teeth to my neck, grazing those wicked fangs over my bite, and I erupted. Pleasure burned me up, coursing through me with more force than I'd ever experienced as I pulsed around his fingers, thighs shaking as I held on to his shoulders for dear life.

"What a good little mate." The words were a deep rumble, his wolf's eyes still glowing as he moved over me, pulling me up to my knees so he could plunge into my mouth, claiming me even as his fangs prickled my lower lip.

The taste of copper tinged the kiss, and my own wolf rose hungrily to the surface. Everything sharpened as he devoured me, the urge to sink my fangs into him nearly overwhelming.

"I need—" I broke the kiss on a gasp, the burning need demanding to be sated.

"What do you need, little mate? It's yours."

"I need the bite. Where—" It was all I could get out, my fangs making it difficult to speak, to think beyond *bite, bite, bite!*

His lips twisted into a devilish grin. He enjoyed driving me wild.

Shuffling back a step where he knelt, he held his arms out wide. "Anywhere you want, hellcat. I'm yours. Use me."

Fuck.

I pounced, and he let me press him back into the soft comforter. It was a heady feeling, dominating this powerful alpha. He could have fought me off, but he didn't, letting me straddle his waist and press his powerful hands into the bed above him.

His pecs were flexed in this position, and my eyes were drawn there, just below his throat.

I surprised myself with the speed at which I sank my fangs into his chest, grinding my pussy down over his muscular belly, chasing *more* even as the bond barreled into me, lighting me up inside and out. He groaned, throwing his head back against the mattress as his hands went to my waist, grip tight as he lost himself to me.

Satisfied that I'd left my mark, I pulled back, licking over the bite to seal it. The coppery tang of his blood was on my tongue when I kissed him, feral, wanting more as a river of emotion opened in my chest, flowing his pleasure back into me, as mine fed his.

It was overwhelming and beautiful, and as the glowing bond filled me, I became a creature of light, every inch of me sparkling with love and wanting.

"Lucien," I panted, bracing my hands on his chest. "I feel... everything. Your love, the way you feel right now, the *caring*." My voice broke, the emotion too much for words.

"You're my everything. And now you never have to doubt it again." He placed his hand over my mark, his features softened by his grin of satisfaction as the bond settled between us. After all the trouble it took us to get here, it felt like coming home.

Can you... Can you hear me? I thought the question, wondering.

Fuck yes, I can.

His words were a low rumble in my mind, just as sexy as his spoken voice, and I moaned, grinding against him as my core reminded me that I still needed him. Very, very much.

More, I demanded in our bond, and he arched an eyebrow at me.

Ready for me to take over already?

Please? I trailed my fingertips over his chest, enjoying his warmth, his strength.

Fuck, you beg so pretty. How could I say no?

He flipped our positions in an instant, surprising me as he pulled me onto my hands and knees. But he didn't stop there, moving my hands to grip the top of the headboard.

Hold on tight, little mate. We're about to set a record.

A record?

How many orgasms one shifter can have in a single night.

He gripped my hips and plunged inside, sheathing himself to the hilt in a single stroke. Over and over, he stroked into me, bringing the lava flow of bliss right back to the surface. He snaked one hand down from my hip, never breaking his rhythm as he played with my clit, igniting me within seconds.

I screamed out my pleasure as he worked, driving me over the edge with ruthless persistence, over and over again until I lost count.

When I could take no more, I begged for mercy.

Too much. I'm going to explode.

He wrapped a hand around my throat, pulling me up from where I still gripped the bedframe. One hand held my back to his chest by my throat; the other reached down, playing with the hood of my oversensitive clit.

Last one for now, little mate. I know you've got one more for me. Come. Now.

My vision warped with stars as I exploded in his arms, clamping down on his cock as he shouted his own release, following me over the edge.

He held me until my breathing returned to normal, gently lowering my boneless body back to the bed, peppering every inch of me with kisses before carefully cleaning me up and wrapping me up in the covers, my head pillowed on his bicep, my back against his chest.

Sweet dreams, my perfect mate.

I drifted off, dreaming of him. And they were very sweet dreams, indeed.

Epilogue

Elodie

The after-party for Olivia and Lucien's bonding ceremony was wilder than we were used to at the enclave. The Hungarians knew how to party, and even though only the top few members of the pack had attended the ceremony, they were all more than happy to come out and dance the night and half the next morning away in honor of their new Alpha pair's bonding. The sun had come up nearly an hour ago, but still they partied on.

It was a good sign considering we needed all the allies we could get. Still, though, there was a thread of unease running under my skin that I just couldn't figure out.

Galyna had been giving me side-eye all night, and right this minute, she was stalking my way, wearing a familiar expression that told me she was about to give me the third degree.

"I'm fine," I started, waving her off as I turned toward the table of nonalcoholic beverages to refill my cup with more cherry punch. Maidens on duty didn't drink, and she and I were on a mission, which meant we were on duty until we were recalled to the enclave.

"You're not fine, and I want to know why."

I sighed. She meant well, in her own bullish way, and I knew it was love that made her be so damn relentless. The best thing to do was just fess up, or else she'd ride my ass all day long.

"I don't know why, okay? I haven't said anything because there *isn't* anything."

She glared hard, and I caved. It was our process.

"Except... this weird feeling that something's up. It's been bugging me ever since the attack at the enclave. Honestly, it's probably just being surrounded by all these unfamiliar shifters. They *just* attacked us, and it's weird that we're... hunky-dory now. I'm sure things will settle as time goes on, and it will pass."

She nodded, mollified for the time being.

We stood shoulder to shoulder, staring out over the impromptu dance floor. People were generally happy, and a few of the younger maidens had come over from the enclave to celebrate with the pack. They danced with the wild abandon of youth.

I missed those days. Most of the time, I felt old, dried up. I had a purpose, and it was honorable. That should be enough, but I couldn't fight the feeling that it just *wasn't*. It was sacrilege and my deepest shame.

Most people would kill to have a calling like mine. And being assigned to Pack Blackwater as they changed history... It was the first time I truly understood the magnitude of what I'd been called to do. The maidens were more important than ever.

We had to deal with the rest of the ODL and whoever had been pulling Varga's strings. The little bits of information we'd found so far indicated it was another species that didn't want the wolves coming back together, but so far, we hadn't figured out *who* the puppet master was.

There was one thing I was sure of, though. War was coming, and this pack was going to be at the eye of the storm. You didn't wipe the floor with a huge contingent of the ODL just to have them vanish quietly into the night. They were prepping to hit back, and hard. I was afraid we wouldn't be ready.

So, I pushed all the angst back down, as I always did. They needed me, and they were family. I couldn't let them down by being distracted. That was how people got killed.

Like Olivia nearly did.

That was another piece of shame to add to my collection. She'd nearly died under my protection. It was only her inherent magic and the sheer power of Lucien's alpha bond kickstarting it that had saved her. I'd been severely reprimanded by the high priestesses and put on probation. One more screwup, and I'd be back cooling my heels on dish duty inside the enclave while history happened without me.

No way in the nine hells was I letting that happen.

So I watched like a hawk, always on alert, waiting for the next threat.

It came sooner than I expected.

Dakota—who was even younger than Oli—danced and laughed with a few other maidens, her platinum-blonde hair easy to pick out from the crowd, when one of the Hungarians decided to get handsy. He yanked her out of the group and started grinding up against her ass before she could even turn around.

I stormed into the crowd, batting shifters out of my way like flies, tunnel vision on the male that thought he could put his hands on a female without her consent.

I grabbed him by the back of the neck, yanking him off her with a warning growl and dropping him on his ass in the middle of the dance floor. Next, I turned to Dakota.

"Anyone puts their hands on you like that without your

permission, you drop them. Immediately. I don't care who it is, they don't get to touch you without your consent, understand?"

"Y-yes, sorry, Elodie."

"Don't apologize. All I want is for you to take care of it next time."

She nodded and darted off, the rest of the younger maidens absorbing her back into their group as they finally left the dance floor.

"Stuck-up bitch," the man volleyed at me from the ground, as if it were some grave insult.

"I dare you to say that again from up here." I fingered the hilt of my butterfly sword, blade gleaming even in the dim lighting they'd set up.

Not taking the hint, the male surged back to his feet, pushing his *maybe* gamma-level dominance my way, as if I'd be impressed.

"That's cute," I said, letting my own dominance out to play. I was more powerful than he was, and I saw the moment his anger turned to insecurity, and he decided to double down on stupid.

He charged, but I saw it coming by a mile, dodging the flimsy attempt at a strike with ease.

"Geza!" A harsh bark from a small distance away had my challenger cowering like a puppy.

Somehow, that just pissed me off more. Why did men always feel like they could bow up to a woman, when they were chicken shit against another male? I could wipe the floor with this guy *and* his five closest buddies.

Valens strode onto the dance floor, expression thunderous as he looked between the gamma and me. I had no interest in boys who thought they were tougher shit than me. But Valens? He was all man, and even I couldn't deny it. His fury was complete as he stepped between us, and I shouldn't have found that hot.

It's been too long since I last got laid.

"You put your hands on an unwilling woman? You are a disgrace to this pack and the honor of shifters. Go to your home. Do not leave it for any reason until I speak with the Alpha about what he wants to do with you. But I'd start packing if I were you."

Geza lifted his chin defiantly, glaring in my direction. "You send me away like a chastised dog. What about that dick-swinging bitch?"

Growing tired of the exchange, I whipped my sword from its sheath, putting one curved blade to his throat with my double-handed grip. "The dick-swinging bitch is right here, and I'm happy to put you in your place myself. You wanna fight? I'll cut your limp cock off and stuff it down your throat before you can cry for your mommy."

He blanched as I smiled, really driving the promise home. But it quickly turned to a frown as a much-larger, masculine hand landed right above mine on the grip of my sword.

Nobody touched a maiden's sword and lived to tell about it. *Nobody.*

"What the *fuck* do you think you're doing?" I snarled at Valens, giving him approximately three seconds to take his hand off my sword before I switched my wrath to him. *One.*

"That is not how we do justice in the Hungarian pack. He will stand before the Alpha for judgment as is right." *Two.*

"I will not have *you* instigating an unnecessary challenge either. Remember your place." *Three.*

I grabbed his hand and twisted, dislodging his grip in one effortless move, tossing my sword to the waiting Galyna—the rest of the partiers had been smart enough to give us some space—and using both of my hands to bend his hand back into a wrist lock.

But Valens stood steady as an oak tree, and he didn't cry out or buckle under the pressure. He stared me straight in the eyes, bringing the entire weight of his alpha dominance into play as he laid his other hand over the top of mine, peeling my fingers free and capturing my hand in his much-larger one.

The air was charged as we stared each other down, that unease I'd been feeling since arriving in Hungary growing to a crescendo.

His eyes began to glow turquoise with his wolf, and I felt my own vision sharpen as my wolf rose in response.

"Mine."

The gravelly word fell from the enemy's lips, and time froze. Maidens oath sworn to the enclave did not have mates, and I could not let this asshole start thinking that was what was happening here.

Oh fuck. Oh no, oh no oh no oh no.

"Guys! Guys!"

Fiona came running up, brushing back her wild blonde hair as she sucked in a deep breath, as if she'd been running for a while. "Blackwater pack meeting. You're needed, now."

I yanked my hands free, spinning and giving Valens my back. "Lead the way."

"They're in the old pack mansion. Come on."

I took one step before Valens dropped a heavy hand on my forearm, making me pause and stiffen.

"Umm, they only requested our pack," Fiona said, confused as she looked from the domineering alpha at my side and then back to me.

"Where she goes, I go."

Fiona's eyebrows nearly shot off her forehead in surprise, but she stayed silent as she led us all back to the pack mansion. I hung back, wanting to tear Valens a new one, but not knowing what to say.

We were up the steps and inside before I'd figured it out, and thankfully, he'd dropped the physical contact along the way.

I did not miss it.

I *didn't*.

Fiona led us straight into the office, and I finally turned, facing him down. "This is pack business. You're going to have to wait outside."

"Actually, Valens has already pledged his loyalty, and we've come to an understanding. He can come in as Lucien's second." Kane waved him in from behind the dead Varga's desk, his expression guarded.

I was shocked when I scanned the room and saw Olivia and Lucien standing there, looking a little bit sleep-deprived but content.

"Shouldn't you guys be in your new cottage, practicing making the next generation?" I teased. Anything to get the attention off me, and the alpha hulking at my back.

"She needed a break and had an idea. But we'll be going back there as soon as we try this out."

Olivia whacked him lightly on the chest, squinting at him. "I did not need a break, thank you very much. But I felt the idea was too important to wait, especially while everyone was still here together."

"What idea?" I asked, confused.

Olivia turned to address everyone at once with the answer. "We've been trying to physically piece the omega stone back together, but it's not just some rock. It's magic, it's power. I thought... I thought we should put all the pieces together, and then all the women who've been marked or given special powers should... I don't know. Pour that power in. Charge it back up." She shrugged, looking a little embarrassed now that it was all on the table.

"It can't hurt, and it's not even close to the craziest thing we've tried," Brielle said, giving Olivia a sweet smile. "I say let's give it a try. You're right, we've got to get back to the enclave soon, before my spell wears off."

Kane pulled a pouch from the desk and poured the omega stone shards out onto the table. They glowed weakly, nothing impressive in their current form. It was hard to believe what the stone was said to do was true, but we needed all the help we could get.

The Goddess-touched women all gathered around, forming a bowl with their hands and placing the pieces inside, as close to how it seemed like they were meant to fit. I watched as lights of varying colors filled the room—Olivia's green healing magic, Shay's white, crackling fae power, Fiona's blue palm, and even a little shimmer from Brielle. Leigh's palm was the only one that simply glowed, her omega mark brightening as they all poured everything they had into the fragments of stone.

The light grew and grew, the swelling power beginning to feel oppressive in the closed space.

Someone gasped—I couldn't tell who—as two things happened at the same time. The stone melded seamlessly back together, and two bolts of what looked like lightning streaked out, one flying out the open office window.

My vision went white as the other bolt hit me square in the chest.

Second Epilogue

Paris Catacombs, present day

Liquid green eyes flickered open as a burst of white light faded into the darkness. The woman's hair lay like a halo around her on her shelf, perfectly curled and vibrant despite the thick dust covering everything else.

She pushed herself up, laughing with glee as she slid off the stone shelf where she'd been laid to rest so many ages ago that time had nearly lost count.

But she hadn't.

She never could.

Footsteps light over ancient stone, the dainty woman with the raven curls stopped in the doorway, clasping her hands.

"My darling Bran, I've missed you."

A warrior stepped forward, seeming one with the shadows as he wrapped his hands around her waist, yanking her close with brutal ease as he took her mouth in a punishing kiss. His leather-and-bronze armor creaked with the movement, but she merely sighed when their lips parted.

"I think it's time we got out of here. Don't you?" She pressed up on her tiptoes, pinning him with a dazzling smile on those blood-red lips. "You'll take care of the guards?"

"Anything for you, Narcissa."

Bran drew a glowing broadsword and turned to stalk off into the darkness of the catacombs.

Narcissa laughed and spun when the screams began, then skipped after him to revel in the destruction.

Thank you so much for reading Fated to the Scarred Wolf! I hope you loved Olivia and Lucien's story as much as I did. 🤍 Elodie will be our last pack mate in The Hunted Omegas series to get her own book... and boy, does she not pull punches.

Grab your copy of the final installment in the hunted omegas series, Fated to the Wolf Maiden:

Oh, and remember Lucien and Oli getting dirty in the shower? Yeah, you can grab that bonus scene here (https://Book Hip.com/MHWQZBW) by joining my newsletter.

And if you would ever like signed copies or special editions, those are available from my website (https://payhip.com/autho raprilmoon).

Playlist

"Fight for Your Right" — Beastie Boys

"Bad to the Bone" — George Thorogood and the Destroyers

"I Don't Care" — Ed Sheeran & Justin Bieber

"You Can Do Anything" — DJ Lucas Beat, Jason Derulo, & SIA

"Honey, I'm Good" — Andy Grammer

"Hold Me" — Teddy Swims

"Let's Get Lost" — Beck and Bat for Lashes

"Kryptonite" — 3 Doors Down

"Imgonnagetyouback" — Taylor Swift (Chapter 31. 'Nuff said.)

"Beautiful People" — Ed Sheeran (feat. Khalid)

"This Town" — Niall Horan

"Ordinary" — Alex Warren

"Hello" — Adele

"Waves" — Dean Lewis

"Burning House" — Cam

"Fearless" — Jackson Dean

"Crazy One More Time" — Kip Moore

Also by April L. Moon

The Hunted Omegas Series

Fated to the Wolf Prince

Fated to the Feral Wolf

Fated to the Warrior Wolf

Fated to the Wolf Billionaire

Fated to the Scarred Wolf

Fated to the Wolf Maiden

Standalone

When Cupid Falls First